The BOOK OF JUDGES

The BOOK OF JUDGES

A Novel

GARY FIELDS

SPARKPRESS

Published in 2026 by
SparkPress, an imprint of The Stable Book Group

32 Court Street, Suite 2109
Brooklyn, NY 11201
https://gosparkpress.com

Library of Congress Control Number: 2025920040
ISBN: 978-1-68463-348-7
eISBN: 978-1-68463-349-4

Interior designer: Katherine Lloyd, The DESK

Printed in the United States

For my light, my love,
my Brooklyn girl, Deb

PROLOGUE: YIN

1260–Beijing

Huang Tse Abdonchai stumbled up the mountainside trail, panting hard, lunging ahead, frantic. For years, he'd awoken each morning all but certain he would not see the next.

Today he was sure.

As he strained against the steep path ascending the Taihang Mountains just west of the city, a thousand voices in his head screamed over one another; a field of banners raced in a blur inside his eyes.

"Softer! Slower!" he begged, desperate to understand their commands. He shook himself, pushing harder. The thousand voices fell to a whisper, replaced by his quickening pulse pounding in his ears, a drum call to the blood-bittering wind. And then, ever so faint, he picked up the sounds of others . . . approaching.

They'd come for *The Words*!

Ten years before, a band of Turkish nomads, the dreaded Mongol "warriors of hell," had thundered across the land on horseback. As each archer, at full gallop, launched sixty arrows with deadly precision, local militias had toppled like dominoes. Fortresses had crumbled before the invaders' catapults and battering rams. The Mongols had needed no help to conquer his beloved Song dynasty.

Ruling, however, was another matter.

And so, Huang Tse, a former local administrator, had been appointed by the regional Mongol overseer as *yin*, the *supreme* magistrate for the entire province—though tightly tethered to his new masters' leash. Year upon year, he'd imposed their savage edicts—until *The Words* had appeared.

He'd first encountered *The Words* in a matter of life and death, with the fate of two young lovers placed in his hands. A Chinese man had dared to marry a "Mansi"—an intercaste union forbidden by Mongol law. Conviction would have ensured executions for both bride and groom. Perhaps Huang Tse had tired of meting out death; perhaps it was the couple's tender ages. At the close of testimony, he'd rushed to his private library—a treasured remnant from the Song dynasty—and wrestled with the matter deep into the night. As he'd traced a weary finger over a series of symbols on a page of a Chinese legal codex, its supple Xuan paper quivered, and a language character seemed to lift into the air.

The symbol for a tree.

He'd shaken his head, but then, from the withered goat-kid-skin parchment of a purple-bound text of Roman laws, a Latin word appeared to rise.

ANIMA

The word for "soul."

Was this a spell, he'd wondered, conjured from a shaman's drum dance? As these apparitions swayed before his eyes, suddenly from all corners of the room symbols and letters flew in to join them, forming what surely must have been phrases and sentences. But before he could dissect any meaning, the mass had split into columns and swirled as whirlwinds.

As the letters and symbols had billowed throughout the chamber, it seemed a hundred voices were screaming in his head—their tones instructing, urging, demanding, but their languages and words unclear. Frightened that he'd slipped past the point of reason, he'd closed his eyes, clenched the edge of his desk, and prayed to be released from the spell. When he'd opened his eyes, the voices were gone, but a message seemed to hang in the air before him:

AS EACH SOUL IS A SEED PLANTED
BY THE GODS, SHALL WE NOT EMBRACE
THE FOREST OF MISMATCHED TREES?

When he'd reached out to touch those words, he'd realized they were not in the air at all, but *inside* his eyes. As the message faded to mist, his mind returned with heightened clarity to the legal issues he'd researched. And a simple miracle was revealed: The Mongol edict had failed to specify a penalty.

The next day, with vigor belying a sleepless night, he'd ruled that the law merely voided the intercaste marriage. The young couple was admonished to leave the territory before the regional overseer could amend the edict.

The Words, as he'd come to call them, had returned innumerable times over the ensuing years, often to aid in his legal decisions, but once, oddly, to guide his choice of horse. Shortly after *The Words*' first appearance, his steed had gone lame. As he was about to purchase a black mare, *The Words* again seized his thoughts. Their message, strange as it seemed, was that he could dispense their wisdom only from a white mount. What mattered the hue of his horse? Yet, afraid not to heed this powerful force, he'd followed its command. Thereafter, whenever he'd ridden into a village in need of justice, the villagers would point to his glorious white stallion and proclaim, "The *yin* has arrived!"

But the wonder of *The Words*, as the years proceeded, had become a two-pronged curse. Their powerful projections had grown so great his mind could scarcely bear them; it was as if the blazing sun of enlightenment would set his inner eye on fire, bringing searing pain inside his head and delusions that lingered ever longer, leaving him begging for relief. The second prong of the curse was the Mongols. He'd come to believe they'd learned of his secret and its powers. They would surely come for *The Words*, or his life.

And now, it seemed, time was collapsing in on Huang Tse Abdonchai. With the shadowy fingers of nightfall tightening their grasp on the mountains, the voices, the banners, came roaring back, as unforgiving as ever. He trembled from the force of *The Words*.

The trees rustled. A quiver of arrows? Was it the Mongols? Or was this all in his mind?

A beam of moonlight shot down through a crack in the charcoal sky, illuminating the path ahead. Huang Tse lurched to a halt in the frigid night air; he was one stride from the cliff. He slid forward and peered down into the endless, welcoming black. Were those footsteps he heard behind him?

The ground swayed and his mind surrendered. He could no longer see past the fire within, could no longer be sure of anything. The voices raged in unyielding fury—*The Words* that had led him to untold miracles and driven him to madness.

Suddenly his body heaved forward, off the edge of the cliff.

Had he slipped? Or was that a hand he felt nudge him? Looking up for his killer, he saw only the unreadable, swirling whirlwinds of *The Words*, ablaze in fireworks across the sky.

As he plummeted into the dark, terror and relief met at the center of Huang Tse Abdonchai. He could no longer live with this dance of power and pain.

The Words were too strong.

UNEXPECTED VISITOR

Something was wrong. The gnawing emptiness in Joshua Sutton's gut was accompanied by an eerie quivering of coming danger.

It had nothing to do with the traffic. Sure, he'd been battling his way through the Friday late-afternoon rush-hour mess for over an hour now, pushing haphazardly southward through western Broward and Miami-Dade Counties, but having done this drive for the past four years, he was used to it. It was his time to settle himself on his way to his night law school classes at the University of Miami, to clear out the mental toxins, to envision some kind of sensible future. But today, instead of growing calmer, he could focus only on this pit in his stomach that wouldn't fade. In fact, it was intensifying.

He stopped for a traffic light in Miami's urban-sprawl suburb of Kendall. To the right was a strip mall with half its stores boarded up and a homeless man sheltering in the shade of the overhang. Another disposable human. The math never added up on this stuff. There were two or three thousand homeless people in the county and at least that many closed strip mall stores. The solution to the housing crisis was staring at him in plywood. Freaking bureaucracies.

Not so easy to solve things for the *emotionally* homeless. His stomach twinged. The roots of that pit were in last night's nightmare, the one he'd had too many times before. His brother was racing frantically ahead through a forest in the fading light, dodging trees as they turned into demons with glistening claws and bloodied fangs, unaware that the cliff and certain death were mere steps away. Desperate to reach him, Dream Josh, terrified but closing in fast, screamed at the top of his lungs, "Seth, stop!" But Seth raced past the last of the tree-demons, gazed back with his face clenched in fear, and, without breaking stride, plunged over the cliff. Dream Josh screamed "No!" as he screeched to a halt at the edge, then burst into tears as he stared down at his brother's body plummeting into the blackness.

Ooof! His ankle lurched forward and he lost his balance. What?! He'd forgotten about the rope. The one connecting them. He careened down into the darkness. To his left and right, small outcroppings burst forth from the ashen walls of the cliffside; one turned into his mother, the other, his father. His parents' arms stretched out like Mister Fantastic's, extending longer and longer, desperately trailing him. Their fingertips grazed his skin but didn't stop, instead racing past him downward into the dark. They were trying to save Seth, not him! He thrust out his hands to grab his parents' arms. As he touched them, a sickening smell of rotting flesh engulfed him; their arms putrefied and then disintegrated.

He'd awoken drenched in sweat, the dream's final image burned into his brain: He was plunging into the abyss, alone.

Beeeeeeep!

Oh. He pulled out and waved an apology to the driver behind him. But he was still suspended between dream and reality, past and present. He'd seen that cliff before, with someone else, not Seth, jumping. But where? Had he read about it in his recent research on those historical judges? Judge Maloch had insisted the project was of "great significance." Or had the cliff clawed its way out of the internal cavern he'd sealed and resealed for years?

Off to the left, he passed the concrete geometric structures of Miami Dade College's Kendall Campus. He'd be at the judge's house in a couple of minutes. He needed to focus; the judge would demand his best. Two weeks ago, just before graduation, Maloch, who'd taught Josh's trial advocacy class this year, had asked if he'd be willing to spend part of his summer researching material for a book the judge was writing on historical judges and groundbreaking cases on human rights. Though

Josh would be busy studying for the bar, Maloch would pay enough that he'd be able to quit his day job in systems design immediately instead of waiting until September when he'd start working with the Palm Beach County Public Defender's Office.

He hoped his notes from this week were strong enough. The first articles the judge had given him were a bunch of ponderous philosophical debates on age-old human rights issues. When they'd met a week ago to discuss them, it felt almost as if Maloch had been testing him, probing to find out if he'd locked in on the history-altering power of these laws and rulings. When the judge had rewarded him with the material for this past week—a fascinating history of a magistrate in ancient China—Josh figured he'd passed the test. The magistrate had devoted much of his career to secretly protecting human rights under harsh Mongol rulers and had paid for it with his life. Josh took his first slow breath in a while; just thinking about the readings calmed him.

He turned his car onto a quiet, leafy street and pulled to the curb. His nerves were back on edge. It was more than the dream; something felt wrong in the present, very wrong. This was a sleepy, suburban neighborhood, and yet, strangely, he found himself scanning ahead and then across the street. He checked the rearview mirror. No one around.

The heavy air of a steamy South Florida summer evening engulfed him as he stepped out of the car. He hopped over a bulge in the choppy sidewalk and steered around scattered coconuts from swooning palm trees that lined the walkway.

Steeling himself, he turned up the path to the judge's aged but well-kept two-story white stucco Spanish-style home bedecked with carved wood window frames and a burnt-orange barrel tile roof. He climbed the three steps to the front door and rang the bell.

Thirty seconds went by. Nothing. He rang again. Finally, he heard what sounded like footsteps coming down stairs.

The door opened. Whoa. Neville Maloch, a renowned appellate judge who wore only finely tailored suits to class, his silk ties in perfect double-Windsor knots, now scratched at a three-day beard and sported a wrinkled T-shirt half tucked into pajama pants. His thinning gray hair pointed in all directions. Even for one-on-one meetings at his house, the man typically never had a hair out of place; Josh had figured he probably woke up each morning in a crisp polo and neatly pressed khakis.

The judge stared at him with a quizzical look. "Josh? What are you doing here?"

"Isn't our research meeting tonight?"

"Tonight?" He hunched over slightly and expelled a heavy sigh. "Sorry, it's been a crazy week."

"You want to reschedule?"

He sure looked as if he did. As if he was struggling to keep his mind in the present. Weird. Normally, the man's every word, every action, seemed purposeful.

"No," the judge said, "that wouldn't be fair. I know you come down from Lauderdale." He straightened almost to his usual, confident posture, shook his head, and smiled. "The sweet surprise of change. I know change has been a theme—er, *issue*—for you, Josh. But believe me, it's the only way to real growth."

"Issue" was a euphemistic way to put it. The judge had been the first person in a long time to whom Josh had given up the goods. Maloch knew about the Microsoft "Emerging e-Genius" award at fourteen that Josh had refused to accept; the high school football stardom he'd run from; Seth's suicide—though not all the particulars—and their family subsequently falling apart.

"*Has* something changed?" Josh asked.

The judge's eyes shot wide. "In three days, *everything* will." He leaned in and whispered, "What *was* will be no more. What *wasn't* will be."

Was this brilliant judge, this once-in-a-lifetime mentor, losing his mind? Could a premonition of this have somehow caused the rot in Josh's stomach?

He waved Josh in. "Let's go up to the study. Your research project is over."

"But I just started reading about the Chinese magistrate—"

"I found the answer I was looking for." Maloch turned for the wooden staircase.

Had he missed something in the material? "What is it?"

The judge spun back. "If we looked at *who* these judges were, and what they must have *seen* . . ." He stopped short. "The significance of this is staggering—almost beyond comprehension." Trembling, he grabbed the banister to steady himself. "But, for your own sake, I don't think I can share much of it with you yet."

For his own sake? What in the hell was Maloch talking about?

They climbed the stairs and were barely two steps into the study when the doorbell rang again. The judge threw his hands up. "Tell me I forgot another appointment."

The man never forgot a thing in class. Was he going senile?

Maloch wheeled to head back down. "Wait here. This research group appears to be growing by the minute."

Josh felt his breath racing again. He let the room wash over him. The large, centered Turkish rug, the oak bookcases along the side walls, with their trove of textbooks and bent-cornered paperbacks, and the classic cherrywood rolltop desk at the far window, its niches crammed with souvenirs from family trips around the world, comforted him. It was a well-lived-in room full of loving memories. Was there any chance his own crap-filled life could ever look like this?

He crossed the room toward the desk and immediately recognized the four stacks of papers on it: copies of the opening statements and closing arguments from him and each of his classmates for the two mock trials this past semester. A half-filled file box, marked TRIAL ADVOCACY PROGRAM, sat off to the side of the desk. Nice. The man actually kept hard copies of all his students' work. But what drew Josh's smile, as always, were the rows of family photos that filled the walls at the edges of the desk: curly-haired grandchildren circling on tricycles; the judge's late wife tossing a ball to their golden retriever; the whole clan at picnics, weddings, graduations. If only.

Wait. He glanced back at the desk. Something was missing. Where was the judge's laptop? It was always on the desk when they met. Maloch made all his notes there. Josh scanned the room. The laptop was sitting open on a corner table to the right of the room's entrance, on a table with no chair. Strange. Maybe he'd had it in his lap when he heard Josh ring the doorbell, and set it down on his way out of the study?

The front door creaked open downstairs, and Josh turned his head toward the study's doorway. In a shaded corner just left of the doorway was an object he hadn't noticed in past visits: a pedestal holding a bronze statuette of a judge swinging a gavel, as if striking a blow for justice. He walked over to it and read the plaque on the pedestal that thanked the judge for his "many years of service to the legal community." Maloch, who had often lectured him about "stick-to-itiveness," obviously had it himself in droves. He'd grown incredibly frustrated with Josh at times, unable to fully comprehend why his student had never stayed the course in his life, why he always ran. But the judge had no idea what Josh had seen, what truly fed his fears. Only Seth had understood.

"Ya'll better hand it over right now," said someone in a deep, angry-sounding voice and a distinct Southern drawl. The voice was coming from downstairs. "I ain't foolin' with ya."

"I'm sorry," the judge responded. "I still don't know what you're talking about."

"Ah think you do."

After a brief pause, the judge spoke again. "Okay, sir, I don't want any trouble. Wait here. I'll bring it down to you."

After another pause, Josh heard the judge's footsteps on the stairs. They came slowly at first and then quickened until they stumbled into staccato bursts. When the judge was probably three-quarters of the way up, something else hit the stairs hard. *Thump!* It hit the stairs again, closer, sounding like a large animal leaping its way upward in pursuit.

Maloch rushed in, panting heavily, and went straight for the rolltop desk. Josh pressed into the shadow behind the open door of the study.

Thump! The floor vibrated, the sound coming from right outside the door.

Before Maloch reached the desk, a metallic object flashed through the air, heading straight for him.

The judge screamed. A large black knife handle protruded from the upper left side of his back.

No! This couldn't be happening!

The judge lurched and then reached behind him, making a frantic grab for the handle as he collapsed.

Josh's chest tightened. He could hardly breathe.

While Maloch's prone body barely quivered, an enormous red-headed man bounded across the room, ripped the knife out, and wiped it clean with two quick swipes on the judge's pants. The man shoved Maloch's now-lifeless form aside and slid the weapon into some kind of sheath inside his shirt as he eyed the stacks of papers on the desk. He pulled out a pair of rubber gloves, slipped them on, and started skimming through the stack closest to him. The mock trial cases? The man tossed them on the floor. Stack after stack went flying.

He opened and slammed desk drawers. He pulled the knife back out and jimmied a locked file drawer, but moments later, he was throwing the contents of that too. Whatever he was looking for, there was only one place it could be. The laptop! The judge kept all his important work on that laptop. He'd just given his life for something that must've been on it.

Josh couldn't let this guy get it. But what chance did he have against a power-forward-sized animal who could throw a knife across a room into a man's back?

The killer had just two more desk drawers to check.

Josh gripped the bronze statuette. It felt solid, heavy. This was beyond insane. He'd have to silently lug this thing across the room and strike with everything he had, and all the man would have to do was turn around in time and use the knife, and Josh would be lying on the floor as dead as his mentor.

OLD FRIENDS

The headline read: "Falun Dafa to Appear at UN Tomorrow." The rats would be spreading their pestilence.

As was his custom, Han Chee-hwa had begun his day in the breakfast room overlooking the flower garden at his palatial estate just outside of Zhuhai in southern China. He pushed aside a dumpling with his chopsticks and stared at the flat-screen monitor across the gilt-edged, hunter-green marble tabletop. He typically scanned headlines from Beijing first, but this morning the news he was interested in came from the West.

The article was brief, revealing little of what this evil cult planned for the presentation and, of course, nothing whatsoever about how remarkable the timing was, how ominous the situation. But then there were perhaps only three or four people in the world who knew the potential horror that was about to unfold, and only because of the email he'd received yesterday.

"Mr. Han," his assistant's mellifluous voice purred through the intercom.

"Yes, Meiling?"

"Which girls shall we provide for the governor's party tonight? I believe his friends have somewhat eclectic tastes."

Not something he wanted to deal with right now. For what was surely the twentieth time, he clicked back to the email from his informant. He'd relied on this girl for years; there was no doubting the message. Incredibly, the dreaded moment the Dafa had prayed for, thousands of years in the making, appeared to be at hand, threatening China's—and the world's—system of order, and with it, his influence and wealth.

"Mr. Han, are you feeling well?" Right. Meiling was still speaking.

"Yes . . . fine. I leave the decision in your capable hands." He clicked off the intercom.

But what of *his* decision? There was no time to explain this to the powers that be. The Party's present concerns with the Dafa were grounded mainly in the group's disloyalty to the People's cause. Most of the leadership were out of touch with this cult's ultimate capabilities.

So, he'd looked to the West. His old prep school friend from the United States, Kyle Fredericks, had an equally fervent interest in stopping the threatened catastrophe—albeit for very different reasons. Within minutes of receiving the email, he had picked up his private line and made the call.

"Chee-hwa?"

There'd been no time for small talk. "Yes, Kyle. I need your help . . . urgently."

"It's happening?"

"So it appears. Within days, unless we stop it. And it seems you're our only hope."

Han shook himself back to the present. His gaze drifted out the window past the colorful flower beds and off to the distant hills. But his mind ran much further afield.

By his own hand, the wheels were now fully in motion—wheels that would later be difficult to brake.

MAD DASH

Across the room, with Neville Maloch's corpse sprawled at his feet on the bloodstained rug, the enormous assassin bent low over the roll-top desk, almost finished skimming through the last stack of papers.

A bead of sweat rolled down Josh's wrist as he shakily eased the bronze statuette off its pedestal; he tightened his grip. It was heavier than it looked, and it would take two hands to swing it. But would he even have the chance?

Returning punts back in high school had taught him a valuable lesson: Once you picked your spot, you couldn't hesitate. You had to burst like being shot out of a cannon. Of course, back then, if you didn't get to the spot on time, you merely got sandwiched, not killed.

The man would be done with those papers any second.

Maloch had taken a chance on Josh, picking him as his research assistant despite Josh's often mediocre work on class assignments. The judge had seen something worthwhile in him—no one else had in years.

Josh exploded out of the corner, raising the statuette. But a floorboard creaked as he crossed the room. The man fired up out of the chair, pulled his knife, and spun.

Josh leaped, twisting his body to avoid the knife, and swung at the man's head.

The blade grazed Josh's forearm as the statuette connected with a crunch, and the killer melted to the floor, face-to-face with Neville Maloch.

Josh dropped the statuette, grabbed the laptop off the corner table, and raced down the stairs. He flung open the front door and flew to his car.

As he pulled away, he brought up the phone app on his car's touchscreen. He'd hit 9 and 1 before he stopped. Not on his cell. He wasn't going through that again.

He passed three gas stations before he found one with a pay phone. "Judge Neville Maloch has been murdered," he told the dispatcher. "He's at 1704 South 122nd Street in Kendall. The killer may still be there."

"And what's your name?" the woman asked.

He dropped the receiver without hanging up.

As he headed northeast, away from Kendall, he checked his speedometer almost as often as his rearview mirror. He couldn't get the image out of his mind: Judge Maloch's lifeless body lying in a pool of blood. He shot a glance at the laptop on his passenger seat.

What was on it?

SAMMI

Fighting off a panic attack, Samantha Bollinger burst through the doors of her apartment building. How would she ever make the upcoming deadline on her doctoral thesis in history and theology when she was still struggling to find any arguable proof that "Engines of Destiny" existed?

She needed her "tunnels of calm"—her banyan trees.

Twice this past week alone, she'd raced out to sit among her favorite families of banyans. To lie back in their broad shade.

A Brooklyn girl, she'd grown up surrounded by concrete. But she'd never been able to get enough of Prospect Park and its Botanic Gardens. She'd built quite the photo collection of her favorite plants and trees. But none compared to the banyan and its mélange of multi-sized trunks, which created artworks of each banyan as unique as a fingerprint.

As she stepped west toward the late May sunset and its lavender-streaked clouds, she reached the closest banyan and traced her fingers down the elephant-skin-like segments. Throughout Coral Gables, rows of immense banyans turned streets into living tunnels. She'd photographed and named some of the unique sculptures created by the interwoven trunks: "The Waterfall," "The Caves." She was half convinced her connection to the banyans would lead to something life-changing. But that was nothing new; every once in a while, something or someone would leave a mark on her, a mark she would tuck away, only to find meaning later on.

Most recently, early last fall, a mark was definitively made by her dear family friend Judge Neville Maloch, who'd been kind enough to hire her as his clerical assistant on campus. It was the judge who'd asked her, "What makes us pursue some of our passions more than others?" That question had launched hours and hours of thought, and found her a thesis topic—a topic still greatly in need of supportive facts. She put two fingers to her wrist; her pulse was as fast as ever.

A puff of breeze rustled the leaves over her head and swirled through the tree's limbs, flicking at her hair. She turned back to the walkway and stepped swiftly along the western edge of campus. It would be dark soon and, to have any chance at calming her nerves, there was one more stop she needed to make.

This was at an old friend: "The Lovers." And her timing was perfect. She arrived as the sun's last rays cast an angelic aura around this banyan's magical formation, which looked like a couple sharing a warm embrace. She smiled as her breaths finally slowed.

The sun melted into the horizon; it was time to go. As she entered an eerily dark thicket of banyans—its trunks resembling prowling ghouls—the fine hairs on the back of her neck rose to attention and a shiver flittered down her spine. Some kind of coldness was suddenly taking hold of the summer evening.

Creak.

She spun to her left and squinted. Was that a tree trunk or a person lurking near the center of the shadowy maze? She quickened her strides. There'd been a couple of muggings near campus this past semester. Just a hundred yards to her building.

A heavy breath came from behind her. A hand grabbed her shoulder, hard.

Before she could scream, she was spun around, with barely time to ball her hand into a fist and swing.

Her punch was caught in midair.

"Josh!?" She yanked her hand free. "Are you crazy? You scared me half to death!"

Panting and dripping sweat, he didn't answer, clearly out of breath. She'd briefly met him a couple of times at Maloch's office and once at her dorm when he'd dropped off some paperwork from the judge. But the deep, almost black irises underneath that mop of dark hair, the slim, athletic build—she wasn't about to forget those; they'd been enough for a minor crush at first.

Those eyes were now red, and his shoulders drooped.

"What's wrong?"

He gasped for air. "Looked for you . . . at your apartment . . . knocked on your door, loud . . . Some girl named Lauren from next door came out . . . said she was your friend and . . . you'd gone for a walk on this side of campus . . . Ran from there . . . figured I'd catch you heading back."

"You caught me, all right."

"Didn't mean . . . to scare you." He inhaled slowly. "Was trying to catch my breath when you showed up."

"It's okay. And, uh, sorry I tried to punch you."

"Can't really blame you." The corner of his lip inched up in a half-hearted attempt at a smile and then collapsed. He seemed to be struggling to hold back tears. He pressed a palm to the side of his face. Was that *blood* on his forearm?

"What's going on, Josh?"

"The whole way here I was thinking about how to tell you. Thought I had it worked out. Now I'm not so sure."

What could be so difficult, so painful, to tell her? And why *her*? She barely knew this guy. The last time she'd seen him, he'd seemed a bit full of himself, the jock who thinks he's so smart. The only thing they had in common was the judge. The judge?!

"Josh, whatever it is, you can tell me. You can trust me."

He nodded slowly and drew another deep breath. "It's terrible . . . But you're the only person I could come to with it."

The only person?

He pointed to a nearby bench under a street lamp hemmed in by banyans. "Maybe we should sit." He had a laptop tightly tucked under one arm. Why would he bring that?

When she joined him on the bench, he set down the laptop and began, "I was at the judge's house tonight, waiting in his study . . ."

It couldn't be real, what he was telling her. Could it? She wrapped her arms around herself as the story unfolded.

". . . I didn't want to believe it," he concluded. "I still don't—but I knew he was dead."

She buried her head in her hands for a second, then quickly straightened, wiped at her cheeks, and eased back. "How did you get out of there?"

"Snuck up on the giant from behind, scared shitless, and knocked him out with a bronze statuette. I'm so sorry, Sammi. I know the judge was your uncle."

"No, that was just his little joke. My mom went to college with him. He called me his 'college niece.' He even teased that he almost didn't hire me as his clerical assistant because of nepotism." She leaned against the bench back and sighed. "What do the police think?"

"I don't know." Josh pushed up from the bench, took a few steps, and turned to face her. "I didn't really talk to them."

"Wait. What? Wouldn't they ask you—"

"I didn't stick around."

"Are you *serious*?"

"I called it in from a pay phone, not my cell. I . . . I didn't want them to have my name."

What was he hiding? "Did you . . . Did you *kill* that guy?"

"He won't be wearing a hat any time soon." He forced a chuckle. "But no, I don't think so."

"Then why not give your name? You were an eyewitness to a *murder*."

"And a possible suspect." Josh paced as he spoke. "Let's say the murderer got out of there before the cops came." He stopped momentarily and pointed to his bloody forearm. "His knife nicked me. My fresh blood is on that carpet." He shook his head. "Not to mention that I took Maloch's laptop and left him there dead from a knife wound. Even I, who haven't passed the bar yet, could make a pretty good case for the prosecution."

"You took his laptop?" He was definitely keeping something from her.

"I was supposed to leave it there for the murderer?"

"But don't you owe the judge something more than just phoning it in? You think he would walk away if he witnessed *your* murder?"

"There's another reason I don't want to be identified yet: the research project. When I got to the judge's house, he told me he'd found the answer he was looking for. He said the significance of this discovery was staggering, almost beyond comprehension. Did you ever know him to exaggerate?"

"Never." What could he have found?

"He said he was afraid—for my sake—to tell me specifics. And then he's murdered in front of me by someone desperate for information that's got to be on the judge's laptop. This staggering discovery, according to the judge, is something happening three days from now. Why would someone kill to get this information before then? What were they trying to steal or stop?" He stepped back to the bench and eyed the laptop. "The answer's in here. I'm not leaving it for the police."

Why not? Did Josh want to steal this discovery for himself? "Isn't it *their* job to solve this?"

"Their job's to catch a murderer. They couldn't care less about Maloch's life's work. Don't I owe it to the judge to at least see what he found? Maybe this leads to a treasure that belongs to his family. Or some historic human rights moment that won't happen without what's on this laptop." He sat down and turned to her. "He chose *me* to help him with this . . . and *you*."

That was true. She'd felt honored when Maloch asked her to research a number of religious, spiritual, and historical issues for his project. But he'd also chosen Josh.

"That's why I came to you," he continued. "In addition to being his 'college niece,' you're invested here. I figured you'd want to get to the bottom of this at least as much as I do."

"But why couldn't the police help?" What *was* he hiding? "You're the only one who can give them a description of the guy."

"All they'll want is an arrest. If he got away, it'll be me." He picked up the laptop. "Maybe we can solve this right now, together." He glanced around. "Not sure it's best to look at this out here. Okay if we go to your apartment?"

Good question. He'd been trying awfully hard to keep the police out of this. But the judge *had* chosen him. Neville Maloch didn't let people into his circle lightly, and once there, he didn't hesitate to dig deep into who you were. He'd done it with her. She'd witnessed him doing it with numerous others. And the judge had a special relationship with this guy. He'd made that clear more than once. This was a matter of faith—faith in the judge. She nodded and got up off the bench.

As they approached the building, he asked, "So, what's your best guess on what Maloch could possibly have found, that someone would kill for?"

"Money, power, or religion have to be at the root of this. Maybe all three."

He raised an eyebrow.

These were the reasons people committed premeditated murder. History books and her Instagram feed were bursting with examples. "Trust me on this."

When they got to her apartment, she took the scattered papers off her desk in the living room, grabbed a bunch of loose clothes from the couch, and headed to the bedroom. "Be right back." She went to her medicine cabinet and then returned to the living room to find him sitting at the desk. She handed him some Band-Aids and a tube of Neosporin and pointed to the kitchen sink. "You should wash that arm off and use these. No telling where that knife has been."

When he finished, she leaned down next to him as he sat in the desk chair and propped open the laptop. "I left it on. I think the password protection was set just for reboots. The judge must've been trying to shut it off when he ran into the room."

The screen lit up, showing incoming emails. There was one unopened item, from qigongzhou@fd.mail.com. The subject was Urgent Message! The body of the email contained only a link: urgent message.

"Think it's spam?" she asked. Sure looked like it.

He shook his head. "It came in around the time I was at the judge's house." He took out his phone, checked something on it. "fd.mail.com isn't an active website. Must be some company's internal mail server.

Let's see if the judge sent this person anything." He clicked on the SENT folder. "They're all deleted." He toggled to DELETED messages. Empty. "Maloch was being awfully careful."

"How about his address book?" The judge was a stickler for organization. All his contacts would be there.

Josh opened it, and there it was: qigongzhou@fd.mail.com. The name assigned to the email address was Master Zhou. So the judge knew him.

"We need to open this," he said.

She nodded in agreement. This Master Zhou was close enough to the judge to send him an urgent message, maybe even warning him that his life was in danger. But why had Maloch never mentioned him?

When Josh clicked on the urgent message link, the screen flickered, flashed brightly, went blank, and turned midnight blue.

He started typing furiously, though nothing was showing on the screen. He hit the ENTER key, then paused and scanned every inch of the display. No change.

"Damn it!" He tried again, typing longer this time, then paused and stared. The screen remained a dark blue void.

He shot Sammi a frustrated glance. "It's got to be malware. If I try to reboot, I'm sure it'll activate password protection. We've got to unfreeze this thing without shutting it off." Josh let out a deep, exasperated breath. He pulled out his phone and started texting.

"Who's that?" she asked.

"Mark Roth. A buddy from my not-so-distant computer geek past. He's literally a space cadet, but he's also Einstein with system failures. And I trust him. I'll let you know what we find out."

"Let me know?"

He pushed back from the desk. "There could be a murderer out there looking for this laptop. If what the judge found is so valuable, others are probably ready to kill for what's on here. I can't expose you to that. I guess I shouldn't have even come here. I'll call you when we have something." He grabbed the laptop, then stood and turned to leave.

"I'm coming with you."

He stopped midstride. "Why?"

Because, no doubt, this was a mark with meaning; Maloch was murdered for something she'd been helping him research. Something the judge had specifically chosen her for. This was a trail of banyan seeds scattered along the path to her destiny. She had to follow it.

"You were right. I want to solve this at least as much as you do. After I lost my dad to a heart attack last year, the judge was there for me through the worst of it. And, like you said, he chose me to help him with this research. I'm meant to be part of this, so you're stuck with me now. One thing, though. I want you to promise that if things get too dangerous, you'll call the police."

Josh pulled out his phone and eyed the screen. "It's Mark. He says to come on over."

"The promise?"

He paused, then locked those dark eyes on hers. "You got it."

She followed him to his car and settled into the passenger seat.

His head dropped as he started the engine. "I keep thinking that I could have stopped it somehow."

She didn't know where her next thought had come from, but there it was: Maybe he wasn't meant to.

HAVEN

Billy Ray "Ripper" Jackson steered his rent-a-car under the faded VACANCY sign and stepped as calmly and steadily as he could to the lobby. His head throbbed like a bobwhite in a quail trap.

The motel was perfect. Run-down, semi-deserted, and not part of a chain. No way would it be up-to-date on police bulletins. A crap-hole where he wouldn't get noticed—no easy thing normally, but even harder now with a softball-sized mound sticking out from the right side of his skull.

"Checking in?" The pimply-faced kid behind the counter barely looked up, which, to Billy Ray, was just fine.

"Yup."

The clerk, eyeing some game on his cell phone, slid over a piece of paper and a pen. "Fill this out, please."

Billy Ray wrote down a bunch of lies.

"How many nights you staying?"

"Two or three; depends on my business here." This was true.

"I'll need a credit card imprint."

"Gonna pay cash. Keeps the budget under control."

"Then I need sixty bucks a night in advance; that's a hundred and eighty dollars. You check out early, we refund the difference."

He took out his gator-skin wallet and paid the boy with well-worn bills—crisp money was too suspicious. He got a receipt and a key, went outside, and pulled the rental car over to his room.

The inside smelled even worse than it looked: cigarette smoke smothered under a layer of Lysol, circulated by a rusty, moaning window-mounted air conditioner. He wasn't quite sure if the room was hazy or he was, but he'd had worse on both accounts. It would have to do; he wasn't showing his mug in the lobby again. Besides, from the overall look of this palace, his room might well be the presidential suite. He got to the bed, dropped his bag, and collapsed.

As an all-state linebacker in high school back in Alabama, he'd had his bell rung enough to know he'd likely suffered a mild concussion. But there was no way he was walking into an emergency room.

Even though he'd gotten away clean, there was the troublesome matter of the eyewitness who had nearly crushed his skull. The Miami police surely had an APB out for a six-foot-six-inch, heavily freckled, redheaded bull of a man.

He needed to rest, though two hours was about all he could afford. With his head still thumping like a flatbed on three wheels, odds were high he'd sleep through his phone's alarm. He reached over to the nightstand and set the cracked plastic alarm clock as a backup. Hopefully the nap would calm his pounding skull and give him the strength to tell the Reverend the triple dose of bad news: He'd had to kill the judge, there was a witness to the murder who was on the loose, and so was the judge's laptop.

VISIT TO A NEIGHBORING PLANET

Sammi followed Josh up the creaky, pitted stairs of a dilapidated building to a second-floor apartment. The three-story catwalk structures in the northwest Miami complex were penitentiary-gray stucco, with pigeon-dropping-streaked asphalt roof tiles that must have once been white. It looked as if the place hadn't been painted or even power-washed in twenty years.

When Josh pressed the doorbell, an extraterrestrial-sounding voice said, "Greetings, earthling. Our leader will be with you shortly. He comes in peace."

What the hell? Sammi shot Josh a look.

"I tried to warn you. He's geek level ten."

A short, pudgy guy in his thirties with thick black-rimmed glasses and curly ringlets of unkempt brown hair opened the door. He wore pajamas patterned with space aliens.

He waved them in. "Hey, Quark," he said to Josh. "What's up? You sounded strange on the phone."

They walked down a hallway past posters of the Starship *Enterprise*, the *Millennium Falcon*, and numerous futuristic-looking cities, and stepped around full-size replicas of Princess Leia, Yoda, Spock, and some unidentifiable monsters. What exactly was this guy's definition of *strange*?

"First I should introduce you to Sammi," Josh responded. He turned and caught what must've been quite the expression on her face. "Once she's recovered from viewing your collection."

"This is nothing. My primo stuff's in the command center."

She was almost afraid to ask. "Command center?"

Josh chuckled and pointed across the way. "The second bedroom. But you might want to finish absorbing our current environment." He took a seat at one end of a worn gray corduroy L-shaped couch, the only piece of normal furniture in the room. It was surrounded by hairy, purple, three-toed ottomans, a coffee table that looked like a flattened asteroid, and side chairs shaped like space helmets. "The command center, Mark, would only cement how warped she must think you are."

Mark sat at the far end of the couch and gave Sammi a smile and a wink.

Okay. He was strange but self-aware. She returned the smile and plopped down on the midpoint of the sofa.

Mark turned back to Josh. "Come on, Quark. Maybe your friend's not as bi-dimensional as you are. Besides, the command center's my creative space, where I build my starship models."

"Speaking of creativity," Josh replied, "your genius is needed." Josh walked over to the dark, star-and-flaming-comet-speckled, nebula-shaped dining room table where he'd placed the laptop when they'd come in. "This thing froze when I clicked on a link from someone I thought I knew."

"Smooth move there, Quark. I'll be right back." Mark went to his bedroom.

"What's with *Quark*?" Sammi whispered.

"His pet name for me. Some *Deep Space Nine* character—a major, intergalactic cynic. Looks like the love child of an orangutan and a vampire." He raised his voice slightly. "Did I mention that Mark spends most of his time in an alternate universe?"

"Heard that." Mark returned with another laptop and a dangling cable. "Doesn't mean I'm not right." He plugged the other end of the cable into the judge's laptop, bent over, planted his elbows on the table, and stroked a symphony across his keyboard while his eyes studied his screen.

"If it's a virus, can't it jump to your computer?" Sammi asked.

"Not with Leia's firewalls. In fact, I hope it tries to attack us. That'll save us some time."

"Yeah, he named his laptop," Josh stage-whispered.

Mark's fingers continued to fly. Then he straightened and his hands shot up, fingers still in motion. "Wow. Gotta be, gotta be. A multi-fragmenter. Nasty son of a bitch."

"English, please." Josh tilted his head toward Sammi.

With a sheepish grin, Mark turned professorial. "All computers fragment information streams. Every time you open a file or run a program, your computer sets up a quick access pathway to that task. Over time, thousands and thousands of these fragments get created. At first this speeds access to your favorite tasks, but, eventually, it slows down the whole system. To get to each new task, your computer has to search in and around all these fragments. That's why computers come with a defragmenter—it typically runs weekly to recapture system performance. It cleans out all these fragments. It's like tuning up your car's engine every few thousand miles to get out the gunk."

"Mark," Josh cut in, "you do realize that no one outside of techies has any idea that a defragmenter even exists."

Good to know it wasn't just her.

Mark raised an eyebrow. "What I'm trying to say is that this virus multi-fragments any computer it attacks. It creates thousands of fragments per millisecond. In minutes it turns your hard drive from a library with a card catalogue to an attic choked with cobwebs."

"Then can't you just run this defragmenter thing on it?" Sammi asked.

"This virus segments a hard drive so fast defragmenters can't possibly keep up. They're not designed to deal with this pace of fragmentation. It would be like the three of us trying to remove a haystack the size of this building, straw by straw, while it keeps adding another apartment load every ten minutes."

"Can you save anything from it?" Josh pleaded. "It's important."

"Maybe some limited data. Are there specific folders or files you're looking for? And why don't you have your data backed up?"

"Because it's not my data . . . or my laptop," Josh said. He'd told her on the drive over that he was going to try to limit what he revealed to Mark, figuring the less he knew, the less he'd be at risk. He locked eyes with her now, shook his head, and sighed. "It belongs to the head of a research project I was involved in about historical judges. He told me tonight that he found the answer to our research question and that it was of staggering significance. I think it's on there. And I need to know what it is."

"Wait, you *stole* this dude's laptop?"

Josh stood up and walked to the window. "Worse. It's, it's been a tough day . . ."

Mark stayed park-statue stiff as Josh took him through most of the story.

"*Murdered* for what's on here?" Mark took a step back from the laptop. "Oh my God. Oh my God." His fingers flittered at his sides.

Sammi couldn't stop herself from staring.

"My hands go a little nuts when I get emotional," Mark said when he'd gotten himself under control. He turned to Josh. "Leave me the laptop for a couple days."

"I need that info as soon as possible."

"You got some kind of deadline?"

"From what the judge said, three days at most." Josh had that solemn look again. "And don't forget, there's a maniac out there willing to kill for it."

THE REPORT

Eeee . . . eeee . . . eeee!

The high-pitched shrieks shook him awake.

What *was* that? Someone gettin' strangled?

Billy Ray gingerly lifted his head off the pillow, squinting. Stains on the walls, crud-covered air conditioner half falling out the window. Oh, right.

Eeee!

He reached out and slapped the cheap motel alarm clock. So much for his nap. He killed the alarm on his cell phone before it could pile on. His head still pounded.

For damn sure he didn't want to report in, not at the moment. But the Reverend preached patience way better than he practiced it. Another kind of agony awaited.

He threw cold water on his face in the bathroom, went back and sat on the side of the bed, then tapped the Reverend's name on his cell phone. The call went out through his encryption app's filter.

"Hello?"

"It's me, sir." Billy Ray softly rubbed his swollen skull. "Got some bad news."

"You okay, my son?"

"Okay enough, sir. But I failed. Information's gone. And please forgive me." He told a PG-rated version of what happened—no reason to burden the Reverend with the gory details: He'd accidentally killed the man; he'd just been trying to scare him when the guy turned the wrong way; another had interfered, and the trail had been lost.

"Injury to any of God's creatures, intended or not, is cause for deep sadness. But the Lord sayeth, 'The evil must wither and die.' You're forgiven, my son. You find anything that could help you move forward?"

"A calendar in the house had a handwritten note for today. Said, 'conference with Josh.' Wish I had more than a first name."

"Let me see," the Reverend responded. "Hold on a second . . . there it is. The conference was with Joshua Sutton, a law school student. He lives at 2470 East Pine Terrace in Sunrise, Florida."

Huh? "How you know that, sir?"

"The Lord works his magic and ours is to wonder."

He didn't hesitate. "I'm out the door."

HOME

"Three days!" Josh blurted. "Uh, sorry." He pulled the car into a space in the parking lot of Sammi's building and turned to her. "Didn't mean to shout. But it might've been nice if Maloch had given a *few* more specifics. *Where* was this thing happening? Time of day? Anything."

Despite Josh's frustrations, Sammi's nerves were settling; it would be helpful to have some time to sort through all this on her own. "If your friend Mark's as talented as you said, hopefully he'll have some specifics soon. You'll call me as soon as you hear from him?"

"Sure." Though the car was in park, he was still clinging tightly to the steering wheel.

She placed a hand on his arm. "You're not alone."

He forced a smile as she got out.

As he pulled away, it hit her: *a few more specifics.*

"Wait! Josh!" she yelled as the car sped off. She reached into her pocket for her phone but her hand came up empty. Unbelievable! She'd checked her texts on the ride back. It must've slipped from her pocket when she got out of the car. She ran into her building.

She hadn't memorized Josh's phone number, so she used her friend Lauren's phone to call her own. No answer. Come on, Josh! She tried again and again. It kept ringing through to voicemail.

HOME

The hand on his arm. She'd just been reassuring him, but still. He'd noticed her before, at the judge's office and when he'd dropped off something from the judge at her dorm. She had pretty, girl-next-door looks: seemingly shy smile, soft hazel eyes and shoulder-length brown hair, lithesome movements. But, man, until today, he'd never seen how solid she was. Sure, the girl was far too much the serious academic for him, but she had grit.

Sammi had seemed about three inches from going full-court press on why he'd kept his identity from the police. No way she'd let that go for too long. At some point he'd have to tell her the whole soul-crushing truth.

With Sammi back in the safety of her apartment and the laptop in Mark's trusty hands, Josh was cruising along the Palmetto Expressway—which was mercifully quiet this Friday night—heading north for I-75 and away from greater Miami. His commute to the city of Sunrise in the outlying suburbs of Fort Lauderdale sort of sucked, but he needed to have a *home*, not an apartment or a dorm room. And, with his two graduate student housemates back up North for their summer break, he had the rental house they shared as his personal fortress of solitude. He'd planned on barricading himself inside for most of that time to prep for the bar, with some breaks to help Judge Maloch with his research. So much for plans.

Bzzzzz.

Was that from inside the car? He glanced at the passenger seat. Nothing there. He took a quick look in back—just his backpack and laptop.

The laptop. The research. Judge Maloch. He should have seen it coming! Why hadn't he gone downstairs when he heard the argument? Why hadn't he slammed the door shut as soon as the judge entered the study?

He shook his head. Guilt was a cruel editor of logic. If he'd acted sooner, he'd be lying dead next to the judge. And that monster would have the laptop. Now it was up to Mark to scavenge whatever scraps he could find in that digital dungeon.

An hour later, Josh turned the car into his driveway.

Bzzzzz.

That *was* from inside the car. He pulled into the garage and went around to the passenger side. When he opened the door, he found a cell phone at the base of the passenger seat. He picked it up and saw a text message on the screen:

It's Sammi. Call me at this number asap!

He took out his phone and dialed.

"Josh?"

"Yeah. You drop your phone in my car?"

"Glad you found it. Remember you said it would be nice to have more specifics on when or where this thing was happening in three days? I may have something on that. You need to get into my phone. I got a text from the judge two days ago asking me to cancel a meeting he'd set for over the weekend. He had some kind of conflict now. I was in the middle of some thesis stuff, so I emailed out the cancellation without paying much attention to it. But I think the text might have mentioned something about his plans."

"I just pulled into my garage." He reached for the pad of sticky notes and the pen he kept in the slot by the gearshift. "What's your passcode? Let me get my stuff inside. Then I'll look for the text." He took down the code.

A few minutes later he found the judge's text, and the key sentence:

I have an event out of town at noon on Monday.

He dialed Sammi and told her.

"Nothing else?" she asked.

"Nope. That's Memorial Day. Was he in the service?"

"Don't think so. He never mentioned it."

And he'd never seen a military photo in Maloch's study or office. "Maybe this staggeringly significant thing's going to be revealed at a memorial for a judge who just happened to serve in the military."

"I would think hundreds did, at least. And we have no idea *where* the event is."

Unfortunately, she was dead right on both. "Yeah. Doesn't narrow it down much."

"Well, at least we have a precise deadline now."

"Not that it matters if Mark strikes out. I'm going to read up on another one of the judges tonight. When Judge Maloch told me he'd found his answer, he said, 'If we looked at *who* these judges were, and what they must have *seen*.' Then he cut himself off. There must be some connection in these stories that helps us. I'll run your phone back down there in the morning."

Soon after, he crawled into bed, grabbed his laptop, and pulled up the file on a second judge from the project. But the day's events had taken their toll. His eyelids dropped.

No! Don't! He tried to fight off the dream, but soon he was staring at the face of a worried captain sailing upriver to imperial Rome. Had he dreamt this before? Somehow, he knew that the man's life would soon be in the hands of a judge . . .

PRAYER AND SACRIFICE

266–Rome

"Quicken your pace!" Claudius Scipio hadn't meant to bark at his crew as they unlashed the ship's anchoring ropes, but he needed to get upriver at once. He'd first arrived at Ostia's busy port as a heartbroken child, having lost both his parents in a matter of weeks to the red plague, but he had been made whole again by his Pappi, his grandfather, who had raised him and taught him the secrets to the sea's bounty. By the time Claudius had turned fifteen, Lutatius had trusted his grandson with his own boat, his own crew. In the seven years since, they'd added boats and fisheries. Markets throughout Rome boasted their catch. His beloved Pappi was still at the heart of his world.

He steered the vessel out onto the Tiber and headed for the city center to sell the morning's haul. He knew the turns of this river like the veins in his hand. His life's blood swam this route: his wife and two children at one end, in Rome, and his business at the other, in Ostia. Ostia was also his Pappi's safe haven, the place to which Lutatius escaped each time the red death reared its wretched head.

Word at the docks was that the demons had returned for the fourth time in sixteen years. And though the losses had been mercifully fewer with each recurrence of the plague, city life had become a shadow of its former self. The air of Rome was choked by the red cloud hanging over it.

Having himself survived a battle with the demons, Claudius knew he could safely care for his family. But his Pappi would, as always, reject any offer to stay with them during the onslaught. Claudius respected Lutatius's independent spirit—the spirit of a former slave, freed by his master in the quinquennial census in gratitude for unraveling the mysteries of fishing. At age sixty, Lutatius was still solid of mind and body. Even so, when Claudius docked at inner-city Rome's end of the Tiber, he intended to see to it that his grandfather sailed for Ostia at once.

As his men moored their vessel amongst the rows of unloading trawlers, Claudius strode quickly from the pungent scents of the docks and along a nearby, shadowy alleyway. He hoped his grandfather was still at his appointment. Claudius stopped at an ash-gray door, and after three rapid knocks, he stepped into a musty room to find Lutatius sitting across a broad table from the fish broker, haggling over rates. A century earlier, Emperor Hadrian had outlawed "middlemen" in the seafood trade, but no fishing business could turn a profit without the efficient distribution networks such men provided. "Excuse my interruption, sir, but my grandfather needs to leave, *now*. The plague is rampant once more."

"We'll see to this on my return." Lutatius waved off the broker. "Several others have expressed interest in our business." He rose to face his grandson. "I can't leave the city quite yet. Other matters need tending to."

"Can I not tend to them?" Claudius asked, not hiding his concern.

"These are personal things. I'll stay wide of anyone with signs of the demons. I sail for Ostia at first light."

"Will you not breathe?" a frustrated Claudius responded. "Not grasp a door handle?"

Lutatius affectionately grabbed his grandson's shoulders. They locked eyes. "I must do what I must do." As always.

They stepped to the alley. At its end, Lutatius bid his grandson goodbye and disappeared around a corner. On his way home, Claudius stopped at the market for fruits and grain. The stalls would be empty soon. As he wove through the city, he tried not to hear the moans that seeped from doorways and windowsills. But in his mind he could still see his mother laid out in her best clothes in the middle of his childhood home, her mouth agape with her tongue awkwardly atop the copper coin to pay the toll for her passage to the underworld; he could still see the uneven quarry of red scabs that overran his father's face, could still feel himself tremble as his father's final scream of agony shattered the night.

The next morning, Claudius rose before the sun to escort Lutatius to the docks but found him shivering in bed, unable to lift himself.

Claudius sent word to his wife, who was sequestered with their children, that he would be tending to Lutatius for the time being. He stayed with his grandfather day and night, caring for him with the same love and compassion that he'd shown Claudius his whole life.

Claudius's childhood nightmares soon reappeared, as he watched his dear Pappi fight for every breath. With the strength of a far younger man, Lutatius took on the demons, but soon the constant seizures exacted their price: His vision blurred, his limbs weakened.

Late one night, as Lutatius asked softly after the health of their fishing crews, his head whiplashed back to the bed. His arms and legs jerked in every direction, like a wild stallion lassoed to the ground. His eyes careened in their sockets. Some supernatural puppeteer was brutalizing Claudius's dear Pappi; the feisty old fisherman could not survive much more of this.

Claudius wrapped his arms tightly around Lutatius, though it was like wrestling that wild horse with his bare hands. Finally, his Pappi's body went limp. Claudius feared the worst, but then he noticed Lutatius's shallow breathing. His grandfather was still alive.

The attacks continued for ten days, each as frightening as the first. When they subsided, Lutatius was left virtually blind, with little use of his arms or legs. After two weeks of living like this, the prayers began.

✦

Claudius had occasionally seen Lutatius pray before his illness. Like his grandson and a growing number of their friends, he'd come to recognize the new god, though it was still unsafe to profess such faith in public. Now his Pappi prayed every day to Christ. For several months his prayers remained the same: a simple request to be granted again the use of his eyes and extremities. But he did not improve.

Lutatius's servants were relegated to cleaning and cooking duties as Claudius did almost everything for him: fed him small bites, cautiously poured sips of water past his quivering lips, bathed and dressed him; the proud old man could not even relieve himself without Claudius's assistance. So, his prayers turned.

When Claudius would leave the room, he could often hear his Pappi's raspy plea, begging God for a release, for safe passage to the afterlife.

✦

Claudius pressed on, while checking in weekly with his foremen and crews. But his heart grew heavier by the day.

One night, as Claudius sat dutifully at his grandfather's bedside, Lutatius, straining for breath, croaked out a whisper: "My dear grandson, it must be painful . . . for you to see me like this."

"Pappi?"

"No, it's all right. My question is: Would it be more painful to live without me, or . . . to continue to see me suffer . . . as something less than a man, knowing I pray every day for death?"

"What are you saying, Pappi?"

"I'm asking . . . if you would help me on my way."

Claudius placed his hand gently on his grandfather's. "Pappi, you *will* get better. God will come to your aid."

"I'm sorry, Claudius, but I believe God has decided for some reason not to hear my pleas. Not to help me live as I did; not to help me die. I am convinced of two things: I will not be improving . . . and you are my only hope."

Claudius stood up. "And because you believe God has abandoned you, you're asking *me* to play God? To break the law? To take the life of someone I love as much as life itself?" How could he ask this? His Pappi *would* improve. He *must*!

"This is no life. I'm a tormented corpse cursed with breath."

"But you're everything to me. You're the road that leads to where I come from, to who I am."

"That road will always be with you."

"This is an enormous request you make of me."

Lutatius trembled. "I know."

"Then know something else, my grandfather. You raised me to treasure two things above all others: family and independence. You showed me how they could coexist, how sometimes the greater need of one must be met at the sacrifice of the other." Claudius knelt and clasped Lutatius's hand. "And so I yield. I yield to the ultimate request for independence, at the ultimate sacrifice of family."

His Pappi closed his eyes and asked for a moment to have a silent word with God. But silence wasn't necessary. Claudius knew well that Lutatius Scipio's final prayer was not for himself.

The bronze door to the alchemist's workshop closed slowly behind Marcus Samsonellus. Stepping through the morning shadows, he felt confident in the potion he'd just received from his old friend; it was something he'd used before to both steady and focus his mind.

In his sixteen years as elected *praetor*, he'd presided at other parricide trials, but the matter set out before him was a case truly of first impression. There'd be no magistrate for this pretrial proceeding. He wished to hear *this* plea with his own ears.

Now, dressed in his *tunic angusticlavia*, its deep crimson borders indicating his privileged judicial status, he entered the towering courtroom in the Roman Forum's Basilica Opimia, observing the reverent looks from the plebians packed in the pews. Little did they know. Though judges had been described throughout history as wielders of great power, most judicial decisions were confined within the four corners of a contract, or constrained by the dictates of a legislative edict. These were the unforgiving boundaries of a judge's dominion.

Even the *kind* of case a judge heard rested on the vagaries of trial assignments, which determined whether a judge's day portended to be an uplifting exposure of the human spirit or a nightmare from the first call to order.

The court was brought to attention. The chamber's quick silence was at once shattered by heavy chains clanging across the stone floor as this member of the *publica vincula*, those incarcerated awaiting trial, was led in. From his podium atop white marble steps, Judge Samsonellus gazed down at the proud bearing of the accused, Claudius Scipio. Facing a gruesome death sentence after pretrial incarceration in one of Rome's filthy, teeming dungeons, most accused murderers staggered into court with head hanging, as if the shackles to their wrists, ankles, and neck had choked off their air supply—but not this one.

"Claudius Scipio, you stand accused of the offense of parricide" were the first words Claudius heard from the judge. "Step forward. Are you prepared to state your plea?"

Though numerous legal orators had offered service, Claudius had refused counsel. He would not ask another to voice the arguments he planned as his defense.

He rose and dragged his chains to the base of the marble steps. "Your Eminence, as I have elected to represent myself, I humbly request the tribunal to educate me as to the legal definition of parricide, so that I may know how to plead."

The judge peered down from his podium, looking as if he could take the measure of a man in one stare. "The edicts provide that this court may grant no special dispensation on account of your decision to represent yourself."

Claudius felt his heart sink.

"However," the judge continued, "on the advice of the court's jurists, I am not prohibited from treating you as I would a novice orator. So, to a degree, I shall indulge your requests."

Claudius nodded respectfully. When he lifted his eyes, he noticed, gazing at him over the judge's shoulder, a white mount—a pristine mosaic of a saddled Pegasus—displayed on the wall behind the marble judicial bench. He'd been to court several times before, for his crewmen, but had never seen anything like this magnificent image of the winged white horse. Why was it hanging over this judge?

"Pursuant to edict," the judge explained, "the offense of parricide comprises four elements: first, that a parent, or someone serving as a parent, has been slain; second, that the death was not accidental; third, that the death was caused by the accused; and fourth, that the accused intended to kill the victim. Do you understand this definition?"

"Yes, Your Eminence." And it confirmed his choice to reject legal counsel.

"Then I ask once more, are you prepared to state your plea?"

Without doubt. Claudius straightened against his shackles. "My plea is innocence."

"So shall it be noted. As you have declined counsel, have you someone who may assist you in investigating the case and in interviewing potential witnesses?"

"Most respectfully, Your Eminence, I have no need of such things."

"Then by what means shall you defend yourself?"

By revealing his heart and praying that was enough. "Not by imposing on friends and associates to testify," Claudius answered. "I am prepared to go to trial at once."

"I see. The prosecution, however, is entitled to organize its case. Trial shall commence in seven days."

The state's orator rose. "Your Honor, there remains the matter of appointing a magistrate."

The judge eyed Claudius one last time. "This trial I shall hear *personally*."

Was that because the judge had already taken his measure? Or, Claudius hoped, because of the two of four elements yet to be satisfied?

The state's orator's first witness, Lutatius's longtime bookkeeper, had been summoned to court—clearly against his wishes—to testify about Lutatius's terribly depleted condition. Below the judge, the jurors perched at rapt attention as the man, unable to look Claudius in the eye, collapsed to tears four times during his testimony.

Claudius turned to the bench behind him where his wife and young sons sat, her face aflame in anger, the boys' heads darting around, lost. He'd urged her to stay at home with them. Why did they have to see this? He'd preferred his internment in the stench-ridden prison to these proceedings.

After the state's orator finished his examination, the judge asked Claudius if he had questions.

"None for the witness, Your Eminence, but, respectfully, one for the tribunal. May I offer to come forth at this time and respond to the questions the state's orator propounds?"

The judge raised his hands to quell the chamber's rising murmurs. "You are aware," he asked Claudius, "that you have no duty to take the stand? The prosecution would then have to prove the elements of the offense independent of your testimony."

"Yes, Your Eminence."

"Then on what basis do you offer to come forth?"

Claudius scanned the room. The jurors avoided his gaze. He hesitantly glanced again at his family and was met by his wife's glare. He knew her greater anger was aimed at his grandfather. "How dare Lutatius ask you to throw your life away!" she'd hissed through the iron bars of his cell. He knew she'd been right. But how could he say no to the man who'd given him everything? Claudius's sons, four and five years old, now stared back at him, their faces scrunched in fear. He nodded calmly at them.

His chains clattered against the bench as he turned back to the judge. "On the basis that I cannot abide such painful inquisitions of my innocent friends and neighbors on matters I am freely willing to admit. I am abundantly aware of the consequences flowing from the path I now choose."

The judge raised a hand to his chin. "So it appears. Please step forward."

As Citizen Scipio strode purposefully to the witness box, a beam of light streamed down from the apse's clerestory windows and glinted off the man's chains, momentarily sheathing him in a sparkling aura.

Before Judge Samsonellus could instruct the state's orator to ask his first question, the accused proceeded. "Your Eminence, of the four elements of parricide you set forth, I believe two are in question: that the death was *caused* by the accused, and that the accused *intended* to kill the victim."

Stepping away from his bench, the state's orator straightened his toga and reassumed his role. "Are you saying that you are not the person who killed your grandfather, Lutatius Scipio?"

Citizen Scipio faced his examiner. "My grandfather caused his own death. He *wanted* his own death. Prayed every day for it. But he no longer had the physical strength to carry out this most fervent wish alone, so he asked for my assistance."

The state's orator slid forward to a position between the accused and the tribunal podium, an adjustment, Judge Samsonellus knew, to force the accused to face the jurors directly when answering the next question. "But when you 'assisted' him, didn't you *intend* to kill him?"

Citizen Scipio, head high, peered straight at the jury. "I never intended to kill my grandfather. My prayers were only for his recovery. But when it became clear to him that there was no hope of his condition improving, he could not bear to have our family endlessly watch him suffer. *He* made this decision, not I. Next to my wife, my children, this was the most important person in the world to me; my heart, my soul. I lost *both* of my parents to the red plague when I was six." Murmurs rippled through the pews. "My grandfather raised me. Even as I helped grant his wish, I did not want him to die."

The man was balancing on the thinnest of threads. Surely the state's orator would sever these last strands.

But the state's orator went round and round with the accused, and the answers never wavered. Having no better witness on the issues of causation and intent, he rested his case. Citizen Scipio did the same.

The matter was now in the hands of the tribunal.

⁂

Staring at Judge Marcus Samsonellus, perched at the far edge of his desk, sat the jar of death. It held the small wax tablets, one side marked with the letter *A* for *absolve*, the other side with the letter *C* for *condemn*. At the trial's conclusion, when each juror rubbed off a side of their tablet and returned it to the jar, the remaining letters would determine if Claudius Scipio lived or died. Now the jar's threatening presence haunted the judge as he struggled with an internal conflict he could not resolve. Should a man's rights and responsibilities ever rise above the law? Above God?

Pulled from the archives and strewn across his desktop were roll upon roll of papyri, peeking out at him from their "purple togas"—their cylindrical parchment cases. He'd immersed himself in the past rulings that lived through those scrolls, along with the annual Praetor's Edicts, but none addressed the conundrum adequately. Here was an act that directly violated Roman law. At the same time, per religious decree—specifically the Judeo-Christian commandments that were a foundation of the Christianity in which Judge Samsonellus secretly believed—this act inhabited a tense void between "honor thy father and mother" and "thou shalt not kill."

And there was the matter of the prayers.

He'd heard that Lutatius Scipio, a rumored believer in Christ, had prayed day upon day, asking for relief from his infirmities. After months of this, bedbound, his sight and limbs ravaged to uselessness, the man's prayers had turned; he'd begun pleading to God—the *one* God—to take his life, to relieve his family of the burden he'd become.

Why had not God answered his pleas?

For God certainly answered prayers. This seemed as accepted a point of faith as the existence of a supreme being. For God must have an interest in his creations and must have an ear open to their pleas. A god of any compassion would surely respond to at least some prayers.

So, the question became: which prayers?

Must a person pray, day upon day, for a goodly portion of their living years, in order to garner God's grace? Such would certainly reward dedication and sacrifice. One might contend, nonetheless, that interminable repetition was but a squeaky wheel, unworthy of God's oil.

Or does God look to the circumstances? If so, how could God—*any* god—have ignored Lutatius Scipio's pleas?

And if God failed him, wasn't the law equally guilty on these facts? It condemned Claudius Scipio for presuming to act in God's place, but what right did the state have to punish a man for the ultimate act of mercy?

As he peered down at a scroll stretched before him, trapped by this collision amongst the legal, religious, and moral, he reached for his goblet, tempted to thrust it against the wall in frustration.

In that moment, a fog rose from the papyrus, and out levitated and spread into something beyond his imaginings, letters that were at first a jumble, hovering, which became then a muddled phrase here, dancing along the windowsill, an exclamation there, tacked above the mantelpiece.

Mist-like, they began to coalesce. Were they all in his mind, *The Words*?

And what exactly were they telling him? As he mobilized every last scintilla of concentration, the haze gave way to roughly defined edges and then the faintest hint of a message. It spoke to morals, to determinism, to man's dominion over his own existence. And then, suddenly, it flashed a response to his questions of God and the law:

THERE ARE SOME PRAYERS THAT DO NOT BELONG IN THE VOCABULARY OF THE YOUNG. PRAYERS NOT APPROPRIATE TO REPEAT, DAY UPON DAY, OVER THE COURSE OF A LIFETIME. PRAYERS THAT APPEAR ONLY AS A LAST RESORT, RISING TO A LEVEL OF EMOTIONAL CLIMAX ALMOST OF THEIR OWN FORCE, JUST AS THE WORSHIPPER IS VIRTUALLY DRAINED OF ANY POWER TO PLEAD. IF GOD IS UNWILLING, AND THE LAW UNAVAILING, TO GRANT SUCH PLEAS FOR MERCY, WHO SHALL?

In a flash, *The Words* were gone. He was left quivering in uncertainty, and yet, *The Words* were surely urging him toward some great good.

He reached for the alchemist's potion to steady his thoughts. Gradually, he forced himself back to his rational legal mind, filtered out all distractions, and arrived at a resolution—the only possible resolution—to the case pending before him. Claudius Scipio was clearly a good man, a devoted grandson. No better man had ever been paraded before the judge's bench. But there was no escaping the law. For it was the law, that ramrod of civilization, that kept the citizens of Rome from devolving back to the pack of wolves from whence they came.

In this case, the law decreed that the intentional killing of a parent, or someone serving in a parental role, was a capital offense. Performing the act at the request of the decedent was no defense.

The hardest part—even more soul-wrenching than decreeing Claudius Scipio a murderer—would be the sentence. The penalty for a conviction of parricide was "bagging."

The guilty party would be taken to a seaside cliff and placed inside a heavy fabric bag. A gamecock would then be tossed inside and the bag tied shut.

The bag would be pushed off the cliff toward the water. The gamecock would follow its instincts and training, lashing out with its razor-sharp striking spur, again and again, in an effort to free itself.

Onlookers at baggings—the citizens of Rome loved a good spectacle—were typically serenaded by haunting screams as the condemned was torn to shreds.

Judge Samsonellus had imposed the punishment before. Each time he'd witnessed its horror, he knew he was being punished as well. As an instrument of a society that sanctioned such atrocities, he was condemned to suffer those screams, condemned to envision what transpired inside that dark and deadly portal of hell.

He glanced over at the far end of his desk. He could almost hear the tablets stirring in the jar of death.

✦

By the next midday, the jury had finished its deliberations. On the table below the judge's podium, his clerk emptied the jar and announced the mark remaining on each wax tablet.

"*Condemno*," the clerk proclaimed, to a chorus of mournful sighs.

"*Condemno*," he repeated, twelve times, as the sighs from the gallery weakened to resignation. Each *C* plunged a jagged blade one notch deeper into Marcus Samsonellus's soul.

The tally finished, his next act was set in stone. He had no choice but to sentence this most honorable man to a terrible, painful death. His "great powers" as a judge were as helpless before the law as Claudius Scipio.

Wait. Perhaps not *completely* helpless, he thought—or had *The Words* just whispered in his ear? Conviction and sentencing would be as required. But there was still room for mercy.

✦

Huddling against the early evening chill as he stepped into the alchemist's cramped workshop, Marcus Samsonellus scanned behind him one last time, making sure no follower lurked in the mist. He'd long ago rejected the notion that alchemists could transmute non-precious metals into gold, but he valued their expertise in potions.

He told his old friend that he needed a poison that would act with precision and swiftness, freezing the body and blocking all senses shortly after consumption. The alchemist went to a shelf in a corner behind his workbench. He examined and pushed aside a few jars, then pulled one from the back and set it on the table. It contained a fine white powder.

"This is from thornapple leaves." He opened the jar and poured a small portion into a packet, then sealed the packet with wax. "Just sprinkle the contents on food. It will take hold rather promptly."

The judge left the workshop with the small packet tucked in his cloak. He could not recall the last time he had been this nervous.

It was not every day that a bagging took place. Half the audience assembled around the plateau of the rocky cliff. The remainder lurked below, just off the shoreline, jockeying for position.

Atop the seaside cliff, Judge Samsonellus's gaze shifted to Citizen Scipio, who sat at a small wooden table eating his last meal. Not far away, a gamecock was being fed as well. The judge stopped briefly by the bird. It happily pecked at its feed.

Next, he walked over and sat down across the table from the condemned man, who was finishing his meal. "May I pray for you?" he whispered. At Citizen Scipio's nod, the judge instructed him to close his eyes; then he extended his arms toward the crown of the man's head, opened his hands, and quietly asked Christ for his mercy.

Citizen Scipio took his last bites. The judge announced that the bagging must begin.

As Citizen Scipio was guided into a large fabric bag, a patch of fine vapor wafted skyward from the sea, like a spirit rising to accept the unredeemed. The rooster was tossed in the bag, the rope at the top tightened, and the bag cast over the side.

The watchers came to attention.

The bag hurtled downward, the outline of limbs thrusting desperately against its sides. Murmurs rose from the crowd. Though no screams came from the bag, the watchers' voices soared with excitement. Damn their bloodlust! They were surely envisioning the panicked gamecock's striking spur lashing out again and again.

The bag crashed into the sea, blasting a crater of white foam. It seemed the cockfighter had done its work. The only movement from the bag was a repeated striking of a narrow point under the outer skin—a rooster cutting its hole to freedom.

The striking spur pierced the side of the bag, and the bird came through.

It was stone dead.

To the end of his days, Marcus Samsonellus had two unforgettable images burned into his brain. The first was the sight of Claudius Scipio coming through the hole in that bag and swimming to freedom, having used the poisoned and paralyzed cock's spur to cut the hole.

The second image was even more brilliant: *The Words*. He could still see every line of the message they'd sent him during the Scipio trial, a message he'd long suspected was a mere blade of grass on an endless field. Over the years, he'd pored over his old research time and again, driving himself back to the precise context. But he'd never been able to see more than that one blade.

In one of those moments, as his years shallowed, Marcus Samsonellus sensed he had arrived at a truth, as inexplicable as it was. His portion of *The Words* had somehow been delivered to him out of the cloud mist of a grandfather's dying prayer.

PREY

Creak!

Josh startled out of his dream, ears locked in.

Creak.

Softer now, but no less certain. Something was being pried apart on the other side of the house. The monster had found him!

Moving quietly, alert to every sound, Josh slid off his platform bed and scooped up his laptop, phone, and running shoes. But where was he going? He couldn't step out into the hall. The man would surely see him. He eyed his two tiny bedroom windows. They barely opened and were too small anyway.

He was trapped.

✦

As Billy Ray set down his crowbar and stepped through the jimmied sliding glass door, he pulsed with energy. Over the years since the Reverend had "saved" him, his special talents had come in handy on a whole bunch of delicate jobs. But never had the Reverend seemed more in a tizzy about one of his assignments.

He unsheathed his hunting knife and slinked down the hall, ignoring his throbbing skull. He took a look-see into each room he passed and listened for signs of life. Not a peep.

One bedroom left to check—the master. He entered the room to find it empty, but the bed was still warm. No one in the bathroom or closet. He spun back to the hall. A backpack and a stack of books were piled on a table near the front door. No laptop, but a cell phone was on top of the stack. A yellow sticky note was next to the phone. Was someone yanking his chain? The note had six digits written out. Could Sutton have just changed his passcode?

Sure enough. Billy Ray quickly downloaded his favorite spy app, then turned for the door that opened into the two-car garage. A white RAV4 was in the dead center. You didn't park in the middle unless you were there alone. He reached in his pocket for the GPS tracker, bent down, and stuck it on the nearest wheel well.

He got up and went back into the house.

Warm bed. Cell phone and car here. Sutton had to be close by.

A low whistle came from his right. A door to the rear of the house was leaking air; it hadn't been closed all the way. He yanked the door open to the dark, moonless night and could just make out a nearby thicket of trees behind the house. He needed his specs.

He raced to his car, his head pulsing harder now. The hunt was on.

"Ow!"

Josh's shoulder hit the tree hard. It was too damn dark and the woods were too dense to fly through at full speed. He started shuffling along in quick bursts, still getting scratched or smacked at every screeching halt or swerve.

He was breathing hard, though not from physical exertion. It was primal fear. There was no doubt who was after him. That monster would've trapped him in the house if not for the platform bed. When he'd found it at the thrift store, he'd liked the idea of the extra storage in the mattress-length, pull-out drawers. Good thing he'd never got around to storing anything in them. Until now. When he'd heard the door to the garage open, he'd slipped out of the drawer and tiptoed out through the rear door, racing for these woods. On the other side was the Sunrise Police Department.

Ow! A shrub stabbed his shin.

Had he just screamed that, or was it only in his mind?

He held his breath, came to a halt, and listened. Somewhere behind him there was a sound that didn't fit the woods. It had to be heavy feet, shifting nimbly. Too nimbly. Like a large, nocturnal animal that could see in the dark.

A car turned onto the road at the back of the woods, momentarily washing the area with its headlights. Josh ducked and looked back in the direction of his house. Fifty yards behind him, every bit as huge as he remembered, was the man. Light flashed across protrusions in front of his eyes. Night vision goggles! He looked directly at Josh and started running right toward him.

Josh spun around and spotted, in the last traces of headlight glow, a narrow path to the end of the woods. He bolted as fast as he'd ever run.

Through the thinning brush, Josh spied a streetlight; he was almost there. As he darted left to avoid a palm tree, something whizzed by his ear. He looked over his shoulder. A large hunting knife protruded from the trunk, precisely at eye level. It had missed him by six inches.

His heart pounding, he slid left to avoid a shrub, then jumped to the right around a tree as asphalt came into view. Finally!

Josh sprang from the woods and raced across the street to the broad, concrete building.

Twenty feet from the edge of the woods, Billy Ray stared out at the large illuminated sign two floors up from where Sutton was standing: SUNRISE POLICE DEPARTMENT. Dang it! He yanked his knife from the tree, wheeled, and sped back the way he'd come. He was about to burst into the open in Sutton's backyard when he stopped cold. Headlights were coming up the street. That was awful quick.

He circled wide, passed through the side yard of a house three over, and, from the shadows, saw the cop car pull up in front of Sutton's driveway. Staying out of streetlights, he made his way back to his car. He'd pick up Sutton's trail in the morning. The cops would be off to other adventures by then.

Not the worst thing. He needed a night's sleep bad; his skull was hammering. For now, he'd leave Sutton thinking about the huge blade that had just missed his head.

Spoiled brat probably thought he'd got lucky. Him with his law school education, house, and SUV. Momma and Daddy been real good to this one. Probably too full of himself to even consider that he'd been missed by less than a foot *intentionally*.

After waiting near police headquarters for twenty minutes, Josh took a circuitous path around the woods back toward his house, not sure if he dared to go in. As he reached the corner, he spotted a car parked out front. A police cruiser. Strange. There was an officer standing near the living room window. Josh watched from the shadows as another policeman came from around the rear of the house. The two spoke briefly, got in their car, and pulled away. What? As it passed under a streetlight, he got a close-up look at the words on the side of their vehicle:

KENDALL POLICE.

WAKE-UP CALL

A knife in midair, slicing through a laptop . . . Judge Maloch on his judicial bench, blood spurting from his chest . . . Josh imprisoned in a banyan's trunks . . . A huge, redheaded man charging out from Mark Roth's command center . . .

Sammi had tossed and turned for hours. It seemed she'd just fallen asleep again when someone knocked loudly on her door.

"Sammi?" The voice was familiar.

She forced her eyes open and slogged across the apartment.

Her friend and next-door neighbor, Lauren, looking less than pleased, was waiting in the hallway, holding out her cell phone. "It's for you. That guy from last night again."

Sammi shook herself awake. "What time is it?"

"Six a.m."

She took the phone and brought it to her ear. "Josh?"

"Were you able to sleep?"

"A little, I think. What's wrong? Why are you calling so early?"

"Been out all night."

"Where? Why?"

"Had a visit from the judge's murderer. Almost got me."

"What?!"

"Broke into my house. No idea how he found out who I am or where I live."

Sammi controlled a tremble as she eyed Lauren. "Okay if I bring your phone back in a little bit?"

"No problem." Lauren turned away, then spun back. "You sure you don't need me here?"

"No, I'm good." She stepped back inside and closed the door.

"Josh, you all right?"

"I'm fine. I slipped out while that goon was looking around. He tracked me through the woods out back, but he took off when he saw me in front of the police station."

"Thank God you went to the police."

"Actually, I didn't. But I knew seeing me there would scare him off. Crazy thing is, after I waited awhile and took a wide path back toward my house, there was a police car out front, a *Kendall* police car."

"How'd *they* find you?"

"No clue. I stayed out of sight until they left. Did me one favor though. No way the judge's killer was hanging around with them there. As soon as they pulled out, I ran in, grabbed your phone, and got in my car. I hauled ass out of there."

"Josh, you've *got* to call the Kendall police. A murderer's after you. He came to your house! Where exactly are you?"

"In your parking lot. Been here three hours. Didn't want to bother you too early."

Josh leaned against the living room wall in Sammi's apartment and switched his phone to speaker as a male voice came on the line.

"This is Detective Gutierrez. You're calling about Judge Neville Maloch?"

"Yes, sir."

"Could you please tell me your name?"

He glanced at Sammi, who sat in front of him at the edge of her couch. "Joshua Sutton."

"Ah, Mr. Sutton. Was it you who called in yesterday to report the crime?"

"Yes, sir."

"Well, Mr. Sutton, we went out there. Neighbor let us in. Place looked fine, no signs of forced entry, no signs of *anything*. Neighbor said she thought the judge might be out of town."

Josh and Sammi exchanged puzzled looks.

"Wasted a bunch of man-hours out there," the detective continued. "Thought maybe this was some kind of sick prank by one of those swatting assholes. But as we were leaving, another neighbor stopped us. He'd seen someone rush out of the house to an SUV and peel out earlier. Took a shot of the license plate with his phone. Turns out the plate was yours."

That's why they'd come to his house.

"And we know about your family and the trial . . ."

He couldn't let Sammi hear this. He took the phone off speaker.

". . . about the murder charge."

He wandered over toward the door, as far from Sammi as the room allowed. He forced a glance back. Her eyes had opened to the size of quarters.

The detective went on. "Got me wondering. Why would someone who'd been charged with a murder call in a phony one? And why would he leave the supposed crime scene in such a hurry?"

"Judge Maloch was murdered. I saw it happen."

"Mr. Sutton, we know you were at the judge's house yesterday, but believe me, no one was murdered there. Are you on any kind of medication?"

He glanced at Sammi again. Threw his hand up. "I'll have to call you back."

"As a precaution, we'd like you to come down to the station. Just a few questions to clear some things up."

"If nothing happened, why do you need me to come in?"

"It's just to make sure we understand everything here. You've made a serious claim."

"I . . . I can't come down there today."

"Fine. I'll give you until 3:00 p.m. tomorrow. I don't see you by then, this will become more than a request."

As he hung up, Sammi's eyes were boring into him.

"Sorry. I didn't want you to hear the personal stuff. I was sixteen when my older brother, Seth, killed himself. Jumped from the roof of my cousin's apartment building. There was . . . an inquest." That was technically true.

Her eyes softened. "Why would he kill himself?"

"He was tormented by dreams, couldn't let them go."

"What kind of dreams?"

Odd question. "Crazy, vivid stories. Characters from across time and all over the world, yet somehow they seemed connected." He hesitated. "I had them too." Oh, crap. Why did he let that slip? He was already on thin ice in the credibility department.

"Really." She opened her mouth to say something more, but stopped.

"He warned me to fight the dreams off. Told me they were killing him. But I never thought he would do something like that."

"I'm so sorry." Sammi's eyes had reddened. "I can't even imagine . . ."

He needed to change the subject before she asked any more questions. "Speaking of things we can't imagine, did you hear what that detective said about wasted man-hours out there? He had to be talking about forensics. The judge must've bled all over the floor in the study, but they didn't find a trace? Something's wrong."

"You're saying the *police* are in on this?"

She had to be thinking he was crazy. Or guilty. He shrugged. "The killer's got to be a freaking Houdini. Think about it. I knocked the guy out. So, he comes to, removes the body, perfectly scrubs the place of evidence, and gets out of there, all before the cops arrive? I called them minutes after I left. Who could do that?" He paced the room. "I need time to think, to go through the rest of the research. And for Mark to come up with something." He eyed her cautiously.

She locked her gaze on him. "That murderer's not going to stop looking for you."

He forced a chuckle. "Yeah, there's also that."

"What would you think about getting out of town?" she said. "At least overnight. My uncle has a vacation place on Sundown Key, out on the Gulf Coast. I could see if it's free for the weekend."

That was a surprise. Somehow, she still seemed to believe him. But why?

BACKUP PLAN

There'd been two brief reports from Kyle in the past twelve hours. His man had failed twice.

Awaiting his overdue guest at his private booth in the back room of the Starlight Club, Han Chee-hwa softly drummed his fingers on the table. He lived in a culture that worshipped patience, a culture that had wormed its way inside him despite his boundless ambition. Well-considered plans and execution had allowed him to painstakingly fashion this club at the penthouse level of a luxury hotel he owned on the beach in Zhuhai, with its dark teakwood wall panels, artisan-etched, floral-patterned Tiffany lamps, and plush leather ebony booths—all having been installed only after touch and approval by his own hands.

Given the exigencies of the current situation, however, he could not afford the extravagance of patience. Yet it had become clear that his hands needed closer contact with the work.

He didn't doubt Kyle's commitment to the cause. And Kyle was clearly convinced of his operative's talents. But there was now ample evidence to support the man's inadequacies.

"Mr. Han, your guest is downstairs," announced Wenqian, his personal server, a woman he'd chosen for her intellect and attention to detail, along with her merely adequate appearance. He did not want visitors distracted when he discussed business matters. "I've sent the hostess you requested to meet him."

The man he awaited, General Fu Chang, stood at the pinnacle of the Party leadership. He'd known Chang for thirty years, done him numerous favors. In return, the general had once come through on a highly sensitive matter. And yet, yesterday, wary of the Party's current leanings, Han had hesitated to call him.

Instead, he'd relied on his gambler's gut and reached out across the world, to the West, to Kyle. But now, with his cards running cold, he needed to hedge his bets. The strongest hedge was a bet on the most powerful.

His late uncle had taught him that having the powerful indebted to you was an invaluable insurance policy. "It's precarious to build a castle without a moat," he'd cautioned. When Han was orphaned for a second time, cast out penniless by his wretched cousin, Zhou, at his uncle's death, he'd clung to his uncle's lessons as his only possessions of value. With no funds for a castle, he'd wondered, was it possible to build the moat first?

He'd headed south to Zhuhai, a tropical paradise of twisting coves and beaches, backed by cascading emerald mountains along the South China Sea. Before their first of several holidays there, his uncle had proclaimed it "China's sparkling pearl." What had drawn Han was the young city's staggering promise.

In his early years in Zhuhai, his smooth, prep-school carriage—acquired on the generosity and insistence of his uncle—had made him an attractive employee for upscale hotels. Despite his youth, he'd quickly moved into midlevel management. Soon, escort services seeking referrals had clamored for his friendship, lavishing him with gifts and other inducements.

He'd noticed that most of the escorts, though well-dressed and delicately made up, could barely read and knew little of world affairs. Their use of language was dreadful, most of them having come from outside of China, where they'd been sold as slaves by their parents, often at an age as young as fourteen. They couldn't carry on an intelligent conversation, and other than their looks, they had nothing to offer that might keep a man interested for more than a brief tryst. Given such limitations, and with so many attractive girls to choose from in Zhuhai, it was difficult for any one escort to build much of a repeat business.

Having been pulled up from the gutter himself, however, he'd seen something beyond their inadequacies: an opportunity to build a moat.

He recruited girls—not always the prettiest ones—who showed an interest in learning. For a small portion of their earnings, he offered to improve their grammar, vocabulary, and elocution, while introducing them to matters of the world: finance, politics, history, religion, sports.

He started with groups of two or three girls, but before long his classes were growing. As he accumulated sufficient funds, he bought his graduates. Because the girls were easily replaceable and had limited periods of profitability before they burned out or contracted a disease that rendered them useless, the escort services were generally willing to sell a girl for less than two hundred American dollars.

Although they were merely disposable assets to him, he told every girl he purchased the same thing: She was not his property, and she was free to go at any time. But the girls rarely left. They were used to being owned and provided for. They'd lost touch with, or never knew, how to live in the real world. They'd been betrayed by their own families, and they felt beholden to him. It served his business purposes to treat his girls far better than they had been treated in the past, but if one crossed him, he would pass word that she'd decided to return to her family. No one dared inquire further.

He constructed a dedicated, unrivaled workforce in Zhuhai. In a town noted for the sex trade, there was a new product available: girls who could carry on a conversation, girls with class and style, girls who could interest a man in maintaining a relationship. And every one of them worked for him.

From early on, he'd reserved his most talented girls for high-status Party members and wealthy businessmen. His uncle had built a moat on bribes; Han's was paid for in a more personal manner.

Over the ensuing years he'd built an empire, acquiring numerous other businesses and substantial real estate, including this hotel, but the backbone of his fortune was still his escort services, and the Starlight Club its most privileged establishment.

The door to the room swung open. The dazzling young hostess was approaching arm in arm with a short, thickly built, uniformed man.

Han slid from the booth and straightened. "Good evening, General."

They shook hands. "Nice to see you, Chee-hwa."

They ordered drinks and briefly caught up on each other's lives. They had not met face-to-face in more than five years, but Han had little use for prologue and, as he recalled, General Chang shared that trait.

At his first sip of *baijiu*, the general said, "Chee-hwa, though it's wonderful to see you again, I'm intrigued as to why you insisted on meeting in person."

"I'm involved in a delicate matter. Something of utmost importance."

"Are you in trouble again, Chee-hwa?" The general furrowed his brow. "In all these years, you've sought my help only that one time."

"We're *all* in trouble, *imminently*. But this is nothing like what you did before." He shook his head. "No public display. And it's outside the country."

"Where exactly?"

"The United States."

"Chee-hwa, please forgive me, but this isn't another one of your Falun Dafa hunts, is it?"

Han lowered his drink. "If it is, why would *you* of all people question its importance? You've led some of those hunts personally on behalf of the national leadership."

The general placed his hands flat on the table and leaned in. "And their feelings haven't wavered on that evil cult. But the Party's direction has. They're focused more than ever on economics, on expanding their foothold on global finance."

"How does that change things with the Dafa?"

"Discretion has become paramount. Our leaders insist, more than ever, on controlling the image the world sees of us. And the ability to control is greatest within our own borders."

"I understand."

"*Do* you?"

"Most definitely, General." Han ran his fingers along the sides of his glass. "This would be an extremely confined covert operation. I've heard our government has some highly specialized agents in the US who can serve on a moment's notice."

The general grinned. "That's a preposterous rumor spread by insurgents."

"So," Han asked, disappointed, "it isn't true?"

"I didn't say that."

INCREASED *DE*

There were so many scenic routes in North America, but the drive across southern Florida from Fort Lauderdale, on the Atlantic side, to Naples, on the Gulf Coast, along a stretch of road commonly known to the locals as Alligator Alley, was certainly not one of them.

Sammi took a deep breath and turned up the music to keep herself awake. She hadn't gotten a ton of sleep, tossing for hours in between nightmares, but given his home invasion, Josh, who was slumped over in the passenger seat of his car, had gotten almost none.

Past Josh's head, out the window, and for miles in front of and behind them, was an endless sea of tall, scraggly, serrated-edged sawgrass—the marshland's unkempt, overgrown lawn—rippling like a choppy green lake in the breeze. Every once in a while, it would be broken up by a patch of spindly pine trees, but then it was back to sawgrass. This part of the Everglades wasn't exactly like those chamber of commerce promotions. No brilliant blue lakes, no airboats zipping around palm-filled islands, no flamingos wading offshore, and not a single alligator sunning itself on the banks. The only wildlife in the past twenty minutes was a bass being pulled out of a dirt-brown roadside canal at the end of a local fisherman's line.

The road ran due west with barely a curve, like a tape measure stretched to the horizon, and the topography was so flat that had Christopher Columbus taken this trip, he might have rethought his worldview. But this was the quickest way to Fort Myers and its barrier islands, the fastest way to her uncle's vacation home on Sundown Key.

The highway clawed endlessly ahead, tires whirring and wind humming steady monotones. It felt good to be putting some distance between them and southeast Florida.

Uchhzzzz.

She glanced over at her snoring companion. The judge had complained to her more than once about Josh—about his lack of effort on written assignments and barely contained anger when arguing in class about issues he took too personally, about the confounding conundrum of his absolute brilliance when a problem was suddenly thrown at him in a mock trial setting.

Despite the complaints, the judge had picked Josh to be his research assistant on this matter of supposedly staggering importance. Did the judge know about Josh's brother? About what that must have done to Josh and his family? Maybe that's why he'd seen past the rough edges. Seen the Josh who, facing the terrifying realities of the last day, seemed rock-solid driven.

But the judge couldn't have known about the dreams. Or that the way Josh had described *his* would hit eerily close to home for her: *characters from across time and all over the world.*

This was another mark with meaning.

Josh was half asleep when he felt the vibrations in his pants pocket. He yanked out his phone. The display read: Spaceman. He shifted upright and took the call on the car's Bluetooth system.

"Hey, Mark. Got anything?"

"Actually, two things. But first, some bad news, Quark. The designer of this multi-fragmenter is an ass-kicking genius. Looks like all I'll be able to extract from the laptop is maybe a few directory or file names. I can't get to any data inside of files."

"Once again, you've blown me away with your talents. What *do* you have?"

"Number one, besides the fragmenter, there was another piece of malware in that link you opened: an address book hijacker. So, when you clicked on the link, the sender of the email got a copy of the judge's whole address book. Since you were the judge's bitch, I'd suggest you stay away from your house for the time being."

He caught Sammi's chuckle. "Great suggestion . . . *eight* hours ago. What was the other useless bit of information you have?"

"You told me to look for files on judges or legal history. I found a directory called 'Judges,' and I think I was able to read the name of one of the subdirectories. But part of it made no sense to me—not as a word, not even as an abbreviation. Take a look."

A text came in on Josh's phone:

Increased De

"Any idea what it means?" Mark asked.

"Not a clue." He turned to Sammi, whose eyes were locked on the road ahead. "Does 'Increased De' mean anything to you?"

"Don't sports people use *D* as shorthand for *defense*?" Sammi asked. "Maybe it stands for some kind of raised defenses."

"They just use the letter *d* for that; this is *d-e*. The judge had season tickets for the Heat and Dolphins. He would've known the difference."

Sammi ran a hand through her hair. "There's definitely something familiar to me about 'Increased De.'" Her hand went back to the wheel. "I'll have to think about it."

Josh thanked Mark, who promised to continue his efforts. He ended the call and entered "increased de" as a search term on his phone's browser. "Let's see what Google tells us. Hmmm. There's a bunch of 'increased de novo,' linking to articles on gastroenterology, and a few 'increased de minimis,' referencing the US tax code. Not real helpful."

He slumped down in his seat and yawned. "We've got two days left and nothing to go on."

She glanced over. "Why don't you rest? The sleep of a laboring man is sweet."

"Huh?"

"It's from Ecclesiastes. Means you've earned a good nap. Maybe something helpful will come to mind."

He couldn't remember the last time someone quoted the Bible to him. "Thanks." He closed his eyes for a second to think but quickly drifted off.

He was lying on his childhood bed. Seth startled him, jumping up on the mattress and screaming, "Don't dream!" But Seth and his warning faded, and another dream soon enveloped him.

Long ago, across the Atlantic, a judge was calling out to an old friend . . .

INNER SANCTUM

1555-London

Has it been twenty years, dear Thomas? Twenty years since last I saw you? Since I heard your words, *those* words? The moments are scattered now; they pass before me as feathers on the wind—most elude my grasp.

But hold, here . . . it comes to me, the very beginning. Each of us a mere thirteen years along, peddled off to St. Anthony's—the finest school in London. For you, Thomas More, proud son of a prominent judge, 'twas a rite of passage. For me, Nigel Tolan, petulant brat, a sentence far less noble.

Wherever your blessed station may be these days, even now must you admit you were a strange young lad. Head endlessly buried in a book, your uniform and hair in disarray, you rarely spoke other than to members of the faculty. And you were always with that journal, that treasure trove where your secrets dwelt. When you weren't writing in it, it was under your arm, locked in position, protected.

We'd had no words; there'd been nothing between us. There was neither rhyme nor reason, at least none beyond the borders of my bitter shell, for what I did. The field trip on that chilled autumn morn led us along a mudded, rocky bank of the Thames. You opened your precious journal, perhaps to admire a passage, perhaps to record a notation.

It was then that I struck.

You went down hard, headfirst, straight to the rocks. Forgive me, dear Thomas, but I think I was even smiling. Your journal took flight out toward the freezing water. Our group was frozen as well—petrified in disbelief. The headmaster, Father Worthington, came to your aid. As he helped you to your feet, your head darted left to right, right to left, up, down. You were looking, searching, frantic. I watched your heart sink—though, back then, I am sad to say, I could not feel it—when you spotted your trusted confidant. It was floating, spine up, pages down, in the water, well off the bank.

You pulled yourself from the headmaster, stumbled down the stony, pockmarked slope, and, to the overriding alarm of the multitude, dove into the frigid torrents. Arms thrashing, you plunged and rose, plunged and rose. As you closed the gap, the journal, saturated, turned on its side and began to fade from view. A few more strokes . . . half the cover was gone. Two thrashes . . . only the spine remained. A final lunge . . . too late! The book vanished; the river had closed upon it.

Down you dove in pursuit, entombed within those icy waters.

We waited. No ripple stirred the river. A few moments more . . . nothing. The group skittered down the bank, edging close to the water. The Father removed his coat, his shoes. And then a splash, your arm smacked the surface . . . a huge gulp for air. You turned and thrashed your way back to us with one hand. And in the other, clenched tighter than a newborn, there was a soaked mass of parchments melted into one great mound and barely clinging to the leather spine.

You dragged yourself ashore. The crowd extended hands and dry vestments, but before you would accept either, you peered down at your beloved, ruined journal, and your legs all but caved in. As a coat was slipped upon you, your focus shifted, scanning the group. Before I could avert my gaze, your eyes found mine. It seemed only I could read the vitriol that flowed within them. It seemed only I could see the anguish bared in that glare. But, of course, dear Thomas, I could never possibly know the full depth of that anguish, nor ever have conceived the twisted fruit it would engender.

"Thirty and five years has it been since St. Anthony's last convened an expulsion inquisition," Father Worthington began. "Woe that these great halls must again be burdened with the plea of the unworthy."

Indeed, I was the unworthy one. But never had I asked to be sent to those great halls. Never had I been heeded, even in the smallest regard. Never had—

"And now," the Father continued, "as we arrive at the matter of final proof, the school requests Master Thomas More come forward and bear witness to the unfortunate events at the Thames."

I sat in the box, on the stage of that grim, teeming auditorium, watching you rise, Thomas, your gait slow, but steady—no hint of uncertainty that might spare my fate. I did not fear expulsion; I almost welcomed it. What I feared were the words you might choose to say, the daggers you might launch, the ugly truths unearthed. I feared your unpredictability, your differentness. But, of course, you knew this.

"Certainly, Father," you said. "I can tell you what occurred at the river. There was a boy to my side. His name is Nigel Tolan. He sits there in the box in front of me.

"I have heard another student testify this day of seeing Master Tolan's arm flash in my direction, immediately before I went down. Of that point, I cannot be certain. But I am most positive of other matters of substance to this case. Master Nigel Tolan is an angry youth, churning on end. I've heard him murmur to others that his father, an advisor to King Henry VII, packed him off to St. Anthony's against his wishes. It seems Nigel bears a grudge at humanity. Ignored in his world, he lashes at ours. He neglects his schoolwork in hopes it will hurt his father. He heeds no one.

"A careful investigation of the matter, however, reveals that Master Tolan and I share a common circumstance: an absence of friends. My classmates shun me—perplexed at my intimacy with textbooks, my cross-examinations of faculty. And Master Tolan shuns everyone. His bitterness harbors no companions."

The faces of the committee members contorted in confusion. The headmaster interrupted you. "Thank you, Master More, but what further can you tell us of the incident?"

"I can report that if caused by Master Tolan"—you motioned toward me—"it was hatched not solely of ill will. It arose from an unnurtured spirit, a soul crying out, unheard."

"But, Master More"—the Father seemed greatly perturbed—"is there nothing else of substance you can relate? Nothing this committee can use for its recommendation?"

You faced the committee. "Why, of course. In point of fact, I can make that recommendation. I recommend that Master Tolan be assigned to study with me for two hours per day for the remainder of the semester."

I can still see the astonished faces of the committee, still hear the gasps from the audience. If you were strange to them before, you had now sailed strangeness to unmapped seas. No one quite knew what to make of this—least of all, the troubled youth in the box.

I know I was difficult. I served my sentence while rejecting your every attempt to interest me in the work. But I began to observe you more closely in class. Your passion for study was beyond comprehension—your furious note-taking; your hand constantly in the air. The instructors' answers were never enough. You insisted on historical context, rationale.

One morning in class brought startling news. An Italian-born explorer named Christopher Columbus had discovered a "New World" out across the great western sea. With a knowing smile blooming on your lips, you leaned my way and whispered, "Lay thy mind open wide as a fertile field, and the winged secrets of life gently shall alight."

"Yes, Thomas," I could not help but reply, "and on your field I'm most certain they'll leave pearls of wisdom in their wake, while on mine, only droppings."

It was the first time I ever heard you laugh.

Sensing my grudging respect, you pushed harder. This time, I finally responded. But, to my credit, I did more than that. As you nurtured my underfed intellect, I began to push back. Not against you, but for you. You needed to be drawn from your shell—not so much for your sake, but the world's—else humanity be denied the harvest of your brilliance.

I prodded you to engage. Remember the school's polo team? You astride your chocolate colt, barreling down the midline, whilst I tracked on my pale, white, energetic mare—even then, you abided my compulsions, my unexplainable need to ride a white mount. As you kept my studies on pace, I loosed my wit, rescuing you, for brief moments, from your solemnity.

But there was one flinty ridge of yours even I could not soften. That internal moral compass with only two settings: right and wrong. I hated to see you tormented, never accepting the conduct of another—or, for that matter, your own—as harmlessly falling into the great grey middle, compulsively assigning absolute accountability to youths and adults for their every action. I tried, Thomas, time and again, to convince you that such an unyielding stance would guarantee a lifetime bereft of friendships but never lacking in disappointments.

And I feared that someday I would again fail to live up to your incomparable standards. Just as I feared that your lofty morals would someday be your undoing.

Was it merely two years thereafter when my father was appointed ambassador to France? I worried for you then. Absent my gregarious presence, surely you would descend back to isolation. For your qualities did not appeal to the masses . . . yet.

In your letters you wrote of becoming a page in the household of Archbishop Morton. It would not be until our next meeting, years later, that I would witness the extraordinary transformation that service had produced.

We had not corresponded in some time. Upon your graduation from

Oxford, your father arranged an internship in a law practice. The crown's relationship with France had soured, so my father was called back to England. Aware of my interest in the law, he found me a similar position.

"Now whose head is immersed in a book?" I'd been dispatched to the courthouse library to research a precedent and was leaning against a stack of treatises, wrestling an incomprehensible ruling, when a nearby voice whispered those words.

I looked up, but there was no need. Partly a sense of decorum—but more fully a fear of reprisal from my extremely conservative law firm—restrained me from boisterous response. Instead, I quietly shelved the book and awkwardly shook your extended hand.

You waved your free hand at the stacks. "So many volumes, such little reach." It was then, for the first time, I witnessed you pull out your pocket-sized Bible, its leather binding worn and misshapen. You held it aloft. "One book, my dear friend, whose orbit bonds heaven and earth."

"Do you tire, so soon, of the law?" I asked.

"Only of its limitations . . . and its misuse."

At our next meeting, we sat in a dark corner of Sklar's Pub—me courting my second pint of ale, you having barely sipped at your sacramental wine—when you announced your intention to join a monastery. I feared that might be the last I'd see of you.

I wish I'd been right.

⯌

"Bring in the accused!" My chief bailiff's voice echoed across the overflowing courtroom.

Lord chancellor of his majesty's courts, I peered down from my perch on the judicial bench, aghast, as they half dragged your enfeebled form into the chamber; you'd been fourteen months in the befouled depths of the Tower of London, rotting with miscreants and guttersnipes.

"In the name of our sovereign, King Henry VIII, you stand charged with the crime of treason." Sitting beneath the royal coat of arms, I uttered those words in disgust. Disgust for the author of that charge.

"Will you now," I asked, hoping beyond hope, "fully cognizant of the consequences of your further denial, agree to take the king's oath?"

"I shall not," was your clipped, defiant reply.

A mournful sigh spread from the lower pews to the balcony. To my utmost dread, the trial proceeded.

"The Act of Supremacy," His Majesty's prosecutor began, "commands that each citizen swear an oath that King Henry VIII is the supreme ruler of the world." Driven by his feud with the Vatican, the king had enacted this tyrannical statute to certify his superiority to the pope. "A citizen failing to so swear is guilty of the foulest of treasons, failing in his primary duty to support our sovereign."

Who in this realm had supported Henry more determinedly than you, dear Thomas? From the time you left the monastery you'd launched into service for the crown, rising to join Henry's Privy Council. You'd resolved his trade disputes. Kept his peace by quelling uprisings against immigrants. Served, before myself, as lord chancellor. And, after you assisted the king in drafting a repudiation of Martin Luther's Protestant rumblings, he even knighted you. Sir Thomas More.

"The duty is the same," the prosecutor admonished the panel of seven judges and twelve jurors, "no matter one's former or current position." That was the burr in Henry's saddle, wasn't it, Thomas? The change in your position. For the years serving him had soured your innards, defied your high morals; his divorces and marriages in defiance of the pope and the Catholic Church, the thousands of beheadings.

And now, it was your head he craved.

Amidst your internment, I'd reread your masterpiece, *Utopia*, in which you fashioned a perfect world—operated by reason and mutual respect. Knowing you as I do, dear Thomas, I should have suspected you would have the audacity to expect even the sovereign to honor those credos.

When, mercifully, the prosecution rested, I anxiously tracked your labored steps to the stand in your own defense. Steadying yourself between sentences, you somehow marshaled the unbound force of that exemplary mind and seized the room with your eloquence.

You assailed the Act of Supremacy on the grounds that it allowed conviction for silence.

"No word has left my lips," you proclaimed as you clung to the podium, "no action have I taken, that can be alleged to make me culpable."

Wait, was it possible that your words were rising above you, aglow as burning coals?

"I cannot have transgressed any law, or become guilty of any treasonable crime . . ."

There . . . they rose up again . . . there . . . Thomas, behind you! Smoke, flames, something emerging!

". . . for no law in the world can punish a man for his silence."

Words, expanding . . . Exploding! My head!

"'Tis God only that is the judge of the secrets of the hearts."

Trembling to my core, all but barren of breath, I announced a recess. Staggering through the doorway to my chambers, I lurched for the desk and pawed at my chair. My brain was on fire, blistering the inside of my skull in jagged agony. The room spun and I was lost. Gone. Irredeemable.

But then, amidst the inferno, I saw them, rising like great pillars of smoke, stoked from the heart of your impassioned plea: *The Words*. Taking form. I reached for them, but they were not of the air; they were pressed into my being. Then the voices came, a siren's chorus, over and *through* one another, foreign and frightening, from deep within me. To my further amazement, there was something eerily familiar about it all, as if *The Words* had always lurked there inside me, an inert fuel, until you, dear Thomas, lit the fuse. Now the explosion had come—messages, meanings, rationales, analyses, encouragements, caveats—striking home in a pulverizing flash. I was overcome by the bludgeoning intensity of *The Words*. And I suspected they'd not deign to again grant me peace.

✦

At next morn's first glimmer, I rose from my chair with channeled purpose. Summoning my law clerks, I instigated an exhaustive study of the history of individual rights.

For seven long days, the panel of judges awaited word from their lord chancellor. Over my years at the high courts, I had worked earnestly to garner the respect of my peers. This, then, was to be the corroborating moment of that respect. At last, I was ready.

Commencing the reconvened proceedings on the offensive, I addressed the panel. "My fellow gentlemen of the bench, before we may place this matter in the hands of the jury, we are called to examine a most fundamental question, a question, I dare say, which casts enormous weight on all future enactments: How far extends the reach of the sovereign into each man's life? Does a man *completely* have rights to anything? Certainly not his goods, nor his dwelling; each may be taken for tax. Not his wife, nor his children; both may be torn from his hands and exiled. Not his own physical being; it may be imprisoned or conscripted into military service. But what of his mind? His soul? Does a man not have some right to think and believe as he wishes? Does the lawmaker have the power to reach *inside* of a man? To know each private thought?"

My emotions were rising with my tone.

"If we acknowledge that power as a rightful grant of legislative authority, then we are saying that a man is less than a horse, less than even a stone. For there's no way to discern the thoughts of a horse, and it matters little to a stone whether it be thrown in the Tower of London. But under this law, a man may be forced to disclose the inner workings of his mind. And if he refuses, he can be tortured, executed, his chattels forfeited, his loved ones left destitute and abandoned!"

They tell me that despite rising passion in my voice, a faraway look possessed my eyes, that, as I continued, I struggled to push the words from my tongue.

"So . . . the question becomes: What right do we have . . . to injure a man who injures no other?! To punish him . . . for no wrongful act?! To deprive him of life and liberty . . . for the sole reason that he keeps his thoughts to himself?!"

They tell me my face ran crimson as a dusk bonfire, that my fellow judges stirred with concern.

"And . . . if we enforce . . . such an invasion into a man's very soul . . . what do *we* become?! Do we fancy ourselves gods?! Dark lords of the underworld?! Are we . . . are we . . . are we . . ."

Midsentence, they tell me, I went down. The distinguished panel of jurists leapt, frenzied, to my aid. I writhed on the floor, screaming rants of words dancing above the flames. They tell me all present concluded—most presciently, as current accommodations attest—that I had lost control of my faculties.

And so, dear Thomas, for twenty years have I inhabited this numb, ungodly tomb—this way station for unfortunate souls afflicted by undefined spirits. I heard that the panel passed my arguments along to the jury, but the king's minions delivered the gravest of threats. The guilty verdict . . . your beheading; I'm uncertain when I received word of those atrocities. But I knew I had failed you again, dear Thomas, just as I'd feared so long before.

Now, as I shiver within these grey stone walls, awaiting the nurse who never comes, lost in the shadows between dreams and nightmares, *The Words*, your words, still claw at my soul, probing, rising from time to time to the surface. I cling to fleeting memories. Ah, yes . . . I did hear from you . . . your words . . . that one final time. Perhaps a year or more after your death . . .

There came a visitor . . . your daughter. She brought the note, the one she said you wrote to me just after the verdict.

Wait, now there it rests, in my nightstand drawer:

> Nigel:
>
> The souls and spirits of your fellow jurists burn with the flame you have kindled. Be not disheartened by immediate results. For that which you have set in motion shall become a

nurtured seed through time. And so shall men see, then accept, and ultimately refuse to reject, that their very thoughts must and will be free.

Your dear friend,
Thomas More

METASTASIS

"Wenqian, have you heard from your daughter?" Han Chee-hwa asked the server, knowing she was childless.

Across the booth, unaware of the cue, General Chang sipped sluggishly at his drink. Several hours earlier, the general's difficulty at detaching his gaze from the evening's young hostess had been apparent. Dinner was pleasant enough, but Chang's war stories had begun to lose cohesion around the time they had switched from drinking Moutai Baijiu to Johnnie Walker Blue.

"How kind of you, sir," she replied, bowing. "She returns shortly."

"Excellent."

A minute later, he cleared his throat to get Chang's attention, then motioned with a slight swivel of his head and eyes as Wenqian held the door for the stunning hostess, who sashayed directly to their table.

"General," she purred, "your journey was long today. Will you honor us by staying the evening?" The corners of her full lips lifted ever so slightly. "I've prepared *special* accommodations."

"Thank you for the . . . dinner, my friend," Chang slurred, sliding effortfully from the booth. He pushed himself upright, accepted the extended arm of the hostess, and leaned a bit too heavily in her direction as they eased from the room. Finally.

As the entry door swung shut, Han reached for his phone and checked the *New York Times*. There it was: "Falun Dafa Demands China Sanctions." The rats had just paraded before the UN Security Council.

Their squeals were nothing new—claims of secret arrests and detentions, along with the usual litany of further mistreatments. The Party denied all charges. Denial, of course, was for media purposes and otherwise unnecessary. As one of the five permanent members of the Security Council, China held veto power over any measure aimed at sanctions.

"Thank you, Wenqian."

His nod was again met with a respectful bow. He rose to leave and laid some bills on the table. The little extras, his uncle had taught him, were the simplest ways to ensure loyalty. Always pay attention to the fine details.

And it was the fine details missing from the *Times* article that stood out. In their diatribe, the Dafa had revealed no inkling of imminent events. Could their organization possibly be uninformed as to what was happening? Had that wretched scum Zhou kept this to himself? If Han could halt this desecration of history, he'd actually have his despicable cousin to thank.

It was painful enough being orphaned twice. But it was his one living relative, Zhou, who'd viciously delivered the final blow. And it was Zhou, consumed since their youth with the troubles of the masses, who'd fallen into the clutches of the Dafa. As his cousin's status had risen in the cult's ranks, Han had followed his late uncle's instructions: "Heed your enemy. Study his ways, his interests. Never suffer the indignity of surprise."

Three years after Han's mother had overdosed, his uncle had rescued him from the slums of her drug-infested world and introduced him to fineries and channels of influence he could not have even imagined. His uncle had drilled into Han the importance of educating himself in order to preserve the advantages they had earned, since their wealth and position rested—as was often the case in China—on fragile underpinnings. When his uncle died, Han had seen his newfound privileges snatched from his grasp on a jealous moment's whim by Zhou.

And so, despite his aversion to anything of interest to his cousin, Han honored his beloved uncle's dogma by uncovering everything he could about Falun Dafa: their covert history, their foundational beliefs, their organizational strategies. He'd become convinced that the Dafa posed the greatest threat to the Chinese administration. And, if the Chinese system collapsed, likewise would Han's hard-earned stature and wealth.

How ironic that at the very moment they were pleading their case on the world stage, it seemed the Dafa, outside of his cousin, were wholly unaware that their cancerous threat was on the brink of metastasis.

QIGONG

Sammi turned north onto I-75, Alligator Alley having mercifully come to a finish outside the Florida Gulf Coast city of Naples. Just seeing something other than sawgrass—housing developments, office buildings, even billboards—was a huge relief. Thirty minutes later, they arrived at their exit, Fort Myers.

"Same crap in every one of these coastal towns," she heard next to her. Josh had finally awoken from his nap.

"And good morning to you," Sammi replied.

"Outskirts with broken-down gas stations and tomato stands," he continued, his tone somewhere between sarcastic and surly. "Suburbs locked behind gates and artificial waterfalls. Half-empty concrete strip malls, and a blighted outer rim of downtown surrounding glass-box office towers. You cross a bridge to a barrier island where they're knocking down anything with history and throwing up zillion-dollar McMansions."

Where was this rant coming from? "Your point?"

"We don't fix broken things in our society. We ignore them. Or worse, we throw them away. Replace them with perfect communities for perfect people, carefully protected from the broken ones."

Was he talking about his family? "We could certainly stand to replace a few security guards with welfare workers."

"Sorry." He straightened in his seat. "Woke up a little cranky. Think I had a bad dream."

"What was it about?"

Josh wrinkled his brow. "Can't remember, but I feel like it was pointing me somewhere."

Sammi nodded. She had to ask, "You ever get the sense that your dreams have an overall direction?"

"That's not the half of it . . ." He caught himself and looked away.

What was the half of it? Or all of it? He clearly wasn't ready to share that. Nor was she. The time would come.

At the Fort Myers shoreline, Sammi rolled down her window and inhaled the brackish air, glad to be leaving the mainland. She steered them across the three narrow bridges and two tiny islets that combined to form the three-mile-long great curling frown of a causeway.

"This is where the gulf feeds Pine Island Sound," she said. "The island up ahead is Sanibel. Stayed here once until my parents discovered Captiva and my uncle's place on Sundown Key. We vacationed down here a lot."

They swung north on the island's main road. Other than some new construction and a few buildings awaiting repair to hurricane damage, the surroundings had changed little over the years: patches of rustic houses and nautical-themed shops framed in driftwood, many with names spelled out in seashells.

Long stretches of the roadway were pressed in on the right by the matted mangroves of the sprawling Ding Darling nature preserve. When she was young, Sammi's dad would take her for catch-and-release fishing in the hollows of those mangroves, where she would spend most of the day entranced by egrets, herons, spoonbills, and pelicans, watching them hover and dive, wade and stab. The first time she saw one with a wriggling fish in its beak, she'd burst into tears. Her dad had tried to explain that birds didn't get to shop at Publix; this was where they picked up dinner. It hadn't helped much.

She caught Josh scanning the leafy morass. "We'll be cutting through the mangroves when we head out to my uncle's place."

At the northern tip of Sanibel, they skimmed over minuscule Blind Pass Bridge—its total distance perhaps fifteen car lengths—to Captiva

Island. Despite all the times she'd been here, the entrance to Captiva never lost its wonder. This was old-time, untamed Florida.

As she drove along the narrow, two-lane road, the bright sky was swallowed whole by an unruly tunnel of trees and scrub. No banyans, just the *p* trees that dominated most of South Florida: pines and palms. The tunnel was dotted along its sides by the ends of shell-rock paths that poked through the thicket, each path sporting an eclectic, nautical-themed mailbox on a post—smiling gray dolphins, neon surfboards, iridescent swordfish.

"This whole island just scraggly trees, bushes, and mailboxes?" Josh asked.

Sammi smiled. "Give it a minute."

Soon the road swung west and the tunnel melted away. They emerged into brilliant daylight on the gulf side of the island. Then the road turned north. To their left, a narrow beach bordered the endless blue of the gulf; to their right, amid patches of vegetation, there was a smattering of inns and homes.

"Something I want you to see," she said.

Sammi pulled over and parked at a cutout that had a mailbox and a few newspaper kiosks. As she stepped from the car, she noticed a headline on one of the newspapers: "Falun Dafa to Appear at UN Tomorrow."

She walked past and pointed at a huge banyan tree off to the side of an inn. Its tangle of trunks looked even broader than the last time she'd been out here; they seemed to span fifteen feet. And the canopy was enormous.

"It's one of the widest banyans I've ever seen." She eyed Josh. "I sort of have a thing for banyan trees."

He smiled and half nodded—oddly, almost knowingly. "Sure are beautiful."

She returned the smile. "I find them incredibly calming."

"Something we can both use right now." He turned back to the tree. "Those trunks. Got to give it to Mother Nature. The old lady did some next-level engineering there."

Next level. She turned back to the kiosk and stared at the headline.

Then she pulled out her phone. "Just had a thought. Give me a sec." She keyed in a search term:

Falun Dafa

Skimming through an article, she found what she was looking for.

"Josh."

He'd stepped away for a closer look at the banyan. He spun back. "Find something?"

"I *remembered* something when you mentioned next-level engineering. I took a course last year comparing religions, spiritual groups, and cults. One of the spiritual groups we studied is called Falun Dafa, which originated in China. The practitioners use a series of mind and body exercises to seek a *next level*, a higher state of consciousness."

He chuckled. "Doesn't every Eastern spiritual group seek that?"

"I guess. But, with Falun Dafa, this higher state of consciousness is supposedly spurred on by what they call 'increased *de*.' And yes, it's spelled exactly like the phrase Mark found."

He stepped closer. "What could this little Chinese group have to do with a book on judges?"

"No idea, but this isn't a *little* group. They've got tens of millions of followers and are actually based in the US now. Their leadership fled here, supposedly at risk of their lives. China's outlawed Falun Dafa."

"Hasn't China banned *all* religious-type practices?"

"Not all, but they heavily regulate most, and they've banned any that are seen as a threat to the state. Publicly, with Falun Dafa, the government claims it's a cult that brainwashes unhappy people. But privately, the Chinese leadership seems convinced that Dafa has some mystic ability to link up its members' brain waves. Some international monitoring groups say the Chinese actually fear their government could be overthrown by a multimillion-man-powered mind bomb. I know that sounds crazy, but human rights groups have claimed China has a long record of abusing Dafa followers. It hasn't gotten the same media coverage as the campaign against the Uyghur Muslims, but there've been allegations that the Chinese have jailed hundreds of thousands of Dafa practitioners, shipping them off to labor reeducation camps where they're tortured, even to death. There's even claims that the Chinese use them as involuntary organ donors."

Josh grimaced. "Eeesh."

"From what I've read, it seems Falun Dafa has started fighting back through media outlets controlled by a few of its wealthy members. There've even been allegations that Dafa's leadership has aligned itself with the alt-right in the US, likely growing out of their shared animosity toward the Chinese government. And I've seen concern about Dafa's positions on homosexuality and interracial relationships, among other things. But look at this." She pointed to the newspaper headline. "That's yesterday's paper. Representatives of Falun Dafa were set to speak at the UN this morning." She scrolled through her Instagram feed. "The meeting was a few hours ago. They pled their case about these supposed atrocities in China."

"Interesting timing." He paused, then shook his head. "But the man went to church every Sunday. You really think Judge Maloch was into some Far Eastern spiritual belief?"

"Whoever sent him the email that froze his laptop was."

"What?"

"Falun Dafa is a spin-off from the ancient Chinese tradition of Xiulian. In the cultural revolution, Xiulian was deemed a religion and banned by the Chinese government. So the practitioners came up with a new name: Qigong. In 1992, one of the masters went public with a form of Qigong called Falun Dafa. The username on the email to Judge Maloch was qigongzhou, and he was listed in the judge's address book as Master Zhou. That's the title given to teachers of Falun Dafa."

Josh's hand went to his chin. "And the mail server for that email was 'fd.mail.com'—*fd* as in Falun Dafa? Does this group have some connection to judges or the law?"

She'd been wondering that same thing. She scrolled down into the article and couldn't believe what she'd missed. "It's right in the name. In Chinese, *Falun* means 'law wheel,' and *Dafa* means 'great law.'" She noticed a cloud in the distance and stepped toward the car. "We should get moving. We need to get out on the water while the weather's good."

Before she pulled out, Josh turned to her. "Let's say you're right, and these Falun Dafa people are somehow involved in this. My question is: friend or foe?"

TOOLS OF THE TRADE

Tracking down and closing in. Inflicting pain. These were his purest, sinful pleasures, burned into him with every purple welt across his backside from the straps and switches of ten different foster parents. As a child, Billy Ray had been punished time and again for his "hobbies." But as "Jackson the Ripper" on the high school football fields of Alabama, the same behavior made him a hero. And now it had been blessed by the Reverend for holy purposes.

He checked the red blip on the digital map again. It was still stuck on some dinky place called Captiva Island. One scraggy road leading in and out. He chuckled. Some of his best tools had been meant for very different users. He'd been in California on a mission for the Reverend a few years before when he'd seen an ad on local TV for the Teen Tracker. The man in the ad had seemed deeply concerned. Were his rug rats *really* at the mall? Maybe they were snorting meth behind a dumpster somewhere. "Do you know where your teenagers go when they use your car? Are you sure? Well, now you can be!"

The Teen Tracker's transmitter, in a matchbox-sized, magnetized box, could be quickly attached to any metal part of a car. Through a GPS signal, the location of the transmitter was constantly displayed on the map in the Teen Tracker smartphone app. The app also sent a text whenever the vehicle left a parked location.

As he turned north from Alligator Alley onto I-75, Billy Ray realized that the throbbing in his skull had finally stopped. For sure, something else had stopped too. The red blip on the map wasn't moving.

Captiva Island. Papa had found his teen.

CONTACT

"Definitely foe." Sammi tracked the minimal traffic and pulled the RAV4 back onto the road.

"I beg to differ," Josh replied.

"You what? They sent an email that destroyed Judge Maloch's work."

"I'm thinking that email was sent to protect, not harm."

She looked over at him. "It locked up his computer."

Josh's arms came up, fingers gripping the air. "And what purpose would there be to lock up his computer?"

"Like I said, to destroy his work."

"The email was from someone in the judge's address book. Someone he trusted. Someone from Falun Dafa, a belief which, you've just suggested, could have a direct connection to the judge's work. I think this Master Zhou got wind that the judge was in trouble and sent the virus to prevent the discovery from falling into the wrong hands."

"And what about stealing his address book?" Sammi asked.

"I don't know. Maybe to warn his other contacts?"

Sammi shook her head. "The murderer didn't even know your last name, but he found your home address. I've kept the judge's calendar for him. He only writes down first names of students. I'm guessing the murderer saw your name on the calendar the judge keeps on his desk; I'm also guessing you're the only Josh in the judge's address book."

"Okay. But if Zhou and the murderer are working together, why would Zhou eliminate access to the information the murderer was sent to get?"

Why *would* he? "Geez, you're right."

Josh took out his phone. "We need to email this Master Zhou."

She steered them toward the boat rental place while Josh typed. After she pulled into the parking lot, he passed her his phone. The screen read:

> I am a friend of Judge Maloch's. He has been murdered. Your last email was successful. I have information that may be of use to you. I also need information from you. Please respond as soon as possible.

Nodding her approval, she handed the phone back and watched Josh click SEND.

She'd dwelled often on the interworking of decisions and destiny. Researched it. Written on it. This had to be one of those moments. One of those choices we make that either expands our fate or seals it.

CAYO COSTA

"Weird knot." From their small, rented motorboat, Josh eyed the anchoring rope bound to a piling at the dock.

"That's a rolling hitch," Sammi said. "I've been tied up with that."

"Huh?"

"One summer out here when I was around eight, my fourteen-year-old brother was into nautical knots. Sometimes, I'd let him tie me up with his latest technique if he promised to take me for ice cream. He'd also promise to let me free after ten minutes if I couldn't escape, but sometimes he *forgot* for a while. So I came up with a trick. When he'd tightened my bindings, I'd ever-so-slightly bow my right wrist, creating a tiny amount of slack, just enough to later slip my little hand through." She undid the knot.

"Your brother sounds like a sadist."

She chuckled. "He grew up; he's a political strategist."

"No comment." Josh steered the boat away from the dock, eastward out of the Roosevelt Channel. Following Sammi's directions, he swung north and kept Captiva to their left as he let out the throttle to cruising speed along the wide expanse of Pine Island Sound.

On this steamy summer day, the water sat still as a welcoming bathtub, disturbed only by the hint of an occasional swell sliding peacefully over the surface. The boathouse operator had assured them that the weather would be perfect for the next few hours along the twelve miles of the sound that led to Sundown Key. No chance of running into one of those violent thunderstorms that pounded the region on summer afternoons.

But another kind of violence had hold of Josh's thoughts.

As they navigated past the resort at the northern tip of Captiva Island and proceeded out to open water, with the gulf off to the left, he found it reassuring that there wasn't another vessel in sight in the gulf or the sound.

He ran his hands over the steering wheel. "I still can't figure it."

"Figure what?" Sammi, bending over her bag, pulled out a hat.

"If the police weren't in on it, how the murderer covered his tracks. It's one thing to get a corpse out of there, but there was blood all over the floor. That would take some serious cleaning. No way he had the time."

The hat slipped from Sammi's grasp. "A *corpse*? You're talking about the *judge.*" Her eyes moistened. "Like his death, his *murder*, is just part of some puzzle you need to solve."

He momentarily studied the floorboards. "I'm sorry." He braved looking at her. "I wasn't trying . . . I just . . . I guess it's an avoidance technique. I deal with logical issues to avoid emotional ones." He'd had years of practice.

"I . . . I'm sorry too." She wiped away a tear. "I didn't mean to go off on you like that. But someone we both cared about was just brutally murdered. And you *saw* it happen. It's no crime to have feelings. We need to deal with them and stick it out."

Not so easy when those feelings become a tsunami. "Judge Maloch told me I needed more 'stick-to-itiveness.' Weird thing, though—yesterday he said that real growth only comes through change."

"Wise man. Most growth I've had came when I made a change, but only when I stuck it out on the new path."

He glanced ahead and steadied his hand on the wheel. "My changes all came from fear. Something about being second best. My brother was the academic superstar, so, in high school, I started refusing to study. He was the All-American swimmer, so I fled the pool, ran to football. When I got out of college, I could've moved back to New York and tried to help my parents work through things, but I took the programming job in Miami, twelve hundred miles away. All I ever do is run."

"We've all got restless souls," Sammi responded. "Something inside told me to come down here for my graduate work, even though my heart's still in New York—my family, my friends, the life and culture of that place. Maybe, like me, you were just hunting your destiny."

Josh shook his head. "I don't believe in destiny."

"You don't think there might be some *reason* you're on this planet?"

"The concept of destiny is a trap. Are we all just crossing guards, waiting for third-graders to get to the corner so we can stop traffic and then return to our posts for eternity?" His brother used to think his dreams would reveal his destiny. Look where that had gotten him. "I'll take free will."

"What if destiny exists, but it's malleable? What if the choices we make and those that others make about us direct us to our destiny?" She scooped up the hat and wiped some sea spray from her hair before putting it on. "Do you know why Judge Maloch asked you to be his research assistant? It started with your argument in class on the DACA case."

That rant? "That was last fall. He didn't ask me until a few weeks ago."

"Well, he told me about it back then. He couldn't believe your passion."

"How would you feel? The twenty-year-old 'golden child' gets to stay in the US without a care, thanks to DACA. His seventeen-year-old brother applies just as it's suspended, so he's deported to El Salvador, even though he's been here since he's three." He pounded the steering wheel. "He doesn't even speak a word of Spanish!"

"Whoa there." Sammi pushed her palms out. "I'm not with ICE."

She was right; he'd sounded like a two-year-old whose brother stole his blankie. "Sorry. It hit a little close to home."

She nodded. "The judge couldn't believe someone with grades as low as yours could argue that well. He told me you were the star of the mock trials all year, but you pretty much sucked on tests and assignments. You don't like to be told what to do, do you?"

Why had the judge told her so much about him? He laughed. "I may have a little problem with authority."

She touched his arm. Again. "And yet you chose to become a *lawyer*?"

"I figured it's easier to take down the system from the inside."

She smiled, then pointed to the northwest. "See that island over there? Let's pull around to the gulf side."

"Is that Sundown Key already?"

"No. It's Cayo Costa, the best shelling island in the world. I think we both could use a break. My folks used to take me here when I was little. All these islands are literally *made* of shells that drifted up from the Caribbean over thousands of years. Shelling's big business out here. On Captiva, the beaches are picked clean by breakfast. But you can only get to Cayo Costa by boat."

Josh steered around the southern tip of the island. Two boats were barely visible well to the north; otherwise, thankfully, there wasn't a soul around.

"Look at how the sunlight's dancing on the tips of the mangroves." Sammi was facing the island with her phone out. She snapped a few pictures.

"Post-worthy?"

"For my collection. I like nature photos—trees and plants mainly. They're the primary living, breathing things that surround us. Like with people, if you look at them carefully enough, you see things you never saw before."

He stole a glance at the case in point sitting next to him.

As the current pushed against the hull, they anchored and waded in through the lengthy shallows.

The island sported a tangled mohawk of mangroves down its middle, outlined along the gulf by an endless, narrow strip of lumpy beach. A seagull landed nearby on one of the "lumps." As bits of the mound fell away, Josh realized they were actually piles of shells—a shimmering rainbow that hugged the shoreline as far as his eyes allowed.

"Conch!" Sammi blurted. She held up a multicolored, eight-inch-long sample, with its distinctive spire, smooth curves, and long canal.

Josh traced his fingers over the sculpted contours. "That's beautiful."

"And completely intact. A lot of this"—she motioned toward the burgeoning shoreline—"is fragments and shells missing chunks. You've got to sift through to find the ones that had a soft landing." Sammi pulled two plastic grocery bags from her pocket, handed one to Josh, and deposited the conch shell in the other. She returned to her search—back bent almost parallel to the ground, shoulders hunched, eyes cast straight downward. "They call this the Sanibel stoop."

As she bent down, a fine necklace slipped out from the top of her T-shirt, dangling from her neck with two small charms: a cross and a Star of David. She'd been concealing a holy war.

"It's sort of unfair," he said. "You seem to know so much about me, and I know squat about you."

She stood up. "What do you want to know?"

"I'm pretty ambivalent about religion. How'd you get so into it?"

"I guess it started at age five, when I found out I had a grandmother. My mom's Jewish and my dad's Irish Catholic. My grandmother was a Holocaust survivor. She lived through a time when six million Jews were wiped from the face of the earth. She couldn't bear to see my mom marry outside the faith. She refused to attend the wedding and refused any contact with my mom after that."

"I'm so sorry."

"Well, my mom, God bless her, never gave up. She kept sending my Nana letters, stories about me, pictures. When Nana heard I was starting kindergarten, I think the grandma hormones finally got too strong for her. She called my mom, came into my life. As I got older, she talked to me about being a child of the Holocaust, and also about why it had turned her against her only daughter. She saw that my mom and dad raised me to respect both heritages, both religions, and she and my mom eventually came to understand each other's choices. They stayed close until Nana died when I was in my teens. The years with her left me with so many questions about religion. Like how could a practice that has served as history's greatest promoter of human rights also be its greatest abuser? Crusades, religion-based genocides—I wanted to understand how these things came about. So, no, I'm not 'into' religion from an orthodox standpoint. Just a very interested observer."

And perhaps not the obsessed, religious academic he'd imagined.

After a half hour of breathing fresh, gulf-kissed air and uncovering aquatic treasures, including a few still inhabited, Josh's tension was easing. Sammi was right—they'd needed this break.

A loud thud came from the gulf. He spun toward the water but saw nothing.

"Wait for it." Sammi's eyes went wide and she ran to Josh. "There!" She pointed to a spot less than one hundred feet offshore.

The long, gray body exploded out of the water and landed with a huge splash. Josh burst into a smile. A second and third dolphin went airborne nearby, their dark forms glistening in the sun. Josh's body tingled; he could feel the joyful energy in those leaps.

Three more broke the surface. One of them dawdled, looked directly at Josh and Sammi, opened its mouth in a huge grin, and squeaked a greeting. Josh watched, captivated, as the family of six meandered southward, one or another launching skyward from time to time.

"That was incredible," he gushed.

"Believe it or not, I've seen dolphins jump almost every time I've been out here. Never gets old."

"Thanks," Josh said.

"For what?"

He waved his arm across the panorama before them. "For this." He looked into her eyes. "For you. You're quite the therapist." And maybe more. "I hadn't fully realized how tense I was."

Sammi smiled. "I needed this just as much. I have a feeling there's a lot in store for us when we get to Sundown Key."

UNWELCOME RELATIVE

Billy Ray scanned the parking lot. Sure enough, there was Sutton's RAV4, off in a corner. He turned and eyed the rickety sign hanging down from the roof of the building: PELICAN PETE'S—BOAT RENTALS AND BAIT.

The place—part shack, part single wide—kicked up bad memories from his childhood in backcountry Alabama. Two creepy portholes, one to each side of the entrance, looked like eyes staring into him, judging him. He stepped inside quickly.

A scruffy, leather-skinned man was hunched over behind the counter, taking a screwdriver to a fishing reel.

"Howdy, sir," Billy Ray said in his warmest, homespun accent. "You Pete?"

"Sure am," Pete replied through a gap-toothed grin.

"You seen mah cousin Josh?"

"Josh?"

"Josh Sutton. He rent a boat?"

Pete laid down the screwdriver and reel and fingered the open logbook on the counter. "Here it is: 'J. Sutton.' My only overnight rental today. Left about an hour ago."

"Damn. Blew it again. Cain't do nothin' right!" Billy Ray let his lower lip slip out in a pout.

"What's the problem?"

"Ah was joinin' him for his birthday. We was gonna rent us a boat and he was gonna pick the place to go. Damn foreman held me up and then ah forgot my dang phone. No way he could reach me, and only place ah got his number is in that dang phone." He shook his head. "Cain't blame him for goin' without me."

"Then it's a good thing he had a lady friend to console him."

Billy Ray kept his surprise to himself. "Ah'm sure they'll have a fahn time without me."

"You could still join them."

"Got no idea where they was headed."

"They said they were going to Sundown Key."

"Sundown?"

Pete spun around to a local map hanging on the wall behind the counter and pointed to a small island. "About twenty minutes north of here." He spun back and eyed the logbook. "Says they're staying at 7 Sundowner Cove. Can't get there by car, but you could rent one of my boats and join them for the night." There was that gap-toothed grin again.

"Y'all are seein' a business opportunity in this, ain't ya?"

"To be honest, yeah. Make my best money on the overnights."

"What if ah just want one for a couple hours? Ah could give mah cousin a nice surprise but leave him with his girl for the evening."

"Wouldn't recommend it." The grin was gone. "Water should be fine for the next hour or so, but later on they're expecting some serious squalls. You go out there, you ought to spend the night."

"That your cash register talkin'?"

"I don't joke about conditions on the water. I'd never put a customer at risk."

"Ah kinda figured you wasn't a man to play fast and loose with someone else's lahf." That made one of them. "How much you git for the overnight?"

SAMSON

"Believe it or not, it's considered Sundown Key's local landmark," Sammi said as they approached Rusty's Bar.

Though unlikely to make the cover of *Architectural Digest*, Josh thought. Thrown together from asymmetrical, misaligned, ragged wood planks of various kinds, the outside looked like a sheepdog in a windstorm. He doubted the structure could satisfy the building code of any nation on earth. But, upon entering, he couldn't help but be intrigued. The walls of the place were decorated, floor to ceiling, with currency.

"What's with the money on the walls?" he asked.

"I think it started as a joke with small tips," Sammi responded, "but now it's tradition. There's currency from all over the world. With all sorts of things written on them."

Josh checked out a few. On an old Italian hundred-thousand lira note, someone had scrawled: "Five more of these and I can buy a pizza." On the back of a US dollar, under the large *ONE*, was written: "is the loneliest number." Instead of *Andrew* Jackson, a fake twenty-dollar bill had a picture of Michael, moonwalking.

He went back to Sammi. "You ever put anything up?"

"Once, by that booth." She walked him over and pointed out a two-dollar bill on the wall. Printed on it in red Sharpie was: "Not found yet."

"What's that supposed to mean?"

"It's that thing you don't believe in: destiny. I've always had this feeling that something or someone was going to find me, to light my path, so to speak."

"And why are you so sure of this?"

Sammi smiled. "Just am."

The hostess came over to take them to their table. An ancient country song squealed from an old jukebox in the corner.

"That's 'Amarillo by Morning,' George Strait," Sammi announced. "About some guy who lost it all—family, possessions—but realizes it's freedom to pursue his path."

Was she trying to ease his mind about his past? What else had the judge told her about him? "You like country?"

"Not much of it. Only know this one because I've been here a hundred times. You won't hear anything in this place from this century or from north of the Mason-Dixon line."

As they sat, Josh checked out the diners spread around the room. A couple at a nearby table looked to be around thirtyish, like the two of them, but otherwise he and Sammi were the youngest by maybe forty years. This was the country version of South Florida's East Coast.

An odd smell wafted his way. He sniffed suspiciously at the air. "You're sure the food's edible?"

"It's okay. I've survived."

"You should put that up on Yelp."

With her soft chuckle that followed, he realized again how being with Sammi was a salve on the tension, a buffering firewall against his thoughts about the murderer lurking out there. Could it possibly be something more?

After they ordered brunch, he eyed the wall next to them. "Hey, check this out." He pointed up the wall near his end of the table. "Someone's created biblical US currency. There's a ten, with a picture of Moses parting the Red Sea, and a twenty with Noah and the ark. Sort of crosses that 'church and state' line."

"You think? And it looks like there's another one behind you."

He turned to see. "Yeah, a five's got Samson destroying the temple."

"Samson?" Sammi's eyes widened. "Wait a sec. What was that again that Judge Maloch said to you yesterday about the historical judges you were supposed to research?"

"He said, 'If we looked at *who* these judges were, and what they must have *seen*.'"

"Do you have the list of judges on your laptop? Last week I saw the list on the judge's desk. I thought some of the names seemed familiar. Now I think I know why."

He took his laptop out of his backpack, powered it on, and brought the list up on the screen:

Huang Tse Abdonchai
Marcus Samsonellus
Nigel Tolan
Nicolau Jephthahpoulis
Henrik of Reibzang
Wesley Jair
Antonio Elonetti

"The second name *has* got *Samson* in it, but I don't see anything familiar in the rest." He spun it around to Sammi.

She eyed the list and let out an exasperated breath. "I do. Okay if I hop on the internet?"

"This place has Wi-Fi?"

"I know, shocking." She started typing, scrolling, reading. She typed some more, then looked up. "Josh, you know what the King James Bible is?"

"Heard the name."

"In the early 1600s, religious scholars in England complained to King James that an accurate English translation of the Bible was needed so the common people could read it. Over the objections of the Catholic Church, which viewed any translations of the original biblical languages as heresy, the king appointed a committee of leading religious scholars and linguists. The project took almost ten years, but the final product is relied on to this day by religious scholars as the most accurate English translation of the Bible."

"Here you go, kids." An elderly waitress slid their brunch plates onto the table.

Josh impaled a home fry with his fork. "And what is it about this religious phenomenon that justifies interrupting my meal?"

Sammi spun the laptop screen back toward him. She had bolded portions of the names on the list, which now read as follows:

Huang Tse **Abdon**chai
Marcus **Samson**ellus
Nigel **Tola**n
Nicolau **Jephthah**poulis
Henrik of Re**ibzan**g
Wesley **Jair**
Antonio **Elon**etti

"According to the spellings used in the King James Bible, the root names of the seven judges on your list exactly match the names of seven of the judges in the book of Judges from the Old Testament. These were leaders of Israel, supposedly sent by God."

This was nuts. "You're not saying they came back to life?" He dabbed his toast at a puddle of yoke. "So big deal. Our judges have biblical names. So does every David, Daniel, or Leah."

"But every David, Daniel, or Leah is not a historically significant judge," Sammi explained. "Judge Maloch gave you a list of seven historical judges he deemed significant, and every single one just happens to share a name with a judge from the book of Judges. He said, 'If we looked at *who* these judges were.' You think that's a coincidence?"

Still sounded crazy. "Okay"—he laid his fork down on his plate—"let's say you're right, and it's not a coincidence." He leaned forward. "Then what the hell does it mean?"

That was a question she couldn't answer. Yet. But Judge Maloch had also told Josh that he needed to look at what these judges must have *seen*.

A woman in a floral-patterned summer dress walked by their table. Sammi closed her eyes for a second, and the woman's image transformed into a flower girl strolling through a Byzantine market. She was sure she remembered this from a dream. A dream about a judge . . .

JUSTICE

530–Constantinople

"A flower of the field," a fishmonger called out at the market to seventeen-year-old Rachel Avdat in tribute to her olive-skinned beauty.

Rachel waved and chuckled softly as she passed his stall, for his words described, too, the object of her daily quest.

Six days per week she rose with the sun's first embers to scour the outskirts of town for wildflowers. Once home with her bounty, she fashioned artful bouquets to sell in her handmade baskets. In the afternoons, shouldering a dozen baskets in her wire amphora tray, she would hawk her wares up and down the aisles of the bustling marketplace, netting, if she were fortunate, enough for a few days' portions of grain for the family. Her mother had passed two years before, and her father was an invalid; the leg he'd injured in his youth had worsened in recent years. So Rachel's flowers and her brother Jason's carpentry had to support the family.

Today she brimmed with excitement on her way home. For the first time in months, she'd sold every last basket. Inhaling the enticing aromas of spices and incense, she toured her favorite food stands and selected ingredients. Bread and vegetables would not suffice this night. She would prepare a sumptuous feast for her papa and brother—spiced fowl with anthotyros cheese, and koptoplakous pastries for dessert—to celebrate her good fortune.

Proudly bearing her amphora tray, now laden with purchases, Rachel passed in and out of the early evening shadows along the dust-clouded road where some merchants towed pull carts while others prodded oxen hitched to wagons, as the neighborhood's brightly colored, stucco-on-stone buildings ebbed to gray.

She reached the family's one-room dwelling, whose exterior evidenced her late mother's joyful spirit—she had plastered over the misshapen brick and stone and painted it all in bright geometric patterns. Rachel set down her amphora tray to open the door. As she bent to retrieve it, a hand was already there.

She jumped.

"A pretty one like you should not be burdened with all this." A thickly built, bearded soldier leered up at her. A tall, thin one stood behind him. She had seen them at the wine merchant's stall at the market, drinking heavily, in their midnight-blue-on-khaki tunics, their shoulders adorned with regimental red stripes. Word was that the emperor's army had returned in a celebratory mood from the war in Spain.

"May the Lord bless your thoughtfulness, kindest sir," Rachel said, repulsed by his foul breath as much as his lustful gaze. "But my papa and brother wait inside to help me."

The half lie had barely lifted from her tongue when she was shoved from behind through the doorway. The two soldiers slammed the door behind them.

"Rachel, is that you, my darling?" called out her father, Benjamin, from across the dimly lit room. His voice was thick with sleep, as if he'd been napping.

The bearded one threw Rachel down on the rug in the middle of the floor. When the other unsheathed his sword and rushed, unsteadily, toward her father, she screamed. A fist came toward her face. Her head snapped sideward; her cheekbone exploded with pain. She went numb and drifted into a dream: All this was happening to actors in a street play. She was merely an observer held back by the crowd.

In the dream, the tall soldier gagged her feeble father and tied him to the bed with his own sheets to look on, helpless, as the man joined the bearded one who had her pinned to the floor.

The bearded soldier reached for her tunic, and the lust in his eyes snapped her mind out of its daze. These animals were going to take her purity, and in front of her papa. And then they'd kill them both.

Her brain issued a short, silent prayer for her papa to close his eyes, his ears. She scanned her surroundings. She needed a weapon. If only she could reach the wooden pyxis that sat on the nearby table. She pushed up against the man's weight. He laughed and held her firm.

The door flew open. Jason! Her scream had been loud enough for him to hear.

The tall one drew his sword and stepped forward. The bearded one turned to watch.

Rachel reached up and grabbed the ornamental box from the table. "Jason, here!" She threw it to her brother.

In one motion he caught it, slid open the top, and removed the ceremonial carpenter's knife. The tall soldier lunged at him, leading with the tip of his sword. Sidestepping the blade, Jason thrust the carpenter's knife home.

As the tall one fell away, the bearded soldier's sword flashed through the air and sliced deep into Jason's shoulder. Jason screamed in agony; his weapon fell from his hand.

The attacker again swung his sword high on an arc toward Jason's neck.

Rachel grabbed the fallen soldier's sword and plunged it into the bearded one's back. The man collapsed alongside his co-conspirator.

Ignoring the pain from his injury, Jason reached out for Rachel as a troop of soldiers swarmed through the open door.

"Arrest them!" barked a lieutenant, pointing at the siblings.

Rachel's father moaned from the bed.

"Free him," the lieutenant instructed a soldier.

Ungagged, her father pleaded, "Release my children. They have done no wrong!"

"Two of your emperor's soldiers have died at their hands," the lieutenant responded. "Justice shall be levied in the emperor's courts."

As she and Jason were taken away, Rachel looked back to see their papa hobble out the entryway, leaning heavily on the humble cane Jason had carved for him, trying his best to keep pace with the troop. For a scant moment, their eyes locked. She saw his fear. He'd struggled enough since her mother died. He'd not survive another loss.

✦

Before he was assigned the case and summoned by the praetor to one of the city's four law courts, Judge Nicolau Jephthahpoulis had already heard the story: the drunken soldiers, the attempted rape of a man's daughter in front of him, the blessed arrival of the son. Though the population of Constantinople was over five hundred thousand, scandalous news spread with a velocity that could challenge any small town.

Regardless of the circumstances, two of Emperor Justinian's soldiers had been slain. As the judge walked west along the Mese, the city's main street, he could feel the emperor's looming presence trailing him. He glanced back at the great dome and towering spires of the Hagia Sofia church and the sprawling facades of the Imperial Palace and Hippodrome. The triad loomed over the eastern tip of the city-peninsula like three giants—*Religion, Governance, Sport*—stationed by the emperor to cast watchful eyes on the populace.

After scaling Constantinople's second hill, the judge came to the gray gypsum-walled praetorium, home of the city prefect, the city jails, and central courthouse. Charged as always to uphold the law, Justinian's Code, with complete impartiality, on this day Nicolau Jephthahpoulis knew exactly where that impartiality would lead. The outcome of the case before him was all but determined before a word of the trial had been spoken: A man was about to lose both of his children.

✦

For his first directive of the preliminary hearing, Judge Jephthahpoulis peered down from his elevated bench and requested the reading of the charges.

The state inquisitor rose at his lectern. "Your Honor, by authority of the emperor and chief consul, Justinian, these defendants stand accused of the murder of two imperial soldiers." As a summary of the supporting facts was provided to the court, the judge shifted his gaze across the aisle.

Shackled in their prison vestments, the young siblings, Jason and Rachel Avdat, listened intently, their expressions a mix of confusion and anger. On the pew directly behind them sat a man whose grimness left no doubt he was their father.

When the state inquisitor finished, the judge called him to the podium. "The two men who were killed," he asked quietly, "were they Orthodox Christians?"

"Yes, Your Honor. Not by birth, but they were Christianized Egyptians."

"And the soldiers who arrived later, are they Orthodox Christians as well?"

"Yes, Your Honor."

"And what of the accused?"

"They are known to be practicing Jews."

"And their father?"

"Also a Jew, Your Honor."

Each kindhearted word, each compassionate look from Benjamin Avdat's friends and relatives as they dropped off a loaf of bread or inquired after his other necessities only seemed to add more weight to his already unbearable burden. He needed nothing but his children.

Five days had passed since Rachel and Jason had been taken, and their trial was still weeks away. He'd journeyed twice to visit them at the jail, hobbling over the hills an hour each way, but was turned back. What torments were they facing? If only they could make it to trial. Then, the truth would save them.

He supported his body against the small corner stove as he stirred a pot of simmering fish stew. It should have been Rachel lovingly preparing the meal as always while Jason set the table and they all shared stories of the day. He prayed, once more, for their safe return. An acrid scent penetrated his prayers; he'd burned his meal. He snickered, for he had no appetite anyway.

A knock came at the door.

Dreading a request to foist his heavy heart on yet another well-meaning visitor, he grabbed his cane, straightened as best he could, and shuffled across the room. Upon opening the door, he tried to hide his disbelief. But he knew he'd failed. There in front of him stood Judge Nicolau Jephthahpoulis, the overlord of his children's fate.

"Citizen Avdat, I think it important that we speak. May I come in?"

Dumbstruck, Benjamin motioned him inside. He closed the door behind the judge, and the two stepped directly across the crime scene. Benjamin hobbled over to his customary seat at the small family table. The judge stood, facing him.

"You understand, of course," the judge said, "that I am in violation of my oath of office by my very presence in this home?"

Still stunned, Benjamin could do little more than nod.

The judge removed his cloak and took the chair at the opposite end of the table. Rachel's chair. "As you, I am a father. And I know what happened in this case. I know your children are innocent."

"Then I am heartened, Your Eminence." Benjamin had found his voice. "You'll set them free?"

"I'm afraid it's not that simple."

"But you said you *know* they're innocent."

The judge clasped his hands together in a prayerful pose. "Citizen Avdat, you understand that in the courtroom I'm compelled to follow the law."

"Yes."

"Well, the law that binds me is the new Civil Code, the *Corpus Juris Civilis*, drafted at the behest of the emperor. It codifies and expands upon the great body of known law. Justinian intends this code to be one of his defining legacies."

"Are innocent people still innocent under this code?" Had the emperor ignored the rights of the common people?

"The issue is the evidentiary rules. There are limitations on what can be presented."

"What do you mean, *limitations*?"

"Justinian wants his code to be followed not only by his empire, but also by the Romans and those under their rule. He intends this to be the seminal legal treatise for all civilized nations."

"What does that have to do with my children?"

The judge sighed. "In order to appease the Romans, Justinian believed the code had to show deference to Christianity."

Oh. The emperor hadn't ignored the rights of the common people, just Benjamin's people. "What exactly are you saying?" The rising smell of overdone fish was not why Benjamin was beginning to feel ill.

"Well . . . Jews are not prohibited from providing evidence. However, under Justinian's Code, a Jew *is* prohibited from testifying against an Orthodox Christian."

✦

Nicolau Jephthahpoulis sat near the shoreline of the Golden Horn, watching merchant ships and small sailboats pass on the calm waters. He'd often come here to focus his mind on troubling legal issues. None had ever vexed him to this extent.

A system of laws was the vertebrae of a civil society. But, if drafted by an emperor, were those truly the laws of the people? Then again, who was he to question the emperor's decisions? He stared out at the white mainsail of a merchant vessel. As a cloud passed overhead, the sail paled to gray; smoke rose from it. He got to his feet, worried for the poor men aboard, for the ship had surely caught fire.

But then the sail flashed back to white, and the smoke left the ship, forming a cloud of its own. This cloud split into fragments, and the fragments, incredibly, seemed to form letters. He shook his head and looked again. The letters were moving, arranging themselves. He glanced to his sides, behind him, at the empty shoreline. Was no one else seeing this? He turned back toward the water. A message was emblazoned in the sky:

IN THE ABSENCE OF LAWS, JUSTICE WITHERS
ON THE VINE. BUT WHICH LAWS ARE JUST?
THOSE DRAFTED TO SATE THE BROADEST REALM?
IN THE NAME OF "JUSTICE," MAY WE SACRIFICE
THOSE WHO LIVE IN THE SHADOWS?

He tried to blink, to clear this hallucination, but could not. He tried to turn his head away, but his neck, his torso, his limbs, were frozen in position. Wait. Had he *heard* the message as well as read it? Was it all in his mind? As the puffs of letters faded into the sky, his body and thoughts became his own again.

One thing seemed certain of this strange miracle: These words were meant only for him.

Benjamin had barely slept in the week since the judge's visit. But then, one night, through pure exhaustion, he finally dozed off. He dreamed that instead of a civil code Justinian had constructed a great wall in the middle of a garden. On one side rows of pastel flowers lined fields of sweet fruits. There, the Christians frolicked and gorged. On the other side the Jews were trapped in a great thicket of bramblebush. Even if they escaped the thorns, there was no way over the wall, and no way around. The more the Jews climbed, the higher the wall rose; the farther they raced, the wider it stretched. In the morning, he awoke suffocating in helplessness, each gulp for air sharpening his hatred for an emperor who, in pursuit of a legacy, had cast him and his people aside.

As he finished changing from his bedclothes, two quick knocks came from outside. He grabbed his cane and limped across the room. When he opened the door, no one was there, but a small envelope lay at his feet.

The note inside was brief:

You are respectfully requested to meet me tomorrow morning at the start of the second hour from sunrise at the Fountain of Purifications.

Nicolau Jephthahpoulis

For what purpose? And why there? To blend in with the crowds? Being Jewish, he'd spent scant time at the Hagia Sofia, but no building in the city swarmed with more people than the Great Church.

Directions to the Hagia Sofia were unnecessary for any citizen of Constantinople. Its gilded octagonal dome, rising high on the city's easternmost hill, dominated the skyline. Justinian's marble masterpiece had been hailed as an architectural wonder and the tallest man-made structure on earth.

The following morning, Benjamin hobbled into this powerful symbol of Christianity and made his way toward the Fountain of Purifications, located in the vast rectangular atrium to the west of the central dome. Cane in hand, he passed elaborately carved marble columns, gold fixtures, holy ornaments, and walls adorned with religious-themed mosaics, gingerly working his way through the buzzing throng of parishioners, visitors, and those assigned to serve—it was said that the church employed over two hundred priests and deacons.

When he arrived at the fountain, he noted the inscription at its base:

CLEANSE OUR SINS, NOT ONLY OUR FACE

He felt a hand on his shoulder. He turned to see a deacon motioning for him to follow. They weaved through the crowd and veered off to a shadowy corner where the judge stood, waiting, next to a priest.

Directly over the judge's head was an icon mosaic, a Palm Sunday depiction of Christ on a white mount, a donkey, entering Jerusalem.

"How are you, Citizen Avdat?" the judge inquired.

"Filled with thoughts only of my children, Your Eminence."

"I must ask you a question, good citizen. Do you know Jesus?"

"Of course I know Jesus. I may be a Jew, but I have some awareness of the world around me."

The judge nodded. "For now, that is all I need to know. Will you meet me here again tomorrow at this time?"

Again? "Your Eminence," Benjamin responded, "it's difficult for me to walk this far." He'd struggled for more than two hours up and down the hills from Yenikapi, the Jewish quarter. "Is it essential that I come?"

"I'm sorry for the hardship. But I need to see you here again tomorrow."

To be proselytized? "Then I will be here." What choice did he have? Rachel and Jason's fate could depend on this.

Over the next few weeks, Benjamin and the judge met daily with various priests. Though the Great Church had many quiet corners, the judge always insisted they meet in the same location, with the judge standing under the mosaic of Jesus on the white donkey. Benjamin hadn't noticed that white mount depicted anywhere else in the church. Did it have some special meaning to the judge?

"Do you know the story of Jesus and the feeding of the five thousand?" the priest asked.

This was not unlike the opening questions Benjamin had heard each day for the past several weeks, every inquiry being about Jesus and his remarkable feats as recorded in the New Testament.

"I believe it's written that he fed them all from only a few fish and a few loaves of bread."

"Do you believe this happened?" the priest further inquired.

As each day before, he was clearly being tested, but he feared telling them anything except the truth, particularly in this place—their most holy sanctuary. "Even in the Old Testament," Benjamin responded, "we understand that not everything is to be taken literally. For this story to have been written, I would think he must have found food for these hungry people somehow."

The priest nodded. "A not unreasonable interpretation."

"In some manner, Jesus was their savior," added the judge. This was the judge's primary comment at the end of each of these stories.

Otherwise, he was noncommittal; he never overtly agreed or disagreed with Benjamin's answers. And yet, at times, it seemed there was something reassuring in the judge's eyes.

As with the tales of Jesus, was this to be believed?

"I was just across the way"—the soldier on the witness bench pointed at Rachel—"when this vulgar temptress lured the men through her door. It was then I noticed her brother lurking nearby with his knife. He rushed in, and the two of them slaughtered my comrades before I could get there." He glared at Rachel and Jason. "This, for a piddling bounty of a few coins."

It was the middle of the third day of trial. Benjamin's nightmare had been nothing compared to this. One by one, uniformed soldiers had marched to the bench and testified, with absolute assurance, to actions he knew they had not seen and utterances he knew they had not heard.

But the greatest betrayal had come not from the witnesses, but from the judicial bench. Even now, the judge was nodding approvingly at this soldier's perjury.

Two days earlier, when Benjamin had requested to make an opening statement on behalf of his children, the state inquisitor had argued that this would violate the law, since it would be based on the testimony of Jews against Christians.

The judge had eyed Benjamin coldly and announced: "Request denied."

That heartless stare had told him the only truth that now mattered. The look of reassurance he'd seen in the judge's eyes at the Hagia Sofia was the judge reassuring *himself*, telling himself that this heathen Jew could never accept Christ as his Lord. Benjamin's answers to the priests' questions had all been wrong. He had succeeded in condemning his own children.

"Your Honor," said the state inquisitor, "being as the accused and their father are Jews, and being as they apparently have no other witnesses to call, we ask that the court move directly to judgment."

From high on his official perch, the judge glanced down indifferently at Rachel and Jason. Then he directed a sanctimonious gaze at Benjamin.

Benjamin responded with a contemptuous glare. How could a religious man, *any* religious man, have allowed this travesty of a trial?

"Come forward, Citizen Avdat," the judge commanded. "The court has questions."

Benjamin did not budge.

"But, Your Honor"—the state inquisitor shot back to his feet—"this man is prohibited from testifying in this matter under the perpetual edicts."

"That is precisely what I intend to confirm." The judge turned back to Benjamin. "Come forward, Citizen Avdat."

Benjamin again locked eyes with the judge. Was it not enough that he was about to lose his children? Was he now to be ridiculed, forced to admit on the stand that he was a lowly Jew, undeserving of even the law's minimal grace?

The judge leaned forward; his lips dipped to a scowl. "This is not a request, Citizen Avdat. Come forward *now*."

Benjamin reached for his cane and rose slowly, his steps coming with great effort. It was not his old injuries that slowed him. It was the thick stew of emotions: vitriol seasoned with betrayal. He limped over to the bench adjacent to the defendants' lectern and peered up at the judge.

"Citizen Avdat, before God and your emperor, Justinianus, do you now swear to speak only words of truth?"

His words would be the first. "Yes, Your Honor."

"How do you spend your days, Citizen Avdat?"

What did he care? "These recent weeks I've been mainly at home, praying for my children, Your Honor."

"And other than praying in your home these recent weeks, have you visited any religious sanctuary?"

Did that matter now? "Yes. I have been to the Hagia Sofia."

Audible gasps escaped the audience. The state inquisitor's head snapped up.

The judge continued. "And how often have you been there in these recent weeks?"

Was he attempting to prove he tried to save this heathen's soul? So he could send Rachel and Jason to their deaths with no mark on his conscience? "Every day, Your Honor."

Scattered mutterings drifted through the crowd.

"Citizen Avdat, I understand you are afflicted with injuries you suffered as a young man, making walking difficult. Yet you traveled to the Great Church every day over these recent weeks. Did you meet with priests there?"

Benjamin steadied himself against the lectern. "Yes. Every day."

Mutterings and murmurs.

"And can you share with us what you discussed?"

"We spoke of Christ, of the people he aided."

The gasps rose, growing in number.

"And when you were not in the church, did you dwell at all upon those discussions?"

"On the long walks home and hours after."

"Citizen Avdat, in light of these many physically challenging trips to our most sacred sanctuary, these weeks of daily conversations with priests about Christ, and these hours each day you've spent contemplating those discussions, I must ask you one last question."

There it was, that look of reassurance again, the one Benjamin had seen in the judge's eyes at the Hagia Sofia, under the white mount. Was he still reassuring *himself*?

"Do you now accept that Jesus Christ is your savior?"

Jesus was their savior. The judge had pronounced this verdict at the end of every Bible discussion. Hadn't he been proselytizing?

Benjamin considered that, considered the judge's question again, the *intent* of the question. As powerful as his doubts had been previously, Benjamin was now possessed by absolute certainty. He would answer the question as he had answered each of the others—truthfully.

"I most certainly accept that Jesus Christ is my savior."

A woman cried out. Benjamin turned, surveying the room. At the back of the crowd, a group of people appeared to be tending to someone.

The air had been sucked from the chamber. It was as if no one could breathe. Not the state inquisitor. Not Jason or Rachel, who were surely unable to even conceive of their father speaking the words he had just uttered—the man who had raised them to be proud, practicing Jews, despite all the disadvantages. A man whose Jewish faith defined him as much as any physical feature or personality trait. His own children stared at him now as if he were possessed by a demon.

Of all those present in the courtroom, only two people seemed at ease. One of them spoke: "The court is satisfied that you are a qualified witness in this matter. You may now proceed with your testimony."

Again, the state inquisitor leaped up. Struggling to form words, he blurted, "But . . . Your Honor, this man . . . is a Jew. Under the Civil Code—"

"Did you not hear what I just heard?" the judge proclaimed. "The witness testified under oath that he accepts Jesus Christ as his savior. There is no better definition of a Christian. I don't care about this man's religious past. All that is relevant for this proceeding is the man's present religious convictions."

"Your . . . Honor," the state inquisitor stammered, gathering his wits, "this testimony was totally unexpected. The state requests a recess so we may investigate further."

"My esteemed inquisitor, as you well know, it is this court's function to administer these proceedings."

"Yes, Your Honor."

"And it is *your* function to be ready for all matters that arise in these proceedings"—the judge's voice was rising—"particularly when I have given you weeks to prepare." A vein bulged in the judge's neck.

"But, Your Honor—"

The judge glowered at the state inquisitor. "Does the state have any evidence"—the volume of his voice continued upward—"to contradict the facts the witness has just testified to regarding his *present* beliefs?"

The state inquisitor apparently had no desire to step in the path of a runaway chariot. "No, Your Honor."

The judge turned to Benjamin. "Citizen Avdat, please proceed with your testimony."

As the years went by, Nicolau Jephthahpoulis rarely got through a day without thinking back to the Avdat case. For it was there that he first saw *The Words*, first found himself in their presence. They had solidified into a commandment—no, a *responsibility*—by the time he stood in the Hagia Sofia in judgment of Benjamin Avdat.

Yes, the judgment had taken place in the church, not the courtroom. *The Words* had left a reminder at the Fountain of Purifications:

CLEANSE OUR SINS, NOT ONLY OUR FACE

Spurred on by *The Words*, he had looked past his oath, past the Civil Code, to a larger purpose. His actions before and during that trial were a betrayal of his training and the law. And yet, he had seen in a new light that it was the only path he could take.

His cleverly crafted plan had relied equally on Benjamin Avdat's parental devotion and intelligence. But, faced with a principled witness and a diligent state inquisitor, the judge had realized that only with the element of surprise could his plan have any chance at success.

He'd also wrestled with the religious ethics of his actions, for he had dipped more than a toe in the waters of blasphemy. It turned out that Benjamin Avdat had asked himself similar questions. But each man eventually took comfort in the same conclusion: The God they worshipped disdained injustice.

At the end of the trial, as he watched Benjamin Avdat escort his beloved children to freedom, it had been difficult for Nicolau Jephthahpoulis to suppress the tears he absolutely could not let flow in public. He knew he had shone the bright light of *true* justice, if only for a flickering moment, on those otherwise condemned to the shadows. And he was heartened by his actions and grew bolder in his good deeds.

But *The Words* grew bolder as well, burning on a signpost through his brain, never letting go.

THE GOOD SOLDIER

A siren blared down on the streets of Gramercy Park. As he packed before heading to JFK, Gao "Steven" Lee could not help but think that he'd received his siren's call as well—it had been evident in General Chang's words when they'd spoken an hour before. In the words and the way they were said.

"Captain Lee, you are to fly to Miami immediately," the general had ordered. "The contact will have details for you when you arrive . . . Do not fail us."

Do not fail us. That was the tell. The general had supreme confidence in him; that had been confirmed time and again over the past twenty years, ever since Steven had been "selected" from his American high school. *Do not fail us.* The general had paused before those words, uttered them not sternly, but almost hopefully, prayerfully. Steven's training had taught him to pay attention to such details. The most critical parts of that training had been at the general's own hand.

Since then, he'd been entrusted with hundreds of delicate assignments at the highest levels. No operative in the organization had been more successful or more often commended. *Do not fail us* could mean only one thing: Events had aligned perfectly. This was the mission he'd spent his life readying for.

He precisely folded and then rolled his clothes into tight cylinders and inserted half of them into their designated spaces along the bottom of his suitcase. Next, he turned his attention to the mission necessities.

From the wall safe in his closet he removed his pistol, magazines, and silencer and set them in place above that layer of clothing. His multistate government-issued permits for the gun were already in his wallet. Ironic. To do China's business, he could legally carry such weapons in the United States as a private citizen, while personal gun ownership was absolutely prohibited in China.

After covering the gun and accessories with the remainder of his clothes, he slipped on a pair of rubber gloves, took out a large plastic container, and removed from it a few gobs of clay-like Semtex. Since this highly efficient and highly concentrated explosive contained no metallic aspects, it was invisible to metal detectors and X-ray machines, making it the perfect choice for this trip. He carefully pushed down the Semtex into an empty, wide-mouth sunblock tube until it was almost full, screwed the top back on, and wiped the tube clean with a cloth. He dropped the gloves and cloth into the trash, scrubbed his hands thoroughly, and slid the tube into his toiletry pouch.

He pressed the intercom button on the wall and asked the doorman to hail a taxi, then took one last look around his apartment. Its slick, clean surfaces and ordered shelves flawlessly reflected his ethos: everything in place. After a final check of the windows, he rolled his bag into the hall and locked the door. The dead bolt hit with a resounding thud.

A new era beckoned.

THE REPLY

Judges who tried cases spread over the past two thousand years. Names in common with biblical judges from God-knows-how-long before that. Ancient Chinese spiritual practices. How could this possibly relate to something happening in two days?

Standing at the curb, Josh tried to settle his thoughts as he watched the door to the quaint little cottage open, revealing an elderly woman in a pink housedress. Upon eyeing Sammi, the woman burst into a smile and smothered her in a hug. The two spoke for a couple of minutes before she handed over the guest key and Sammi came back down the walkway.

"I've known Mrs. Adria since I was eight. She keeps an eye on my uncle's place," Sammi said as she steered Josh around the corner and down the block.

They stopped at a fish-shaped mailbox that read 7 SUNDOWNER COVE – MAXWELL. Pale gray sanded-wood siding served as a canvas for bright white trim and colonial shutters on the pretty tropical home. Its Old Florida cedar-shake roof, which had aged to a deep charcoal, was tufted with scattered golden pine needles dropped from the soaring trees huddled around the two-story structure. An elderly Ernest Hemingway could have lived here.

Sammi unlocked the front door and let Josh in. The interior was decorated like a typical, beachy second home used only a fraction of each year. A few pieces of rattan furniture graced the living room, along with two framed watercolors of sailboats, a couple of fake plants, and some nautical-themed accessories. Sage tiles covered the floor; the walls were textured almond. Against this neutral background, the couches and chair cushions erupted in bright blue and copper flowers.

"I'm going to put on some tea," Sammi said.

Josh scratched his temple. "Why now?"

"Because I like green tea after a meal?"

"No, sorry, I meant why is this incredibly significant event happening in two days? The judges on the list are from hundreds to thousands of years ago. The biblical judges are even older. Why is something happening *now*?"

"Things that matter happen when they're supposed to happen."

"Not letting go of this destiny thing, are you?"

She chuckled and handed him her bag. "The bedrooms are upstairs. You can have the master. I'll take the one at the top of the stairs. It's a study they converted to a bedroom, and it shares a bathroom. But it's my favorite. You should check it out."

When he got upstairs, Josh immediately understood. The soul of the house lived in this room. Its beating heart was a white-washed-maple, four-poster canopy bed with pastel drapes. A complementary bookcase ran the length of the opposite wall, split down the middle by a light-gray stone fireplace, a feature Josh hadn't seen in a South Florida home. Probably got used every tenth Christmas but definitely enhanced the ambience. At the far end of the room, double French doors framed a small balcony shaded by a huge jacaranda tree. The midday sun illuminated its colorful blooms, creating a soft purple, magical backlight to the room.

He smiled. How lucky to walk in just then, to see that effect. *Things that matter happen when they're supposed to happen.* Wait, was it that simple?

Josh put down Sammi's bag and his backpack, took out his laptop, and placed it on a corner table. He powered it on, patched the Wi-Fi through his phone, and checked the dates of the key human rights cases tried by the judges on his list . . . Not quite. He looked for the dates of birth and death for each judge . . . That wasn't it either. Then he pursued one last idea . . . Incredible. He went back to the list of judges, reordered them chronologically, and keyed in the date for each.

Sammi walked in.

"Come look at this." He could barely believe his eyes as he stared with her at the updated list:

Marcus **Samson**ellus	250
Nicolau **Jephthah**poulis	500
Henrik of Re**ibzan**g	750
Wesley **Jair**	1000
Huang Tse **Abdon**chai	1250
Nigel **Tola**n	1500
Antonio **Elon**etti	1750

"They're all *exactly* two hundred and fifty years apart," she said. "That's amazing. Is that their birth years?"

"It's when each of them became a judge." He shook his head. "Some were elected, some appointed, but in *every* case exactly two hundred and fifty years after the prior one and two hundred and fifty years before the next one. How could that be?"

"I have no idea," she said, "but it's got to mean *something*."

"Well, it at least may explain *one* thing. How about that last date, 1750?"

"The Seven Years' War was around then. Some consider it the actual first world war."

"Didn't know that, but not what I'm looking for. What date is two hundred and fifty years after that last date?"

"2000." She gasped.

He shook his head again. "I wouldn't even consider this crazy theory if it wasn't Judge Maloch behind all this. He must have realized that the years these people became judges aligned perfectly in sequence. And that another one of these special judges was alive now." He bent down to the laptop to run a search. "Let's see how many of these leaders of Israel are mentioned in the book of Judges." He skimmed through the results. "Looks like there are thirteen."

"So," Sammi said, "if the pattern actually continues, one of the other six names should be a root name for the current judge."

Josh frowned. "Even if this nutty theory's correct, all we've got is that somewhere on the planet, some judge with a biblical name was or is possibly involved in an important human rights case and has discovered something valuable."

"Don't forget the 'increased *de*' clue."

Another level of crazy. "Okay, you're saying these historical judges may have had some higher-level mental abilities? I guess that could actually be the case, since they each were apparently ahead of their time in dealing with human rights. But Judge Maloch said the significance of what was about to happen was *staggering*. Someone killed him to get this information. Could what some current judge found during a human rights case be that crucial?" He cupped his chin. "Let's try two of the more-modern-sounding names from the book of Judges: Deborah and Gideon." He cross-referenced Deborah and Debra with "human rights" and entered the search. "There's a zillion Deborahs involved with human rights issues. It would take forever to figure out which ones are judges and when they were elected or appointed." He threw up his hands. "And a bunch of these are from other countries. Not sure I can even get to those records." He ran the second search. "The only thing I find for Gideon is *Gideon v. Wainwright*, a 1963 Supreme Court case that established the right to counsel in criminal cases. Huge decision, but Gideon was a guy wrongfully convicted of burglary, not a judge, and he died back in the seventies." He sighed. "We need more."

Sammi patted his shoulder and let her hand linger momentarily. Their eyes locked for a second, then she stepped back. "Don't be frustrated. I know there's a lot to consider here. And a deadline. But, as wild as it seems, we've clearly moved beyond coincidence. I think you've got us on the right path. Hopefully Mark will have something soon to help us narrow it down." She waved him forward. "Now come see the balcony. It's the highlight."

He followed her across the room and out the French doors. The far end of the balcony was notched so part of the jacaranda tree's broad trunk could pass through; branches flush with purple flowers hovered above and around them. A wooden bench sat off to the right side, but Sammi led him to the railing on their left and had him lean out; the view past the front of the house stretched all the way to the island's marina.

His phone vibrated. "Maybe it's Mark . . . No, look."

It was an email from qigongzhou@fd.mail.com. He held the phone out so they could both see it.

> Although I am greatly saddened by your confirmation of the judge's death, I am most heartened that you have contacted me. I believe it is imperative that we confer in person without delay. I will be glad to meet you at eight o'clock this evening for dinner at the Szechuan Grill in Boca Raton.
>
> Sincerely,
>
> Master Zhou

"Great. Maybe *he* can fill in the blanks," Josh said.

"You're sure it's safe to meet him in person?"

"It's a public place," he responded. "And the email's clear; he wants to do this face-to-face. I can go by myself if you want."

Sammi shook her head. "Not a chance."

Josh chuckled.

"What's so funny?"

"Maybe this Master Zhou *is* that someone you've been waiting for—to light your path, as you put it."

"Guess we'll find out at dinner." Sammi leaned out over the railing. "At least we can stay for a little bit before we have to head back."

Josh looked out past her toward the marina. He froze.

Even from two hundred yards away, there could be no doubt—the massive size, the orange-red hair, the spring in his step that seemed so out of sync with the enormity of the man. "We're not staying at all," he said grimly, and pointed.

"Oh my God." Sammi quivered. "Is that him? How'd he find us?"

The man was making rapid progress toward the front door of the Maxwell home.

"Stay here; I'll get our stuff." Josh ran through the open French doors, raced to the other side of the bed, grabbed their bags, then hustled back. He pointed to the jacaranda. "We'll climb down and go to the boat. We'll be off the island before he's finished searching the house."

Sammi nodded, but her eyes leaked concern.

Josh slipped his backpack on. Sammi stepped over the railing, got a foothold on the jacaranda, and started climbing down. Josh was right behind her.

Halfway down, he realized the backpack was too light. "Oh, crap!"

"What's wrong?" Sammi asked.

"My laptop's up there, with my research. Here, take this."

She took her bag from him.

He slipped off his backpack and dropped it to the ground. "Take my backpack and run to the boat. If I'm not there in ten minutes, get out of here."

"Don't go back up there," Sammi pleaded. "You can't risk it."

"I can't let him get the laptop. I'll be right behind you." He reached for a branch above him and pulled his body upward. His biceps strained as he latched on to another and another, climbing as fast as he could.

He saw Sammi reach the ground as he stepped onto the balcony.

There were sounds coming from downstairs as he burst into the room. Before he reached the corner table, he heard sickeningly familiar catlike leaps coming up the steps.

As Josh scooped up the laptop, the redheaded giant appeared in the doorway, his face a menacing snarl.

SPIN MOVE

Sammi was hyperventilating; her heart pounded and her pulse drum-rolled as she sat, riveted to the driver's seat of the boat, one hand white-knuckled on the wheel. Josh had to be coming. Please. She sucked in a deep, calming breath, then another. Screw his ten minutes. She wasn't leaving. Not yet. Her head darted back and forth, searching the patch of trees between the houses in the distance, and the edges of the nearby boathouse. Her breathing quickened as she envisioned not Josh, but the judge's killer, hurtling around one of those corners.

No sign of either of them. She checked the time on her phone again and again. How could she just leave? But Josh was right. If, God forbid, something had happened to him, someone needed to see this through. Fighting back tears, she pulled in the boat's anchoring rope and started up the engine.

✦

Josh was flying along, pushing his body to its limits. His lungs begged for air, his muscles burned from toes to neck, his chest ached. But he had to keep moving. He could barely believe he'd escaped.

Trapped in the corner of the bedroom with the murderer just steps away, he'd calculated in a flash—like he had, innumerable times, on the high school football field—figuring the approximate speed of his enormous but supremely athletic opponent and the angle the man would likely take.

As the dirtbag had been about to speak, Josh, cradling the laptop like a pigskin, had broken for the balcony with every ounce of acceleration he could harness. But his pursuer had taken a far more aggressive angle than anticipated, launching his bulk toward a point well short of the balcony doors, bound to crash into Josh with incredible force.

As the massive body went airborne, inches from delivering a pulverizing blow, the punt returner in Josh had emerged. Planting his forward foot, he had slowed his momentum. But again, his opponent was way ahead of him.

In mid-flight, recognizing Josh's move, the man had thrown out his left arm. That powerful forearm, with enormous inertia behind it, was aimed to deliver a blow Josh could not avoid.

With contact inevitable, Josh had reached out and pushed down on the massive limb, hoping he could force it to slide past him. But as Josh pressed down with the stiff-arm, the man had opened his huge hand, grabbing Josh's thigh. The tackle was about to be completed.

That was when the *feel* took over—that moment when an athlete's mind stepped out of the way. Josh had found himself spinning. Not against the blow, but with it. As his enemy's fingers tightened on his thigh, the downward pressure from his own arm, combined with his spin, had caused the man's hand to slip off. Instead of taking Josh down, his opponent had flown past and crashed headfirst into the base of the wall near the balcony doors.

Josh had come out of the spin move with a burst. His heart hammering, he'd darted to the hall, leaped down the stairs, spurted through the open front door, and raced toward the marina.

Now, blocks away, he lurched to a halt, gulping at the air, feeding his starving lungs. As his head began to clear, he broke back into a sprint.

He intended to stay alive.

Ready to pull out, Sammi turned her head one last hopeful time.

Josh?

Exploding from a thicket of trees, there he was—a blur, sprinting faster than she thought he could possibly move. Her heart was pumping probably harder than his. As soon as he jumped aboard, she gunned the engine and they flew out of the marina.

"Give it . . . everything you've got!" He was gasping for air.

She kept it floored. "He's coming?"

Josh's eyes were focused far out over the water. "Wasn't so much . . . thinking about him, as I was . . . about *that*." He pointed ahead.

"Shit." Massive, dark clouds were sweeping in from the gulf, on a path sure to intercept them on the way back to Captiva. "Should I turn around?"

"Can't do that."

"He *is* coming, isn't he?"

Josh nodded glumly. "Not sure how much of a lead we have."

She glanced behind them, then peered back out over the gulf. Far off, a charcoal cloud sparked with lightning. The wind howled, and the water was getting choppy. It was hard to hold a steady course. She was strong for her size, but she'd never had to pilot a boat at this speed in these kinds of conditions. She eyed the flexed muscles in Josh's forearms as he gripped the dashboard alongside her. Those arms needed to be on the wheel. "You up for driving?"

"Got it." He took the helm and handed her his laptop. Sammi slipped it inside his backpack in the boat's watertight storage compartment and held on tight in the seat next to him. They seemed to be traveling more by air than water. Despite the bumps, the boat was rocketing along. But so was the gathering storm.

A row of huge cumulonimbus dominated the skies ahead, sporadically turning into ebony mushroom clouds bursting open in torrents of rain. It was the middle of a summer day, yet the view in the distance was so black Sammi could barely differentiate between water, land, and sky.

✦

The wind pressed hard on Josh's cheeks, and the waves and sky spit at his eyes. Squinting in the darkness, unsure of his bearings, he stood firm, tightened his grip on the wheel, and refused to let up on the throttle. The judge's killer was back there, somewhere, coming.

Josh had witnessed his share of Florida's powerful electrical storms, but he'd never been out on the water for one. He was concentrating so hard on maintaining their course that he was caught completely off guard when the jet-black sky suddenly lit up like a bonfire. A thunderclap detonated, and he flinched, jerking the wheel to the right. The boat twisted violently and rammed into a wave. Josh lost his balance and plunged to the deck.

Grabbing for a hold as the boat wobbled, he scrambled back up and latched on to the wheel. The sky was going black again. He focused his vision and saw they were headed directly at an island. He yanked the wheel to the left, and the outboard motor screeched and kicked as it briefly scraped bottom. He strengthened his grip on the wheel, keeping the boat turning as it pulled free.

"Whew. Sammi, you okay?"

No response.

She wasn't in her seat. He checked behind him, around him.

The boat was empty.

EXPOSURE

Billy Ray lifted his head, tried to shake out the cobwebs. His stomach turned as he came to grips with the sickening truth.

He had missed the tackle.

As he staggered to his feet, his skull pounded. The pain knifed through his groggy haze, followed by rage. He'd smashed his head into the wall on the same damn lump! Sutton was a dead man!

After a quick check of the house, he sprinted back to the docks. When he got there, three marina workers were securing anchor lines.

As he approached his boat, huffing, one of the men stepped in front of him and asked, "You're not thinking of going out *now*, are you, mister?"

Billy Ray sucked in a breath and tried the polite route. "Ah'm 'fraid ah got somewhere ah need to git."

He started again toward the boat, but the man wouldn't back down. "Look, some crazy couple headed out into *that*"—he pointed to the dark clouds over the water—"before we could stop 'em. Mister, believe me, you don't want to go out there." The other two men joined him in blocking Billy Ray's path.

Throwing a slack-jawed gape at the blackening skies, Billy Ray nodded respectfully. "Ah see what y'all mean. Any decent man be thankin' y'all." He smiled and placed his hands gently on the shoulders of two of the men. Be gone, chickenshits. He pushed them both off the dock.

"Guess ah ain't no decent man," he said as they splashed into the water.

The third man rushed him. Billy Ray bent to the side and with a sweep of an arm he sent the man's head crashing into a piling. The man groaned and collapsed on the dock.

Billy Ray unleashed his boat, bounded in, and gunned it into the bay. The skies ahead were as eerily dark as that filthy cellar his foster dad would chuck him in back when he was seven, when the whippings hadn't been enough. He'd been sure there were monsters in that cellar, and the monsters were surely out here this afternoon lurking in those black clouds. He could feel the static electricity in the air, the raging waters gathering. As the boat's engine strained to meet his demands, he felt like a floating target, a bobbing six-and-a-half-foot, two-hundred-and-forty-pound lightning rod.

Hairs on his arms stood up as a huge bolt of lightning split the near sky to the southwest. Thunder rumbled. The boat shook. Buckets of rain came down.

He squeezed the wheel as the heavens darkened again, afraid the boat might flip in the churning waves and howling wind, finding it harder and harder to see in the pitch-black sky and driving rain.

He could almost hear the Reverend trying to calm him, telling him to trust God's plan. At the moment, he wasn't so sure God's plan agreed with his own.

"Sammi!" Josh frantically scanned the water but could barely see anything in the darkness. He yelled again at the top of his lungs: "Sammi!"

Nothing. Where was she?!

He reached for the boat's toolbox. There had to be a flashlight in it.

A windswept plea, barely audible against the wailing torrents, came from the water. "Jahhhsh. J . . . ahsh. Josh."

"Sammi!" he screamed.

"Here, Josh! Over here!"

He could just make out an arm, thirty feet away, swinging wildly above the waves.

"I'm coming, Sammi!"

He pulled the boat close, bent down over the side, and reached in vain for Sammi's flailing arm as the craft careened at the whim of the elements. He had to get her before she drowned! He tightened his left hand's grip on the edge of the boat and stretched his body down, reaching out as far as he could with his right arm. The hull lurched at Sammi's head and she went under. No! The boat swung back, but there was no sign of her. He leaned out to dive in. Wait, there! An arm suddenly burst up through the surface. He lunged down a third time, and their hands found each other. She latched on to his forearm with her other hand. He tried to pull her up with his one arm, but with her waterlogged body and clothes pressed up against the side of the boat, the resistance was enormous. His biceps cramped. Panicked that he'd lose her, he arched backward for leverage and used his weight, with his legs pinned against the inner frame of the boat. He slowly dragged her up the side and hauled her in.

They collapsed to the deck and she threw her arms around him, pulling her soaked body to his. She was panting.

He held her tightly. She brought her lips up and found his mouth.

A bolt of lightning flashed to the west. As they pulled back from the kiss, he could see a nearby island illuminated. "You're sure you're okay?" he asked. "I thought you—"

"You're not getting rid of me that easily. Though I *have* been on better dates." Thunder growled over the gulf. "We should get moving."

Josh scrambled to the driver's seat and sent the boat hurtling southward at full throttle. They'd lost valuable time. The killer was surely not far behind them.

Sammi found a dry blanket, wrapped herself in it, and sat by his side. He glanced over at her and caught the hint of a smile as cracks of blue poked holes in the sky. The lighting storm moved off, flickering occasionally in the distance. But, just as their ride softened, a gathering wind whispered a low howl off the water, swelled into a mighty roar, and drenched them with a deluge that seemed to be moving sideways. Mercifully, a few minutes later, they pulled up to Pelican Pete's as the rain finally stopped.

Pete secured the boat while Josh and Sammi grabbed their gear and climbed onto the dock. As they headed inside, Pete asked, "Weren't you staying the night? Some hellacious crap you just came through."

"Sort of an emergency," Josh responded. "Hey, did someone come here looking for me?"

"You mean your cousin? Didn't he find you?"

Josh exchanged a glance with Sammi. "Yeah, big redhead found me, all right. Such a prankster. What name did he use?"

Pete went over to the log book. "Can't read his scribble."

"Typical. He give you a credit card?" Josh asked.

"Paid cash, even for the security. Why's that matter?"

Josh waved him off. "Long story." He picked up his backpack to leave. "Go ahead and charge my card. We gotta go."

"You can change out of those wet clothes in the bathroom," Pete offered.

"Thanks," Sammi interjected, "we're sort of in a rush."

Pete shrugged. "It's your pneumonia."

Josh checked his cell phone as they walked out. Three missed calls from Mark.

Mark picked up on the first ring. "Wondering when I'd hear from you, Quark. Been trying you for a half hour."

"Sorry. I was a little distracted. Look, Sammi and I are fine, but we took my car out to Captiva for the weekend, and the man who killed the judge almost caught us out here."

"Check the wheel wells on your car. Look for a small metallic object. He probably planted a GPS at your house last night. It'll take a nice tug to overcome the magnets."

Josh switched the call to speaker, handed the phone to Sammi, bent low at the driver's-side front wheel, and yanked out a matchbox-sized metal box. "Got it. Thanks, MacGyver. Call you later. We need to get on the road."

"No biggie, Quark," Mark replied. "I'll want details. And, oh yeah, when you call back, I've got something for you too."

✦

"Wait," Sammi said as Josh headed for a nearby dumpster. Why let that transmitter go to waste? "Give me that."

She took it from him and ran across the street to the rear of a tractor trailer parked outside a convenience store. The truck had a Georgia license plate. Perfect. She stuck the transmitter on the chassis just inside the bumper, raced back, and hopped into the car. The truck driver emerged from the store with a bag of jerky, a piece dangling from his lip, climbed up into the cab of the truck, and pulled out. He was headed along the main road that led off the island.

They followed the truck off Captiva, through Sanibel, over the causeway, and into Fort Myers. When they reached I-75, the semi took the north on-ramp, Georgia-bound.

"How brave are you?" Josh asked.

"Sort of a silly question at this point."

He nodded. "Well, I'd like to know at least once, for sure, where that ginger giant is headed." He pointed to a gas station on the south side of the street. "We can park the car on the other side of that gas station and watch for him around back. I'm sure he's crazy enough to follow us off that island in the storm. Unless we're lucky and he got hit by lightning, I think he's going to show up in the next half hour. If he gets on the northbound ramp, we'll know for sure we have some lead time when we get back to Miami."

She wasn't sure if she was *that* brave. "What if he sees us?"

"Yeah, I'm not thrilled about that possibility either. But he'll be focused on that GPS heading north. If somehow he spots us, we'll jump in our car and dial 911 on our way to the nearest police station." He tapped at his phone. "The Florida Highway Patrol's got an office a minute from here."

It *would* be nice to have some certainty about where their pursuer was going. "All right. Let's do it."

They pulled to the far side of the gas station, got out, and moved around to the back by the bathrooms. Pressed tight to the building, Sammi sensed Josh's edginess next to her as she nervously eyed the roadway.

Waiting on a killer.

NEXT BOAT IN

Drenched to the bone, head still throbbing, Billy Ray finally arrived back at Pelican Pete's. He stepped inside, dripping puddles.

"Never seen a manatee out of the water before." Pete grinned from behind the counter. "Was your cousin surprised to see you?"

Billy Ray scowled at him.

"Why'd the hell you come back in this weather? I figured your cousin just got caught in it, but you could've waited."

Abandoning his charming Southern drawl, he barked, "When did they leave here?!"

Pete's head snapped to attention. "About . . . twenty minutes ago."

He extended one of his massive palms. "Be needin' that deposit back."

As Pete opened the cash register, Billy Ray pulled out his phone. Sure enough, the Teen Tracker GPS had sent him a text eighteen minutes ago when Sutton's RAV4 had left Pelican Pete's. Now the blips showed the car on I-75—heading *north*. Good luck with that.

✦

Twenty minutes had passed when the dark gray Buick stopped at the traffic light. The car's single occupant was a large man with matted-down red hair.

At the back of the gas station, Josh fought off a shiver and tugged Sammi's arm. "There."

While he waited for the light to change, the man in the car looked off in the opposite direction, toward a strip mall.

⁂

Sitting at the traffic light, Billy Ray glanced to his left—a furniture store and pizza place—nothing exciting. He spun quickly to his right and eyed the back of a gas station.

No one around.

The light changed. He went under the I-75 overpass and turned north onto the highway. The map on his phone had the red blip about thirty miles ahead. Still heading *north*. His prey must have figured they'd lose him by going in an unexpected direction. He'd seen this move before. They were on the run now, panicky. Easy pickings.

⁂

Josh peeked out around the door of the men's room and expelled a burst of air as he watched the car get on the northbound highway ramp. "Sorry I yanked you in here like that. I had this creepy feeling he was going to look right at us."

"It's okay. I was freaked out enough just seeing him." Sammi tapped the bathroom door. "Good thing this wasn't locked."

Good thing they were still breathing. "I guess someone was looking out for us."

"Speaking of someone to look out for us," Sammi said, "maybe you should call that detective again."

"And tell him what?"

"That our lives are in danger. That the man who killed the judge is after us. That he almost got you *twice*."

He stifled another shiver. "Why would he suddenly believe me?" He shrugged. "I sent the police to the crime scene, and all they were able to prove is that I'm a liar. Now I'm going to tell them I'm being chased by the same man they found no trace of, whose name I don't know, and whose whereabouts I can't be sure of?"

Sammi stepped outside, her eyes fixed on the highway on-ramp. “There’s got to be some way to convince him.”

He shook his head. “Let’s meet with this Master Zhou. Maybe we’ll have something then.”

Sammi sighed. “I sure hope so.” She tugged at her damp top. “Be nice to get out of these clothes.”

Josh jerked his gaze back toward the highway. “How about we head south for a bit first?”

As they pulled out, he glanced at the dashboard clock: almost 2:00 p.m. Forty-six hours to go, and all they had was a bunch of questionably sane theories, with nothing close to an answer. Sure, their pursuer was now going in the wrong direction, and Josh and Sammi at least knew where they were headed.

It didn’t make them any less lost.

NEW BEGINNINGS

Zhou Yuanxin's flight looped west from LaGuardia Airport, then south over the Hudson River. From his window seat on this luminous afternoon, he could see the glistening towers of New York City reaching skyward like the highest branches of the wish trees from the Daoist temples of his youth. He had pinned many a leaf-shaped note to the wish trees, hoping the wind might lift his prayers to heaven.

A sense of uneasy excitement crept over him. Perhaps he was reaching heavenward as well, as his window on the world delivered him to his next new beginning.

The seeds for his first new beginning had been planted by his mother.

He'd been only five years old when she took him to the orphanage that first time. The dingy rooms and dark hallways had frightened him. But the smiles on the orphans' faces—when he'd read them a picture book or as his mother opened the bags of fruit and rice she'd brought them—overcame his fears. From that day on, in his notes on the wish trees he'd prayed for a life of meaning, of purpose. He'd wished for a path that might help him change the world for the better.

His mother had introduced him to Falun Dafa—to enrich his soul, she'd said. Its exercises and meditations had quickly brought him such peaceful joy. He'd prayed that when he was old enough he might spread its blessings to others, and in his early teens he'd desperately clung to those blessings when his mother died. Six years later, when his father also passed, Zhou had inherited staggering wealth. Though it couldn't heal the hole in his heart, it brought freedom from financial need and freedom to pursue his one true passion.

It was the time that he considered to be his new beginning, his rebirth. It had been easy being so young and so committed.

"Would you like something to drink?" A courteous female voice interrupted his reflections.

A flight attendant hovered.

"Ginger ale, please." He ordered it only on flights. It soothed the pellet of air travel anxiety that typically sprouted in his stomach.

He sipped the tendered beverage, set it down on his tray table, leaned back, and returned to his memories.

By the time of his father's death, Zhou had progressed through Falun Dafa's lotus movements with ease, finding an innate ability to connect mind and body in the process. Upon devoting his full time to this spiritual pursuit, he had sometimes reached moments of astounding clarity. He turned out to be not just a natural student but also a gifted teacher. He advanced quickly through the ranks, was bestowed the title of master, and within a few years was considered one of the leaders of the Dafa movement in Beijing.

But rumors of government atrocities against his fellow practitioners—internments in "reeducation" camps, torture, and worse—eventually grew into hard-to-ignore absences from the local Falun Dafa community.

One day, almost five years after his father died, as Zhou prepared to instruct a class of beginners, his home was raided by the police. He was handcuffed and thrown in the back of a squad car, certain he was destined for prison and torture, when someone approached the officer in charge of the raid. Zhou could barely see the man's face. Was that—? It couldn't have been. But it was: the provincial deputy governor, a man who had been a guest on several occasions at his father's table. The deputy governor said a few words and appeared to hand something to the officer before leaving the scene as quickly as he had swept in. Moments later, the squad car door swung open. Zhou was pulled out and released from his cuffs. The officer told him he had three hours to vanish or they would be back for him.

He'd left that day for the United States. Presciently, he had already shifted a substantial portion of the family wealth to international holdings. Whatever else he could not arrange to ship out or transfer from China in those few hours he simply left behind.

Back then, his English had been rudimentary at best. But a number of trusted friends in the Dafa leadership had moved to New York. There, he would embrace the second stage of his new beginning.

"Oops. Sorry." The fidgety businessman seated next to him had failed in his attempt to simultaneously answer emails, eat, and read a paperback. The book now sat in Zhou's lap.

"We all seek our own space, but no space is our own." Zhou smiled and handed over the runaway book as he noticed the title: *Finding Focus*.

The years in America had introduced him to individuals unlike any he had known in China. As technology transformed the world—email, cell phones, virtual conferencing, social media, artificial intelligence—Westerners seemed increasingly distracted. Multitasking created conflicting channels of mind flow. "Finding focus" had become an illusory goal. Thus, the paths to higher levels of consciousness were less discernable, the leap far more difficult. What had once seemed reasonably possible—bringing true enlightenment to the Western world—was vanishing in a haze of undisciplined minds. His once youthful enthusiasm for his spiritual journey was waning.

But, in the past six months, he'd found reason to hope. Judge Neville Maloch had lifted his spirits—initially, with a theory that buttressed Dafa's deepest beliefs in the power of the evolving human mind, and, in recent days, with the startling revelation of an imminent awakening.

And then they'd murdered him.

As horrifying as that news was, Zhou had immediately known what it meant. He must pick up the mantle. Although unsure what might transpire with this supposed friend of the judge, he'd calmed his mind and accepted as primal truth that their meeting was predestined.

And so, as his flight pushed southward, Zhou found himself, despite his deep sadness about the judge, strangely at peace. It was as if he were returning to his first new beginning, when the greatest of possibilities had first appeared. Perhaps a note he'd long ago pinned to a wish tree was finally ready to bear fruit.

PRECEDENTS

Billboards flew by as Josh drove south on I-75. It felt good to be piling up the miles between them and the judge's killer—and to no longer be soaking wet, thanks to a brown wad of gas station bathroom paper towels and a change of clothes.

"Shoot." He glanced at Sammi. "I forgot to call Mark back." He voice-dialed on the car's Bluetooth.

"Quite the day, Quark," Mark said, after Josh had filled him in on everything. "And here's a little something to pile on top. I cracked another directory name."

Long pause. Mark loved to milk the moment.

"Okay. Let's have it."

"Higher Precedents."

"Higher Precedents," Josh repeated. "I can see that." He nodded at Sammi. "I've only read the material on one of the historical judges on our list, a magistrate in ancient China. But he rendered a decision that caused a change in the way criminal laws were written by the Mongols who ruled China back then."

"So, it was a 'higher precedent' because it was a groundbreaking ruling?" Sammi asked.

"I think there's more to it than that. The case was about basic human rights. The Mongols banned marriages between what they decided were different classes of people."

"A caste system?"

"Exactly. This magistrate tries the first case where a man marries someone of a supposed lesser class. A 'guilty' verdict probably means death. So he conducts pretty extraordinary research for the time. He reviews texts of Roman and Chinese laws and ultimately finds legitimate grounds to rule that the law simply voided the marriage. Thus, no finding of guilt."

"He saved them." Sammi smiled.

"With a ruling that refused to punish people for exercising basic human rights. His stand for human rights in that case defined the rest of his life. All the judges on our list supposedly handled groundbreaking human rights cases."

"'The righteous shall inherit the land.'"

"The Bible?"

"Yes, Psalms," Sammi replied. "And maybe it's my theology classes talking, but what about the judges' names all being from the book of Judges?"

He still hadn't quite wrapped his head around that one.

"Those biblical judges," Sammi continued, "were involved in matters of much higher import than simple judicial decisions. They led Israel out of dark times. They were *also* saviors."

They passed the first sign for Naples. Josh scratched his temple. "So you're saying this judge who's alive now is some kind of savior?"

"No. I'm saying that 'higher precedents' may not just mean rulings on important human rights cases, but more moral, more *righteous* ways of thinking. Maybe Judge Maloch is telling us that these judges were operating at a higher level of moral conscience. That would tie into the 'increased *de*' concept from the Falun Dafa—that these judges had each somehow reached a new plateau of human thought."

"And how would they have reached that plateau?" Mark's voice crackled from the dashboard speakers. "Without *help*, I mean?"

"What kind of . . . help," Sammi asked, not seeing Josh shaking his head, "did you have in mind?"

"Extraterrestrial. Gotta be. You really believe that greatly advanced thinking just *happens*? They planted an algorithm for it here. To arise at their command. Or, these judges could be *them*, infiltrating."

Josh blew out a breath. "Oh yeah, infiltrating at a rate of one person every two hundred and fifty years. Brilliant takeover strategy."

"But, Quark—"

"Sorry, Spaceman"—he waved at the air—"let's get real. Judge Maloch was just *murdered* over this. They murdered a *judge*. How often does *that* happen?" Holy crap, the dreams—*characters from across time and all over the world, yet somehow connected.* "Just realized, he may not have been the only one."

"What?" Sammi shot him a look.

"What if Judge Maloch wasn't the only one who died for this information? I think the Chinese magistrate might have. He died after falling off a cliff on a trail near his home, a place he'd probably walked hundreds of times. And he wasn't that old when it happened. So why does a highly respected judge suddenly fall to his death, from a trail he knows well?"

"Think he was thrown off the cliff?"

"Or maybe he jumped on purpose."

"Why would he do that?"

"What if he'd discovered something so valuable, and so dangerous in the wrong hands, that he gave up his life to protect it? Sound familiar? I'm getting the feeling Judge Maloch wanted me to research these particular judges for more than just their human rights cases."

"So," Sammi replied, "two judges lose their lives for the same unknown reason, a thousand years apart. Money, power, or religion—what's your best guess?"

"I'll take 'No Freaking Idea' for two hundred, Alex."

The highway swung them southeast in a broad arc into the long straightaway of Alligator Alley.

"We need to read up on those other judges," Sammi said, "and see what else, besides human rights cases, they had in common." She paused. "Can't do it at my apartment."

"Yeah. That tracker was on my car when I parked there this morning. Mark, you still with us?"

"Like I have a choice?"

"You think the mother ship could hold a couple stowaways for a few hours?"

⯌

What those judges had in common. Why was it that Sammi felt she knew something about that?

"I think," Josh said as he ended the call, "I dreamed about the Chinese magistrate two nights ago. The night before Judge Maloch was killed."

"Well, hadn't you just finished reading about him?"

"That's the crazy thing. I feel like I've dreamed about him before. Maybe even months or years ago."

Mind . . . freaking . . . blown. *That* was it! She had to tell him. "I think I might have too."

"How is that possible?" He stared at her for a beat longer than his eyes should've been off the road.

She shrugged. "I wish I knew." But maybe she did. As painful as Josh's dreams had been for him, she'd always embraced hers, felt they were tied to her destiny. This had to be yet another mark with meaning. "Have to think on that." But did she, really? This was a matter of trust. She had to trust her instincts, her long-held beliefs.

A landfill rose off to the north of the highway, rolling green hills in stark contrast to the surrounding flatness.

Trust. She'd seen rolling green hills like those before. *Dreamed* them. She closed her eyes and saw the hills of Normandy, sensed the air filled with great battles to come. There would be a historic channel crossing, and a judge faced as well with a matter of trust . . .

LOVE AND TRUST

1035-1068–Normandy and England

Until that frost-tipped December afternoon when he arrived at the stables for his midday ride, Phillip, the Count of Cotaine, had never seen the grubby child. Surprisingly muscled for his apparent age, the young boy sweeping the stalls had light blond hair and sky-blue eyes—clear markers of his Nordic heritage. Despite Phillip's best efforts, his township in western Normandy had been overrun by hordes who looked just like the boy.

"Giles!" the count called out for his chief stableman. Where *was* the man?

Giles Merogin rushed in from the other end of the building as quickly as his burly body would allow and flashed a hopeful smile below his mustache. "My lord, I see you've met my son, John. He's ten now and well hardy enough to help with the horses."

Those filthy immigrant hands were not getting near his stallions. And this Nordic stray was clearly no son of olive-skinned Giles. "I'll not have his kind about. I believe they need laborers in town."

The sound of hooves at a gallop came from a distance, reaching a crescendo moments later as Phillip's ten-year-old daughter, Anne, rode in, nodded curtly at her father, and dismounted. She was always angry at him over something. Seeking an explanation, Phillip trailed behind as Anne walked her mare into its stall. With a loud bray, the horse startled and reared, kicking up a cloud of dust and extending its powerful forelegs; they had come upon the sweeping boy.

Before Phillip could react, the boy sneezed.

Inexplicably, the horse relaxed and dropped to all fours. Anne and the grubby boy burst out laughing.

The boy bent down, picked up a long shaft of beech wood that had a sharpened tip, and tossed it to the side of the stall. "Don't want your fine mount to trip on my lance." He knelt and extended his hand. "May I tend to my fair maiden's steed?"

She chuckled and handed him the reins. "Certainly, my brave knight."

This wretched stray was her brave knight? Let them have their moment, Phillip thought. He'd instruct Giles shortly that the child was never to return.

But to Phillip's dismay, a fast friendship had been born. At Anne's insistence, the boy, John, became a regular at the stables. On many an afternoon that spring, Phillip looked on with disgust as this bastard Nordic laborer accompanied the count's only heir on lengthy rides through the hills.

✦

Book four of the *Deeds of Emperor Berengar* sat on the flat surface of John and Anne's "reading rock" on a shaded bank of the Seine at Cotaine's northern edge. Two years had passed since Anne had begun his lessons, soon after they'd first met. Now John prided himself in being able to share in the reading of this epic poem. He flipped the page and leaned back so Anne could take her turn. As she bent over the stone, he admired her profile; her beauty seemed to increase by the day. So had his love for her.

From the moment he'd first glimpsed those steel-blue eyes, that auburn hair, he'd been fascinated by Anne. He'd watched her boldly defy her father time and again and had welcomed the rewards: their daily rides, the reading lessons. Under her father's glare, she'd even shown

John the proper placement of dinner utensils at the weekly meals to which she'd insisted he be invited. She was everything he was not: poised, confident, refined. His "fair maiden." Yet, somehow, she'd seemed equally charmed at his ability to scamper up a tree in a flash; and he'd never forget her awed smile when he'd hurled his homemade wooden lance and brought down a brown hare in midstride. Her "brave knight."

"It's him!" She was staring at a line of the manuscript. "The emperor was just like my father. Flattered, adored, and arrogant. Is it not enough for these monarchs to rule their realm? Must they insist on ruling our hearts?"

Clearly, something else was on her mind. "What's happened?"

"I didn't wish to trouble you with this, but I feel if I contain it a breath longer my soul would surely burst from my being and sever in two. Last evening, my father had me called to his study. He announced that as a woman of almost twelve, the day had come for me to 'cast off childish fantasies.' That I was to find a more suitable companion, for, as he's lectured too many times in the past, you are"—she deepened her voice—"'no more than a devoted servant, whose station is, and always would be, far beneath mine.'" She spun, picked up a small, fallen tree branch, and hurled it out into the river. "I'd suffer a thousand hells before I'll let him chart my course."

Would she? He liked to believe her feelings for him were as strong as his for her, but he couldn't help but wonder. For just that past week when he'd dined at the castle, a server had brought Anne the wrong tea.

"You useless fool," she'd spat at the poor girl. "Perhaps I should ask one of the hounds to bring it next time."

She'd never launched such venom at him. But, in recent months, there'd been several of these incidents. Were they merely the release of pent-up anger at the count? Or was her father's arrogance working its way downstream?

John awoke to a nearby rustling. He turned from the wall to see his mother and Giles hovering over his cot. Their hands were empty. They'd always awoken him on birthdays with gifts—simple and practical, but wrapped and bowed.

Giles seemed to notice his look of concern. "Happy twelfth birthday, my son. Our gift this year defies wrapping. We have for you a journey . . . to Falaise in Normandy's south."

"Why *there*, Father?"

"There's someone who desires to meet you. Another twelve-year-old."

"In Falaise? You can't mean—"

"Yes, John. The child duke, William."

"But, Father, what interest would our sovereign have in me?"

"No more, I imagine, than any child might have in meeting a cousin of the same age."

What? "Father, I don't understand."

"Your mother and I have kept your background to ourselves. These are dangerous times, with heritage more curse than blessing. But you, just as the duke, are a direct descendent of the great warrior Rollo, the first of the Normans."

Could this be real? "I am?"

He nodded. "And despite our efforts, the duke has known your secret for some time. He's sent word he'd like to meet you." Giles motioned John to the window. Ten soldiers on horseback waited outside, adorned in glittering mesh and conical helmets, each carrying the long shield of the duke's battalions. "Perhaps more than just *word*."

Incredible. He was galloping amidst the duke's personal guard. John glanced over time and again at his official escorts as they rode through the day, thundering across Normandy's golden valleys and emerald hills. At last, in fading light, the group reached the great castle of Falaise. They crossed the lowered drawbridge and were ushered to the duke's stable.

Emerging from a swarm of servants and soldiers, a boy in royal dress strode forward and called out: "Is that you, Cousin?"

John dismounted. "Yes, my lord."

The young duke approached. He and John stared at each other.

How could they help it?

For he and the duke shared something far beyond their blond hair and blue eyes. Though John was small in stature, he had the gait and muscular physique of a man ten years older. It was something he'd never witnessed in another twelve-year-old—until this very moment.

There was little doubt that he and his cousin flowed from the same powerful bloodline.

As the great boar was rolled to their table, its flesh crisp from the spit, John rescanned his surroundings. It seemed the entire castle at Cotaine could fit in this chamber. A hundred servers scurried about filling goblets. To think of it—a grand feast thrown in *his* honor.

"They technically run the duchy until I'm of suitable age," William whispered to John, motioning down the dais toward his three custodians. "When my father died, I was only eight. Though I'm his sole heir, I was born illegitimate, as you. So there are nobles who would challenge my claim. But, through the influence of these gentlemen—my father's most trusted advisors—I have taken the throne, and intend to keep it." He grabbed John's arm. "I've had no living relative with whom to share this." He smiled. "Until now."

Over the next two weeks, William showed John every corner of the castle, from the workings of the drawbridge to the best positions on the walls for archers. At daily training in swordplay and archery, the boys held their own against experienced knights. Evenings brought dinners with advisors at the command table outside William's quarters.

"A siege at Bayeux is the only means to control the baron." William launched this opinion in direct contradiction to his custodians' views. Yet all heads bowed in agreement with John's twelve-year-old cousin. "But," William asked, "what if others are involved?"

The next night, a soldier rushed to the table. "I'm afraid, my lords, your suspicions are confirmed. Four families of Your Lordship's enemies ready to join forces against the duchy."

William turned to John. "The challenge expands. I'll need to deal with this in the field." Might he ask John to join him? "I wish you were ready for such endeavors." He patted John's shoulder. "Best you leave in the morning." As John nodded, trying to shield his disappointment, William added: "I'll have you back at my side before long."

✦

The moment John reached home, he rushed off to find Anne, anxious to share with her his stories of Falaise. He found her outside the stables, cinching her saddle for her morning ride.

"Could you have told me you'd be gone for almost two weeks?" she asked as he dismounted. She gave not so much as a glance in his direction.

"I didn't know how long I'd be there. Just that the duke wanted to meet me."

She glared at him. "And did you *ask* to leave, or did he tell you it was time to go?"

Why such anger? "I don't understand—"

"You certainly do. You abandoned me on your birthday. If you truly cared about me, you would've excused yourself after a few days. Father was right. Never depend on people of inferior breeding." She climbed into her saddle and rode off.

They were each still but twelve, he counseled himself, calming the pain in his chest. With time, she'd surely come to know that love and duty are necessary companions.

✦

"I dub thee Sir John of Cotaine." Ringed by a deep crowd of his soldiers, William lifted his sword from John's shoulder and asked him to rise. "My dear cousin," he continued, "my fervent wish is for you to join my royal brigade as 'special advisor to the duke,' to aid my quest to unite all Normandy under the duchy. Will you accept this commission?"

John had been training for this moment for the past five years, as a frequent guest at the duke's castle, having joined William in countless strategy sessions with his advisors and perfecting, alongside his cousin, imposing battlefield skills. At seventeen, there was only one other thing he wanted as much as this. "It would be my great honor to so serve Your Lordship and the realm."

A joyful clamor exploded from the surrounding throng.

As John rode home to Cotaine, all he could think of was Anne. He was bursting with excitement to tell her of his knighting and new title, yet wary of her reaction. She'd often rejected him when he returned from Falaise, but she'd always softened in a matter of days, showing him every kindness, integrating him—despite her father's disdain—into her world.

He caught up to her at the stables and nervously shared the news. "Perhaps," he quickly added, "after I've held the title for a few months, your father might deem me worthy of your hand."

A smile burst from Anne's lips. "We must celebrate, immediately."

With wine and blankets stuffed in their saddlebags, they rode off to Echo Cave, one of their secret hideaways. There, Anne laid out the blankets as John poured the wine. When he turned to hand her a goblet, she was spread out on a blanket, unclothed.

"I thought you wanted to wait until—"

"No need," she said. "*Special advisor to the duke*. Father will have no choice."

"You've earned your prize," William said as John rode by his side at the head of the duke's army. They'd been four unrelenting months at battlegrounds and sieges, crushing all resistance to the duke's reign. It was time to go home to ask for Anne's hand.

As soon as John crossed the drawbridge at Falaise, an aide raced toward him holding out an envelope. "Lord Merogin," the man huffed, "a letter from Cotaine, marked 'urgent.'"

Urgent? "When did this arrive?" John demanded.

"Three weeks past, sir. I'm so sorry, but we were instructed not to bring such things to the battlefield."

John recognized the seal immediately. What had happened?! He ripped open the envelope. The letter was but one sentence:

Dearest John—Please return home at once. Your Anne

"Saddle a fresh horse!" he barked at a stableman.

With barely a few minutes of rest, he was off to Cotaine.

Twenty-six years later, as he sat at the head of the long table in his castle in England's shire of Southborough, John Merogin watched the last of the guests exit his retirement feast. They'd shared stories of his years serving William, advising his cousin and fighting his battles—the conquests of Normandy and, two years past, the invasion and domination of England. His closest friends and many of his comrades in arms had come. King William had insisted on stopping in beforehand, so as not to draw attention from the honoree.

But now, as the servants cleared the plates, John stared at chair after empty chair. Over the years, he'd been blessed with the finest of friends, civilian and military, but he had no family to share his table. For he'd never met a woman who rose to the image of his first.

"My lord." His chief manservant entered the room. "A woman who calls herself Anne of Cotaine is at the door and has requested entry."

Now? After all these years? And why was she here after what she'd done?

They'd been only seventeen when he'd rushed home at her urgent request to find that he hadn't been worth even a three-week wait. Her father had married her off to Harold Godwinson, the brother of the queen of England.

And why was she here after what *John* had done? Anne's husband had risen to the English crown shortly before William's conquest of the country, and, in the Battle of Hastings, it had been John's own sword that had run Harold through.

His astonishment was soon overcome by a question: Why *Anne of Cotaine*? Her rightful title was "Anne of Wessex." What was she telling him?

After being escorted to John's table, Anne lowered her hood. Her braided auburn hair was ablaze against her porcelain skin; her steel-blue eyes sparkled like polished gems. The fiery teenager he remembered had matured into a stunning woman.

"After Harold's defeat," Anne explained over dinner, "I fled the country and took shelter back in the castle at Cotaine. I never loved Harold. As the years passed, I thought only of you."

"Then why did you leave me at seventeen for him?" The old wound was still fresh.

"Didn't you get my note, begging you to come home? For weeks I waited but heard nothing. I was desperate for a husband. I was . . . with child. It was stillborn in my eighth month."

Astride his white mount, in the cresting shadows of dusk, Wesley Jair gingerly weaved his way from the courtroom back to his temporary quarters amidst the still-bustling, smoky streets of innermost London. Though he was an elderly sheriff of a small shire, his integrity and impartiality were legendary in his corner of the realm. He'd been told these—along with his distance from London's political quagmire—were why King William had chosen him as trial judge. But, until this prosecution of Lord Merogin, which had begun three days prior, he had never tried a case of treason. As his pale steed's flame-like breaths pierced the chilled night air, he once again weighed the matter before him, and, once again, found the proceedings supremely disturbing.

Lord Merogin had opened his heart and home to the former queen—taken "his Anne" back. In return, over a course of weeks, she'd steadily plied him with wine until he let slip some details of troop movements, details she passed along to rebels in Ely who sought to upend William's rule. How hard must it have been for the king to levy charges at his beloved cousin! No horse, hound, or knight had ever been more loyal to the crown.

Under the laws Judge Jair was charged to enforce, Anne of Wessex's letter to the rebels was fully admissible as evidence, even though neither the drafter nor recipient were available to vouch for the letter's authenticity—the former queen having fled the country and the leader of the rebels having been killed in battle before the letter was discovered in his cloak. And, most remarkably, the fact that Lord Merogin had been drugged and duped was of no consequence. The jury had merely to find that Lord Merogin's actions had contributed, in some manner, to rebellion. The case against John Merogin was clad in iron.

During breaks in the trial, Judge Jair had scoured every treatise he could find on the essential elements for conviction of a criminal act. Seven hundred years earlier, Augustine, a primary founder of the Roman Catholic Church, had established the concept of *mens rea*—"guilty mind" in the Latin—for use in church penitential determinations. Augustine proposed, in essence, that "sin was the result of a guilty mind." Bad deeds were the misbegotten heirs of evil motives.

Under Norman-English law, however, motive could be proven simply by the fact that Lord Merogin had let go of the intelligence used by the rebels. A man was held responsible for the results of his actions, notwithstanding being seduced, drugged, and betrayed.

Judge Jair wrestled with the absurdity of this interpretation. How could someone who had no desire whatsoever to commit treason be liable for information obtained from him wholly by trickery? He'd heard about Lord Merogin's history with this woman. Despite his unceasing devotion to her since childhood, she'd constantly rejected him in jealous rages in response to his loyalty to his cousin, and then, as he'd readied to marry her, she'd tossed him aside for a more advantageous match. What's more, he'd killed her husband at Hastings.

After all this, how could he have trusted her? Yes, she'd apparently extended to him some kindnesses in their youth. But trust must be earned. The pocket change of dependable responses needs be invested over a steady course until the ledger runs flush. How could Lord Merogin have ignored all these past markers?

That night, in the midst of reexamining a manuscript on criminal procedure, desperately hunting for some helpful precedent he might have overlooked, he found what he thought was a small fissure in the deficient logic of the time. He stared, repeatedly, at the phrase he had been reading. Nothing of aid. Suddenly, amber-crested peaks seemed to rise from the print, dancing above the page. His mind had surely fogged from overconcentration. He lifted his head and gazed past the manuscript at the fireplace. Amidst the crackling sparks, was that a message rising from the flames? What was happening? This much was clear: The phrase he'd been pondering had no significance at all to his dilemma; the opening he had seen was not contained on the parchment before him—it was teased from some hidden chamber of his mind.

Focusing on the ethereal wisps of smoke as they ascended and vanished, he found the fissure once more. Calming his mind, he peered through. What he observed at first seemed a collection of meaningless symbols. But the symbols fell away and *The Words* burst forth. They began with a justification:

**LOVE IS THE TRAPDOOR TO TRUST.
IT IS A REALM OF FANTASY WHERE OUTSIDER
PASSES FROM STRANGER TO FIDUCIARY IN THE
FLICKER OF A WAYWARD GLANCE. WORSE YET,
LOVE BECOMES THE ERASER OF HISTORIES REPLETE
WITH UNDEPENDABLE ACTS. LOVE IS NOT ONLY BLIND,
IT IS DEAF, DUMB, AND UNEDUCABLE.**

The Words led him along a journey through the thoughts of a thousand great legal minds out to the very border of human freedoms. To the line that separates an individual's most fundamental rights from the rights of the state. There he found the answer that satisfied him:

Without some credible proof that a person actually *intended* to commit a crime, conviction for a criminal wrong was an egregious violation of any system of free men.

And *The Words* told him so much more. He could not, however, contain it all. The power of the messages, the volume of information, was too great to hold all at once. Exposure to *The Words* was pressurized. Like diving into the sea, it seemed the deeper he delved, the weightier the atmosphere became and the less likely he'd ever safely resurface. So he clung to what he could, and he determined to seek out the fissure again in the future, hopeful he might train his mind to cope by returning for small doses. Yet he somehow sensed that even small doses might accumulate into an all-consuming addiction.

As for now, he was flush with a level of enlightenment that was wholly useless in the present circumstance. In fact, it served only to inflame his anger, since he well understood his responsibilities in the matter. He was mandated to instruct the jury that it could convict a man who clearly never intended to commit any wrongful act.

At the close of the evidence, that is precisely what he did.

The jury deliberated for three days. Despite several chastisements from the judge, the group was unable to arrive at a unanimous decision. When they ultimately came in with seven favoring conviction and five for acquittal, Judge Jair felt a great weight lift from his shoulders as he prepared to announce a hung jury.

Before this pronouncement could be made, however, the prosecutor motioned to the judge and snatched a large, leather-bound text from his counsel table. He brought it up to the judicial bench and flipped furiously through. Stopping at the desired page, he rotated the book to face the judge.

Wesley Jair could not believe what he was reading. Although he admittedly was not completely versed in the recent Norman changes to English law, the ones he'd dealt with all seemed fairly reasonable. But this one made no sense at all, particularly in a criminal case.

Norman law employed a bewildering twist on the English requirement for a unanimous verdict in a criminal trial. The Normans recognized a deadlock only if the jury were half for conviction and half for acquittal. If a majority voted one way, the judge was required to deem all the minority votes to be for that same verdict, thus transforming consensus to unanimity.

Though utterly confounded as to why a country would allow a criminal conviction so easily, Judge Jair knew his duty, as distressing as it was. After sending counsel back to their stations, he addressed the court. "Will the accused please rise."

Lord Merogin came to his feet.

The judge continued. "Under the legal code as adopted by our sovereign, King William, a deadlock may be declared only where the jurors are locked at six all. If, to the contrary, there be a majority in one direction, this court is compelled to convert such majority to unanimity. As seven of our twelve jurors cast in favor of conviction, it is hereby ruled that the five dissenting votes are reversed, resulting in a unanimous verdict of guilty."

Lord Merogin stood stone-faced.

Under the law, there was still one matter of discretion. If there were no doubt in the trial judge's mind as to a jury verdict of guilty for the crime of treason, he was required to levy a sentence of death. On the other hand, if he were unconvinced, the judge could order an additional trial "by ordeal." The death sentence, Judge Jair knew, was generally far more merciful.

"There remains one matter for judicial determination. Inasmuch as the jury was less than certain, it is hereby ordered that the convicted be subjected to trial by the ordeal of hot iron. May the ordeal leave no doubt. This inquest stands recessed pending preparation of the ordeal."

As the judge spun to vacate the chamber, he thought he noticed a shudder crossing the countenance of Lord Merogin.

John Merogin had witnessed an ordeal by hot iron when, several years before, one of the king's soldiers had been accused of raping and killing a young girl in the outskirts of London. The man was convicted on highly conflicting evidence, and his demand for a trial by ordeal had been granted by the judge. A large metal vat had been filled with water and hung over a firepit. Once the water boiled, it was poured into two troughs. An iron bar was placed in each trough and left to absorb the heat. When the bars turned red-hot, the accused was brought into the room and the bars were lifted from the troughs and extended toward him. He was given two choices: immediate death or grabbing the two bars—one in each hand—and walking with them a distance of twenty strides.

The man had chosen to hold the bars. At first grasp, his face contorted to an ugly mask, and his screams paralyzed the chamber as the iron rods crashed to the ground. In untold agony, he begged to be killed at once. The last of his screams echoed as the executioner's axe came down.

John had heard of peasants, with hands thickly callused from physical labor, who had lasted somewhat longer. But, to his knowledge, no man had ever held the scalding irons for even half the distance.

John's hands were among the most powerful in England. He could swing and maneuver the heaviest weapon with ease. Years of battle and practice had hardened the skin of his palms and fingers to horsehide. But red-hot iron bars for twenty strides?

As a solemn Lord Merogin was led into the expansive chamber, the several hundred observers hushed. From the room's center, Judge Jair glanced above the crowd at King William. The monarch sat on his pedestal, his face grimmer than a pallbearer's. The judge turned to watch the steam rise from the two bubbling troughs; within them, the iron bars glowed red.

He approached the prisoner and extended his hands. Lord Merogin took them in his own as the judge looked him in the eye and explained the choices ahead. Lord Merogin nodded in affirmation.

The judge let go and announced: "The prisoner is informed. Let the trial by ordeal commence."

Lord Merogin was escorted to the troughs, and the scalding iron bars were raised in front of him. Eyeing the bars warily, he reached out and grabbed hold.

The judge shot another glance up at King William and swore the sovereign flinched, likely imagining the searing steel against the flesh of his cousin's palms. Lord Merogin took his first step, his face clenched hard. As one effortful stride led to another, the judge wondered what the crowd might be thinking. Was the prisoner about to collapse in unbearable pain? Or could he miraculously continue this superhuman exertion of will?

When a bailiff proclaimed "Ten strides!" with Lord Merogin's expression unchanged and his hands still firmly on the bars, the murmuring of the crowd betrayed their sentiments: This man was either a god or falsely accused. Perhaps both.

At the pronouncement "Twenty strides!" Lord Merogin let go.

The bars clattered against the stone floor, and the chamber erupted. The king's head dropped into his hands, clearly shielding tears of disbelief and joy. Lord Merogin composed himself with a series of lung-filling breaths, and then his stoic countenance relaxed.

Judge Jair approached and asked Lord Merogin to extend his hands. The judge examined them closely as murmurs flooded the room, then stepped back and proclaimed: "Unbowed and unmarked."

The crowd roared its approval.

Lifting his voice over the din, Judge Jair announced: "Lord Merogin is hereby declared innocent of all charges."

That night, as Wesley Jair said his bedtime prayers, he thanked God and *The Words* for this little miracle. Only God's grace could have ensured that the thick, flesh-colored clay he'd slipped into Lord Merogin's hands would protect them long enough. And but for *The Words*, he'd have lacked the nerve to undo this injustice. Though wary of their power, and puzzled at their origins, he hoped *The Words* might deign to visit him again someday.

There were paths ahead to be paved.

STATUS CHECK

A spasm tugged at his forearm. Han Chee-hwa eased his hold on the elliptical's handgrips. Thirty seconds more.

He had begun the morning with unharnessed energy born of mounting frustration. Now his legs churned and his quadriceps were on fire. Fifteen seconds. He swiped at his eyebrows, redirecting rivulets of sweat from his forehead. Time. He slowed his pace, drew air deeply to his lungs, and stepped free as shards of the day's first sunlight glinted off the steel limbs of the exercise equipment spread across his private gym.

He punished himself further with ice-cold water in the shower, toweled off, and donned a robe. But the workout and biting shower had served as no more than minor distractions. What of the wheels he had set in motion? What was happening on the other side of the world? He needed answers, and he needed them soon.

"Mr. Han"—the intercom crackled with the sweet voice of his assistant—"your morning massage?"

This distraction he welcomed.

"Yes, Meiling, please."

He removed his robe and moved to the massage table as she came in. Carefully selected from the upper echelon of his escort service, she'd worked for him for more than three years, yet Meiling's youthful beauty still surprised him every time she entered the room. This morning he had a pressing phone call to make, so the massage would be the extent of her services.

"Shall I start with your back?"

"Yes, Meiling, please." Merely saying her name soothed him.

"Maximum pressure?" she purred.

"Yes, Meiling, please." How perfectly she could keep him lingering between pleasure and pain.

"Your late uncle," she asked as she applied the oils, "today is his birthday?"

"Seventy-four," he said.

She chuckled. "How did you know I would ask his age?"

"You do every year." His thoughtful assistant was probably the only other person in the world who knew or cared. He couldn't imagine his cousin gave a damn. He opened his eyes. On the wall near the massage table was a favorite picture: his uncle sitting up at the front of a lounge chair on the beach at Zhuhai, his arm wrapped around the young Han's shoulders. Everything he had, he owed to that man.

Orphaned to the streets of Beijing at age nine, Han had learned the back alleys and illicit occupations of the city, running with the pick-pockets and the highwaymen. At twelve, after one of his numerous arrests, his uncle had tracked him down through police connections. His uncle swore on the grave of Han's drug-overdosed mother that Han would be straightened out. Though firm on rules and discipline, his uncle had taught him the value of possessions and power while mixing in the joys of horseback rides and fishing trips to Zhuhai. He was sent for a year to a military academy to learn structure, then for two years to a private preparatory school to catch up on academics and, per his uncle's mandate, to master English. Before long, he'd worked out how to blend in with the entitled heirs to some of the wealthiest families in China.

When Han had turned fifteen, his uncle had arranged to send him to the United States to an exclusive prep school in Boston. The plan had been for Han to get into a leading American university, from which he could bring back the newest secrets of technology, science, and economics, to keep China competitive and preserve the family's position of privilege.

"Wouldn't your son be a better choice?" Han had asked. They'd been close when Han had first come into their home, but as his uncle had taken Han under his wing, his cousin had pulled away.

"Zhou is an embarrassment," his uncle had spat back through sour lips. "He has a weakness for the common people. He doesn't understand who we are, what this takes, what we can too easily lose. I crawled from the pit to build my fortune, crawled over whatever was in my way. I see that potential in you. But power and wealth can too easily slip from a barebacked horse. They require a saddle of ruthlessness. I can give you power and wealth, but to keep them you must constantly ask yourself: 'How ruthless am I willing to be?'"

So, he went off to America. To a breeding ground for its capitalist elite. To bring home their secrets.

By then, his English had become more than passable, but his accent, skin tone, hair, and eyes had made him a target of the class bullies. And his scrawny frame didn't help. A week into school, two of his larger abusers had cornered him behind the assembly building. One had pushed him down from behind, knocking a stack of books from his hands.

"Y'all better be picking those up quick," came the booming voice of Kyle Fredericks, the tallest boy in class—two heads above Han.

From the dirt, Han watched his attackers scoop up the books, stack them neatly in front of him, and run off.

Kyle extended a long arm to help him up. "To them Yankees, I'm about as welcome as you are. All I got going for me is my height."

Kyle said he was from a place called Gatlinburg, Tennessee. His father had sent him north for a better education before he went into the family business. They were religious Episcopalians, and his father owned a string of television and radio stations across the South that emphasized wholesome, Christian-oriented programming.

Maybe Kyle had taken to Han at first as a fellow outsider, but the ultimate glue to their long-term friendship was something else they shared: an unshakable dedication to their goals.

Han's mission in America had proceeded on course for almost two years. And then came the phone call.

Late one evening, near the end of spring semester, Kyle came running into the dining hall. "Chee-hwa, your cousin's on the phone from Beijing."

Why would *he* call? They'd barely talked in years. Han raced to their room and picked up the phone.

"Zhou, is everything okay?"

"I'm afraid not. I—"

"What's happened? Tell me!" He prayed his uncle was okay.

"My father suffered a heart attack yesterday."

"Are you at the hospital? Can I speak to him?"

"He . . . they couldn't save him."

Back came the frightening sensation Han had known only once before—something long walled off from his memory. It was as if he had swallowed a stone that was rapidly expanding in his abdomen, pinioning him to the ground and suffocating him from the inside. He'd not felt this since the day he came home as a nine-year-old to find his emaciated mother dead on the floor, an emptied syringe in her opened palm.

His uncle's nurturing had almost allowed him to forget that unbearable pain. But here it was again, crushing his insides and his future. For just as sharp as his anguish was the unwritten message in the wind: At age seventeen, he was to be cast adrift a second time.

He was on a flight the next morning. Still in a state of shock, he attended his uncle's funeral. After the ceremony, Zhou pulled him aside and explained that Han's uncle had never updated his old will and that it contained no mention of Han. Zhou had been left the bulk of the family fortune, and he had no desire to waste any of it on Han, his father's "pet project." Instead, Zhou proclaimed, he intended to use his newfound riches for the betterment of the masses. Han had known exactly what that meant: His uncle's hard-earned wealth would be squandered on a dangerous cult, Falun Dafa—an enemy of all his uncle had stood for.

Zhou told him there would be no funds for Han's return to America, no funds to pay for Han's further education. So much for the betterment of the masses. The bastard gave him a small sum in exchange for his agreement to gather his things and vacate the family compound within two days.

Shattered, he'd drifted for weeks, knowing that the six-month traditional Chinese mourning period for a "father" would be woefully inadequate. But eventually he'd invoked his strongest inheritance from his uncle: the steel in his spine. Somehow, someway, he'd vowed, he would crawl from the pit again. And then, when the timing was right, he would deal with his cousin.

Now, all these years later, it seemed that day was finally at hand.

"Mr. Han, will there be anything else?" The massage was finished.

"No, Meiling. Thank you." He stole a glance as she departed; his call could wait no longer.

He walked to the window. Drawing strength from the surrounding mountains, he picked up his private line and dialed.

"Chee-hwa?"

"Yes. Any news?"

Kyle hesitated. "My man's been down there less than twenty-four hours. Give us a chance."

"He's had several chances already." Han drummed his fingers on the windowsill.

"You have a better option?"

Han did not respond.

"Look," Kyle continued, "my man's truly gifted in this area, blessed. He's never let me down. I'm confident we'll have results by tomorrow."

But would tomorrow be too late? His meeting with General Chang had been about more than seizing the glory for himself. This was a battle for the imminent survival of the world order. Kyle, of all people, understood that, in pursuing crucial goals, cold, hard decisions were often necessary.

Particularly once an asset became an obstacle.

CONNECTIONS

"We're missing something major," Josh said to Sammi, momentarily pulling his eyes from the road as he piloted them north on I-95 on their way to meet this Master Zhou. "Biblical names and human rights cases can't be the only links between them." They'd barely had two hours at Mark's to research and skim through the histories of all the judges on Neville Maloch's list. "I wish we knew more about their lives."

"What about their deaths?" Sammi asked.

"You talking about the Chinese magistrate? We know his death was suspicious."

"How about Henrik of Reibzang, the one who served under Charlemagne? It seems pretty clear he took his own life. And the British judge, Nigel Tolan."

"He died in an insane asylum," Josh said. "But we don't know how. And we don't know how the rest of them died either."

"You said earlier that maybe the Chinese magistrate gave up his life to keep some valuable secret out of the wrong hands. What if Henrik of Reibzang killed himself and Nigel Tolan was institutionalized for the same reason?"

"Okay," Josh said, "let's say all of that was to keep something secret. We still have no idea what that *something* is."

"Maybe we won't find it just by looking at these judges. To understand history, it helps to look at more than just individuals. The actions and interests of countries, organizations, and religious groups can often tell us things individuals can't. Maybe the key is to find out who's been so desperate to learn this secret."

"I guess I should've asked the guy that was trying to kill me." He glanced over again to catch her response.

"Pity you let that chance slip by." She grinned. "Well, maybe Master Zhou can tell us." Her lips leveled off and she steeled her jaw. "But even if he can't, we're going to figure this out."

As Sammi turned away, he kept his eyes on her for a beat. There wasn't a whisper of quit in that profile. And she'd taken up his cause from the moment he foisted this nightmare on her. In the past, he'd hightailed it for the nearest exit in the face of far less pressure. But he was going to stick this one out, despite the risks, despite the dark corners of his dreams, despite his brother. This was no longer solely about the judge. He'd see this through for Sammi.

Along I-95, through northern Miami and southern Fort Lauderdale, Florida's lush green landscape was nowhere in sight. They were surrounded by concrete: big-box stores, warehouses, overpasses, and urban highway wallpaper—those bland sound and sight-line barriers that ran for miles on end.

Squeeeak!

Josh snapped to attention as the car in front of him squealed, its taillights glowing red. He braked hard as traffic skidded to a halt.

"There's an accident a mile up according to Waze," Sammi said. "No exit before then. We're stuck."

They inched forward for ten minutes before Josh heard sirens. Two Broward County Sheriff's patrol cars, an ambulance, and a tow truck whizzed by on the shoulder. It was another fifteen minutes before they finally passed the accident scene.

"We don't have Zhou's number," Josh said. "Why don't you call the restaurant so they can tell him we're running late."

As Sammi made the call, his mind fell back to the judges they'd been discussing, the possibility that their deaths were not coincidental. Destiny. That's what Sammi would say. It was a dirty word to him. How could it not be, with his past? But Sammi's belief in destiny had been eating at him since her shocking revelation a few hours earlier. Maybe it was time to ask the question.

"This morning you said you think you also may have dreamed about the Chinese magistrate. Have you dreamed about any other judges?" Out of the corner of his eye, he thought he caught a hint of a shiver.

"I'm pretty sure I have. But I was always more focused on the historical aspects of my dreams. Pieces were so vivid. For a while I figured they were simply tied to my love of history. But, at some point, I started to believe there was more to them. That this past was somehow linked to my future. I didn't necessarily realize that judges were involved." She paused, then touched his arm. "Until this weekend." She gently wrapped her fingers around his forearm. "What's happening between us?"

REDIRECTION

Billy Ray plowed south on Florida's Turnpike, still pissed off beyond all get-out. He'd been played for a fool, had wasted precious time in the process, and had gotten reamed out by the Reverend to boot.

He'd left Captiva hours ago and had headed north on I-75 along the west coast of Florida, twenty minutes behind the red blip on his Teen Tracker app. The blip had kept moving at eighty miles per hour with no signs of slowing down, which meant it would be a long time catching up, since he didn't dare exceed eighty-five, not wanting to attract attention.

By the second hour, he'd started wondering just where Sutton and his girlfriend were headed. Were they leaving the state? What did they know?

Outside of Tampa, the red blip had left the highway and had finally come to a stop. He'd closed the gap in ten minutes, pulling into an old diner just off the exit ramp. When he entered the parking lot he'd screamed "Damn it!" at the top of his lungs. The blip on his phone's screen wasn't coming from Sutton's car. It was coming from a semi with Georgia plates.

After a few more choice words and a quick scan to make sure the coast was clear, he'd slipped under the truck for a look-see.

"Excuse me, sir," he'd heard an official-sounding voice say, "you got a problem?"

He'd slid out to find a county sheriff gazing down at him. "No, Officer. Heard somethin' clang off the bottom a way's back. Checkin' to be sure she's okay down there."

The sheriff narrowed his eyes. "Want me to stick around in case you need help?"

"Thank you, sir," he'd responded. "I can see she's just fine."

After the man had left, Billy Ray had found the transmitter under the truck, near the rear end. When he'd gotten back in his car, he'd slammed his fist so hard into the dashboard that he'd left a permanent impression of his knuckles. Steaming, he'd turned the car around and headed back south.

Maybe he'd underestimated his prey.

Once again, he'd cut across the crappy center of this godforsaken swamp of a state to get to Florida's Turnpike, the fastest route to the Fort Lauderdale/Miami area, where he was sure Sutton must've returned. His head still not right, he'd had to look twice at the name of the town where he caught up to the Turnpike: Yeehaw Junction. Too starving to go on, he'd found a barbeque joint for lunch and was just finished licking the rib sauce off his fingers when he'd heard "Amazing Grace" coming from his pocket. Shit on a stick.

"Amazing Grace" was the personal ring tone he'd chosen for the Reverend. He had tones for all his special callers.

"Hello."

"Thought I'd have another report before now. Everything under control?"

". . . Sort of."

"What's that supposed to mean?" The Reverend's tone was far from amazing.

"I tracked the man, caught up with him."

"You get the information?"

"Uh, no." He hated admitting failure, especially to the Reverend.

"He wouldn't talk?"

"Can't really say." That was stupid.

"You being coy with me?" The Reverend's voice was rising.

"'Course not, sir." Knew it.

"Then what *are* you saying?"

It hurt to say the words. "He escaped."

"Again?!"

During the tense pause that followed, he pictured the veins rising into high ridges down the sides of the Reverend's neck, as they always did when the man clenched his teeth in anger.

"Kid's a bit more resourceful than I'd expected." As soon as the words fell out of his mouth, he'd wished he could've stuffed them back in.

"Than you'd *expected*?!" Now the Reverend was hot. "My son, we both know the unexpected is exactly what one must be prepared for. The expected is routine. *You* are not routine. You weren't selected to serve our holy purpose because of your incredible capacity to deal with the *expected*! Now please tell me, after his 'escape,' did you get back after him?"

How come the dang phone company never dropped a call when you needed it to? "Got a little detoured."

"Detoured?!"

It was the second time in a row the Reverend had turned Billy Ray's words into a question—never a good thing with the Reverend. The sermon was about to launch into high gear.

"Yes. But, sir, now's not the time for explanations." This was their code phrase for "Other ears may be listening." Finally, he'd felt his wits coming back. Why was it always so hard to find his brain when he talked to the Reverend?

His prayer answered, the Reverend had backed off. "Do you anticipate being back on course soon?"

"Absolutely. Using my alternate plan." Weren't no lie.

"Then I'll await your next report."

"Thank you, sir."

"And I assume it will be more positive."

"Yes, sir."

"And without as much delay."

"Yes, sir."

"And, since it is *your* report, perhaps *you* will actually call *me* to deliver it."

The man was a barrelful of chuckles. "Right, sir."

It was astounding how the Reverend could pulverize him with just words. No, not even words—with the thoughts Billy Ray figured the Reverend had in his head. Billy Ray had felt this way ever since that speech at the stadium in Tuscaloosa, fifteen years back.

Though he'd been a prized incoming-freshman linebacker at the University of Alabama, he'd torn up his knee so bad in summer drills that the doctors, though they'd patched him up as best they could, said he'd never play again. With football ripped away, he'd packed his things to leave school. He'd become what all those wretched foster parents had sworn he was: an outsized freak with nothing else to offer.

But as he was zipping his duffel bag closed, his roommate told him there was something happening that night at Bryant-Denny Stadium that was way bigger than the Crimson Tide. And the school's cheerleaders, the Crimsonettes, were the opening act—he'd had his eye on that Heather, the tall blonde. He'd figured it wouldn't hurt to check her out one last time.

He'd limped on his crutches into the packed, buzzing stadium as the school band broke into "Sweet Home Alabama" and the Crimsonettes danced on a stage that had been set up in an end zone. When the music stopped and Heather and her teammates sashayed off, a man at a podium was alone on the stage. The man gazed down at a girl in a wheelchair who was at a microphone near the stage's edge.

"Reverend," the girl's voiced echoed through the stadium, "why must I suffer like this? Why am I less than those around me?"

"My child," Reverend Kyle Fredericks had responded, "I have no answers for you . . ."

The crowd fell to a hush, everyone catching their breath at once.

"But Exodus does. 'And the Lord said unto him, who hath made man's mouth? Or who maketh the dumb, or deaf, or the seeing, or the blind? Have not I the Lord?'"

Billy Ray's roommate nodded in agreement. But Billy Ray had heard hogwash like this too many times.

"And John tells us the rest," the Reverend boomed. "'Who did sin, this man, or his parents, that he was born blind? Jesus answered: Neither hath this man sinned, nor his parents, but that the works of God should be made manifest in him.' And then," he added, "comes the crucial passage: 'I must work the works of him that sent me, while it is day: the night cometh, when no man can work.'"

Billy Ray was ready to leave.

But then the Reverend bore his eyes in on the wheelchair-bound girl. "Each of us are made differently by our creator, different vessels for different holy purposes. Even with our *wounds*, all that matters is that each of us employ these blessed differences to their best effect while the light still shines upon us."

A shudder had crept down Billy Ray's spine. Was the man saying that he and his bum knee could still, somehow, have value? He needed to know more.

Hours later, Billy Ray had waited outside with a whole bunch of stragglers determined to see the Reverend as he left. When he came out, the Reverend shook every hand and had a kind word for every last soul. He stopped when he saw Billy Ray, looked him up and down.

"Aren't you Billy Ray Jackson, 'Jackson the Ripper'?"

Billy Ray had felt the shiver again. "You . . . know me?" he'd stuttered.

"Know you? I'm quite the Tide fan. Did my graduate work here. Can't wait to see you on the field." He eyed the crutches. "Going to be ready for the season?"

"Afraid not. Doc says I'm done. I heard you say we all got to use what we've been given. My gift's been taken away. To folks I'm just a big old freak. What do I do now?"

The Reverend looked him over again. "The Lord has seen a greater purpose for you than football. Perhaps the world has not sufficiently evolved to fully appreciate your 'perfected form.' But the two of us, and the Lord, we'll push the world there together. Son, I'd be truly honored if you'd come join me in my holy work. I promise your talents will not be wasted." He pulled a card from his pocket. "Here's my ministry's number. You give them a call and tell them who you are."

Talents. Someone actually still believed in him. Maybe these preachers weren't all full of manure. He'd stifled another shudder.

And still, after all these years, the Reverend could so easily unsettle him. It was a heavy load disappointing your father and your Lord all at once.

Determined not to let the Reverend down again, he'd gotten back in his car and picked up the southbound Turnpike. An hour later, still on the highway and wondering whether his "alternate plan" would kick in any time soon, he heard "Three Blind Mice" coming from his cell phone. Perfect timing.

He hit the MUTE button and listened in on the call.

"Szechuan Grill," a man was answering. "How can I help you?"

A woman responded about running late.

He pulled over and, after a few misspellings, got "Szechuan Grill" to show up in his Google Maps. It was in Boca Raton, only twenty-five minutes away.

SPACIAL GEOMETRY

Zhou's restless mind was soothed for a moment by the swirling aromas of the Szechuan Grill. The scent of brewing oolong tickled his nasal passages; his lips tingled in anticipation of the peppercorns to come. From where he sat in a booth near the rear, facing the cherrywood swinging doors of the kitchen, he watched servers hustling back and forth and weaving through a platoon of busboys. A constant low clatter of silverware against china served as a backbeat to the echoing conversations that filled the room. He'd almost forgotten how large and popular the restaurant was; his last visit had been several years before, after a nearby regional spiritual gathering.

In an abundance of caution, he'd set this meeting in a public place. He'd selected the Szechuan Grill not because the location was ideal—in fact, it was somewhat inconvenient to both the Fort Lauderdale and West Palm Beach airports—but due to the quality of its food. How better to settle himself than with a bowl of first-rate hot-and-sour soup?

He wished today's outcome was more predictable. Life would be so simple if it were confined to one plane. All its angles would have no choice but to add up to 360 degrees. Every surprise, every nuance, could be calibrated and put in place.

But alas, life, from its very essence, was a mystery. Drafting in the tailwind of every short-term solution was a long-term enigma. How incredible, then, when the long-term enigma was solved. Judge Maloch had divined a previously undetectable pattern—a wondrous convergence of paths—leading to an imminent miracle.

Could it be snatched away at its very moment of actualization?

Of course it could be. In this multidimensional reality, it was precisely when the angles appeared to add up that the playing field often changed. And it already *had* with the judge's urgent message and then his murder.

A pot of oolong arrived. As he poured it, he deeply inhaled its jasmine-tinged aroma and tried not to think just how predictable the source of that death had been. It was Han Chee-hwa, his cousin and childhood playmate, who'd become the sworn enemy of Falun Dafa. It had to be.

Recently, Zhou had been alerted that his computer was being monitored and that extremely sensitive emails had been compromised. Convinced his cousin's probing fingers were involved, he'd immediately alerted the judge, and the two of them had coordinated the emergency email message. Zhou would know the moment anyone clicked on the "urgent message" link he'd embedded into that email, and that same click would lock out the person while delivering a copy of the judge's address book to Zhou so he could get in touch with the judge's contacts if the judge suddenly were to go missing. Though Zhou's assistant had assured him that their IT people had removed the spyware from his computer, out of an abundance of caution he'd used a terminal at the local library when he'd responded this morning to the judge's friend's email.

"Excuse me." A female voice snapped him back to the present. "The rest of your party has arrived."

A young couple stood next to the hostess.

Two of them? And so young. The email had indicated only one person, and he had assumed that any friend of Judge Maloch's would be closer to the judge's age. Though neither looked over thirty, the twosome evidenced a solemn demeanor, each assessing him with delving eyes.

He straightened, bowed his head slightly, and motioned across the table. "Please have a seat."

The couple slid into the booth, the girl first. The young man extended his hand. "I'm Joshua Sutton and this is Samantha Bollinger."

Of course. Ms. Bollinger offered a slight smile and returned the nod.

He shook the proffered hand. "Zhou Yuanxin. My pleasure to meet friends of Judge Maloch. I wish the circumstances were better."

"He was my mentor," Mr. Sutton said. "I just graduated from law school at the University of Miami."

"I worked for him as a student-clerk," Ms. Bollinger added.

"You were also his research assistants."

Their eyes widened.

"He spoke highly of you both." He fumbled nervously for the teapot. "You emailed that he was murdered."

"I was there." Mr. Sutton eased forward and recounted the incident he'd witnessed at the judge's home, admitting that he'd taken the judge's laptop and opened the link in Zhou's email, which had frozen the hard drive.

Though Zhou had learned about his dear friend's death hours earlier, hearing the grisly details was something else. He gripped the edge of the table as he shakily poured himself more tea. His cup was newly heavy as he guided it to his lips.

"What have the police found?"

"Nothing." According to Mr. Sutton, there was an astounding lack of evidence at the judge's home.

Sammi had closely observed the man's reactions. Zhou Yuanxin was deeply upset by the judge's death. It was clear they had been close. This man was a Falun Dafa master, and Falun Dafa was definitely a part of all this. If she and Josh shared what they'd learned, maybe he had the rest of the answers.

She was about to speak when Zhou expelled a heavy sigh. "I must tell you how I came to know the judge," he said, "how we became friends." He awkwardly guided his teacup back to its saucer, where it clicked into place. "Are you familiar with Falun Dafa?"

"Somewhat." Out of the corner of her eye she saw Josh's hesitant nod.

"I'm a Falun Dafa master and part of the leadership. About two years ago, the judge contacted me through a mutual colleague. Unlike most people I hear from, he had little interest in the exercises. He was far more concerned with the Dafa's history—its roots. At first, he led me to believe this was purely an academic interest, but we ended up in many stimulating discussions. We shared philosophies and backgrounds, and a friendship formed. Eventually, he took me into his confidence. He was seeking information from the archived manuscripts we maintain at headquarters."

"What information?" Josh nearly demanded.

"If you don't mind us asking," Sammi offered, apologetically.

"Not at all. This was the part of his research he told me he felt it best to keep from you both for your safety. He wanted to examine the Xiulian writings about laws. Laws both spiritual and legal, along with rulings passed down from the ancient dynasties."

"Was there any specific theme to the laws and rulings he wanted to see?" she asked.

"Most definitely. He was focused on the development of human rights. He was interested also in certain judges who had been deemed significant by the Xiulian historians."

After meeting her eyes, Josh asked the question pressing on her mind. "Did he tell you *why* that line of legal precedent and those judges were important to him?"

He smiled. "He didn't have to. He was looking for the link to the pathway."

"The pathway?" she asked.

"The best way I can explain—" Zhou's head jerked back, his lips freezing in midsentence.

Was he having a seizure?

A crash came from the kitchen. Sammi spun toward the source of the sound.

When she turned back, Zhou's eyes were glazed over; his mouth hung open. And a hole in the center of his forehead was leaking blood. His head plunged forward and smashed into the table.

As a crimson pool spread on the tabletop, a woman in an adjoining booth screamed, "He's been shot!"

Waiters dove under tables. Trays of china smashed to the floor.

People sprang from their seats. A frenetic crowd started pushing toward the front doors of the restaurant.

Sammi grabbed Josh's arm.

He tugged at her hand. "We have to leave. Now."

"But . . ." She stared at Zhou's motionless head in the puddle of blood. Why? How?

"Now!" Josh commanded, fixated on the restaurant entrance. "Look!"

She followed his gaze. No! At the front door, a pair of eyes bore into her from a head that towered over the crowd. How could he have found them?

Josh pulled her from the booth and toward the front of the restaurant. Was Josh crazy? They were going right to him! "What are you doing?" She pulled back, trying to get him to turn in the direction of the kitchen.

He tugged her hand harder and grabbed her elbow. "Trust me."

They merged into the panicked crowd edging toward the door. She trained her eye on the killer while keeping her head down. The man repeatedly tried to push farther into the restaurant, but, even with his massive size and strength, he was having trouble against the crush of bodies determined to flee.

Sammi's heart pounded. She realized Josh must have been afraid they'd get trapped if they ran into the kitchen, since they didn't know its configuration. But where was he trying to take her? They were now within thirty feet of the murderer. Josh clenched her hand tighter as the dense crowd pressed forward around them.

Ten feet closer, she saw Josh looking to their left. There, partially obscured by a floral ornamental screen, she spotted it: an emergency exit door! Josh was trying to steer himself and her in that direction, but the frenzied mass of bodies kept pushing them toward the front door, where two evil eyes still glared at her from above the fray.

From now five feet away, the monster reached out with an enormous hand and barely missed grabbing her free arm before the throng knocked him back. Josh pulled her close as the man gathered himself. While Josh fought, in vain, to move the two of them sideways, the man lunged again. Huge fingers grazed Sammi's shoulder, but then Josh pulled her to the left through a fissure in the riptide. She glanced back as the crowd's inertia caused the man to lose his balance and go down.

Josh shoved open the emergency exit door. Hallelujah! But they weren't safe yet. With bodies spilling out behind them, he kept his grip on her hand as they rushed to his car.

A STRANGE FEELING

Damn! Shoes kicked at Billy Ray's legs. Ow! Someone stepped on his arm. Sprawled flat on his back, he pulled in his limbs, protected his face with one hand, and launched an elbow at a beer belly rolling over him. Fuming, he let loose an earth-shattering roar. The legs around him stopped churning for a moment. He peeled off two writhing bodies, grabbed hold of some upright limbs, and yanked his way to his feet. The tide picked up, pushed him outside, and shoved him free. Two people fell to the concrete next to him. He stepped to the side and scanned the area. Folks were skittering through the parking lot like headless chickens. But no sign of Sutton or the girl.

The cops would be there any second. He'd kept them off his scent so far with his neat trick after killing that judge. Clever move to wrap the man's body and mess of papers in the rug he died on and haul it out. Made his exit look like a carpet cleaner on the job while he got rid of the body, the mess, and the blood. It had been worth the two minutes it took, plus the drive to the Everglades to dump it all. There was nothing left for the cops to find.

He wasn't about to let them find him now.

But what in holy hell had started that stampede? He'd just stepped inside the place when all crap broke loose. He couldn't believe it when Sutton and that girl headed right at him. Now how in hell was he going to explain to the Reverend that Sutton got away *again*?

He hauled it to his car and got moving; he'd pick up the trail later.

Barely a mile away from the restaurant, a strange feeling hit his gut. He'd been doing his missions for the Reverend for years, and he could spot a police tail in his sleep. He'd checked his mirrors a bunch of times since he left the parking lot. Nobody was back there. Yet, his hunter's sense told him something else, like it had a few times on those nights alone, deep in the woods, rifle at the ready for twelve-point bucks.

Eyes were on him.

THE WHOLE TRUTH

Sammi's neck hurt. She must've twisted it in the mob—the frenzied horde set off by a murder that may have been her and Josh's fault. She looked over at Josh behind the wheel.

"That's it," she insisted. "We're going to the police *now*."

"Let's get out of here first, okay?" Josh responded. "I'll head west to the Turnpike. He'll be looking for us on 95."

"We need to get to a police station. He found us even after we switched the tracking device. Where do you think we can escape to?"

"Just about anywhere. He didn't track us this time."

"He just *happened* to choose the same restaurant we were at? Out of thousands in South Florida?"

"I just realized," Josh said, "that Zhou's computer must have been hacked. *That's* how the judge's killer found out where I lived. He had the judge's address book that was emailed to Zhou."

Oh boy. "And since Zhou emailed us about the meeting at the Szechuan Grill—"

"He told the killer where and when to find us."

"So, without the tracking device or any more emails between us and Zhou, he has no way to know where we are." Thank God.

"As long as we stay away from anywhere he'd expect us to be."

Sammi massaged the side of her neck. "But shouldn't we go to the police anyway? I mean, this time we *both* witnessed the murder."

"Along with two hundred other people," he replied. "The police are definitely after that guy now. Not sure we'd be any additional help. Look, that detective wants me to come in by three tomorrow. We barely got to skim through the research this afternoon. What if we spend the night going through it all in detail and see if Mark finds anything else? We can organize our notes and hopefully go to the police with something that makes sense. At least enough so they stop focusing on me."

What? "With everything that's happened, you're *still* worried about that?"

He stared ahead, clearly not wanting to look at her. "I'm sorry. I haven't told you the whole truth about my older brother's death. I said there was an inquest. It was actually a murder trial. I was accused." His eyes stayed glued to the roadway.

Now he was telling her? "You were tried for murder?"

"When Seth jumped off the roof of that building, I was trying to stop him. My aunt saw us arguing and thought I pushed him."

"Why would she think that?"

"We'd been screaming at each other on the roof. About the dreams. Like I told you, he wanted me to fight the dreams off. Told me they were killing him. He threatened to jump if I didn't promise to try."

"Did you?"

His head dropped. "The dreams were my escape. I was the family rebel. He was the family star. I didn't want to let them go. I ran to him. Begged him. Didn't really believe he'd do it. Just as I got there, he said: 'Don't follow your dreams.' I reached for him, but he jumped before I could grab him."

Her eyes moistened. "I'm so sorry."

"Yeah, me too. Sure, I was jealous of him, but I adored him. He was my best friend. My idol. And then they tried me for murder—as an adult! At sixteen. Can't even do that anymore in New York. But in the end, my aunt refused to testify at the trial." He drew a deep breath. "Destroyed my family, though. Like I said, he was the star. Admitted to Stanford. A Division I swimmer. Brilliant. My folks broke up within six months. It's been fifteen years now, and my dad still doesn't talk to me;

and my mom . . . well, a lot of her went over the side of that building with Seth." He finally braved looking over at her.

She felt a tear on her cheek. "I can't even imagine . . . No wonder you didn't give the police your name. All they know about you is that you'd been charged with murder in the past."

"Now you see why I'd rather not go to that detective until we have enough to show him that I don't need to be a suspect. I hate to say it, but Zhou's death probably makes that easier."

A shiver ran down her spine. She saw Zhou's face—his expressive eyes, his lips in midsentence, frozen in a death mask. "You're *sure* that guy can't find us again?"

He reached over and placed his hand on hers. "Not a chance. We'll go to Mark's. We're safe there."

Goose bumps crept up her arm. "Do you think he meant to kill Zhou, or was he aiming at one of us?"

"He meant to kill Zhou."

"How can you be sure?"

"He still needs whatever it is we have. And I'm thinking he doesn't want anyone else to have it."

"I guess you're right."

She exhaled; they were safe for now. That was small comfort, however, for a bunch of reasons—including two horrible murders, the fact that they had less than forty hours left to figure out how to possibly save some unknown thing of staggering importance, and that their best chance at an answer might have just died at their dinner table.

FLASH POINT

It was too easy. An operation of such significance was not supposed to go off this smoothly.

When Steven Lee had arrived for a late lunch at the Szechuan Grill several hours earlier, he'd taken a bathroom break with a "mistaken" turn into the kitchen. After eating, he'd walked around to the rear of the restaurant to verify that the outside door to the kitchen was left unlocked during business hours.

He'd returned at 7:30 p.m., staying in his car in the parking lot. Shortly before eight, after Zhou Yuanxin had entered the restaurant, Steven had walked up to the front window and watched Zhou be seated in a booth near the kitchen.

After returning to his car for fifteen minutes, Steven had walked back to the front window to verify Zhou's guests had arrived. He'd wanted Zhou occupied. An occupied man was the easiest target. As Sun Tzu had written in *The Art of War* thousands of years before:

> *Engage people with what they expect; it is what they are able to discern and confirms their projections. It settles them into predictable patterns of response, occupying their minds while you wait for the extraordinary moment—that which they cannot anticipate.*

He'd circled the building and entered through the rear kitchen door. He'd barely been noticed as he'd stepped deftly through the bustling food prep areas.

When he'd reached the swinging doors separating the kitchen from the patrons, he'd glanced out, found Zhou Yuanxin seated and engaged in conversation, and eased the gun from under his shirt. The room's roaring din had aided his silencer in muting the shot.

As he holstered the weapon, he'd taken another quick look to confirm his assignment was completed, then spun back into the kitchen, purposely brushing against a busboy to get him to drop a tray full of plates. He'd been two steps from the back door when he'd heard the first scream. The kitchen staff had barely lifted their heads, and he was gone.

Driving off, he was floating. It was actually occurring. *The* mission.

He'd taken out an enemy of the state at the highest level, silencing a man whose finger was on the button of the weapon some in the Party leadership feared more than they did any foreign power. And this was just step one.

He bathed in the glow of history.

REVELATION

Stark images had stabbed at Josh's brain in the quiet he'd shared with Sammi for most of the ride back to Miami: Judge Maloch reaching in vain for the knife plunged into his back; Zhou's head smashing down in a pool of blood; and then, from nowhere, could that be a man carrying two molten steel bars in his bare hands and another man and a gamecock trapped in a sack, plummeting off a seaside cliff?

Now he sensed new images scaling his walls, probing for entry points. Fight them off or let them in?

He glanced over at Sammi, who sat at the other end of the couch in Mark's "command center," balancing one of Mark's spare laptops on her knees while poring over her share of the research on the judges. Her expression betrayed no hint of having witnessed Zhou's brutal murder just hours ago. But it had to be eating her insides. It was still devouring his.

He turned back to his own laptop. Focus. He needed to finish his share of the reading and building their combined notes. There had to be something in this research that would get them home. They had less than thirty-seven hours until "*everything* changes." No way they were solving this by then with what they knew so far.

"Ahem." Mark leaned over from his futuristic captain's chair, which faced a mock starship navigation console. Two laptops sat open in front of him, one of which he was staring at. "Got one for you, Quark."

"What is it?"

"Another file name. Pretty sure it's 'White Mountain.'"

"Pretty sure?"

"It actually says 'White Mount,' but the right side of the final *t* looks truncated."

"And what does that mean?" Sammi asked.

Mark tapped random buttons and rotated a knob on the instrument panel in front of him. "Bits were damaged in the defrag process, causing part of the second word to get lopped off."

"Why are you so sure the word is *Mountain*?" Josh asked.

"What other word starts with *Mount* and would be preceded by *White*?" He turned another knob. "Gotta be. Maybe your secret's locked away in the Himalayas."

Josh stood up, walked to the window, glanced outside, and then paced the room. Sometimes he thought better on his feet. But he couldn't come up with a more reasonable continuation of the word *Mount* that would follow the word *White*.

He considered the clues to date. Sometimes he thought even better out loud. "Let's see. We've got judges from around the world, spread over the last two thousand years, each involved in an important human rights case. Some were killed, died suspiciously, or were institutionalized.

"We've got Falun Dafa, a widespread spiritual pursuit of higher levels of consciousness that are spurred on by something called 'increased *de*.' The movement's somewhat controversial and supposedly under attack by the Chinese government. Per Sammi, there've been claims that Dafa leaders are being treated like some of the historical judges—murdered or tossed in a cell.

"We've got 'Higher Precedents,' which could relate to these decisions on human rights, or could refer to higher or more moral levels of thinking."

He circled back to the window and stared out. "The judges, Falun Dafa, these precedents—we know they add up to something of great value, something Judge Maloch gave his life to protect." He glanced back at Mark. "I guess it could make sense that the answer to how this all ties together is stashed away in a white mountain somewhere, so the wrong hands can't get to it." He paused, then pounded the windowsill with two fists. They had a day and a half *at most* left to solve this thing. He turned back to the man who, at the moment, was spinning dials, appearing to be adjusting their warp speed. "Spaceman, do you have any idea how many freaking white mountains there are in the world?! We need more clues!"

Rather than rattling Mark, the outburst seemed to trigger his analytics. He typed manically at his keyboard and scanned his monitor, then pulled his eyes from the instrument panel and rocked forward and back a few times, his arms in minor orbit. "My defragmenter's killing itself holding off the rate of deterioration. Less than one percent of the hard drive is still scannable. I think we're done."

"You've got to be kidding me."

Josh dropped onto a furry arm of the couch near Sammi and put his head in his hand. Maybe they *were* done.

Sammi tugged gently at his sleeve. "I see another possibility."

"Please, anything," he responded.

"Money, power, or religion. Remember?"

"Yeah, the things you said people historically kill for."

"Remember I thought 'Higher Precedents' could possibly refer to more *righteous* ways of thinking?"

"Got that in the notes. But don't see how it relates to a white mountain."

"It doesn't. But what Mark actually found were the words *White Mount*." She glanced over at starship central. "Mark, you said the word *Mount* had the right side of its final *t* cut off. But you don't know for sure that the word or phrase continued after that *t*, do you?"

Mark adjusted his glasses without looking up from his console. "Not without more data we'll never get to."

"So, the complete phrase could actually be *White Mount*?"

Mark close-mouthed "Mm-hm."

"Then it's possible," Sammi proclaimed.

"What's possible?" Josh was totally off the scent.

"That religion is our answer." Sammi popped up off the couch, shaking her head in wonderment, clearly excited. "That we're looking at some kind of resurrection."

"Well, yeah, we already figured another one of these judges is due," Josh said.

She looked skyward. "I forgot I'm dealing with a pagan." She chuckled. "Josh, I assume you've heard the term *messiah*?"

"How does *White Mount* lead you to a messiah?"

"I'll show you." Sammi sat back down with the laptop and keyed in something. "Growing up in Brooklyn, my mom took me to museums in the city all the time. That's where I got my first taste of religious art. There's this image of Christ on a white horse I've seen hundreds of times. And there's a reference to it in the Bible. Revelation, chapter nineteen. Look at verse eleven." She ran her finger to it.

And I saw heaven opened, and behold a white horse; and he that sat upon him was called Faithful and True, and in righteousness he doth judge and make war.

"For centuries, religious scholars have said this passage describes the arrival of the Messiah. There's some dispute as to what kind of white mount it'll be. Revelation says a horse. Zechariah 9:9 says a donkey." Her eyes widened. "Wait a minute." She was typing again. "Look at this. It's from chapter five of the book of Judges." She pointed to a phrase:

Ye that ride on white asses, ye that sit in judgment.

"Back then, nobles and magistrates often chose white mounts. So the 'White Mount' clue directly connects the judges from the book of Judges and the Messiah."

This was getting uber-crazy. Was she seriously saying a *messiah* was coming? Josh was ready to voice his doubts when the word *judge* flashed through his mind. "Go back to that sentence from Revelation about the Messiah." He stared over Sammi's shoulder as she brought it back to the screen. "That description . . ."

"Pretty powerful, huh?"

"Sure is. But I was focusing on the last part: 'and in righteousness he doth *judge*.'"

An eerie silence crept over the room.

REDEVELOPMENTS

Kyle Fredericks hurled his phone against the wall, shattering it to pieces. He'd held his composure throughout Billy Ray's report, but he was clenching his teeth so hard it felt as if his temples would explode.

He shook himself, slowed his breathing, massaged the sides of his head. He stepped over to his liquor cabinet and selected a bottle of single malt, settling on a limit of one glass and ten minutes to calm down. He wanted to be in possession of all his faculties for his next call.

That two-faced jackal.

Drink in hand, he sank deep into the dark leather couch in the corner of the private office in his Gatlinburg mansion and stared, as he had so many times, into the unlit fireplace across the room, contemplating the crisscrossed lines of ash that rose from the hearth like lost souls searching for redemption. He'd corrupted himself for those souls.

He'd long believed humanity was falling apart, imploding on itself. While hellfires burned at home and across the globe, he'd watched his stomachless colleagues do nothing more than blabber about heeding the words of Our Lord. Corinthians demanded we do the Lord's work. But what if that required no longer turning the other cheek?

He'd grown convinced that the time had come for someone to do more, to take on the forces of the Antichrist, before it was too late. Someone needed to be willing to dive into the trenches of this holy war and fight fire with fire, using unconventional means and unconventional soldiers in the name of God. If the Lord would not vanquish heaven's enemies, then he, Reverend Kyle Fredericks, would carry the load. Terrorists, white supremacists, hate-mongers; he'd cull the forces of evil and save as many lost souls as he could.

Would God condemn him or sanctify him? He'd long passed the point of wrestling that dilemma. What mattered was that the Lord had fallen asleep at the switch. Someone had to step up for humanity.

But now, as he readied to face Satan's ordained emissary, there was a serpent in his own house.

Kyle lifted his drink to eye level, swirled its dwindling amber contents, inhaled the honeyed cedar of its aroma, and sipped. It wasn't helping.

He had not been this angry in a long time. Or felt more naive. He'd been double-crossed, but he should've seen this coming. Han had destroyed entire communities on a moment's whim to get what he wanted. *Redevelopment*, he'd called it. Crushing Kyle's plan was a minor audible in the man's playbook.

If Kyle had learned anything over the years, it was how to push people's buttons in the service of the Lord. As the leader of one of the largest megachurches in the country and the owner, face, and voice of a major Christian television network and streaming service, he was unaccustomed to being the one manipulated. Others were too respectful or too afraid of him to play such games. Apparently, that healthy dose of respect and fear did not hold up across oceans.

When Billy Ray called in, Kyle had been expecting to hear about the Ripper reconnecting with his targets. Instead, their talk confirmed that the Reverend and his loyal servant had been used, *worked* like sidewalk marks playing three-card monte.

He gazed down at his glass. Empty. It was time. He grabbed a phone from the study annex.

Han answered on the first ring. "Hello, my old friend."

"*Friend*? You insult me by calling me your *friend*?" One scotch and ten minutes had clearly not been enough.

Han was caught off guard. "What's troubling you, Kyle?"

"*You. You're* troubling me. What in hell do you think you're doing?"

"What have I done?"

Kyle was tired of the feigned innocence. "This is the United States of freaking America! You don't throw a 'Redevelopment Day' here and assume everyone will look the other way. How dare you sneak in your own people, after all my man's hard work, all the risks he's taken."

"'Redevelopment Day'. . . I forgot you knew about that. That's a low blow."

"Low blow? In the middle of my operation, you take out someone who could've provided crucial information. And you do it in a crowded restaurant, with my man there—just the kind of attention we don't need. You do this in service to some hidden agenda and still have the gall to call me your friend?"

"When your man failed repeatedly, I thought help might be needed. And when that traitor Zhou got involved, we had to act."

"Without telling me?"

There was no answer.

The silence spoke to Kyle perfectly. Han had wanted him to take all the risks, to pinpoint Han's targets for him, but Han had never trusted him. He was a marionette in this puppet show.

Leaning hard against his desk in Zhuhai, Han swallowed his pride. "You're . . . right. I should've called before acting on my own. I'm sorry. I didn't mean to make things uncomfortable for you. But we can't afford to be divided now. We can't risk the consequences."

Before he started his next sentence, he was listening to a dial tone.

ENGINES OF DESTINY

Through fuzzy morning eyes, Sammi glanced quizzically at the instrument panel in front of her: screens filled with weird-looking planets and futuristic outer-space vehicles, multicolored groupings of knobs and dials, three-dimensional graphs with captions in unrecognizable languages. Oh, right. She was on the sleeper sofa in Mark's "command center."

"Maybe it's *random* that the judges on the list happen to be arriving once every two hundred and fifty years." Josh's voice, agitated, was coming from the next room.

She opened the door to find Josh pacing.

Mark was running his fingers through the long mane of a green, human-sized model of an alien standing next to him. "Nothing is coincidence."

"So, you're taking Ms. Destiny's side?" He'd spotted her leaning in the doorway.

"And good morning to you," she said. "You've decided that these judges coming along precisely every two hundred and fifty years, all having names from the book of Judges, and all dealing with important human rights cases has got to be coincidence?"

He spread his palms. "It's a bit much, don't you think?"

History-changing events often were. "Maybe I should speak to you in your own language," Sammi responded. "Picture a massive computer program you guys created."

Josh and Mark shot each other a look.

Sammi went on. “What if you change one command near the beginning of the process? Can’t that have multiple effects on results down the line?”

“GIGO,” Mark chimed in, as he plucked a few Cheetos from a bowl in the alien’s extended hand.

“GIGO?”

“A programmer’s acronym,” Josh advised. “Garbage in, garbage out. You start off with bad data, you screw up the results.”

“So, one simple cause,” Sammi said, “let’s call it a ‘precipitating event,’ creates a series of coinciding changes. Because, in this ‘system,’ everything is connected.”

“True,” Josh countered, “but that’s in a confined environment.”

Sammi stepped into the room. “According to physicists, action on any single particle in the universe affects every other particle. *Everything* is a confined environment.” She’d noticed Mark had a whiteboard on a wall near the window, with complex calculations scrawled across it. She went over, picked up a marker, and, on an open area of the board, drew a dot with long, radiating lines flowing out in all directions. “Everyone understands this in time travel. If you go back in time and do something that was not done before, it supposedly can affect innumerable things in the present.”

“Supposedly.”

“Well,” she said, “what about today? Using the same principle, depending on what actions you currently choose to take, the future could be vastly different. Correct?”

“I guess so.”

“Then would you consider all these changed, future events to be mere coincidence? Or did they just flow from a ‘precipitating event’—your current choice of action?”

“For a theology person,” Mark interjected, “you seem really into science.”

“Science and religion exist for the same reason—to explain things we otherwise wouldn’t understand. Why limit ourselves to one explanation?”

"Sammi," Josh asked, doubt filling his voice, "you have any thoughts on what could *possibly* be the 'precipitating event' in our situation, two thousand years ago?" He took a seat on the couch, studiously folded his hands in his lap, and gazed up at her.

Two thousand years ago! How had she missed that? "Josh, pull up that chronological list of the judges you made."

He reached over to his nearby laptop, keyed in something, and started over to Sammi.

"Don't show me," she said. "Show it to Mark."

While Josh and Mark eyed the screen, she shook her head and cracked half a smile. "These judges show up every two hundred and fifty years from the year 250 to 1750. We've been so focused on the fact that another one should be due now, trying to see what the clues we've got could tell us about this person, that we never looked back to the beginning. Who was alive two hundred and fifty years before the first judge on our list?"

"Jesus Christ!" A dozen orange pellets spewed from Mark's mouth with the proclamation.

"Bingo. There are two primary schools of thought about Christ. Christians, almost a third of the world's population, believe he was the son of God. The other two-thirds of the world—Muslims, Hindus, Jews, Buddhists, atheists, and the rest—generally agree he was an incredible man, an incredibly good man. In either version, as the Dafa put it, he was a man of 'great inborn quality.' That means he could access the *de* at very high levels."

"Not seeing how that becomes a 'precipitating event,'" Josh said.

"Falun Dafa shows us how. Before I passed out last night, I looked deeper into their beliefs. They believe that *de* is a primordial spirit that connects all of us. A spirit that's been continuous throughout time. Among other things, it's supposedly a warehouse of human knowledge, the cumulative essence of great minds and spirits. To go back to computer-speak, the Dafa say that people with 'increased *de*' can not only download, but also upload information to this system. So what if Christ uploaded his goodness, his devotion to the condition of man and man's freedoms, to the *de*, along with his belief in the crucial function of the judges as sanctuaries to carry mankind through godless times? Could this create a destiny?"

Josh's hand found his chin. "You're saying the judges on our list connected with this *system*?"

"They were all exceptional minds. They all had powerful beliefs in human rights. And every one of them was faced with a case that pushed them to reach beyond the prevailing laws of their time. Per Falun Dafa beliefs, they were primed to access the *de* to look for answers."

"Sounds like the Trills." Mark sorrowfully eyed his empty bowl. "Humanoids from *Star Trek* who merge with symbionts. When the merger happens, the Trill receives the memories from all the lives the symbiont had merged with previously." His fingers flickered. "Think about the power of all that accumulated knowledge."

"And the *weight*." Josh shot to his feet. "One of these judges ended up in a mental institution; at least two others likely committed suicide. Is it possible they accessed all this information at these high levels of the *de* but couldn't handle it?"

"According to the Dafa," Sammi responded, "it takes accumulation of *de* for extremely long periods before a person of great inborn quality arrives who can fully channel it. I'm thinking that person will be the last of the six remaining names from the book of Judges." Goose bumps fluttered down her arms. "Crazy, but this whole thing is right out of my thesis."

"What?" Josh and Mark uttered as one.

"It's called 'Engines of Destiny.' It theorizes that significant historical moments flow from specific precipitating events. Events that often seem unconnected, sometimes occurring at points far in the past, or across the planet."

"But some of this," Josh said, "has still got to be coincidence. Like the fact that our judges happen to have names right out of the book of Judges."

"Each of these judges cared deeply about human rights," she replied. "So what about their parents?"

"You're saying their parents raised them to care?"

"More than that. If their parents also felt strongly about human rights, is it possible *they* connected with the *de* at some level and were sufficiently influenced to name their child after a humanity-saving judge from the Bible? That makes their name no longer a coincidence, just a future event flowing from an Engine of Destiny."

Josh started to pace again. "Something still doesn't add up. Even if every piece of your theory is true, why is someone willing to kill just to find out who the current link in the chain is? If there are six judges to come before this next 'person of great inborn quality,' what is it that this current one can do, or knows, that's so important?" He jerked to a halt. "It just hit me. What if Judge Maloch's killer doesn't *want* something from this person, but just intends to kill them? To prevent whatever great thing they're supposed to do. What if we're the only ones who can stop him?" He shot a frustrated glance at Mark. "We've got no more clues coming." He eyed a meteor-shaped digital clock on the wall and threw his arms up. "And, at most, we've got twenty-eight hours. We need answers *now*."

"I think it's time we got some outside help." She pulled out her phone.

"You have someone in mind?"

"My thesis advisor. Brilliant. An expert in Bible study, religions, and spiritual groups." She tapped a contact on the phone and put it on speaker.

"Richard Harper here."

"Professor, this is Samantha Bollinger."

"Ah, a thesis question?"

"Not directly. I'm involved in a research project that's raised some issues of biblical interpretation. I think there's some historical religious aspects we're missing. Any chance you could help? We're sort of under a time crunch."

"I'm home for the week, working on an article. If you want to come on up after lunch, I could give you a couple of hours."

"Thanks so much. Um, Professor, there are three of us on the project."

"Bring your friends along."

Though Mark appeared deeply focused on his green-haired companion, his chest seemed to puff out a little as Sammi ended the call.

"A research project?" Josh asked. "I guess that's technically true."

"Wasn't sure what to tell him."

"Yeah, we'd better think about that, considering what happened to the last person we consulted who knew something about all this."

THE CONDUCTOR

The organist blasted eerie chords as images of a magnificent stallion, luxury car, limousine, jet, and helicopter flashed on the huge screen behind Reverend Kyle Fredericks on the podium. As he'd instructed, every image was white.

And they kept coming: white horses, white BMWs, white Cadillacs, white Lincoln Town Car limos, white private jets and helicopters. He turned to the packed pews of his Gatlinburg megachurch, pleased to see his parishioners' confused expressions. The thousands streaming this at home or watching on his network's simulcast had to be equally intrigued. With the world perhaps twenty-four hours from Armageddon, he could not miss this chance.

"The white mount!" he roared from the stage, knowing the images still alternated behind him. "You think it brings joy?!"

"No?" predominated the muddled mix of conflicted responses from the crowd.

"Salvation?!"

"No!" responded the throng, now almost as one.

"Don't be fooled!" He pulled the microphone from its stand and spun back to face the screen. "There!" He pointed to a giant BMW. "There!" The image of a Learjet soared past. "Beware the white mount!"

He turned again to the crowd. "Are we only to know the easy path, the answers always at hand? Is that our Lord's way?"

"No!" shouted the united chorus.

"But our Savior, we've been told, shall arrive on a white mount. Then surely all we need do is pray for, and await, this blessed arrival. Isn't that true?"

The voices from the pews fell to murmurs.

He shook his head and peered heavenward. "Yes, dear Lord, of course. You did not create your flock to sit and wait. You gave us legs, to move. Hands, to work. Eyes, to see. But we see not!"

He panned over the breadth of the room. He widened his eyes. He bared his teeth. "Revelation lays the matter clear before us. This"—he pointed at the screen—"from chapter six." A thunderous chord rose from the pipe organ and the images were replaced by words that he let his parishioners absorb in silence:

> *And I saw, and behold a white horse: and he that sat on him had a bow; and a crown was given unto him: and he went forth conquering, and to conquer.*

"*This* rider on a white mount comes not to save, but to conquer. An agent of the devil, and *deceit* shall be his calling card. Thessalonians speaks to us." With another organ blast, the Reverend let the congregation take in the next words that appeared:

> *Even him, whose coming is after the working of Satan with all power and signs and lying wonders, And with all deceivableness of unrighteousness in them that perish; because they received not the love of the truth, that they might be saved. And for this cause God shall send them strong delusion, that they should believe a lie.*

He came down from the podium and patrolled the aisle, ricocheting his gaze from face to face and stretching his arms wide. "See the world around you. Genocides. Pandemics. Conspiracy theories. Intolerance. We no longer agree to disagree. We hate!"

The rows of heads bobbed up and down. He could feel their shame.

He leaped back onstage. "The only thing missing from this orchestra of suffering is a conductor—the Antichrist! Revelation and Thessalonians tell us he's coming. Shall we sit and wait and risk falling prey to his deceptions?!"

"No!" answered the resounding chorus.

"Shall we stay ever vigilant to rise up and meet the challenge?!"

"Yes!" The stage vibrated with the room's passion.

He pivoted to see the screen fill with all the earlier images at once. A discordant tone screamed from the organ. He faced the worshippers, raised his arms, palms turned upward, and spread them wide in front of the screen.

"May you keep our eyes open, Lord, so we may discern the form of the evil one's arrival."

He brought his arms forward, pointing with both hands at the crowd.

"Beware the white mount!"

THE LONG WAY HOME

Sammi returned the phaser-like hair dryer to its holster at the end of the vanity. She glanced at her image in the bathroom mirror as she ran her fingers through her clean, reasonably dry hair. If only the shower and shampoo could've scrubbed away the horrors of the past two days. Her stomach growled. She checked her phone; it was almost 10:00 a.m.

"You got to admit," Josh was saying as she stepped out of the bathroom, "that was a crappy system we put in. Had to kludge that sucker up the wazoo." He was sitting on a purple, three-toed ottoman, watching Mark fidget with bendable alien figurines on an end table.

Mimicking a robotic voice, Mark had one of the extraterrestrials say, "If the droids in management had any clue how to set a deadline, Quark, maybe we could've tested *before* we installed." He shot Josh a look and switched to his own voice. "GIGO."

"While you're on that subject," Sammi interjected, "I need some garbage in. I'm starved."

Mark released his alien captives. "Hadn't realized you'd beamed down. The galley's pretty bare."

"Nothing?" No way she was facing this day on an empty stomach.

"Maybe some leftover Cap'n Crunch from a light-year ago."

Ugh. "Could we order in?"

"The only place I like for breakfast doesn't do delivery. It's about half a mile from here. Quick on takeout, and awesome breakfast burritos.

I've got a global chat in twenty minutes with my orbital team. Mind bringing me something back?"

"You're going with her," Josh said. "I need a shower, but no way she's going out there alone with that maniac on the loose."

"No comment on the shower," Sammi responded. "But agreed that none of us should be going anywhere solo right now."

"Fine," Mark grumbled at Josh. "Let's hope the world isn't attacked in the next half hour." He turned to Sammi. "It's quicker if you order by phone. Place is called That's a Wrap."

"Okay. I'll pull the menu up on my cell."

"No need. Menu's on the counter in the kitchen."

She found no menus on the kitchen counter, just a foot-long metallic alien spacecraft. "Don't see it."

"Talk to the spaceship."

Sammi peered out from the kitchen pass-through. "*Talk* to it?"

"Say the name of the restaurant."

Really? Sammi turned and addressed the spacecraft. "That's a Wrap."

The dome of the craft popped open and a screen scrolled up. The screen flashed once and a menu for the restaurant appeared. You had to love this nerd.

Wedged in the corner of a strip mall, the walls of That's a Wrap boasted a collage of overlapping movie posters. It was oddly comforting to be stared at by Bogie and Bacall, Leo and Kate, instead of Vulcans, Klingons, and, particularly, murderers. The order was already bagged and waiting with a teenage girl at the register. Sammi paid, grabbed the food, and she and Mark headed back to his car.

As they got there, a soft, wet cloth was pressed hard over her nose and mouth.

"No!" Her scream was muffled by the gag. How could he have found her there? She tried to twist free, but a bearlike arm was clamped around her in a stranglehold. To her left, Mark was trapped in the same position.

The cloth on her face had a clean, not unpleasant aroma and an almost sweet taste. Within seconds, she felt the bag slip from her limp hand.

As her surroundings faded, they were replaced by images from one of her oft-repeated dreams: a dark castle and an ominous cloud lurking over an ancient courtroom. Though her own voice was silenced, she could hear a judge's desperate pleas for help . . .

THE DEVIL'S PERSUASION

802-804–Reibzang and Bonnburg

Journal entry—11th of December, 802

My shoulders bear two great stones this bitter, wintry evening: the needless killings of both a child and a man-child. May my lord forgive me that as I suffered late witness to the one, I did compel the other.

Roused early morn three days past by my chief manservant, I was summoned to my law court. My groomsmen had readied the gray stallion, the fleetest horse in my stables, but I waited, instead, for my trusted alabaster mare. From my earliest days dispensing justice—uncountable years past—I've suffered from an inexplicable compulsion to arrive at my court appearances only on a white steed.

Riding hard from castle to courtroom, I traversed the unyielding, ice-gray countryside through the misty, semi-frozen dew, the consistent clack of hooves my only comfort against the chill. Brought before me upon my arrival was Tomas Schreier, a local peasant accused of murder. At once I empaneled seven men from my village of Reibzang to stand as jurors and parse the facts of the matter.

The testimony:

First, a neighbor who squinted at the jury, pointing aimlessly as he spoke: "There were a straw-haired peasant lad, looked to be no more than eleven or twelve. I'd spotted 'im, time to time; he were thin as a leaf. Walked uneven, leaning on a stick, and always with that raggy gray dog. Whenever they came 'round, Tomas would pitch a rant. He was bad-hearted toward that poor boy . . ."

Tomas's father, respectfully attired and stoic as an elm, addressed the jurors directly: "Tomas is a sweet, guileless child; though twenty and eight years of age, he lives still with us, able to cope merely with the simplest chores. He's not advanced his thinking since age five. Tomas can count only to ten, and, for that, requires his fingers. He confuses colors. Yes, he can be flustered, but he'd never grow angry. My boy would not harm a field mouse, let alone a child."

Another neighbor, clad in dirt-caked vestments, an impression of a plow handle pressed into the chest of his tunic, spoke as if delivering the gospel: "I swear ye, this be what occurred. Day last, whilst seeding my field, there came shrieks out from the Schreier plot, following a mongrel's growl. A gray mutt and a small boy were circling Tomas. Without doubt, I saw Tomas reach and violently push out. That boy fell to the ground, he did. I come running with all haste. The boy's neck was snapped. Dear Lord, he was dead as he lay."

Tomas—upon my questioning—pawed at his clothes and pondered the floor, his head shaking: "I not, I not . . ." Tears burst from his eyes, and wrenching sobs followed. Try as I might, I could not divert him from this state. He was wholly unable to explain his actions.

Tomas's mother, eyes reddened, voice hoarse, hands clasped tightly as one: "My Tomas is deathly afraid of that dog. The boy would bring the animal by solely to torment my son. When Tomas begged them to leave, the boy would yell cruel things in return; he'd call Tomas a 'dumb head.' Tomas would cry like a little child but would never lash out. If Tomas hurt that boy, it was an accident. I'm sure the dog must have attacked Tomas and Tomas was merely defending himself."

Save Tomas, none but the neighbor with the plow handle mark were witness to the incident. The jurors gave faith to his testimony and found that Tomas had pushed the boy to the ground, killing him. Under Frankish law, this was murder.

Though I harbor doubt as to the full facts, I am well familiar with the law of my land. My sovereign, Charles the Great, issued his

Capitulary of Herstal in 779. Under it, a vassal who fails to render justice risks losing his office and his family's stake. And "justice" means, per that same Capitulary, "that judges shall judge justly, according to the written law and not according to their own judgment." The facts are to be parsed by the jurors, and my charge, as vassal and judge, is to pronounce a ruling in accord with those same findings. In essence, I have no "judgment."

And so, I wielded that second great stone. I ordered poor Tomas Schreier put to death.

Respectfully submitted, Henrik of Reibzang

Journal entry—12th of December, 802

Having escaped a tortuous overnight, fending off apparitions fed of ale and fitful sleep, I staggered out in the bitterness in my bedclothes, wandering in dawn's grim grasp, searching for . . . I knew not what. Lost for hours on familiar ground, as fir trees bowed to angry skies, I was whipped in the winds, beaten and shredded bare, until, properly punished, I reversed course. Nearing the soulless portal of my homestead, I stumbled on a craggy stone, slipped, and fell back, my eyes forced skyward. There, in the crevasse of a coal-colored cloud, clung a specter lurking over me. In eerie transformation, it ignited into a blazing message:

ALL MEN ARE CHARGED WITH KNOWING THE LAW.
BUT, IS KNOWING THE LAW EQUAL TO
COMPREHENDING THE LAW?

Was that truly in the heavens? I blinked, shook, stared up once more. The message stood fast. Terrified, I fled to the safety of my manor.

Back inside protective walls, I found myself unprotected. It was then that I first suspected I could take no adequate cover. For I had seen them: *The Words*.

Shivering, I raced up the stairs to the warmth of my study and its hearth, seeking refuge. But *they* followed me. I took shelter at my desk with stacks of legal manuscripts surrounding me like variegated castle walls, but *The Words* leapt over, insisting that the answers to my torment lay in this room. Frightened and confused, I tore into the texts.

Page upon page, volume upon volume, no edict came to my aid. But *The Words* would not release me. There was something else *they* knew, something *they* were trying to tell me. And then *they* pulled me in.

Could it be possible that they sent my mind over a thousand years into the past, back to the days of Romulus, as legal concepts crawled from the abyss of chaos? It seemed I heard the voices of the ancient forum crying out, debating contrasting merits of future legal systems.

A fantastic image arose before me: the Greek goddess Astraea, astride a towering platform, holding out her great scales of justice. But those sacred scales shook and teetered; she could scarcely stay upright as she held them, for her platform rested on a single, unsteady stanchion. And then it struck home. True justice could not rest on the single pillar of legislation. A curse had been laid upon us by the Romans: the civil law.

For the civil law honors only the will of the sovereign, the legislator. It allows for no free thought, no "judging." Its bounds are of hardest rock, immovable, yet, as a foundation for justice, when facts are applied, it proves precarious; it provides far too narrow a base.

Our ancient senators had considered, and regrettably rejected, a better way, built on two balanced fortifications: the legislative will and the judicial temperament. Together these could fashion a wondrous framework. It would allow judges to *interpret* the written law, based on the facts of a matter, to arrive at rulings that would serve as precedent in similar cases. What the legislator enacted would no longer be in stone; it was malleable within common reason. Even the act of killing another might not be murder given appropriate circumstances. Had such a system been adopted, judges and legislators would each contribute to decisions that were truly just.

And then, as quickly as they had appeared, *The Words* were gone, evaporated in the wavering light, abandoning me to a most wretched state. I was trapped beneath a third great stone: my sovereign's civil law.

For that enactment commanded a judge to rule "according to the written law and not according to their own judgment."

The civil law is the barbed tether that pins, pierces, and strangles me.

Respectfully submitted, Henrik of Reibzang

Journal entry—9th of February, 803

No longer can I endure these images. Men strung from ropes, ashen faces drained of life, bulging eyes fixed and pleading: "I not . . . I not . . . I not . . ." These phantoms haunt my dreams and stalk my waking hours, week upon week. Everyday tasks are unbearable. To look my servants in the eye, to mete out justice to my townspeople, to hunt, to eat, to sleep, each adds interminable weight to the stones I bear. And so, I can avoid it no longer. I must ask the question.

I am somewhat fearful corresponding with our sovereign on what he may deem a trifle of domestic affairs, with his vision focused on expanding the kingdom. Nevertheless, I recall his kinship in our youth and his forthright compassion at the death of my father—how he swore to protect my family and lands just as I paid homage to him. But so many years have slipped past. Now I am merely one of countless pledged vassals to our sovereign lord. How dare I question his word and his wisdom. Yet, I fear these great stones I bear shall be slung eternally upon the most innocent and feeble if the tide is unturned. And so, I craft my dire plea:

> To my lord and sovereign, King of the Franks and Emperor Charles Augustus:
>
> I most humbly apologize for imposing upon your time as you tend to important affairs of the realm. I pray this missive finds you stout in health and spirits as you lead us with your kind and steady hand. In fulfilling my role as Reibzang Township magistrate, and my pledge of homage, I have always diligently applied your laws, taking comfort knowing you seek only true justice for your subjects. However, in one matter of late, I am uncertain as to whether justice has been achieved.

> A man was brought before me on a charge of murder. He had lashed out at a boy, knocking him to the ground with such force as to kill him. The jurors found these facts, which equate to guilt under the law. I duly sentenced him to death. However, the man was not of sophisticated mind. His thoughts had always been those of a child. There were questions of provocation, and I am most certain the man was unaware of the consequences of his action.
>
> My lord, please forgive my impertinence, but I wish to inquire as to whether the sovereign might consider a caveat to the law of murder, whereby a man who is truly unable to understand what he has done may be treated less harshly than a man who acts with knowing malice.
>
> I accept in complete faith your good judgment in this regard.
>
> Your loyal vassal and humble servant,
> Henrik of Reibzang

I posted the letter this day, with my most trusted rider, off to the king's castle at Aachen. I pray I have not sentenced myself to some even graver hell.

Respectfully submitted, Henrik of Reibzang

Journal entry—30th of March, 803

I sit nearby my stables, dear Charles, on what might otherwise be admired as a sun-drenched, promise-filled spring day, watching my groomsmen lead my steeds through their morning paces. But the weeks lie heavy in ambush. *The Words* barely allow me to draw breath as I await your answer, or any sign that you may reply to my cry of desperation. Though sixty years have passed since our first days together—more than a life's span for most men—the weeks since I sent you my letter seem a far greater eternity.

Will you trust in me now as you have before? We were only each ten years of age, when your father, King Pepin, took me on as a page. Your heart had not yet warmed to the rigors of education. When the tutor appeared, you would run off to ride and hunt. But, after your father allowed me to join your siblings at class, you asked that I boil down the meat of the lessons into bites more palatable. We'd sit by the creek skimming stones—you towering over me even then—as I recounted the morsels of the day. I'd like to believe I helped kindle the spark that ignited your current passion for learning and the arts and inspired your engagement of the brilliant faculty from across the realm who populate your castle school and teach your children.

You once trusted me with your mind. I now trust you with my life. I pray that your knowing hand shall guide me out of this cursed forest; else I may wander, tormented, for all time.

Respectfully submitted, Henrik of Reibzang

Journal entry—10th of May, 803

With each month passed since my unanswered plea to the sovereign, I have descended deeper into resignation. The ghosts have become my constant companions, their baneful cries as regular as the morning cocks. But lo, this day, a king's emissary rode in at dusk, announcing delivery of royal correspondence. After welcoming him to dine on boar and pheasant at my table and inquiring of activities at my king's court, I offered shelter for the evening. Having barely partaken in the meal, I excused myself and made off to my study, sealed letter in hand.

Fingers trembling, I beheld the sovereign's red wax insignia: KAROLVS IMP AVG, which I knew to stand for "Karolys Imperator Augustus," the Latin title bestowed upon King Charles by Pope Leo III three years past in gratitude for Charles marching into Rome to smother a rebellion against the church. I gently took my knife to the envelope, wishing to preserve the seal. Inside, two sheets of fine scented linen held my fate. I slid them out and read his words:

> To my loyal vassal, Henrik of Reibzang:
>
> I thank you for your kind tidings and thoughtful query. Your correspondence arrived at a most opportune juncture. These past two years, I have dispatched a large contingent of loyal servants of the crown—archbishops, abbots, and pious laymen—to

the far reaches of the realm, to the Moors, Saxons, and Gauls, to learn of the disparate local legal customs, so that I might issue comprehensive Capitularies harmonizing the law for all in my kingdom. At your letter's delivery, our scribes had just begun a draft of the new laws; hence, the delay in reply.

Considering your valid concerns, I insisted upon an inclusion in the revised Capitularies, which, at last, are readied for distribution. Henceforth, where a jury determines that a murder was "persuaded by the devil," it shall be resolved in full by the paying of compensation to the victim's family; the victim's family shall be barred from any other form of retribution.

In honor of your dedicated service and your sensitivities in this regard, I hereby appoint you to a specialized judgeship in Bonnburg. All murder cases in which the defense appears to be persuasion by the devil shall be transferred to the Central Law Court at Bonnburg where you shall preside. I confidently rely on your good sense to guide the jurors in these delicate matters.

By the King Himself, signed with his own hand,

Charles R I

I noted that he now followed his name by both the regal *R* and the *I* reserved for emperors. I fell back against my chair. The most powerful man on earth had deigned to hear my plea, had amended his own law on my word, and had entrusted to me a direct commission so that I might carefully shepherd the new law's application.

But my moment of reverence and awe dissolved to an unsettling realization: Any murderer could henceforth avoid the penalty of death by convincing a jury he was "persuaded by the devil." This stood far short of the standard *The Words* required, but then, I imagined, no one else in the realm—not even King Charles—had been enlightened by *The Words*. And so, I now fear, my desperate plea has worked only to seal my fate. The great stones that burden me are primed to multiply.

Respectfully submitted, Henrik of Reibzang

Journal entry—15th of November, 803

Thrice have I been summoned to Bonnburg this last month. On each arrival, its sights and sounds startle me anew. Serving as military fortification and government center, its soaring walls pace the Rhine River to the horizon. Its stone buttresses, originally built solely of wood, once sheltered several Roman army legions, more than ten thousand soldiers. Today it stands a walled city of rock, crosshatched by lanes lined with government buildings and the core of King Charles's battalions, and overflowing with an industrious peasant population to service them. After half a day's ride from Reibzang, this imposing, thriving metropolis should fire my blood, but its walls have come to encase a brewing evil that, I fear, may boil far beyond its bounds.

This day I presided once more at a murder trial. One of my own Reibzang peasants was charged with killing another in a dispute over the sale of a horse. The accused appeared most rational; indeed, both charming and cunning. I observed with care as he lured the jury in, convincing them that the victim had tried to swindle him on the sale by unfairly denigrating the treasured family horse. Then he came almost to tears as he explained that he was parting with this dear animal—a favorite of his late mother's—to help feed his starving children. To conclude his tragic tale, he recalled how the "devil himself" had possessed him in his weakened state, as images of his dead mother and hungry children filled his head. He swore he was unable to recall anything further concerning his actions.

Other witnesses revealed that the horse in question was old, withered, and semi-lame, and that no man was willing to proffer in the least for the wretched animal until the victim appeared. Townsfolk averred that the accused was commonly regarded as ill-tempered, and a neighbor swore she'd seen the victim walking away from the negotiation when the accused cut him down.

Unduly swayed by the perpetrator's mournful mask, the jurors ignored all contrary evidence. They found this murder to be "persuaded by the devil." Accordingly, I had no discretion but to set the murderer free with but a nominal restitution.

The hour late, I chose to bed here in Bonnburg. The house steward drew my bath to ease me toward a night's rest, that I might marshal my strength for the morning's ride home. But rest will not come. Instead, I sit shaking in my quarters, penning these notes to ward off the demons of the evening. *The Words* have returned.

They surround me, scattering my thoughts. *They* enter me and press outward against my skull. *They* ask why I do nothing to right these horrible wrongs. *They* warn that the great stones are multiplying, gathering at the cliff's edge, a looming avalanche. *They* demand action, anon.

I steel myself and focus for my response. I plead that I am helpless—against a jury's verdict, against a sovereign's dictum, against an era incapable of the necessary leap in legal reasoning. But *The Words* care not for my protestations. *They* burn themselves into my brain, searing, scarring. I scream in anguish to no avail. I fear *they* will leave me dead or mad. And then, amidst my desperation, a moment of clarity bursts forth, and I remember the truth: *The Words* have presented me with a miracle; I have seen where justice must go.

But this miracle has a price, and my appeal to the king did not satisfy my debt. I must continue to take action toward true justice. I cannot waver in this commitment. But if I can't bend the sovereign or the verdicts, what can I do?

Oh no, not that! You cannot be asking me that!

Respectfully submitted, Henrik of Reibzang

Journal entry—11th of February, 804

Each trip to Bonnburg has become a journey to hell, an unalterable notch on the dungeon wall of my terminal sentence.

I have now condemned society to accept twelve murderers into its midst, twelve men acquitted of their crimes for being "persuaded by the devil." A thirteenth murder occurred this day, in my own township, in my presence.

A boar hunt organized weeks ago began at dawn's first light. I joined several nobles from surrounding townships, each with members of their staff, their trained bay dogs and catch dogs, and a group of local peasants serving as groundmen. We watched in the early chill as the groundmen and bay dogs stormed the nearby woods, the men rattling sticks on the trees as the dogs raced about, barking and howling. After a time, we heard the familiar sound of a large animal moving quickly through the brush, seeking refuge from the tumult. My staff captain spotted the boar as it burst from the thicket. Horns were sounded, and the bay dogs took chase.

Our group rode hard, circling a corner of forest, kicking up clouds of dust as we followed the rising uproar. At a clearing we lurched as one to a halt. The bay dogs had the pig surrounded in a hollow. The great animal—at least three times a man's weight, in my estimation—paced nervously, measuring its surroundings, its mighty breaths rising through the air like a battalion of specters. Its coat ran charcoal-on-black; silver bristles rimmed its snout.

The groundmen arrived with the catch dogs. As the dogs moved in to grab the beast's ears to keep it in place, the agitated boar lowered its head. Its razor-edged tusks glinted in the early light, thrusting upward. A catch dog cried out and was catapulted through the air; it lay dying, its belly sliced asunder.

The remaining catch dogs moved in and held the boar; we nobles took aim as one, raised our spears, and let go with all force. Several of the other nobles' spears brought down the pig. My own spear, to much surprise, struck home in the back of one of the groundmen. He expelled a startled cry, reached behind him in vain, and collapsed to the earth.

Amid the chaos, the death of the groundman was begrudgingly accepted as an unfortunate consequence of an invigorating outing. Not one of my peers seemed to ponder a further thought in this regard. But I had dwelled on the matter even before I threw the fateful spear.

When the groundmen had first emerged from the woods, I'd recognized him. He was the charming scoundrel who had escaped justice in my Bonnburg courtroom three months past. At the moment the boar attacked the catch dog, sending the other dogs and our group into action, my opportunity arose. The man had moved to a line almost directly between me and the boar. A spear aimed squarely at his back would appear but a slightly off-target launch.

And so, the twelve murderers I released into society are now eleven. And the great stones pile higher upon me.

Respectfully submitted, Henrik of Reibzang

Journal entry—20th of June, 804

Damn *The Words*! They have at last taken my soul. In slaying the scoundrel at the boar hunt, I had barely a moment's pre-thought. Sudden emotion ruled. But yesterday's morn I awakened with premeditation in my heart.

Three weeks past, a peasant came to trial for the brutal murders of a mother and her two young children. The man claimed "voices" led him to these deeds—though ample evidence exposed the calculated, hateful acts of a spurned lover. To my horror, the jurors found the killings to have been "persuaded by the devil."

To my sovereign and lord, I swear that I tried to accept this verdict. But *The Words*, unforgiving and relentless, thrust their torment upon me at all hours over this travesty of justice. Only with greatest effort might I sleep some precious minutes, consume more than a few morsels, or haphazardly conduct my daily affairs.

Awakening this past morn, frenzied, with *The Words* clawing at my innards, I scoured deep within my cellar. At the bottom of a storage barrel lay the bag of white powder once foisted upon me by a Moorish trader, a parcel buried in the depths of my castle so that even I might not recall to find it.

This poison—the Moor had named it arsenic—was said to be silent to the tongue, undetectable in food. Of equal import, he had assured, it caused a death akin to common illness.

I rode off to visit the murderer on the pretense to verify no relative of his victims had sought retribution. He invited me in to dine and apologized for the meager stew he offered. On his momentary absence from the room, I mixed a spoon's worth of white powder in his bowl.

As we finished, spittle escaped his lips and he rushed from the table. I excused myself to more pressing matters. This afternoon I received word of his passing, a violent illness being the cause.

I pen this entry as I lie in bed, unsettled and unmoored, uncertain I shall ever scale the wall to divine sleep. It is not *The Words* that erect the barrier. I am now constructing my own.

Respectfully submitted, Henrik of Reibzang

Journal entry—9th of July, 804

My own hands! How could I have done so? *My* fingers below me, stretched fully round his throat and pressed with all strength.

Had *his* deed been so far worse?

As the rage cooled, as I drew back, I rued the purplish gouges where my fingers had been. I'd strangled his life away.

What now is left of mine?

Respectfully submitted, Henrik of Reibzang

Journal entry—12th of October, 804

'Neath the overpowering aura of *The Words*, where once I glimpsed daylight and its hope, now grow only deceit, darkness, and despair. Now *The Words* themselves are the great stones. They swell in number and heft; they conspire to crush and suffocate me! I wither away in a nightmare of my own moral collapse.

I've grown unworthy to sit in judgment of other men. I've violated my most sacred oaths. My cause is now truly beyond hope.

At last, in this moment, all is clear: My further actions can only damage my sovereign's good name. And so, I pray that what I have marked down shall be of use to he who next happens upon *The Words*. May he be blessed with the Lord's strength to find a purer path.

I can endure this no longer. My sole relief shall be by means of my own blade. I must find my sword! Though, as I ready to fall upon that rapier, a thought occurs:

My death shall truly be by the devil's persuasion.

Respectfully submitted, Henrik of Reibzang

THE PASSCODE

Sammi forced her eyes open as she groggily emerged from her haze. Everything, however, stayed dark. A blindfold pressed tight around her head, heavy tape pulled on her cheeks, and a wadded gag filled her mouth. Some kind of thin, strong cord was wrapped securely around her arms and legs, binding her to a chair.

What was he going to do to her?

Someone was tightening her restraints from behind. Keeping as still as possible, she bowed her right wrist ever so slightly.

"Ain't you up yet?" a deep, gruff voice barked from her side. A huge, meaty hand nudged her shoulder.

While pretending to still be out cold, she focused her available senses. A low, clapping sound was moving away from her. The chair she was tied to was wood, the floor under her shoes felt like matted-down carpet, and there was a pothole out on a nearby street that cars kept thumping through. The air hinted at cigarette butts and beer. This had to be a cheap motel or the back room of a bar.

The clapping sound crept close.

"No way you're still out." Now the voice was right in front of her. "You don't raise your head right now, I'm gonna slap you awake."

She slowly lifted her head off her chest.

"More like it."

She tried to ask, "What do you want from me?" but the gag in her mouth turned her words to gibberish. She twisted in the chair.

"Settle down now." The man checked her restraints again. "Ain't gonna hurt you unless you make me. Now listen up. Do you know what's in that laptop your boyfriend took from the judge's house?"

She shook her head vigorously.

"You sure?"

She nodded just as affirmatively.

"Now, I'm gonna take off that gag and get a little more specific. Do I need to tell you what'll happen if you scream?"

She shook her ahead again, slowly.

"That's a good girl."

Ow! The tape was ripped from her cheeks, and the gag was yanked out. The clapping sound moved a few steps away and then came back.

"Now you stay real still. You ever had a fine hunting knife against your skin?"

She felt a wide piece of cold, flat metal on her cheek.

"If you move a hair, it'll scar that pretty face. And it won't take but a little twist and out comes an eye."

She froze, afraid to even breathe.

"Now, you're *sure* you don't know what's in that laptop?" He pulled back the blade.

"Really, I . . . have no idea." Her voice quivered. Thank God he couldn't see her eyes. Lying had never been her strong suit.

"Then why'd your boy take it?"

"He said he thought you might've wanted something on there. But he hasn't been able to figure out what." Now that was true.

"I'd sure like to believe you." A meaty hand pawed at her fingers. "Got this lie detector test. Never fails. I start by cuttin' off a finger. Usually get the truth before I need to cut off anythin' else." He grabbed the end of her pinky.

"Please!" she pleaded. "He's just one of the judge's law school students. He was there for a study session." She started crying. "Please don't! I wish I had the information you want." She cried some more. "Please!"

He stretched the pinky away from the rest of her hand.

No! "Please!" she pleaded again. She braced for the horrible pain.

He stretched the finger a little more . . . and held it still. She clenched her jaw, squeezed her eyes tight . . . Then he released it. The clapping sound moved away and came back.

"Let's go with plan B."

Oh God, what was *that*?!

"You're gonna call Mr. Sutton on your phone. You're gonna say just what I tell you."

She was breathing again.

"We're gonna arrange a little trade—you for that laptop."

She gathered herself. "Can't . . . use my phone blind."

"Got a point. I guess you seen me before anyways."

The blindfold was peeled off over her head, and she squinted at the glare as her eyes adjusted to the light. She'd been right. A dingy motel room—a B-movie murder location. Most of it was blocked out, though, by the massive man in front of her, dressed in a grungy T-shirt and jeans, and—she should've guessed from the clapping sound she'd heard—flip-flops. Seeing him again brought home how menacing, how dangerous, the man was.

You seen me before.

Sure had. She and Josh were eyewitnesses to the man's murders. If he got the laptop, why would he let them live?

"I'm not calling him. I don't trust you."

The man scowled at her, turned to his side, and lifted his arm.

She stiffened, anticipating the blow.

"We could just go back to plan A." He eyed her with an evil grin. But instead of striking her or retrieving the knife, he stepped over to a ratty desk against the wall and picked up a phone with a violet cover . . . *her* phone. He brought it over, glaring at her. "*Sure* you don't want to make this call?"

She shook her head. Her heart pounded.

"Fine." He chuckled. "I'll make it myself." He held the screen in front of her and entered her passcode.

How could he have known that? Was it the drugs? Had she talked in her sleep?

He flipped through her contacts. "Let's see . . . here it is: Joshua Sutton."

RETRACED STEPS

Josh stepped down on the gas, running most of the red light at the intersection. He slammed the wheel. Why had he let them go without him? It had been over thirty minutes since Sammi and Mark left to pick up the food, and he hadn't heard from them. They weren't answering their cells either.

He pulled up to That's a Wrap to find Mark's dinged-up Ford Taurus sitting in the lot. Had they just gotten there?

He jumped out and went into the place. The teenage girl behind the counter said she remembered them coming in but had seen nothing out of the ordinary, and certainly no huge, redheaded man hanging around. Josh spun and ran out to the parking lot.

A bag was on the ground near Mark's car. He picked it up to find three untouched wraps. Then he noticed movement in the front seat. He rushed to the driver's-side door and yanked it wide. Inside, Mark shook himself; he cracked open an eye.

"What happened?" Josh asked. And where was Sammi?!

"I think we were drugged."

Iced prickles ran down Josh's spine. The beast had her.

He pulled out his cell phone to call the police. He pressed the 9 and the first 1, and the phone vibrated. He almost dropped it.

The screen read: Sammi.

He put the call on speaker so Mark could hear and answered hesitantly. "Hello?"

"Sutton?"

The prickles intensified. He'd heard that voice only once before—when Judge Maloch was murdered.

"Sutton, you there?"

He looked at Mark. "It's me."

"Your lady friend's a charmer. Sure you want to see her again?"

What had he done to her?! "I do."

"Then listen up. You're gonna meet me where I tell you. No friends, no police, just you and that laptop. You give me the laptop, I give you the address and the key to where I left your girl. I got a buddy watchin' over her. I see one cop, or you screw this up any other which-way, you ain't seein' her again."

"How do I know she's okay?" No way he trusted this animal.

The phone went silent for a moment.

"I'm okay, Josh." It was Sammi's voice. "He hasn't hurt me." Her tone was flat; he could feel her fear.

"Satisfied?" the killer said.

"You've got to bring her with you. I need to see her before I hand over the laptop."

"Sorry, bud, ain't happenin'. She's too much trouble as it is. I ain't draggin' her along. If the setup ain't good enough for you, maybe I'll just stay here and see what I can carve out of her. Come to think of it, I might even prefer that. You got five seconds to decide."

He couldn't take that chance. "Okay, we'll do it your way."

"That's my boy. I'll be slippin' her gag back on now. Need her to be a quiet little mouse while I'm out doing our business."

Mark nudged Josh's shoulder and lifted an index finger. He mouthed, "One hour."

Josh nodded in acknowledgment. "Where should I meet you?" he asked the man.

"There's a park at Northwest Seventeenth Avenue and South River Drive."

"I . . . don't have the laptop with me. By the time I get it and drive there, it could be an hour."

There was another brief pause. "Ain't playin' that game. You got fifteen minutes. And like I said, I best not see a cop within a mile of that place. You do anything stupid, my buddy's gonna have a fine old time with your girl."

THE BACKPACK

Sammi flinched as the man tried to tape the gag in place again.

"Get your ass still!" He grabbed her hair behind both ears and yanked down hard, jerking her head back.

"Oww!" Her neck felt ready to snap. "Okay!" She let him put it on.

He walked over to the bed and pulled out a large hunting knife from a backpack. "Maybe I need to make *sure*," he said, pointing the blade at her, "that you won't be doin' nothing else stupid." The evil grin was back. "Been a bit since I skinned anything." He stepped toward her.

Her heart pounded through her chest. She'd served her purpose; he didn't need her anymore. She pleaded with her eyes, her screams for mercy turning to mumbles in the gag.

He chuckled and returned to the backpack. "I'll let you get by for now. Might still need you." He pulled out a leather sheath and slid the knife in. "Gonna scout out the scene early, make sure your boyfriend ain't pullin' nothin'." He stepped toward the door, then looked back. "And I wasn't joking about my man outside. You think *I'm* nasty?"

On the rooftop across the parking lot, Steven Lee crouched low at the ledge and watched Jackson step outside, alone.

He'd been tailing him ever since the man fled with the panicked crowd at the Szechuan Grill. He'd stayed in the distance, seen the kidnapping, knowing that if he waited, the moment would present itself. When he could control all the X factors. Bend them to his will.

As Jackson strode to his rental car, Steven realized the man had left behind not only the hostage, but also his backpack. He'd definitely be returning.

Jackson pulled out of the lot. No need to go after him this time; the tracker on his car would show where he was. The prize, for now, was in the motel room: the girl. He'd wait a bit, keeping an eye on the GPS map on his phone to be sure Jackson got far enough away.

The latest X factor had come into focus. He'd find out what the girl knew. Thanks to his training with China's secret police, his methods for extracting information were surely far more advanced than Jackson's. Maybe he wouldn't need the man at all anymore.

He took out his phone. Jackson was heading west.

As much as he liked control, the purest thrill of his assignments came with in-the-moment decisions, choices ranging from explosive action to subtlety. Back in his military days, General Chang had encouraged Steven to absorb the wisdom of millenniums past. It was then he'd first studied *The Art of War*, the timeless strategies attributed to a general of the Eastern Zhou dynasty: Sun Tzu. Others in his unit dutifully read the book as any other required text. Steven had absorbed it into his being.

Once again, the words of Sun Tzu would now guide him:

All warfare is based on deception.

The backpack.

Immediately after her captor left the room, Sammi's eyes went to it. Why would he leave it here if he was getting the laptop and giving Josh directions and keys to this place?

He *was* going to kill Josh! And her. Once he had what he wanted.

Wait . . . what was that? A small, rounded corner of violet protruded from the bedsheets near the bottom of the backpack. Her phone! He must have tossed it on the bed when he'd put the gag back on her. She had to get to it! The bedside alarm clock read 1:17 p.m. She had maybe ten minutes. In fifteen, Josh would be dead.

But ten was all she'd needed at age eight.

Just as she had back then to defeat her brother's nautical knots, she'd instinctively bowed her wrist minutes ago when her captor had been cinching her restraints. Now, she flattened the angle of her hand and twisted it. She pulled with all her strength, but it wasn't working. She bent the wrist inward and tried to slide it while holding it tight against her other hand. Nothing! She kept bending, twisting, pulling, contorting, but couldn't slip her hand through. Her brother had been a teenage amateur. Now she was dealing with a professional.

She looked at the clock: 1:22. Five minutes wasted!

She had to fight off the panic, keep her head clear. After two deep breaths, she thought about the cheap motel chair she was sitting on. If she could just loosen one of its legs, she'd have enough slack. She leaned forward then rocked back hard, smashing the wooden chair legs into the floor. She did it again, and again, and again. It was 1:25! She tried again to slip her hand through but couldn't.

With sweat streaming down her face, she kept rocking and smashing, rocking and smashing. She heard a *crack*. She tried her hand again. The rope wasn't budging. It was 1:27. Ten minutes were up!

Breathing in labored gulps, she rocked and smashed even more frenetically, again and again. More cracks, but no give. It wasn't working!

She was almost afraid to look. It was 1:31. Fourteen minutes gone! She burst into tears.

It was too late.

THE PARK

Josh jumped out of his car, dodged a pickup truck as he scampered across the intersection, and tore through the park's bordering clot of trees. He burst into the open, stopping on a small grass field dotted with tall palms. He scanned beyond them, out along the Miami River, but saw no one. He eyed the nearby playground. Empty. He checked his phone again. He'd just passed the fifteen-minute mark.

He looked right, left. Not a soul.

Would that maniac kill Sammi over a few seconds?!

He frantically traced the tree line.

"Sutton."

The voice came from off to his left, from the shadows of a huge banyan. A shiver skittered down Josh's spine. "Yeah."

"Step over here, outta the light."

Josh squinted. One of the banyan's thick, twisted trunks had separated into the absurdly large shape of a man. He'd almost forgotten how massive this guy was.

The man took a stride forward in the shadows and extended a hand. "Give it here."

Standing his ground, Josh brought the laptop to his chest, clenching it in the football "high and tight" position, not ready to give it up just yet. "I want the address where she is, and the key."

The man reached down and pulled out his enormous hunting knife. "Soon as I check out that laptop."

This guy was going to kill him. "I'll place it here on the ground and go back behind those far trees. You look it over, then throw the key out to me and shout out the address where you've got her."

"Nice try, pal. But I want your ass right here in front of me, case you're tryin' to pull somethin'. You bring it here *right now* or I call my buddy to take care of your lady, and we'll see if you can make it outta this park ahead of my knife."

Damn it. Mark's bluff had better work. Though Mark had asked for an hour, he'd had less than fifteen minutes to do his magic. He'd downloaded a ton of judge-related articles and links to an extra laptop, along with a bunch of stuff on Falun Dafa, figuring this guy, or whomever he worked for, had to know at least that much. He'd also thrown in some random note files and email folders, working mostly in the car before he'd hopped out a few blocks back.

"Okay. I'm coming. Can you at least put the knife away?"

As Josh stepped toward the darkened thicket, the man sheathed his blade. The concession had little effect on Josh's rising tension.

From two arm's lengths away, he reached out and handed over the laptop.

The man placed it on a waist-high stump, lifted the screen, and knelt in front of it. As the man scanned through the contents, Josh slipped his left hand in his pocket, on his phone. He inched back a couple of paces.

The man's head shot up. "Don't be movin' away now."

Josh froze.

After some further inspection, the man furrowed his brow, tapped at the keypad a couple of times, and then shook his head.

Oh no.

Josh's phone vibrated. He stealthily slipped it out. It was a text from Sammi:

I'm free.

"This is horseshit!" The man glared at Josh and reached for his knife.

Josh quickly tapped an icon on his phone.

A stream of liquid shot out of the laptop and splattered across the man's face. "Aahhh!" he screamed, dropping the knife and pawing at his eyes.

Josh spun and raced for his car, serpentining through the trees, ducking his head. Hoping the blade would miss him, again.

THE MAN AT THE DOOR

Sammi wriggled free from the last of the cords wrapped around her limbs. A minute before, her seesawing had finally cracked off one of the chair's legs and created enough slack so she'd been able to free a hand, crawl over to the bed, and grab her phone. But had it been too late?

She picked up the phone again. Still no response from Josh.

She dropped her head, prayed he was okay, and turned for the door. She had to get out of there.

Eeee. The rusty latch was moving.

He couldn't be back already?!

She needed a weapon. The chair leg! She scrambled over to it. As the door creaked open, she raised the leg and spun to face her captor.

What?

The person at the door was a well-groomed Asian man in his midthirties. She hadn't believed for a moment that her kidnapper really had an accomplice outside. But at least this guy was normal-sized. She waved her weapon over her head.

"I'm getting out of here."

The man lifted his hands in front of his chest. "Absolutely." His voice was calm; his smile looked almost sincere. "That's why I'm here. My name is Henry Kwan. Agent Kwan of the FBI." He pulled out a small wallet and flipped it open. The top half held a card with "FBI" printed next to his picture; the bottom had a gold badge.

She lowered the chair leg. Thank you, God. "How did you find me?"

"I've been tailing your kidnapper. He's a person of interest in an investigation."

"He was supposed to meet my friend at Sewell Park minutes ago. I think he planned to kill him. Can you get someone over there? I haven't been able to reach him."

He took out his phone and speed-dialed. "Kwan here. Get a unit over to Sewell Park. Suspect reportedly there, threat to a civilian." He glanced at her. "Get an EMT there too. I'll call back shortly." He pocketed the phone. "I'll explain everything once I get you out of here. I just need a minute first." He quickly surveyed the room, then walked over to a pair of sneakers at the foot of the bed. "Do you know what kind of shoes he was wearing when he left?"

Strange question. "Flip-flops."

"Perfect." He took out what looked like a flattened black pen, coaxed a thin blade from its end, and cut a fine slit into the heel of one of the sneakers. He pried up the top of his wristwatch, removed a tiny thread, and slid the thread into the opening. Then he pulled a tube from his pocket and unscrewed the cap. Holding the hairline fracture in the sneaker open, he squeezed in a drop of goo from the tube. When he put the shoe down, the slit sealed itself closed.

"What's that for?" Sammi asked.

"A little bureau tracking technique. He won't stay in flip-flops for any serious travel; these are his only other shoes." He motioned for the door. "We should go."

She stepped out into the sunshine and gulped at the fresh air. As he closed the door behind them, she glanced back at the room and fought off a cold shiver.

"You okay?" Kwan asked.

"Not really."

"You're safe now."

Please let Josh be safe too.

He ushered her to his car while speed-dialing on his cell phone. "Kwan again. I've acquired the hostage without confrontation. Need time to debrief. Send an unmarked local until another agent can get here. Let me know if the Sewell Park intercept happens. Otherwise, suspect expected back shortly. Out for now."

"The bureau's been following this guy for a while," he said as they pulled out of the parking lot. "Believe it or not, he works for a highly visible Christian religious leader."

"Really? Who?" So religion *was* part of this.

"Sorry, it's an ongoing investigation, so I can't say. All I can tell you is that our regional office tipped us off a few days ago that your captor was about to pop up on the grid down here on some questionable business. I was assigned to track him."

"What's he up to?" Sammi asked.

"Not exactly sure yet. Only been on him since yesterday. Highway Patrol ID'd a rental car under one of his known aliases going southbound on the Turnpike. I caught up to him in Boca Raton. Been on him since."

"Do you know," Sammi interjected, "what he *did* in Boca?"

"I think so. Zhou Yuanxin, a leader of the Falun Dafa spiritual group, was murdered at a restaurant there. I spotted your captor returning to his car in the restaurant's parking lot and found out later that that was right after the murder."

"You know why he would've done that?"

"No clue. But we didn't let the locals arrest him yet. We think he's got bigger fish to fry. Speaking of that, do you know why he kidnapped *you*?"

"Supposedly to trade me for a laptop. He killed someone dear to me who it belonged to. My friend Josh ended up with it. That maniac's been chasing us around the state ever since. That's why he left the motel—to meet Josh and get the laptop." She took a deep breath. "Josh and I have both seen his face . . . and seen him kill. If he got the laptop, do you think . . . ?"

"Let's hope my people get there in time."

SAVED BY THE GEEK SQUAD

Josh pulled his car to the curb. Mark was standing inside the Starbucks, his face pressed to the window. Josh beeped the horn and waved, then dialed Sammi.

"Josh?" Her voice came from the dashboard speakers as Mark hopped in the car.

"Yeah. You okay? He didn't hurt you, did he?"

"I'm all right. What about you?"

"Fine. Left him in the park."

"Did you have to give him the laptop?"

"Sort of. Before I explain, where are you? I'm coming."

"No need. I've got a ride with the FBI."

"What?"

"They've been tailing our guy for a while. They were there when I escaped."

"Do they know what he's after?"

"No. But they're as anxious as we are to find out. I told Agent Kwan about Judge Maloch and about our theories so far. Surprisingly, he doesn't think we're crazy. But he wants to know every detail we've put together. We're on our way to Mark's now."

"Wait a minute. If the killer found you so close to Mark's apartment, should we be going back there?"

"We think it's okay. Agent Kwan had me check my cell phone. There was a spy app on it that listened in to all my calls. I called That's a Wrap to place the order, remember?"

"How'd he get into your phone?"

"The night you had it—"

"Oh crap. I wrote down your passcode. It was next to the phone when he broke into my house."

"I figured. What was that you said about *sort of* giving him the laptop?"

"Mark phonied one up. Didn't fool him. You texted just in time."

"What do you mean?"

"The guy was about to get nasty when I got your text. So, I used Spaceman's secret weapon." He turned to Mark. "You tell her."

Mark straightened in the passenger seat. "I've got this prank squirt-module that inserts into a laptop. It shoots water at the user when I tap a link on my phone. When I first moved to Miami, my mom made me bring some pepper spray to protect me in the big city. I put that in the module for Josh."

"Yeah." Josh chuckled. "Saved by the geek squad. I left that guy screaming. So, now that the FBI's on board, what's our next move?"

"They want us to go ahead with the meeting we've got this afternoon with Professor Harper."

"Wait. You set that up on your cell phone."

"That's actually going to work to our advantage. Before I deleted the spy app, Agent Kwan placed a call to my phone pretending to be the professor's assistant moving our meeting to tomorrow. Our guy's going to have a nice welcoming committee waiting."

A NEW LEVEL

Blind in his left eye, his face on fire, Billy Ray barreled down the road toward the motel. The bitch was going to pay for his pain.

Somehow the spray had missed his right eye, or no way he'd even be driving. The water fountain at the park had done nothing for his left, and his skin from the neck up was a herd of blisters all trying to peel off at once. He remembered the possum he'd hit with bear spray for laughs back in his teens and how that thing had jerked around like a roller coaster at the county fair, spitting and gagging. Now it was him spasming and coughing his lungs out as he tried to keep the car going straight. No fun being the possum.

He'd take this out on that girl's hide.

He pulled into the motel, half stumbled out of the car, and jabbed at the door with the room key until he got the danged thing in. He turned the knob and shoved the door open.

"Damn! Not again!" With every ounce of fury he could muster, he flung the room key and its clunky, metal holder at the empty chair, missing it by five feet. It took a chunk out of the far wall.

He glared at the room. Raging, he crossed to the bed, where his backpack sat open. He pawed through it. At least everything was still there.

He eyed the chair again. No way she got out of those ropes without help. He'd tied deer to his gun rack and swerved through the Smokies at eighty miles per hour and never had one budge.

The door hadn't been forced open. Local police would've kicked it in. Besides, if it were the cops, they would've been waiting for him when he got back.

He should've known. When he'd driven away from that restaurant in Boca Raton, he'd felt it: Someone was on his tail. But, even with his usual tricks, he hadn't been able to spot the car. This guy had serious skills. Had to be a fed. Or maybe the man working for the Chinese, the one the Reverend had said killed that guy at the restaurant.

He checked every inch of his bag and belongings to see if he'd been bugged. Nothing. He put on his sneakers, packed up his stuff, and hustled out of the room.

Before he left the lot, he bent down and checked all the wheel wells on the car. Then he flipped over onto his back to look under the chassis. Not a damn thing. He popped the hood. Nestled up just left of the radiator he found a round, two-inch-wide, black tracking dot. Slick. He yanked it out. No cars around to stick it on, so he tossed it in the dumpster. Let them think he was still there, at least till the trash got picked up. It would buy him some time. He needed his head clear for his next move.

Like it or not, the game had reached a new level.

ONE OF TWO

In the back seat, Josh looked up from his laptop. Sammi was at the wheel of Agent Kwan's car, with the agent next to her. To Josh's left, Mark was hunched over his phone, playing some intergalactic warfare game. They'd traversed most of the ninety-minute route north on I-95 and were slicing through West Palm Beach. Weedy patches of roadside greenery bordered the drab, windowless rears of big-box stores and shopping malls that had turned their backs to the fumes and din of the highway; billboards blared everything from medical marijuana dispensaries to gun stores.

Josh shifted his eyes back to his screen. He'd spent the last hour running searches and rereading chapters of the book of Judges, coming up with nothing of use. Sammi had said there were probably religious issues they'd missed—things that she'd assured him were well within the expertise of Professor Richard Harper—but there had to be some further clue in these chapters, something even *he* could find.

Frustrated, he glanced over at Mark. "Someone really important could be murdered tomorrow if we don't figure this out. And while I'm racking my brain here, you're in some freaking galaxy far, far way."

Without looking up, in a weak attempt at a motherly voice, Mark replied, "Now, Joshua Hayes Sutton, if you can't say something nice—"

"Joshua!" Sammi blurted out. "Oh my God! Joshua! Joshua was a prophet considered by some biblical scholars to be the first of the judges."

The car went silent.

"I thought . . ." She eyed Josh in the rearview mirror as she continued. "I'm sorry if this sounds creepy, but I had a feeling early on that we were meant to be part of the same story. And those dreams we've both had about the judges. How did I not see this?"

What exactly was she saying? "Can you be more specific?" Josh asked.

"I'm named for my grandfather Samuel. Samuel was also an Old Testament prophet. The biblical period of the judges ran from Joshua to Samuel. They were both *judges*."

As Sammi shook her head, the car went quiet again. No freaking way. *Both judges*. Something about these *judges*. Judges? Judge? What if . . . ?

He could have asked a simple question of a chatbot or relied on Google's AI response, but he wanted to be absolutely certain the answer was correct. So, he went old school. He loaded a webpage with the King James version of the book of Judges. Back in his college computer classes, he'd been one of the best at composing Boolean searches—logic-based search strings set out like algebraic equations—to search texts and articles for specific, connected pieces of data. What he needed now was a search string that would scan the book of Judges for the words *judge* or *judged* within, he estimated, thirty words of any of the thirteen leaders of Israel mentioned in that book.

"Northlake Boulevard," Sammi announced. "We're getting off here."

Let's see . . . He began to type:

(judge OR judged) AROUND (30) . . .

"My GPS says we should take the exit after this one," Kwan said.

(he OR she . . .

"There's a reason I want to go this way," Sammi insisted as they turned onto the ramp.

OR Othniel OR . . .

Moments later, as Josh continued to type, Sammi slowed the car.

"Look left," she instructed. A huge banyan tree with a massive canopy and innumerable trunks of all sizes sat in a circle of grass, splitting a roadway.

After his quick glance at the banyan, Josh finished adding the thirteen leaders of Israel mentioned in the book of Judges, then submitted his search:

(judge OR judged) AROUND (30) (he OR she OR Othniel

OR Ehud OR Shamgar OR Deborah OR Gideon OR Tola

OR Jair OR Jephthah OR Ibzan OR Elon OR Abdon OR

Manoah OR Samson)

Sammi pulled over and stared out the driver's-side window. "That magnificent banyan marks the official entrance to the city of Palm Beach Gardens. A classmate who lives up here told me about it. It looks like one now, but was originally two."

Two. He looked down at the results of his search. Could it be? "Sammi, I think I found something. I was thinking about that quote from the Bible you showed me about the arrival of the Messiah, how it said he 'doth *judge*.' Well, I just ran a search on the book of Judges for the leaders who are specifically said to have *judged* Israel."

"Didn't all of them?" She turned her head to face him.

"Actually, only nine did. And every one of our seven is on the list."

"Really? Who are the other two?"

"Deborah and Othniel."

"So, this current judge could be the second to last in the chain!" she replied. "Incredible."

Yet frustrating. "That still takes us back to my question from this morning," Josh said. "Why would someone kill just to find the latest link in the chain?"

"Occam's razor," Mark announced, his eyes never leaving his phone.

That made sense. "Could be."

"What the heck is Occam's razor?" Sammi asked.

"In competing hypotheses," Mark said, "the odds favor the one with the fewest assumptions."

Josh jumped in. "Occam's razor is a principle that essentially states that the simplest solution is often correct. The simplest solution here is that the maniac was willing to kill people because he was after the most valuable judge in the chain, the *final* one. Which would mean that perhaps an Othniel or a Deborah was a significant judge at the time of Christ, but wasn't on the list Judge Maloch gave me."

Mark stopped playing on his phone. Agent Kwan cocked an ear toward the back seat.

Sammi's eyes went wide. "You're saying—"

"This could be the *one*."

THE PROFESSOR

Sammi hopped out of the car and pressed the intercom button on a call box mounted on a granite-sheathed pillar. They had not even entered the grounds, but from the pillars, the spiked wrought-iron gate that hung between them, and the ten-foot-tall ficus hedges shielding the property from the outside world, Josh could see this guy had more than a professor's salary going for him.

"Who's there?" came a man's voice.

"It's Samantha. I have three others with me, Professor."

"Come on in."

The call box beeped, and the gate slowly swung open. Sammi jumped back into the car and pulled forward. As they proceeded along the curving entry drive, the view was still blocked by thick hedges. When the path cleared, a tennis court and gazebo sat off to the right. To the left of the main building, separated from it by a long walkway under a vine-covered trellis, was what appeared to be a guesthouse. Looking through the opening, Josh could see the intracoastal waterway at the rear of the property.

The huge main house, like the gate pillars, was covered in irregular sections of gray granite. The home ranged in parts between two and three stories under gabled roof sections of dark concrete tiles. Antique bronze windows, along with a great turret-shaped entrance, dominated the front elevation.

After Sammi parked the car to the side of the wide circular driveway, the group approached the towering, dark wood front door, the center of which was adorned by a brass knocker in the shape of a satyr's head.

As Sammi reached for the knocker, the door opened.

Really? Josh had assumed that a professor of theology would have some hint of the clergy about his appearance, or at least that Professor Richard Harper would look *professorial*. The man standing in front of them, however, could easily have passed for a high-end real estate developer: well-tanned, with thinning slicked-back hair, golf shirt, alligator belt, and expensive-looking jeans. His loafers matched the belt.

Harper gestured toward the interior. "Please come in."

To their right rose a two-story-high library, all cherrywood and polished brass accents, with rolling wall-mounted ladders. Ahead of them and to the left was an enormous living room. Josh couldn't help but to notice the conflict before him: bold modern furniture at odds with walls of Renaissance art.

"You've added to your research team since this morning?" Harper asked. "Didn't you say there were three of you?"

"Sorry, Professor. It did start out as a research project," Sammi said. "It's far more than that now."

They'd decided on the way up that there was no choice but to tell him the real story. Besides, they hadn't been able to solve this thing with every fact they had. How could they expect him to do it with less?

"These are my friends"—she motioned toward them—"Josh and Mark. And this is Agent Henry Kwan of the FBI."

"The FBI?" He took a small, deferential step back.

"We've got a bit to tell you, Professor."

"I imagine." He guided them toward a section of the living room where white leather couches and chairs nestled around a red, trapezoidal, high-gloss composite coffee table. "Make yourselves comfortable. I'll be right back."

A beam of light glinted off a corner of the table. Josh gazed up from his new vantage point on the couch to see a large skylight in the center of an angled, cedar-beamed ceiling that soared three stories above the room.

Harper reentered and set down a serving tray stocked with fancy-looking cheeses and crackers, a large pitcher of iced tea, and cups. Mark immediately reached for the crackers. They'd never gotten to eat those wraps.

"So, Samantha," Harper asked as he dropped into a nearby chair, "what's going on?"

As Sammi summarized the significant details of the past forty-two hours, from the death of Judge Maloch to the present, Josh watched Harper's eyes slowly transition from moist and reddened to narrowed and focused.

"And your research on these clues and on the judges, you have that with you?"

"We put together a summary for you," Sammi answered. "It's all on Josh's laptop."

Harper stood up and grabbed the serving tray. "Let's go to my library."

They followed him out of the living room. Josh expected him to turn right, toward the room of bookcases they'd passed on arrival, but instead Harper steered left, heading deeper into the house.

"Isn't the library the other way?" Mark asked.

"That's the reading room," Harper replied matter-of-factly, "for my nonacademic collection. My research library is back here."

He led them into a rectangular, low-ceilinged space, about twenty-five feet long by fifteen feet wide. The white melamine, do-it-yourself bookshelves that lined most of the walls were filled primarily with bulky, hard-bound volumes. There were three small desks, two covered with books and papers, and a third, near the door, holding a laser printer. The linoleum floor was a skating rink of scratch marks, probably from the casters on the five or six rolling secretarial chairs scattered across the room. Against one of the short walls, two desktop computers sat on a table under a window.

Something was off about the window. Josh took a closer look.

"It's fake," Harper said.

Josh turned around. "What?"

"The window's fake. This is also my hurricane room. It's built internal to the house, surrounded by steel-reinforced concrete walls and ceiling, with a six-inch-thick solid steel entry door. I had the fake, back-lit window installed so I don't feel like a prisoner when I'm in here, since it doubles as my research library." He handed Josh a slip of paper. "That's my Wi-Fi info and email address. Can you email me your summary? I work better off the printed page."

The group settled into secretarial chairs as Josh opened his laptop on a desk. Soon, the laser printer spat out the summary pages.

Harper left them to the refreshments while he skimmed the material. When he was finished, he spun his chair around to face the group, closed his eyes for a moment, then snapped them open. "Fascinating."

"Do you see anything we missed?" Sammi asked.

He chuckled. "Look at my fingernails." He'd extended his arm fully, perpendicular to his body. "While your focus is there, can you tell me what color my eyes are?"

No one offered a guess.

"Sometimes," he continued, "we stare so deeply at our subject that we look right past the obvious. You tied the names of your historical judges and even your own names to the book of Judges, but what about my colleague who was murdered and whose laptop contained the clues you found?"

"Judge Maloch?"

"Maloch. In Hebrew his last name means 'messenger,' and in the Hebrew version of the Old Testament, the word *malakh* is used for a specific kind of messenger."

"An angel!" Sammi exclaimed.

"Precisely."

The room went silent. Josh's mind raced. An angel delivered the information to Joshua and Samuel, two biblical prophets, who followed a list of historical judges that paralleled the key judges from the book of Judges, on a mission that led to some kind of messiah.

No freaking way. Josh turned to Sammi. She was shaking her head in wonder.

"That's crazy," he blurted out.

"Sure is." Harper smiled. "With more crazy to come."

ADMONITION

Buried beneath silk quilts, Han Chee-hwa, deep in Ambien-infused REM sleep, stirred slowly to the ringing of his phone. His bedside clock read 3:00 a.m. The caller ID on his private line was blocked. A government number.

"Hello?" he rasped.

"Chee-hwa?"

"Yes, Chang . . . I mean General." Why was he calling at this hour?

"My superiors received word."

"Of what?" He was still groggy.

"Of the Zhou Yuanxin sanction."

"I see." Weren't they pleased that he'd had a traitorous Falun Dafa leader erased?

"So public. So many witnesses."

"Sorry, General. I had precise information for your man. Time. Place. Most crucially, he was able to act before the further flow of this malignancy."

"So, the crisis has passed?"

"Not yet."

"Then you must tread carefully. I've been asked to inform you that our leadership is in no mood to see some new foreign incident become a public indictment. Our belt now encircles the globe. We'll not have it loosened."

THE THIRD EYE

"There's more?" Josh locked his eyes on Harper.

"I noticed your note about your brother, Seth—your concerns with your dreams." Harper turned to Sammi. "Samantha, what can you tell us about Joshua and Seth, or Sethur, from the Bible?"

Her brow lifted, then fell away to a smile of acknowledgment. "Of course. The scouting of Canaan." She eyed Josh. "Moses appointed twelve spies to scout the land of Canaan as the potential future home of the Jewish people. Seth, or Sethur, was one of the ones who were afraid of the challenges ahead. So he came back with lies about cities being protected by great armies they couldn't defeat. Joshua, on the other hand, reported that the land held great promise and that it could be theirs. Of the twelve spies, only Joshua and Caleb, who had reported truthfully, were permitted by God to enter the Promised Land. Seth and the other false prophets all perished in the desert during the years of wandering."

"So..." Harper turned to Josh. "Seth and Joshua saw the same things, but Seth was consumed by the struggles that lay ahead, while Joshua could see past to the land of milk and honey. The parallels, as eerie as they are, are just too strong. You needn't fear your dreams. Somehow, they've led us here."

Really? Seth and Joshua, *both* from the Bible? But then, all those other names *had* lined up. Even Judge Maloch's. Now Harper was saying that *Josh* was the golden child? Those dreams had killed his brother. How could he trust them? He grabbed his face with both hands. As nuts as all this was, something else was even more incredible. "Do you really believe *here* means the direct path to the arrival of some kind of *messiah*?"

With a gleam of excitement in his eye, Harper hopped up on a desk, addressing the group like a study session. "Think of it this way. The Falun Dafa believe in a primordial spirit shared by all mankind, and that, with proper training, certain individuals can greatly increase their *de*—the positive side of this spirit—and reach higher levels of brain functioning sufficient to activate what's known as the 'third eye.'"

"What's that?"

"It's a centuries-old concept referring to the pineal gland, which sits in our mid-brain; it's a focal point of yoga and meditation, with some science behind it. The Dafa believe this 'third eye' is an opening to our sixth sense—for those able to handle higher levels of *de*, a path to such things as telepathy and clairvoyance."

"Isn't that stuff all smoke and mirrors? Like those fake freak shows?"

Harper smiled. "I'm sure some of it is. But we've had da Vinci, Einstein, and so many others who've seen beyond what was 'possible.' The concept of a messiah could certainly align with that one special person of 'great inborn quality' who the Falun Dafa envision accessing the *de* at the highest levels of all."

Josh scanned his team. Mark was still hovering by the food. Agent Kwan was leaning against a bookcase, locked in focus on Harper. Those FBI guys were intense. Sammi, seated nearby, exhaled a long breath, took a sip of her iced tea, then looked up at the professor.

"What about my theory," she asked, "that we're following a human rights chain of *de* that started with Christ?"

"It's a practicum for your thesis, isn't it?" he said, with a semi-awed shake of his head. "You may have found a true engine of destiny." He glanced downward, paused. "But, like you, I'm at a loss as to why someone would kill to find out who the current judge is, if the final one in the chain, this 'messiah,' isn't coming for another two hundred and fifty years. *That* person would be the potential threat the Chinese fear. Why send a killer now? I saw your note about the possibility that Neville Maloch neglected to list a judge from Christ's lifetime, which would make the current judge the *one*. Having spent more than a few hours with Neville, I have a hard time believing he'd miss anything so crucial."

"But as you know, Professor," Sammi replied, "a number of biblical chronologists have predicted the arrival of the Messiah to be early in this millennium. Isn't it the Jewish Talmud that ties the arrival of the Messiah to a lost article and a scorpion? Well, Judge Maloch's laptop is our lost article, and our scorpion is his killer."

Enough with the academic analysis. Josh rose to his feet. "I guess what really matters is, according to Judge Maloch, we now have less than twenty-four hours before 'everything changes.' If that really means the arrival of this quasi-Messiah, and this 'scorpion' was hired by the Chinese to kill them, it looks like we'd be the only people who would know." Hold on. "What if the Chinese figure out who this person is without us?" He turned, hopefully, to Agent Kwan. "Your people are tracking Judge Maloch's murderer, right?"

"They were," he replied dryly, "but they lost contact a few hours ago."

Great. Even the FBI couldn't stop something if they didn't have a clue as to where it was supposed to happen. Josh locked his gaze back on Harper.

"I couldn't find a single Judge Othniel anywhere, and there are so many Debras and Deborahs in the judiciary in this country alone that I wouldn't know where to start." After everything that had happened, were they really just going to hit a dead end? He threw up his hands. "We're running out of time. You have any idea how to find this person?"

RECONNAISSANCE MISSION

Billy Ray's latest rental car blended into the herd of traffic plodding along northbound on I-95. Whether it was the feds or a Chinese agent, some folks were a little too slick. He chuckled. Awfully coincidental that right after she got rescued, Sutton's girlfriend *happened* to get a call to reschedule her meeting. Billy Ray may have been born on a farm, but it wasn't in the henhouse. He pressed the first number on his speed dial.

"Hello, my son," the Reverend answered. "How are things?"

"Falling into place, sir. Found out about a meeting today. I'm almost there."

"Who's it with?"

"A Richard Harper."

"What do you know of him?"

"Some kind of professor of religion."

"A theology professor . . . They're getting close. As you know, they'll be looking for a name—a judge's name. You need to get that from them."

That, and a little something for his aggravation.

A VIEW FROM AFAR

"I wish I did know how." Harper dejectedly slid down from the desk. Great. Josh looked around at the blank faces. Clearly, no one had a clue how to connect the final dot.

Suddenly, Mark, who had detached himself from the food tray, spoke up, after having apparently pursued his own line of thought on one of the professor's computers. "I think you guys are missing something." His arms lifted slightly at his sides. "Let's apply some *logic* to this. Who's behind this whole thing, all these coincidences? These historical judges whose names sync with the Bible, who show up every two hundred and fifty years like clockwork; Josh and Sammi's names fitting right in the story; even Judge Maloch's. Who wrote the *code* for this? You're saying Christ? If so, who wrote *his* code? God? Assuming you all believe in God, have you ever considered exactly what God is? Could God be the collective mind-power of an advanced civilization? One that has some master plan for us?"

Here it came.

Mark's hands flapped around like angry sparrows. "If you look at the actual language used in the Bible—the King James version—God's appearances could easily be that of an extraterrestrial." He began typing as he continued. "Professor, I'm going to email you some stuff. I saw you've got a projector over there on the shelf." He pointed at a wall screen. "Can you put it up on that screen?"

Harper nodded and took a seat at one of the computers.

Did they really have time for this? If Judge Maloch's killer somehow tracked down the right judge, a history-altering tragedy was less than twenty-four hours away. Josh shook his head in frustration and got up to refill his iced tea.

Moments later, Mark stood at the screen. "This is from Ezekiel."

And I looked, and, behold, a whirlwind came of the north, a great cloud, and a fire infolding itself, and a brightness was about it, and out of the midst thereof as the colour of amber, out of the midst of the fire.

"Isn't it obvious? They were witnessing the landing of a spacecraft using reverse thrusters."

"Isn't that a bit of a reach?" Josh asked. He sipped at his drink.

"Actually," Harper interceded, "I've heard this argument made before, by some fairly well-respected theologians."

With a sideways glance at Josh, Mark pressed on. "And even by the founder of Falun Dafa."

Now this was getting ridiculous.

"Impressive, Mark," Harper said. "I'd almost forgotten about that. The *Time* magazine interview."

"What the . . . ?" was all Josh could get out. Sammi seemed equally mystified. Even Agent Kwan, who'd been wall-leaning at his usual stoic attention, looked on eagerly.

Smiling broadly with his newfound standing, Mark said, "Professor, it's the next article." He spun back to the refreshed screen. "Look at these quotes from a man whose teachings are followed by millions of people."

[S]ince the beginning of [the twentieth] century, aliens have begun to invade the human mind and its ideology and culture. . . .

The aliens have introduced modern machinery like computers and airplanes. They started by teaching mankind about modern science, so people believe more and more science, and spiritually, they are controlled.

Mark's arms shot forward. "Don't you guys see it? We're all being manipulated."

Josh glanced around. He noticed a hint of a sneer from Agent Kwan. Sammi looked distracted; she'd wandered over to a far corner of the room.

He let Mark's words filter through his mind. *Logic* is what Mark had asked for. *Logic* told Josh that every Bible passage was not meant to be taken literally. *Logic* dictated that perhaps the Falun Dafa founder had gone slightly off the rails in that interview. Mark's argument was like an overhyped software program—a lot of flash, but minimal substance. Enough with this crazy tangent. But how to solve the problem at hand?

Frustrated, Josh returned to his seat and stared blankly at his laptop screen. His fingers had been off the keys for a while, and his lock-screen slideshow had kicked in. In front of him was a beautifully strange image of a banyan tree. He cocked his head at an angle. The tree's interwoven trunks looked almost like a human couple embracing. He lowered an eyebrow in disbelief. Two of them *together*?

He typed a search-engine query: "Othniel Deborah"

Unbelievable. "Professor," Josh asked, "can I email you something to print?"

The article from the *New York Times* came spitting out of the laser printer near the door. Josh set it on the desk for the group to see. The headline said it all:

Industrialist George Othniel to Marry Judge Deborah Fenton

"Othniel *and* Deborah!" Harper gushed. "Remarkable. How did you think to look for Deborah and Othniel *together*?"

Josh leaned against the desk, facing the professor. "The only theory we had that led to a messiah now was that Judge Maloch had missed one judge when he compiled his list—an Othniel or a Deborah from the time of Christ. But that would mean he was unaware of that judge; he wouldn't have been expecting the final one yet. So he wouldn't have sent an alert to Master Zhou about some messiah's imminent arrival. But we know he did, because that brought a killer to his door."

"I see." Harper's eyes narrowed. "But that still doesn't explain how you decided to look for Othniel and Deborah *jointly*."

"I've got Sammi to thank for that." Josh went back to his laptop. "Sammi, do you recognize this picture?" She came over, and he brought back the image that had appeared as part of the slideshow.

Her eyes went wide and she smiled. "Of course. It's 'The Lovers.' How did you get that?"

"A few months ago, I'd admired some nature photographs on the wall in Judge Maloch's office. He told me you'd taken them. The next day he emailed me copies. They show up all the time when my screen's locked. Good title, by the way." He turned back to Harper. "This picture Sammi took came up on my screen. It's a banyan tree with its trunks shaped into a sort of sculpture that looks like a man and a woman embracing. It made me think: What if Judge Maloch didn't miss a judge at the time of Christ? What if both of these names were in one judge now?"

"Hey, am I crazy, or does that look like a halo?" Mark, excited, pointed to a place on the photograph just above the "woman's" head.

Now Josh saw it: a glint of sunlight poking through the banyan trunks, creating a small, faint golden circle.

"'And the Lord gave Deborah dominion over the mighty,'" Professor Harper announced. "I believe that's from chapter five of the book of Judges."

"The wedding's in Manhattan," Josh said, "at St. Patrick's Cathedral, tomorrow at eleven. By noon she'll be Deborah Othniel." He turned back to his laptop. "Let me check one more thing." With a couple of search queries, he found what he was looking for. He spun to look at Sammi. "She became a judge in 2000."

Harper let out a small groan and reached for his stomach. "Excuse me for a minute." He opened the door and stepped out, closing it behind him.

Josh eyed Agent Kwan. "Now you know where and when."

As Kwan was about to respond, the lights in the room and on the computer screens all flickered. A red light next to the door went on. Under it was a small sign that read GENERATOR ACTIVATED.

Josh tapped the touch pad on his laptop. "Wi-Fi's been cut off."

Sammi went to the door. The knob turned freely in her hand, but the steel door wouldn't open. She leaned into it, then yanked hard; it still didn't budge. "I think it's been bolted shut from the outside." She turned to Josh. "Why would he do this to us?" She seemed equally confounded and furious.

The four of them reached for their phones like gunslingers.

Agent Kwan drew first. "No bars."

A SCORPION IN THE WEEDS

Even a cracker like him knew the difference between money and big money. The ones with money, Billy Ray figured, wanted the common folk to gape at the splendor of their McMansions—what those realty jokers called curb appeal. The ones with *big* money didn't even want a curb—just walls too high to climb and hedges too gnarly to mess with, hiding their palaces from the peasants.

This neighborhood was big money.

He parked his rental, then strolled cautiously along a few blocks of walls and hedges until he found the alleyway next to the property. The hedges were higher than a single-wide, thicker than a bog's swamp gas. He could barely make out the concrete wall behind them. This was not going to be a joyride.

With a quick look-see around to make sure no one was watching, he wrenched open a small crack in the dense hedge and found a foothold. He stepped on, then reached up and yanked another space open. Ow! Rrrrr. His arm got stabbed by the sharp end of a branch. As he climbed, the stabs kept coming: shoulder, shin, forearm, quad. He'd definitely be taking this out on the folks in that house.

Poking his head over the top, he surveyed the security camera locations. He looked for a midpoint between two cameras. It was less likely to be noticed if you stayed near the edges of the coverage. He hoisted himself up over the wall. Damn. The inside had hedges every bit as thick. Lately he'd been about as lucky as the farm's fattest pig the day before Christmas dinner. That was about to change. He worked his way, stab by stab, halfway down, then jumped off softly to the ground.

While giving his arms and legs a rub, he eyeballed the huge house. Another thing about these palaces: There were so many doors and windows that you could bet your Sunday finest there'd be one they'd left unlocked.

ALTERNATIVE ANALYSIS

Josh watched from across the room as Kwan checked the seams on the doorframe. The agent stepped back a few paces and lowered his shoulder, then barreled forward and launched himself at the steel door, crashing his body up against it. The door didn't give an inch. Kwan gathered himself, grabbed the knob with two hands, set his feet against the base of the wall next to the door, and, uttering a low-pitched groan, pulled with his full body weight. The door still didn't move. Wonderful. Kwan shook himself, walked to a nearby chair, sat down, and pondered.

Josh slammed down his fist on a desk. "What possible reason could he have to lock us in here?" he said to no one in particular.

"Can't believe I missed this." Sammi had drifted back to the far corner of the room, where he'd noticed her during Mark's rantings. She was staring at some textbooks.

"Missed what?"

She turned to Kwan. "You told me Judge Maloch's murderer works for a Christian religious leader, right?"

"Right."

"Then why would he suddenly be working for the Chinese government?"

Kwan shrugged his shoulders.

"What if he's not?" Sammi continued. "We've been focused on why the Chinese might fear a '*de*-enriched' higher-developed human. But can anyone tell me why a Christian religious leader would have someone killed just to find out who this person is ahead of everyone else?"

Josh had no idea. "You obviously have an explanation."

Sammi came back from the corner. "I do. And it's pretty dark. Professor Harper pointed out that Judge Maloch's last name is Hebrew for a messenger angel. But I realized that his first name, Neville, or *nephil* in Hebrew, was used for fallen angels, those who followed Satan. Why would the professor ignore that when his academic subspecialty is Satanism?"

The room went momentarily silent.

Incredible. "He's a devil worshipper?" Josh asked.

Sammi shook her head. "No, just an expert in theology's evil side. That corner of the library"—she motioned to where she'd just been—"is filled with books on the subject, some written by the professor. I've heard he gets paid huge fees to lecture on the topic around the world."

"But," Josh said, "maybe the professor ignored Judge Maloch's first name because all the other clues lead to a quasi-Messiah."

"Not necessarily. A 'white mount' is supposed to deliver the Messiah, but, per the Bible, it will first deliver the Antichrist, a deceitful conqueror who'll appear godlike, filled with 'all powers . . . and wonder.' Does that description sound familiar to any of you?"

"An extraterrestrial?" Mark asked, hopefully.

"Close, but I'm thinking more DC and Marvel than *Star Trek*."

Was she really headed *there*? "A superhero?" Josh guessed.

Sammi nodded. "Bingo. I was thinking about what Mark showed us: that the founder of Falun Dafa claimed the unprecedented technological advancements of the last century have conditioned us to accept greater and greater influence by science. It made me consider another phenomenon that exploded over the course of the last century: the superhero. Think about it. Mankind has worshipped superheroes for thousands of years. The Greek and Norse gods captured the imaginations of civilizations and pervade our literature. But in the last century we perfected the superhero. First in comic books; then television made them prime-time stars. And in the last twenty years, with digital graphics, superheroes made a seamless transition to the big screen. Every conceivable kind of superpower can be displayed in a way that's truly convincing. Superman, Wonder Woman, the Avengers. Even the way some superheroes are created aligns with modern science—like simple gene mutations. For all these centuries mankind worshipped superheroes, wanting to believe they could exist. And now, we see them in action all the time."

Mark's arms were attempting liftoff. "What you're saying is that we're ready."

"Maybe *conditioned* is the better word. And the problem with that is that if an actual superhero comes along who looks good and acts good, we'll all follow along like little lambs, believing that superhero *is* good. But, if the Satanists are right, the 'white mount' might not be bringing a savior. It could be delivering us to the abyss."

Kwan, hovering by the few remaining scraps of food, had his eyes locked on Sammi. He seemed particularly intrigued by this line of reasoning.

"What about the other clues?" Mark asked excitedly.

"I can see it," Josh said. "The judges who couldn't handle the 'increased *de*.' Nigel Tolan, committed to a mental institution. Henrik of Reibzang going from human rights crusader to bloodthirsty vigilante. And Abdonchai, the Chinese magistrate, if he *did* throw himself off that cliff, what had happened to *his* mind?"

"Exactly," Sammi added. "These men were revered in their communities. So, what if Deborah Othniel embraces the 'increased *de*' at first and is able to elevate her mental abilities far beyond anything previously imagined, but then, after she becomes a powerful, and possibly even worshipped, world figure, what if she reaches a point where she can't deal with the increased level of *de* anymore? What if she decides to draw up her *own* rules for right and wrong? I can't believe I'm saying this, but she could end up being the Antichrist."

Mark stared at the books behind Sammi. "You think the professor *wants* that to happen?"

She shook her head. "He just believes in the biblical theory that great evil serves an essential, though painful, purpose—that it creates the opportunity for a true savior to come."

"So," Josh said, "that's why the redheaded lunatic is on the loose. He and his boss think they're stopping Satan."

"It's the only thing that makes sense," Sammi replied. "But Professor Harper wouldn't want this Deborah Fenton killed, even if she's the Antichrist. That's why he won't let her identity leave this room."

Great. "If that's the case, why would he *ever* let us out?"

No one responded.

Josh eyed the steel door. Even though he knew there was no other exit, he paced and scanned the room again. Their prison. Perhaps their tomb.

He hadn't noticed *that* before. Sitting by itself on a shelf, occupying a rare space between textbooks, was a small colored-glass figurine. Images flashed through his mind. Venice. The islands of Murano. A prison of another kind for a frail teenage boy and a judge . . .

THE MERCY OF THE WIND

1789-1790–Venice

Gabrieli Triani peered into the beckoning mouth of the glassblower's furnace, numb to the scorching, blinding, yellow-white flames. Three weeks had passed since his father, Giuseppe, the factory's master craftsman, had taken ill, leaving Gabrieli no choice but to take over the work. If production stopped, Signore Vittoria would have no reason to continue their wages or provide their tiny Murano apartment. Gabrieli and his father would be out on the street.

A row of still-cooling glass figurines filled his workbench. Enough for the morning. He set down his metal tongs, anxious to get back to his laboratory. He wrenched his body upright and limped through the dark halls toward a storage closet in a far corner of the factory.

"Is today the day?" Sofia Orzano, the daughter of the plant manager, who had been dusting a nearby lamp as Gabrieli approached, offered a hopeful smile.

"Let's find out together." He'd been experimenting with combinations of chemicals and pigments on glass beads since he was twelve, convinced he could improve the colors inside his father's glass creations. At least Sofia took him seriously. His father thought it a waste of valuable apprenticeship hours. Signore Vittoria just wanted the "cripple" to stay out of Guiseppe's way. But Sofia, who, at seventeen, was only two years older than Gabrieli, and his only friend, understood how it felt to be young and trapped, along with your dreams, inside a factory.

After they entered the cramped workspace, Gabrieli turned up the flame under the ceramic bowl he'd left on the tabletop. Once the hydrochloric acid it contained boiled, he dropped in some colorful glass beads, waited a few seconds for the acid to thoroughly clean the beads, and then removed them with tongs. As he reached to drop the last of the beads into a bowl containing his carefully measured mixture of clays, pigments, and chemicals, his elbow grazed a nearby vial of sodium hydroxide. He grabbed for the flask, but missed, and its contents spilled into the mix.

No!

He'd spent months refining this formula. Now it was ruined. He wheeled to hurl the mess into the trash, but Sofia was in the way. He circled her on his path to the waste bin.

As he tipped the bowl to pour out his latest failure, Sofia shrieked, "Wait!"

He saw it before the contents reached the edge; a transformation had taken place.

The colors in the beads were suddenly different. It was not their hue, exactly, that had changed, but something even more profound; it was more like they had developed *energy*. They were radiating.

Carefully cradling the bowl, he dragged his withered leg across the factory with Sofia by his side and set his experiment down at the end of his glassblower's workbench, close enough to the fire to keep the beads from hardening. He needed to make a figurine. He picked up a steel rod and immersed its tip in the main furnace, extracting a small glob of molten silica. Then he blew this soft glass into a bubble and rolled it on the marble marver to elongate the shape. After he'd repeated the process to add more glass, he used his crimps and shears to shape the bubble into a small clown. Finally, he grabbed his fine-tipped tongs, removed the treated beads from the bowl, one by one, and passed them through a small opening he'd left in the figurine.

"That's incredible," Sofia said with a gasp.

As the beads took shape with the firming glass around them, the effect he had witnessed in the laboratory was multiplied tenfold. He'd sculpted hundreds of clowns, many more finely wrought than this one. But the colors at the core of this clown danced with an otherworldly glow; it was all but alive. Surely there'd never been a work of glass anything like this.

He wanted to scream for joy. He wanted to see the ecstatic face of Signore Vittoria. But there was someone he had to show first. He set the clown in the annealing oven to cool. When the workers were finally released that evening, he slipped his creation in his coat and rushed to the street.

A strong wind pressed against his face. The wind had always been against him, from his mother's death at his birth to his lifelong frailty—his walk forever a limp, his attempts at running always something between a hobble and a skip. But he'd never let that hold him back. Determination was his ballast against the gales.

And no wind could hurt him today.

He raced, as fast as he could, the few blocks to the little apartment. He opened the door to his father's room. "Father," Gabrieli gushed, "I have done it!"

There was no response from where Guiseppe lay on the bed. While Gabrieli was at work, his father had passed away.

"There's nothing like this elsewhere on our island of Murano or, for that matter, anywhere on earth," Nicolo Vittoria boasted to a group from Milan.

Greedy bastard. Sofia listened from behind the stock-filled rows of glass shelves. Prices had soared at the Vittoria factory as word had spread of its remarkable, intensified-color glassware. The showroom buzzed with hordes of new buyers. But wages, even Gabrieli's, had not changed.

His working conditions had.

A few weeks after Guiseppe Triani's funeral, Sofia had been sweeping an adjacent hallway when she'd overheard the signore speaking to Gabrieli. "Gabrieli, you're as a son to me. But our business . . . our family . . . we've fallen on hard times. Even with your new pieces, we barely meet expenses. We're at the mercy of the shippers and suppliers—every one of them a thief! I'm so sorry, but we can no longer afford your apartment."

"But . . . Signore," Gabrieli had stammered, "where will I live?"

"Right here, child. We've made you a room at the back of the factory near your workshop. Since your father died, we've been worried about you—you're sick so often. Here we can take better care of you."

From that day on, security guards had been posted at all the doors. When she'd spotted Gabrieli stepping outside for a breath of fresh air, one of the guards was always watching him. Signore Vittoria could profess all he wanted that he was simply looking after his sickly ward, but it was evident that Gabrieli was no longer a free man.

Not that it seemed to matter to him.

Something inside him had died along with his father. She watched Gabrieli slog through his chores at the furnace and his workshop, lost in his work. His eyes had always sparkled with purpose despite his infirmities. When he glanced her way now, those eyes were as battered and damp as the seawall.

Sofia, on the other hand, found her mind exploring thoughts long buried. She'd been taken out of school to help support the family, and she'd slowly resigned herself to her menial station. But as she watched Gabrieli accept *his* fate, she asked herself why Nicolo Vittoria should be the only one to benefit from Gabrieli's remarkable talents. It occurred to her that there was money to be made, a life-changing kind of money.

Gabrieli sat at the cramped desktop in his laboratory, readying to remove a strand of treated beads from a vial. He barely felt the hand on his shoulder.

"Gabrieli," Sofia whispered softly, "I must speak with you."

He didn't move. "Sorry," he responded stiffly. He couldn't bear what was surely another one of her attempts to lighten his spirit. "Busy now. Perhaps tomorrow."

"The time has come!" she barked.

He'd never heard this tone from her. Startled, he laid down his tongs and slowly swiveled to face her.

Sofia softened her voice. "Look at you. You've cut yourself off from the world . . . from the other workers . . . from me."

"But my designs, my inventions—"

"Is that all there is of you? Are you no more than a piece of pretty colored glass?"

Gabrieli felt his eyes moisten. "What am I supposed to do? My work is all I have left."

She held up a package he hadn't noticed. "The world outside this room and your furnace still lives. Use *this* and you could too. Tomorrow is our Carnevale, the one day Vittoria lets us join the celebration."

For those who were in the mood to celebrate. At least this explained the commotion he'd heard outside the past few weeks as he'd tossed on his cot at night. He took the package and opened it. Inside, he found a handmade burgundy cloak, a pair of dark boots, and a devil's mask.

Sofia kept her voice low. "We'll need to be discreet . . ."

Early the next morning, Nicolo Vittoria's factory bustled with strange activity. Heartfelt greetings rang out around him as harlequins, gypsies, dancers, and knights scurried about, hanging streamers. In a corner of the room, a devil in a burgundy cloak, who had limped out from the back of the factory, and an angel with a silver halo chattered away.

At noon, a roast ham was brought forth, accompanied by trays of cheeses and barrels of wine. By midafternoon, the wine had flowed freely. Even the devil had his due. When Vittoria announced that the workers could go home early, vigorous *buona sera*s filled the air.

Signore Vittoria chuckled at the sweet irony, as the warmest goodbye of all—a lingering embrace—was shared by the angel and devil. As the other employees left, Vittoria watched the little devil shuffle off to the room at the back of the factory and noted a happy half-skip in that usually sullen, awkward gait.

✦

Fighting his nerves, Gabrieli tried his best to hide his limp as he joined the rest of the Vittoria workers in the small piazza outside the factory. If even one of them realized that Gabrieli was now wearing the angel costume, Sofia's plan, and his chance at freedom, might be gone forever. Minutes later, their group merged with a mass of masqueraders in an unofficial parade through the streets of Murano. A few blocks along the route, he turned and headed off down a narrow, high-walled passageway. By a canal at the end of the street, a *gondoliere* waited at a wooden post. He helped Gabrieli into a black gondola, and they were off.

✦

On a canal that sliced through Venice from the north, they passed rows of street-gutter-gray buildings and scores of broken-down boats. Awash with acrid scents of decaying fish, a cold breeze whistled down the corridor and clawed at Gabrieli's cheeks. Finally, after sailing under a number of stubby pedestrian bridges, the gondola emerged into the brilliant sunlight of a great channel.

As the gondola entered Saint Mark's Basin, directly across from Gabrieli was the famous "church island." San Giorgio Maggiore monastery, with its towering orange-and-white spire, seemed to rise directly out of the water, as if it had been constructed by a submerged holy spirit and coaxed skyward. Until now, he'd seen it only on the paintings in the factory showroom and heard about it only from Sofia, who'd been lucky enough to visit Venice twice. But neither the paintings nor Sofia had come close to capturing the magnificence of the real thing.

The gondola swung west, and Gabrieli caught his breath as he peered up the Grand Canal into the land of waterside palaces. It was something out of a fairy tale.

The *gondoliere* finished the turn into the docks at Piasa San Marco, where a horde of bartering fishermen, traders, and craftsmen were surrounded by wonders Gabrieli had seen only in those same showroom paintings: the winged Lion of Venice high atop its granite column; the great red, thirty-story Campanile, where, word was, Galileo had pointed his telescope at the stars; and the Basilica, with the storied bronze Four Horses of St. Mark in midstride over the entranceway.

"Master Triani." A neatly dressed man reached down from the dock. "Senator de Conti awaits."

The man escorted Gabrieli toward a rectangular structure that dominated the waterfront, the Doge's Palace—the seat of the Venetian government and the residence of the Grand Duke of Venice—unmistakable in its cloak of pink and white marble geometric patterns, sitting atop two levels of ornate, white arches.

The man identified himself to the guards at the entry, then guided Gabrieli through the arched doorway, across the grassed central courtyard, and up a marble staircase to a great hallway filled with Renaissance paintings, frescoes, and mosaics.

His guide removed a black bandana from his pocket. "Forgive me, but your eyes may not witness this next part of our tour."

Blindfolded, Gabrieli heard a door crack open nearby. He was led up a creaky staircase past several landings and through a series of musty rooms. When the blindfold was removed, he was standing in a narrow, dimly lit passageway.

"When the Council of Ten was established to investigate political crimes," his escort explained, "they required a secret place to conduct their inquiries."

The man located a movable panel in the wall and slid it to the side. As he stepped through, Gabrieli shielded his eyes to adjust to the brilliantly lit room. Its walls were covered in paintings by masters; tiled images danced on the soaring ceilings.

An immaculately dressed man approached. "Good afternoon. I am Francesco de Conti." The man stroked his trim, graying beard. "All is prepared. The Council of the Black and the Red awaits you." He pointed to a doorway across the room. "You are to tell them precisely how you create the pulsating, colored centers of your glass figures. If you convince them that your technique is truly original, they have the power to grant a *privilege*."

"And that will protect my work?"

"Far more than that. With a privilege granted, no one can copy this invention without the privilege-holder's permission. It's the power to profit directly from every sale in which your creation is part."

Amazing. He'd barely believed Sofia when she'd told him this.

Gabrieli crossed the room and entered a great hall, its walls and ceilings covered in grand paintings encased in ornate, gilded moldings. Benches, backed by low, dark wood paneling, ran the length of two sides of the room.

"Master Triani."

Gabrieli snapped his focus to the long wooden desk at the front of the chamber. Three men sat rigidly behind it, staring at him—two were in black robes; one wore red.

The man in red took notes as Gabrieli described his process. Then the panel launched questions at him: "What are the precise ratios of each chemical and substance in the formulation?" . . . "Did you record the initial temperature of the mixture per the Santorio thermoscope using the Anders Celsius scale?" . . . Finally, he was excused.

As he left the room, Francesco de Conti strode right past him, saying, "Have a seat at the bench; I'll return shortly." De Conti entered the council's chamber and closed the door. When he emerged, he held a certificate in his hand. A smile creased de Conti's lips. "The council has granted a privilege. This certificate denotes that grant and the basis of the invention."

"Kind sir," Gabrieli responded earnestly, "I truly appreciate how you've helped me." He extended his hand to receive the document.

"This certificate does not belong to you," de Conti responded coldly.

He folded the paper and tucked it in his cloak. "It has been issued to *me*. In exchange for my arranging your escape from Vittoria, you've come here and voluntarily described your invention to the Council of the Black and the Red. I'd already presented the case for a privilege to be granted in my name. Your testimony provided them with the details of the invention."

Gabrieli sprang to his feet. "But, sir, it's *my* invention."

"Not anymore!" de Conti boomed. "If you desire ever again to make those exquisite glass figurines with exploding colors, you must do it for me. I'll be glad to employ you, and I'll pay you much better than Nicolo Vittoria."

Some promise of freedom. All he'd found was a new jailer. Gabrieli scowled at de Conti and scrambled to the council's door, but the room was empty. He spun around. "I want to go back." He could barely believe he'd said the words.

"Where? To Vittoria? You don't know what you're saying."

"Yes, I do. Keep your damned certificate. I'll never work for you. Take me back *now*!"

First to arrive, as usual, Antonio Elonetti scrutinized his fellow senators as they filed into the grand rectangular chamber in their heraldic-patterned, red velvet robes, taking seats to his left and right beneath the towering crown of gold-framed ceiling frescoes. He tried to decode their respectful greetings, searching for some inkling of change in their thoughts on the issue at hand.

Elonetti relished his position on the Council of Ten—sitting as a judge, rendering decisions on vital state legal matters, was the high-water mark in a distinguished career of service to his beloved Venice. But this morning, as he churned over the case the council had heard the day before, his thoughts flowed not with pride, but with irony.

It was the first counterfeiting case tried within these walls in a hundred years. Most local inventors had long ceased seeking a government "privilege" for their products, since a competitor could simply obtain the same right in another country and flood the market. The very concept of legal protection for intellectual properties had originated in Venice, only to flounder due to lack of comity between nations. Yet, in this instance, a citizen—this boy, Gabrieli Triani, who had properly registered his invention with the state—was not suffering from foreign competition; Venice itself now barred him from making his own product.

But the more encompassing irony, Elonetti thought, was that the local economy was crumbling under the weight of rampant thievery of Venetians' ideas, in a city-state whose most sacred symbols had been stolen from others by Venetians many hundreds of years before: The gilded bronze Four Horses of Saint Mark were the spoils of a raid on Constantinople in 1204; and the remains of Saint Mark himself, Venice's patron saint, had been dug up in Egypt by Venetian merchants and spirited out of that predominantly Muslim country by concealing them in a barrel of pork.

On the surface, the current case of thievery before the council seemed clear enough. A patrician, and member of the Senate, Francesco de Conti, owned a privilege for a technique that involved the amplification of color inside blown-glass figures. The Vittoria factory on Murano was found to be using the technique without a license from Senator de Conti. The factory's owner, Nicolo Vittoria, apparently was unaware that a privilege had been granted for this invention. On the other hand, the evidence had shown that the factory's glass blower, Gabrieli Triani, the inventor of the technique, knew the privilege existed, yet persisted in producing the counterfeit goods.

The council was likely to impose but a modest fine on Signore Vittoria, as he had given his word that he would cease manufacturing the color-enhanced glass figures. A far more severe punishment seemed appropriate for the young man who knowingly broke the law to his own financial advantage. The council was particularly eager to make an example of someone who had intentionally infringed on the rights of the holder of a Venetian privilege.

But there was something very wrong in all of this. Something, Antonio Elonetti feared, he alone had seen. He'd examined the official records at the grand chancellor's office. This privilege was applied for during the early part of Carnevale, when the Council of Ten was in recess and the Council of the Black and the Red sat as an executive committee.

The two patricians serving on the Black and Red at the time were close business associates of Francesco de Conti, a man whose family's fortunes, per recent murmurings, had been plummeting along with the local economy. At the previous day's hearing, Elonetti learned that de Conti had never even met the inventor until the day of the application.

There was no dispute that Gabrieli Triani had created the technique he was now accused of counterfeiting. But his appeals to the Council of Ten—that he had testified in support of Senator de Conti's application only because he was deceived—had fallen on deaf ears. De Conti explained that the boy had approached him through an intermediary and they had agreed to an arrangement. He would free the boy from his shackled life in Vittoria's dungeon-like factory and provide him with a rewarding permanent position where he could pursue his art. In exchange, Gabrieli Triani would testify in support of the privilege to be issued to Senator de Conti.

As the council reconvened, Senator Elonetti was certain his brethren were poised to deal harshly with Gabrieli Triani. But Elonetti was unconvinced that this poor child was guilty of anything other than misplaced trust hatched of desperation.

Elonetti had spent much of the last evening immersed in law books. Unlike most in the Senate, he was trained as a lawyer. And there was a point of law that began troubling him midway through the prior day's proceedings.

Late that night he had assembled the dilemma in his mind. Was there anything more personal, more private, yet of greater value to mankind, than an individual's creative thought processes? When something a person creates was so special, so unique, that it was entitled to legal protection, how could society fail to ensure that the inventor was protected as well?

He'd scoured old cases and treatises, Venetian and otherwise, searching for anything to buttress his reasoning. He found precious little of use. Frustrated and heavy-eyed, as the hours slid well past midnight, he'd shoved a rejected tome aside. It teetered at the edge of his desk—like a nervous hatchling prepping to flee the nest—and then crashed to the floor.

Unsettled, he'd stretched out and performed his breathing exercises, the meditative regimen taught by a friend who had traveled to the Far East. Renewed, he sat back at his desk and examined a decision from centuries before, under English law. It was clearly not on point, so he pushed it aside. Or at least he tried to.

The book wouldn't move.

Or his mind wouldn't let him move it. The case would not let go; he read it again.

There was a message pushing its way out, but it wasn't on the printed page. It seemed to seep from the bindings, oozing into the air as liquid slowly solidifying. He'd close his eyes, reopen them, look off to the far wall. The message was still there, growing clearer.

He'd feared he might be at some dangerous precipice, beyond which the cliff fell away to a sea of irrevocable insanity. But there was no place to hide. There was no escaping them.

The Words.

On their edges he could almost see something else. Wait, there it was: a corner . . . a bend. And around it the beginning of a path . . . multiple paths. He strained his focus; where did those paths lead? Somehow, he knew the answers were down those roads.

Then the voices came. He felt the presence of others. Not in the room, but gathered deep in the recesses of his mind. *The Words* were on their lips.

He'd found no cases to bolster his legal theory, but *The Words* supported him. They started by forming a message that showed him the *why*:

OFTEN, THE ARTIST FLOATS UNDIRECTED,
ADRIFT WITH NO SOURCE OF FUEL OTHER

**THAN THE IMPETUS OF IMAGINATION.
FROM TIME TO TIME, THESE FRAGILE CREATIVE
VESSELS PUT OUT TO SEA, CARRYING WITH THEM
MAGIC SEEDS CAPABLE, UPON GERMINATION,
OF PROPELLING A CIVILIZATION FORWARD.
THEIR COMPASS, HOWEVER, IS OF LITTLE AID
AGAINST THE TORRENTS. AND SO, BOTH THEIR
SAFE HARBOR AND THE REALIZATION OF THEIR
GENIUS ARE DETERMINED BY FORCES BEYOND
THEIR CONTROL. AS THEY BRACE THEMSELVES
ALONG THE JOURNEY, THEIR RIDE IS PINNED
TO THE ETERNAL QUESTION:
WHITHER THE WIND?**

There was no doubt that he and the Council of Ten were the *how*. They were supposed to be the wind, guiding and sheltering Venice's most precious vessels.

As *The Words* flowed through him, his thoughts had crystallized. His reasoning became irrefutable; his conclusions, unassailable.

Now, as the moment neared for the council to pronounce judgment, he requested the chairman's permission to address the panel. He was the senior senator on the council, one of the most respected minds in the service of the Venetian government. Accordingly, the chamber grew still in anticipation.

Antonio Elonetti rose from his seat and began. "My fellow council members, before you hear my thoughts on the matter at hand, I ask that you consider our role in the evolution of this republic.

"Are we but stiff-necked arbiters, frozen in a dead-straight stare at the matter before us, unable to see to its left or right? As the tide of time carves its way through our beloved Venice, constantly changing the world around us, must its passage have no effect on our rulings?

"I need not remind you, my dear colleagues, that our great city-state now fights for its very survival. And I submit"—his voice rose—"that this is no day to surrender. Rather, it is ever more urgent that we take firm hold of the direction of this republic, lest its remnants"—he slammed his fist on the table—"crumble down upon us!"

Heads jerked upright. He'd never addressed his colleagues with such force.

"Five hundred years ago, our forebears in the Senate authored legislation that was the first of its kind, allowing a privilege to be issued to an inventor. Yet these last decades have seen our intellectual might shipped out to points west. So, the question we must ask ourselves is: How have we failed our own people? For the creative sparks have not ceased to ignite here in Venice; we've just fallen short in protecting those precious flames."

All eyes were riveted to him. It was time to proffer a solution.

He softened his tone. "But *we* have the power to assure our creative community that their ideas will remain their own. We can start with the case before us. We must find that Gabrieli Triani could not have bartered away a priceless creation of his own mind without a written, signed, and witnessed document, proclaiming his intentions and executed under trustworthy circumstances.

"We would require no less for a transfer of land. How can we allow the transfer of a man's own original thoughts, and all their infinite value, on the mere testimony of an interested party?"

As he concluded, a majority of the council nodded in agreement, the faint glow of enlightenment revealed on their faces.

Ten months later, on a frigid February afternoon, Antonio Elonetti shivered as he ascended the stairs to Piombi prison, at the top of the east wing of the Doge's Palace. Its infamous lead roof kept the cells blistering in summer and freezing in winter. He'd made this trip several times per week since the trial; each time, it brought him back to what happened following his final argument.

As the chairman had called the matter to vote, numerous council members nodded subtly at Senator de Conti. Despite each term of service on the council being limited to twelve months, these patricians had spent their lives together: first as schoolmates, later as junior senators, and finally, in year upon year of joint service to the community. Acquitting Gabrieli Triani meant rejecting one of their own.

Elonetti approached the dank, gloomy prison cell where Gabrieli huddled in a corner, wrapped in a blanket. He'd come so regularly to see the boy partly from a sense of guilt. But there was also something about Gabrieli, a spark that wouldn't fade, despite, as the boy had put it, "the winds always being against him." That spark was something Antonio Elonetti fondly recalled in his own son, who had been lost at sea three years before. As he'd talked with Gabrieli, whether about the political issues of the day or their favorite colors through blown glass, a bond had taken hold: the father missing his son with the son missing his father.

"I've met a friend of yours," Elonetti said. "Her name is Sofia."

Gabrieli's smile went sour. "She's no friend of mine." He shuddered. "She delivered me to de Conti. I was so naive; I thought she actually cared." His eyes moistened. "She reached for my heart on the way to my wallet."

Elonetti held up a small package. "Are you so certain of her motives? She asked that I give you this."

Gabrieli took the package and tossed it under his cot. "Perhaps I'll open it later."

They talked for a while until Elonetti announced, "I'll be back tomorrow, midday." He motioned toward the package. "Be sure to open it by then."

The next day, the fourth day of Carnevale, Elonetti arrived clad in an angel's costume. To his delight, Gabrieli had not only opened the package, but was now attired in a handmade burgundy cloak, a pair of dark boots, and a devil's mask.

"We haven't much time," Elonetti said as he glanced up and down the empty hallway. Using a copy of the prison master key for which he'd paid handsomely, he unlocked Gabrieli's cell.

A short time later, Elonetti, now wearing the devil costume, left the cell and snuck over to a window. Out by the docks, he spotted an angel with an odd gait approaching a gondola that bore Elonetti's family crest, the winged Lion of Venice, in ivory, with one of the senator's ancestors astride it, proudly riding that white feline.

The gondola would take Gabrieli to a merchant ship for the trip to France. There, Gabrieli would be met by representatives of Elonetti's cousins, wealthy Parisian businessmen interested in expanding their glassworks production line. The family had already applied for a French privilege, in Gabrieli's name, for his invention.

There was someone waiting for Gabrieli on that gondola: Sofia, who had tracked down Elonetti, suggested the escape plan, and even insisted on providing the costumes.

As the gondola pulled from the docks, a flag at the pier snapped open. The wind had changed.

It was finally with Gabrieli.

The wind had changed for Antonio Elonetti as well. He'd failed with the council this time, but *The Words* would not let go. This was only the beginning.

DEPARTURES

Mark tugged Josh's sleeve and gazed longingly at the empty food tray. "He's got to let us out of here eventually," he whispered. "Right?"

"Sure," Josh answered, as reassuringly as he could. One thing they didn't need was panic. But tell that to his insides.

They were trapped within solid-concrete walls and a bolted steel door, with all communications shut off. It was clear that Mark had finally been correct about something—Professor Harper's intent. By locking their group away, Harper was keeping their discovery from the world.

Agent Kwan sat off in a corner, his eyes panning from the door along each of the walls and then around the ceiling. He appeared to be weighing the next directive on the FBI emergency checklist.

Until a few minutes ago, Josh and Sammi had been in charge of this research team, with Mark serving as technical support and Agent Kwan as security. But now, their think tank having morphed into a potential tomb, all eyes had shifted to Kwan.

Just as Josh opened his mouth to ask Kwan about their next move, he heard a faint scraping of metal. It sounded like the outside bolt on the steel door.

Hugging the wall, inching forward, Kwan reached under his shirt, drew his gun, and trained the weapon on the doorway. He motioned for everyone else to back away.

The door slowly creaked open.

Professor Harper leaned into the door as he entered, his arms hanging at his sides. His eyes were eerily still. A moment later, he slid toward the floor.

The huge redhead emerged from behind him with a gun, and fired.

Kwan screamed before collapsing.

Waving the gun at the three of them left standing, the murderer stepped over the dead professor into the room. He took a quick glance down at the closest desk and then stared. Josh knew what would be staring back at him from the printout of the newspaper:

Industrialist George Othniel to Marry Judge Deborah Fenton

The man grabbed the paper with his free hand and faced them. His freckled face, framed by a heavy brow and orangey mullet, split open in a flash of teeth. He aimed his gun at Josh's heart.

"Noooo!" Sammi yelled as the gunshot went off.

There was a high-pitched squeal of metal. Josh's hands went to his chest, but he felt nothing. Had his body gone numb that fast? The man spun and raced from the room. Agent Kwan sat up slowly, a trace of smoke seeping from his gun and blood oozing from his shoulder. His eyes flashed to the steel door; Josh's followed.

There was a bullet-hole-sized dent right next to where the assassin had been standing. Dazed and wounded, Kwan had just missed.

Sammi looked from Kwan to the professor. She stammered, "I-I-I'll go call an ambulance."

"No . . . we . . . don't have time." Kwan grabbed his shoulder and grimaced. "I have to . . . go after him." He straightened and headed for the door.

"What are *we* supposed to do?" Josh asked.

"Stay here!" Kwan barked.

"Wait!" Sammi pleaded. "How will we know if you're okay? If everything's okay?"

Kwan winced as he pulled a card from his wallet. "It's got the direct number to my team in the New York office."

As Kwan left, Sammi, frozen in place, holding Kwan's card at her side, stared down at Professor Harper's lifeless form. Two people about whom she cared deeply had been murdered this weekend; a third person had died sitting with her at dinner. Josh's own gut was churning. He couldn't imagine what Sammi must've been feeling. But as he stepped toward her, she clenched her jaw and narrowed her eyes.

"We can't just stand here."

"What do you propose we do?" he asked. "We just got a direct order from a federal agent."

"We've got to get out of here. What if Kwan doesn't make it? How does it look that we came here for an appointment with the professor and he ended up dead?"

Not great, particularly if a certain Kendall detective found out. "Been happening to me a lot lately."

"And if Kwan dies, who's going to believe our story? And who's going to stop that maniac from killing Deborah Fenton?"

"Hold on—do we want him stopped?" Mark asked. "After all that stuff you told us about the arrival of the devil's all-powerful emissary, maybe that big dude's doing the world a favor."

"Are you willing to risk humanity's future on a *maybe*?" Sammi replied. "When I brought up all that, I was just voicing my concerns about Professor Harper. About why he never volunteered anything on that theory even though it fell directly within his expertise and even though all the clues were there. And the clues *are* there. But if we take the moderate approach—what I consider the more reasoned interpretation of the Bible—reading its most dramatic passages more as metaphor, then just look at the world around us: terrorism, genocide, a chasm between the haves and the have-nots. A lot of people think the devil's worst work is already happening. The time could be ripe for a savior."

Josh jumped in. "Sammi's right. We've got to stop this guy. I'm not buying the Antichrist crap. Deborah Fenton could be our only shot to turn this screwed-up planet around. How can we let someone kill her?"

A faint smile briefly lightened Sammi's expression. "You sound convinced."

"*You* convinced me. You and someone dear to both of us. Judge Maloch gave his life to protect Deborah Fenton's identity. I don't think he would've done that for Satan. And one more thing."

"What's that?" Sammi asked.

"All that positive *de* accumulated for thousands of years, contributing to all those amazing people. I know some couldn't handle it, but I find it hard to believe a force that positive is about to create a super-powered monster."

"Okay, I'm with you guys," Mark said, nodding. "But how would we know if we're wrong?" He turned to Sammi. "Any clues from your biblical scholars?"

Sammi sighed. "Darkness. If she's actually meant to serve evil, darkness will be in the air. Counterfeit signs will replace authentic ones. We'll need to be there to see it. We should get going."

"What about the professor?" Mark asked.

Josh glanced down at Harper's frozen expression and stifled a shiver. Judge Maloch, Master Zhou, and now Harper. "I'm sure Agent Kwan called this in," he responded. "Probably not a good idea for us to touch him."

Given that Kwan had left with their transportation and they didn't want to be picked up at this address, they walked the half mile back to the main road.

"Just found us three seats one-way to New York." Sammi eyed her phone. "Leaving in a couple hours out of West Palm."

As Josh was about to open his Uber app, Mark pointed. "See that plaza with the Walmart? We need supplies."

"You've got to have a clean pair of boxers in the morning?"

"No, Quark. But in the course of stuffing your brain full of law school mumbo jumbo, you've lost your street smarts. Picture the three of us showing up for a one-way flight to New York with no checked luggage and only your laptop as a carry-on. You want to spend the next six months at the Homeland Security Hilton?"

Ten minutes later, they emerged from the store rolling cheap carry-on bags filled with travel toiletries and underwear.

On the ride to the airport, Sammi tapped Josh's shoulder. "Should we check on Kwan?"

And attract attention? “What if they order us to stay put?”

“He could be bleeding to death.”

Like the FBI would let that happen. “Okay, give me his card. I’ll do it.”

He dialed.

After a brief delay, a woman answered. “FBI, Manhattan. How can we help you?”

“My name is Joshua Sutton. I’ve been working with Agent Henry Kwan, and I need to speak to someone familiar with his present assignment.”

“Yes, he told us to expect your call. Agent Kwan wants you to know he’s fine. All alerts are in place, and the resources are being coordinated for tomorrow, if necessary. Oh, and one more thing—he asked me to thank you and your friends.”

He ended the call and met Sammi’s expectant gaze. “Kwan’s okay. They’ve got alerts out for the maniac, and the bureau’s set for tomorrow if they don’t catch him here.”

“Thank God.”

“They even passed along a ‘thank you’ to the three of us.”

“Nice. I noticed you didn’t say anything about our plans.”

“I figured I was on a roll. Why spoil it?”

Three hours later, having just strapped himself into a middle seat on the plane, with Sammi at the window and Mark on the aisle, Josh felt his phone pulse. It was a text:

> You were due in my office 2 hours ago.
> If you don’t come in voluntarily this
> afternoon, we’ll be glad to escort you.
> Detective Gutierrez

Shit.

The feds were thorough. But they were also predictable. Staying off the main roads, Billy Ray worked his way north out of Palm Beach Gardens.

If the feds were in on this, he was dead meat at the West Palm Beach airport, and likewise, Fort Lauderdale and Miami. Even Orlando, two hours north, or Tampa, three hours west, would be dicey.

Fortunately, previous assignments had turned up some blind spots in the local radar. He called ahead for a charter pilot at Witham Field, the Martin County airport, thirty minutes away in Stuart. He'd used Witham once before. It was one of those sleepy little general aviation facilities scattered around South Florida, an outpost for prop planes and small jets. The operation was barebones and the runways were too short for commercial aircraft. Some charters ran gambling hops to the Bahamas, but from what he'd heard, the only steady money was from lawyers and lobbyists. Flights to Tampa for depositions and to Tallahassee when the legislature was in session were the meat and potatoes of the Witham operation.

With his flight confirmed, he pressed his speed dial.

"Hello, my son," answered the familiar voice. "Where are you?"

"In motion, sir. Got the name you wanted. Even better, got a place and time."

"Tell me."

"Tomorrow morning at eleven, Judge Deborah Fenton marries George Othniel at St. Patrick's Cathedral in New York City."

"She'll be Deborah Othniel!" The Reverend's excitement all but jolted the phone. "The moment is here."

"Sir," Billy Ray asked, "could you kindly get me the phone number of your New York City friend who helped me out the last time I was up there?"

"Surely, my son. May I ask what your plans are?"

So that's how much this mission meant. In all the years, the Reverend had never once asked him how he was going to do his work. Billy Ray laid it out.

As he hung up from his next call, it hit him how glad he was to be leaving South Florida. After winding his way up the coast past stuck-up golf courses, swampy state parks, semi-dead retirement communities, and raggedy strip malls, he finally pulled into the dinky airport. It was a few hangars, some small planes scattered around, and a triangle of short, paved runways hiding behind Florida crabgrass.

He parked, grabbed his bag, and made for the closest hangar, where he found his pilot waiting. Billy Ray told him he was a tomato farmer heading to Tallahassee to lobby state representatives so they'd get the feds off his back about the pesticides he was using.

He *was* heading to Tallahassee to get the feds off his back.

The pilot pointed to the tiny doorway of the plane and said he'd be there in a minute. Feeling like a barrel-shouldered ox about to squeeze through an inner tube, Billy Ray paused at the top of the stairs. Compressing himself, he got inside and took a seat.

He mentally checked off the rest of his itinerary. In Tallahassee, he'd catch a flight to Atlanta for a late connection to Albany in upstate New York. The feds wouldn't be looking at flights from Tallahassee to Atlanta, or Atlanta to Albany. In Albany, he'd catch a few hours of shut-eye. That's all he ever needed, anyway. Then he'd take a wee-hours drive down the New York State Thruway to Manhattan, which would put him in town plenty early.

He patted himself on the back for remembering the New York City contact. Everything had to be in place that evening. By morning, there'd be too many trip wires.

✦

A connecting flight from Zhuhai to Beijing followed by an overnight to New York would have cut things too close. But General Chang had come through again, providing his personal plane to Han for the trip—though not without a further admonition.

"Chee-hwa," the general had said, "be mindful of our last discussion. This must be quick, clean, and untraceable."

"I assure you, General," he'd asserted, "everything is in order."

Now, as the Chinese military jet hurtled across a darkening horizon, he convinced himself again that his statement was true. The general's own highly trained professional was on this and had proven in Florida that he was up to the task. And this was New York City; the man lived there. He knew the territory.

Han had been to New York only once, back in prep school, with his old friend Kyle. A friendship he'd now incinerated. Their last phone call had made that clear. Kyle's crack about Redevelopment Day still lingered. Han hadn't thought about that career-defining event in quite some time . . .

Many years back, after his escort services had secured exclusive arrangements with every elite hotel in Zhuhai, his competitors repurposed part of a condemned slum into a world-class resort; they even stole some of his top girls. But, in their rush to build, they'd not obtained permits.

Shortly after its grand opening, twenty huge Chinese army tanks, delivered by General Chang, flattened that slum, resort and all, sparing no structure or person.

The local municipal administration, valuing the lives of prostitutes even less than the condemned land, and having been well attended to by Han's personnel, issued an official letter of appreciation to Han Chee-hwa for having cleared out this "pox" on the community. The city newspaper dubbed the event "Redevelopment Day."

And so he'd answered the question his late uncle had posed for those determined to sustain their pinnacles of wealth and power: "How ruthless am I willing to be?"

He'd answer it again tomorrow.

For tomorrow would be Falun Dafa's death knell. And he, Han Chee-hwa, who had twice risen from the gutter, would be China's hero. It was *his* network that put this together. There was no way he was going to miss the big event.

His old friend Kyle's angry dig had actually been right on target. This was to be the ultimate "Redevelopment Day."

Home. As Sammi gazed down from thirty-five thousand feet, tracing the Eastern Seaboard's juts and hollows, her thoughts slipped forward to the place that, regardless of where she lived, would always be home: New York City. Wasn't it also home to the world? What city had a greater impact? A greater conglomerate of souls? Of religions? What city was more deeply enmeshed in every triumph and tragedy, every family, everywhere?

Somewhere in that city, prior to her imminent wedding, what was Deborah Fenton—soon to be Othniel—doing? What was she thinking? And, of far more importance per Judge Maloch, what had this judge *seen*?

Suddenly Sammi recalled, rising from her mists of dream memories, that among the city's countless legacies lay a tiny, desperate battlefield from the Middle East, born of a father's incalculable grief . . .

THE ANGUISH OF SALVATION

The two letters lay side by side on the coffee table in front of Deborah Fenton, each written by the same man, the handwriting and English far shakier in the first. But there was no dilution in the anguish. The man's suffering had been greater than any parent should have to endure.

✦

Yaron Levy counted himself a good husband and a good father. Being one of the most respected thoracic surgeons in Tel Aviv certainly brought him satisfaction, but nothing like the pride he had in his marriage and his two children.

His son, Arik, was the adventurer in the family. At age seventeen, Arik received a military deferment and an opportunity to intern for a year at the United Nations while attending Columbia University in New York City.

Arik called often to update the family on his explorations. He devoured Manhattan's museums—from the T. rex at the Museum of Natural History to van Gogh's *The Starry Night* at MOMA—jogged in Central Park, feasted in Little Italy and Chinatown, and walked the Brooklyn Bridge. On weekends, his fellow students and interns dipped him in the lavish suburbia of the Hamptons and led him on rustic adventures upstate.

One Sunday, two months after Arik had left for America, as Yaron was chatting with his wife, Tova, and daughter, Danit, at the kitchen table, enjoying their midday meal, the phone rang and Tova answered it. After listening intently for ten seconds, she screamed, "No! No! Noooooooo!"

She dissolved into reeling sobs and collapsed. Yaron leaped from his chair and barely caught her before her head hit the tile floor.

While Yaron clung to his wife, fifteen-year-old Danit picked up the dangling receiver and, unsure what to do, placed it at her father's ear. With great effort he tried to listen, but, like his wife, he lost himself to hysteria. And so, seemingly steadied more by shock than composure, Danit pulled back the phone and dutifully jotted down the pertinent information.

The next morning, the three of them were on a jet to New York City.

Shortly after landing, Yaron learned the details from the police. Arik and two other UN interns had been upstate in the Catskills. Hours before dawn on Sunday morning, as they headed home on a narrow, winding mountain road, a drunk driver barreling north in his pickup truck swung wide out of his lane as he approached their car. Arik's friend who was driving swerved to avoid the pickup, but the car hit a patch of ice and spun out of control. The truck smashed head-on into their front passenger door, crushing it in on Arik. All involved were rushed by ambulance to the nearest hospital. Arik's friends and the drunk driver—who was later arrested—all had relatively minor injuries, but Arik had suffered massive internal damage. Within an hour after he arrived at the hospital, he was pronounced dead.

Devastated, Yaron arranged to fly Arik's body home to Israel for burial. Before Yaron and his wife and daughter left the hospital, however, an administrator pulled him aside. Since Arik's duties as a UN intern had included chauffeuring Israeli representatives around the city, the man explained, he'd been encouraged to obtain a New York driver's license. Because on the application he'd checked "Yes" in the box that read ORGAN DONOR, the hospital had removed Arik's left kidney. His injuries from the crash had left no other suitable organs.

✦

From the King David Lounge of Tel Aviv's Ben Gurion Airport, the Arab banker eyed the smooth touchdown of the jumbo jet from New York. He prayed the plane would land as softly upon its return to the United States. In the seat next to him, curled uncomfortably in a fetal position, his twenty-two-year-old son was gravely ill.

✦

Early on the morning of Arik's funeral, Yaron Levy switched on the lamp at the end of the living room sofa and sat down with his daily *Haaretz*, hoping its articles might briefly tug his mind from his anguish. A page-three headline mentioned a notorious Palestinian businessman he had once met. The man was reputedly a financier for the Palestinian Islamic Jihad, a terror group responsible for untold deaths of innocent Israelis.

Yaron was about to flip past the story when he took in the entire headline:

Son of Muhammad Arani Flown to US for Kidney Transplant

Paralyzed, Yaron forced himself through the rest of the article:

Hassan Arani, son of prominent Palestinian banker Muhammad Arani, was flown yesterday to the United States for a kidney transplant. The younger Arani suffers from lupus, a disease of the autoimmune system, which damaged his kidneys when he was an adolescent. Complications from years of dialysis have contributed to a further decline in his health.

The transplant procedure is to be performed at Memorial Sloan Kettering Cancer Center in New York City. The surgery is expected to take place in the next several days.

The facts not in dispute, the matter was to be heard solely on briefs. Judge Deborah Fenton, of the New York State Supreme Court Civil Trial Division, had been advised by medical experts that a delay of even two or three days could be life-threatening to the proposed transplant recipient.

Pacing her chambers, feeling the weight of the hardbound case law crammed into the surrounding bookcases, she replayed the highlights of the submitted briefs and affidavits—the pertinent facts already committed to memory: The decedent had clearly checked off "Yes" in the organ donor box on his driver's license application. By statute, New York, like most other states in the country, allowed minors to be bound by their signed contracts at the age of eighteen. Arik Levy, however, had been only seventeen. In the place for parental consent on the application, he had signed his father's name.

Thus, the initial analysis was easy. Since Arik was seventeen, New York State technically had no right to remove his kidney for transplant purposes. The first problem, however, was that the state had done no wrong. The doctors at the hospital, acting under statutorily mandated procedures, and medically mandated time constraints, had reasonably relied on what purported to be a validly executed parental consent for organ donation.

The second problem was that the kidney had already been removed from the body, and the body had already been buried in Israel.

The third and most troubling problem of all was that another young man was likely to die in the next several days if he did not receive that particular kidney.

She leaned over the credenza behind her desk; the pleadings were splayed across the surface. Staring down at the plaintiff's brief, she ran her index finger under each line of the case caption:

YARON LEVY, INDIVIDUALLY, AS NATURAL GUARDIAN, AND AS EXECUTOR OF THE ESTATE OF ARIK LEVY, A DECEASED MINOR,

Plaintiff,

vs.

THE STATE OF NEW YORK and MEMORIAL SLOAN KETTERING CANCER CENTER,

Defendants.

The judge shook her head. She knew the real case was *Levy v. Arani*.

Born and raised in Brooklyn, Deborah Fenton had close Jewish friends. And she'd had a wonderful Palestinian law clerk two years ago. She was well versed in the Israeli–Palestinian conflict: its horrors, the apartheid versus security-from-terrorism arguments, the settlements issue, two states or one, the claimed right of return, theocracy versus democracy. But she was not about to let emotion, politics, favoritism, or religion sway her judgment. She would rule based on the mandates of applicable law. The hard part, whichever way her decision went, was the pain it was sure to inflict on one family or the other.

Dropping into her desk chair, she gazed up at her walls of precedent, wondering where ultimate guidance might come from. Her reverie was broken by a knock at the door.

Her law clerk entered. "Your Honor, the bailiff just brought this up."

It was an express mail envelope—from Israel.

As the law clerk exited, Judge Fenton sliced it open. Inside, a handwritten letter was addressed to "The Esteemed Trial Judge, Devorah Fenton." It read:

Dear Ms. Judge:

In advance I apologize for my English, but I must send you this most urgently, there being time not for review.

Being a medical doctor, I am very knowing that the matter that rests before you is concerning more than just legal cases. However, I cannot sit here with my wife and daughter, and our many other family, all in the shiva (our mourning), and look anymore on their faces, knowing what we have already lost, without saying to you what is in my heart.

We live here in Israel not in a very large country protected by great seas, but in a small room, with cracks in the walls. We live each day with the knowing of many other countries surrounding our borders, each leaning to push our cracked walls in onto us. We are also knowing, that we have few friends in our struggle only to survive.

Due to the vigilance of our government and insufficient number military, we keep daily the walls from falling. But our greatest horror is from the devils that slip through the cracks.

These devils come not as large, bright red scary men with horns and tails that are so easy to recognize. They come, instead, as women and beggars. They come as businessmen. Now, more and more, they come as children.

On any one morning, we may walk our young one to the school bus, or maybe by car take our mother to the market. We know, just as we bring them to these places, that the devil has again slipped through the cracks. But we never know to where he is going. So, every of our days, our choice is to either be prisoner in our own home or to live a little our lives, hoping today is not the one the devil has picked to come to <u>this</u> market. Hoping <u>this</u> is not the same school bus the devil is riding.

Please understand. We are never wishing for such things to happen to another bus of schoolchildren or to another busy market. But we are knowing it will. So our choice is only to pray: "Not today, not to <u>my</u> child, not to <u>my</u> mother."

In most recent time, my family has its own great horror. But this, not from the devil that slips through the cracks.

This week, my son Arik, a very good boy 17 years aged only, has been from us taken. He was in your great country, at university (Columbia). He was also part-time working for the United Nations. On weekend holiday, the car with him and his friends was crashed by a drunken driver.

I am not knowing if you are a parent. But I can tell you, even from only these few days, that I feel my life never again can be the one it was. When can I wake up and not think of what my Arik should be doing today? When can I stop my thinking of how he will find his dreams? Of why he can never have chances to find his own love? Have his own family? Hold his own babies in his arms?

How does a father live for even one day longer than his son? From now, I must live this <u>every</u> day!

But I write to you not so much to share you my burden. It is because of the devils, I write.

In the morning the day we are placing our Arik in the cemetery, from what I am reading in the newspaper, I am learning that the son of Muhammad Arani comes to New York to receive Arik's kidney.

I again ask that you understand. My objection is not because this is a Palestinian. I am very knowing how the Palestinians suffer. My wish is not to cause them further pain. And, as I earlier write, I am a medical doctor. If the kidney from my son can help another to live, this I am in favor for.

But this person's father is a banker who raises the money for the worst terror makers of the Hamas. Those who lie and cheat their own poor. Who tell fairy stories to the little children. Who promise those with nothing that they will find great treasures in the world that comes after life.

The terror makers teach these poor ones to become the devils that slip through the cracks. This army-of-no-hope takes with it many of our children and our mothers each year.

And so, if you are allowing the kidney of my son to be used in this Hassan Arani, you are, for sure, giving the power to the devil.

But please I beg you to see, to completely know, <u>all</u> that this devil is doing. It is his work that takes down <u>two</u> worlds, that destroys the chances for there to ever be peace in this region. For this devil destroys both Palestinian and Jew. He most surely steals their hopes as he does our dreams.

And so, just as I am knowing that my dear Arik's kidney can now do him no longer good, I am hoping you to see how much the harm this kidney can bring.

I pray you are deciding well.

May God Bless You,
Yaron Levy

Late into that evening twenty years ago, on which she had received Dr. Levy's letter, Deborah Fenton was again patrolling her chambers, deep in thought, occasionally glaring at an untouched dinner salad that sat, intrusively, at the corner of her desk. She was wrestling with the concept of property rights versus personal rights.

There was nothing more personal than someone's own body parts. And yet she knew that a body part, removed under legitimate circumstances, became by legal definition a fungible item, covered, like a banana or a television set, by the Uniform Commercial Code. It was now subject to being part of a commercial transaction. Any hospital could buy it for a negotiated price from the state-sanctioned organ depository.

But how could this be? How could law have sauntered so far down the halls of logic that it lost sight of our very essence as human beings? Weren't we more than a collection of interchangeable parts?

Her frustration mounting, she grabbed the offending salad and angrily thrust it in the trash. She needed to calm herself. Dropping to the floor in a corner of the room, she crossed her legs, let her arms hang freely at her sides, sucked in a controlled breath, and let it go. Then another . . . and another . . . deep and slow . . . smooth and steady. She relaxed and meditated. Her mind cleared.

As she stood and refocused, something caught her eye just past the corner of her desk. A streetlight's beam, diffused by the leaves of a wind-swept tree, flickered through the window, tossing shadow-flames at the base of the wall.

And then, incredibly, *The Words* emerged.

Wisps at first, they rose and mushroomed to cumulus, filling the room. The clouds were wrapped in phrases: instructions, explanations, questions, flowing in and out of each other, multiplying at blinding speed. The phrases took voice: plaintive queries and pleas for action. The voices were male and female, adult and adolescent, amassing, rising.

The Words overpowered her. Her every neuron was stressed to its limits. With what meager strength she could muster, she begged for mercy.

And then realized she didn't need to.

For this was no assault; it occurred to her all at once that these strange messages were simply reaching out. Sure, it was more a bludgeoning than an intervention, but perhaps that was only because they had so much to convey.

The moment she arrived at this notion, *The Words* transformed; they swam deep inside her in tender undertones, their messages clear, enlightening, and purifying, caressing her beliefs in personal rights, while soothing her fears of the choice ahead.

Yet she could still feel the agony of one father's heartbreaking loss, still hear his impassioned pleas, and she could still picture the other father watching his son wither away. She still knew how devastating her decision would be to one or the other, still had to face her own anguish over that call. But then, somehow, *The Words* stepped in again and flooded her thoughts, eerily in her own voice, first, with questions and answers:

WHY MUST THE MOST VALUABLE LESSONS BE THE MOST PAINFUL? DO WE REQUIRE THAT KIND OF HURT TO UNDERSTAND LIFE'S DEEPEST MESSAGES? OR PERHAPS, LIKE THE ILLUSORY BORDER THAT SEPARATES MADNESS

FROM GENIUS, THERE IS AN INTANGIBLE LINE BETWEEN PAIN AND PERCEPTION. WHAT IF OUR MINDS HOUSE UNTAPPED VAULTS OF LIMITLESS KNOWLEDGE, CREATIVITY, COMPASSION, AND REASONING, AND THE ONLY WAY TO OPEN THESE DOORS IS THROUGH UNBEARABLE AGONY? WHY IS IT THAT SO MANY OF OUR MOST GIFTED PAINTERS, MUSICIANS, ACTIVISTS, AND SCIENTISTS SUFFERED DAUNTING EMOTIONAL WOUNDS ON THE ROAD TO EXPLODING PREVIOUSLY SUFFOCATING BARRIERS?

And, last, with one hopeful query:

IF OUR GREATEST LEAPS MUST BE NOURISHED BY OUR DEEPEST TRAUMAS, WHAT MIRACLES LIE IN WAIT AS THE PRODUCT OF HEARTACHE?

After what felt like hours, but had been mere minutes, *The Words* marched on. Deborah Fenton collapsed, exhausted, into her desk chair.

Her quest for answers sated, physical hunger at last took hold; she was famished. As the punished dinner salad taunted her from the wastebasket, she got up, grabbed her jacket, flicked off the light, and headed for home, a weary smile creasing her lips. It was not the food waiting in her apartment's refrigerator that sparked this moment of joy; it was imagining the wondrous dreams that surely awaited her night's sleep.

✦

Deborah Fenton reached toward the coffee table for the silver antique teapot that sat sentinel to the two letters from Israel. After she refilled her cup of morning matcha, she eyed the letters and thought back to that first time, when *The Words* had startled and comforted, educated and inspired. Then, as later, they broadened her vision and impelled her to rule in ways immensely more far-reaching.

Over the years, *The Words* had set her on many wonderful paths. But *The Words* were wayward winds, coming and going as they pleased. They seemed not to be there for *her*, but she for *them*—a conviction that deepened with time.

On a few occasions, when she had arrived at peak relaxation of mind and body in her lotus position, she reached some new level. It was a place so supremely tranquil that the last traces of static were wiped away.

It was then *The Words* burned in a new light.

There was no pain or exertion, as there had been at times in the past. Instead, with her focus pure, *The Words* burned not as an out-of-control blaze, but as beacons.

In those moments, she could separate and categorize them. And with this new clarity, she saw that *The Words* were far more than the messages at the surface. The messages led to passageways, along which hung keys to vaults guarding vast collections of related wisdom.

The Words, the passageways, the keys, the vaults of accumulated knowledge, these had somehow been formed from the accrued insight of countless minds that had come before—minds and spirits that had connected with *The Words* and nourished them. So, *this* was how mankind took its great leaps. Access to the appropriate portals of this comprehensive library of human thought, reasoning, and experience had helped lay the groundwork for the future.

Though the totality of *The Words* apparently went far beyond human rights into every area of human endeavor, her passion for human rights is what must have opened a crack in her mind's eye, allowing her to connect with that subdivision of *The Words*. If she were destined to forge a path as human rights crusader, she hoped *The Words* would continue to guide her.

Without destroying her.

For their power was immense, and they arrived so often in explosive bursts—roaring blazes she might briefly calm. She worried what would result with undiluted exposure, where the tipping point might be.

Yet, despite her fears, she'd long ago accepted her relationship with *The Words*. Regardless of their transitory and volatile nature, she had no doubt that their influence—or, perhaps more accurately, their inspiration—had instilled her actions with a greater good.

In the Levy case, she'd awoken the next morning with her entire ruling in her head. It boiled down to a single principle: "The greatest property right of all is life."

And so, she had decided that the dignity of prior life and the potential threat to future lives could stake no claim equal to the saving of one life in the present.

Hassan Arani received Arik Levy's kidney.

The second letter had arrived five years after the first, this time as Deborah Fenton lunched in her chambers on a gray, rainy afternoon. Her bailiff had just brought in the mail. Having spent the morning refereeing a custody war—watching a once-loving couple treat their children as chattel—she'd welcomed the distraction, thumbing through the envelopes while she picked at a bowl of quinoa and sautéed vegetables. As sporadic raindrops clattered against the window, her mind slipped to a custody battle from years before, where the prize was not children, but a vital organ.

And then, peering up at her from the pile of correspondence, she spied an envelope with nothing exceptional about its appearance, until she noticed the country and name on the return address: Israel . . . Yaron Levy.

She dropped her fork. Why would he write her again after all this time? Had his bitterness about her decision, harbored for five long years as he mourned his son, finally boiled over? Or, heaven forbid, had Hassan Arani committed some grievous act of terror?

Her impulse had been to toss the letter in her wastebasket—better yet, to run it through the shredder. But she couldn't. Instead, with a queasy sense of foreboding, she sliced it open.

It was handwritten, just as the first. This was an old-fashioned man who clearly preferred to put his personal touch to his work, as he did with his surgeon's scalpel. This time, however, the command of the English language was markedly improved.

The letter read:

Dear Judge Fenton:

I write to you today so that I can be sure you have heard the rest of the story you helped make. Despite my personal plea to you five years ago, you allowed my son's kidney to be used to save the life of the son of a terrorist. In the years since, the devils have continued. One month ago, my daughter Danit, my only living child, who had just celebrated her twentieth birthday, was out at a nightclub with her friends. There were over two hundred Israeli youths there, dancing and having fun. It was the kind of evening in which an Israeli can perhaps forget, for but a short couple of hours, about the devils who slip through the cracks.

Into that crowded nightclub came a Palestinian man. You may remember his name: Hassan Arani. He was in the company of five others from the group he commands.

Without warning, in the middle of a loud musical number, while the dance floor was packed with young Israelis, Arani and his men took control of a corner of the room. Before anyone realized what was happening, his lieutenants had pinned down one of the dancers, four of them holding the young girl's arms and legs, while the fifth tied a gag tight around her mouth.

Arani stood over her. He knelt down and unbuttoned her blouse. Then he took a small blade out of his pocket and, aiming it carefully, plunged it down three times.

His men lifted the girl's body to their shoulders as the music faded. Arani stood tall and let out a scream. He was holding his right hand high up. In it, he held a detonator.

The place fell into chaos. Israeli youths ran in every direction.

Some dived behind furniture. Others thought about rushing the Palestinians.

But none of their actions mattered. Nothing the young Israelis did could change the outcome of that evening for any of them.

The bomb that was brought into that club was one of the most powerful a Palestinian had ever carried into Israel. Hassan Arani knew that. He also knew that on this evening he wanted to make one of the loudest statements ever made in this war of terror.

So he struck, with precise information and tactical efficiency.

As the Israelis panicked, he waved the detonator high over his head. Then he brought it to his lips and kissed it.

He had carefully cut it off the suicide bomber who had been sent to destroy the club and everyone in it. He screamed again in celebration. Then he and his men handed the girl over to the Israeli police.

The news spread like wildfire on both sides of the fence. To us Israelis, this is a bellwether of true hope. To the Palestinians it is a gift far greater. Now, when the devil makers approach an innocent, the recruit has already heard the stories of the new resistance. Offers of afterlife rewards ring hollow against the likely shame of failure and imprisonment.

The Palestinian poor are being dissuaded, for the first time, from false hope. Though the bombast and frightful actions of politicians on both sides, whose minds are tethered to the past, continue to fortify the walls between us, the word on the street is that more and more of our downtrodden neighbors are starting to be willing to work peacefully toward real solutions, with Hassan Arani leading the way.

Incidentally, my dear daughter Danit, who helped me write this letter, was a few steps away from the suicide bomber when Mr. Arani disarmed the girl.

May God Continue to Bless You,
Yaron Levy

Deborah Fenton leaned forward and set down her teacup on the coffee table. Tears flooded her eyes as she gently picked up the two letters—each now dog-eared and wrinkled from endless readings—and held them to her chest. No wonder, that even on this, the morning of her wedding day, she needed to be in their presence. Several decades had passed since the Levy case, with the Israeli–Palestinian situation unfortunately rising to even greater, unthinkable horrors. But the Levy case had marked her forever. Hope, it reminded her, was often but a tiny seed crushed under an avalanche of hate; and yet, starved of nutrients, it could somehow birth a root, wind its way to the surface, and grab a foothold on the future. These two letters and *The Words* had fashioned an unbreakable bond with her soul. The man who was about to take her hand was getting a woman who had evolved beyond her wildest imaginings.

ARRIVAL

"Totally unnecessary, Quark."

As they passed over the Fifty-Ninth Street Bridge with the windows of Manhattan's infinite skyline ablaze in morning sun, Josh didn't need to look in the back seat to know Mark's arms were out of control.

He was still complaining about Josh insisting on staking out the scene an hour before the wedding. Rather than blow their budget, the three of them had shared a cheap motel room near LaGuardia Airport, but Josh wanted to make sure they got into Manhattan by 10:00 a.m. So they'd gotten up at eight thirty—far too close to the crack of dawn, in Mark's view—grabbed some bagels and cream cheese to take along for breakfast, and caught an Uber. They'd been assured that the FBI would be fully prepared, but nerves had told Josh that he needed to see it all in place.

"Sorry," Josh parried, "didn't realize your beauty sleep was more crucial than saving the world."

Through his bagel, Mark huffed an unintelligible response.

Ten minutes later, their ride dropped them off on Fifth Avenue across from the entrance to St. Patrick's Cathedral. This striking remnant of Civil War–era New York, with its neo-Gothic white marble spires and intricately patterned windows, stood in sharp contrast to the surrounding forest of modern office towers.

Josh turned and eyed the office building behind him. Guarding the entrance was an immense bronze statue of Atlas holding up the world. Sort of the way he felt at the moment.

"He's planning to shoot her from this rooftop."

"And you know this how?" Mark asked.

"He wouldn't shoot from the street—too easy to get caught. Look around. We're surrounded by skyscrapers with windows that don't open and roofs that are way too high. This building's only six stories." He pointed up at the roofline and across at St. Patrick's. "He's got a perfect angle to the front doors of the church."

"I don't think so," Sammi said.

"Why?" Josh asked.

"Wouldn't the sound of a gunshot echo off all these tall buildings?"

"I guess."

"Which would make it hard to tell where the shot came from."

"So?" Mark asked.

"So, if echoes make it hard to locate the shooter, why shoot from an obvious place, directly across the street on a low roof? Wouldn't that be one of the first places the police would look?" Sammi pointed at the next building south, just across Fiftieth Street. "That building's also six stories high, with a clear, diagonal view of the cathedral doors. That's got to be just as good a location for a shooter, but not one people would look at right away."

Josh smiled. "I stand corrected. Can't argue with that logic. I bet the FBI has that covered."

They crossed Fiftieth Street. The building Sammi had identified was part of Rockefeller Plaza, which sat kitty-corner across Fifth Avenue from St. Patrick's Cathedral.

The three of them passed the front of the building and turned right into the plaza. Its long stretch of decorative planters separated two pedestrian walkways that were bordered by glass retail storefronts at the foot of six-story office buildings. The walkways were bustling.

Josh glanced around. "An awful lot of people."

"Memorial Day Weekend is the official start of the summer tourist season," Sammi said.

"Yeah." He scanned again. "But I don't see a single cop."

As Han walked past St. Patrick's Cathedral, the old white-marble church seemed an unappreciated elder, all but ignored amid the whirl of surrounding office-tower youths.

Not for long.

He turned into Rockefeller Plaza. Families snacked on benches surrounding its colorful flower boxes and fountains adorned with playful bronze statuettes. Smiling children held bags from the LEGO store and tour groups gathered in circles, all blissfully unaware that their futures were about to be radically changed.

It was early yet. He found an open bench, sipped at his coffee, and unfolded his *New York Times*. Across the way, two young men and a woman huddled at a storefront, looking around. One of the men, the thinner one, seemed somewhat perturbed.

Han went back to his paper. His goal was to blend in. Later, he'd walk unhurriedly to the front of the plaza and adopt an admiring vantage point of St. Patrick's. For the moment, he'd wait in the background.

Until *his* moment.

Sammi shrugged. "Maybe the FBI doesn't want to scare this guy off with a lot of uniforms. Wouldn't they want to catch him in the act?"

"So, we're surrounded by undercover federal agents?"

Mark didn't miss the opportunity. "You bet we are. Couldn't be this many people in New York who *chose* to get up this early on a holiday."

"Okay, Spaceman, leave the phaser on stun."

They sat down on a bench. Josh silently eyed passersby. Most were obvious tourists, gawking at everything—New Yorkers didn't gawk; they stared straight ahead and sliced their way through the hordes. Workers in the retail stores readied display windows. Maintenance men swept detritus from the edges of nearby buildings as the smell of warming hot dogs from a corner Sabrett stand wafted in. Taxis screeched to the curb. Hand trucks full of supplies rolled through doorways. A FedEx delivery man carried a stack of packages.

An *extremely large* FedEx delivery man.

Josh nudged Sammi and motioned with his head. Her eyes followed. "Oh my God. Is that him?"

"Who?" Mark asked, glancing around.

"Him," Josh said softly, pointing. "The giant with the FedEx shirt that looks five sizes too small."

Josh got up and signaled the others to do likewise, while putting his index finger over his lips. He led them into the camouflage of a tour group.

As a guide expounded on the history of Rockefeller Plaza, Josh's eyes stayed glued to the FedEx man. There was no mistaking his animal-like gait, no forgetting his deadly capabilities.

The man pulled out his cell phone and uttered a few words into it. He turned right, toward the entryway of the office tower. Instead of entering, he stopped at what appeared to be an emergency exit door and waited.

The exit door swung out. The man stepped inside, and the door began to close behind him.

Josh broke from the crowd in a frantic sprint. He dodged an older couple and raced around another tour group. The door was closing fast. A woman with a stroller stepped in front of him; he leaped sideways and swerved past. As the door reached the frame, he lunged and caught the handle just before it latched.

From behind him, Sammi rasped, "Don't go in there!"

He had no intention of doing so. He put his ear next to the tiny slit of opening that remained and waved to the others to keep their voices down as he listened to the footsteps climbing the stairs. He counted out quietly: "two . . . three . . . four . . . That's it. Four." He let the door close.

"The landings?" Sammi guessed.

"Exactly. He's on the fourth floor."

He looked around. No one was coming toward them. No one was entering the building. Had he been the only one who'd spotted the guy?

He spun back to Sammi. "Where the hell is the FBI?"

It had been a long night. Though the bullet had been removed and the wound had been stitched up hours ago, his shoulder still burned.

Playing FBI Agent Henry Kwan had gotten Steven Lee crucial information; one troubling detail, however, still needed resolving. As he marched toward Rockefeller Plaza, he appeared to be casually observing his fellow pedestrians, but he was actually looking for one man, and one man only. Was Jackson in range? There was no way he was letting that man interfere with this chance to steer the tides of history.

Josh pulled out his cell phone and dialed.

After a pause, he heard, "FBI, Manhattan. How can we help you?" It was the same female voice from yesterday.

"It's Joshua Sutton. Can I speak to Agent Kwan? I'm in New York, and I have urgent information."

"You're in New York?" The woman hesitated. "What's the information?"

"I just spotted the man Agent Kwan's looking for. He's on the fourth floor of the six-story office building on the north side of Rockefeller Plaza."

"I'll let Agent Kwan know right away."

He had to ask. "Where are your people?"

Another hesitation. "We've got it covered. Now get out of there before you screw it all up."

"What did she say?" Sammi asked as he ended the call.

"That they've got it covered. Oh, and also, 'Get out of there before you screw it all up.' That's twice the FBI's given us a direct order to stay away."

Sammi's jaw hardened. "I'm not leaving."

"Me either. Mark?"

Mark adjusted his glasses. "I just hope they put us on the same cell block."

✦

When they stepped out of the stairwell, Billy Ray's escort led him to a door marked Suite 414. The man pulled the door open, waved Billy Ray forward, and said, "He's waiting for you inside."

"Who's waiting?"

"You'll find out shortly." The man headed for the elevator.

Billy Ray tracked the guy for a moment, then shrugged and entered the room. It was a small, barely furnished reception area with an office next to it. Empty desktops, a couple of chairs, and nothing on the walls. The place was clearly abandoned except for a familiar figure sitting on a chair by the window.

Billy Ray tossed down his packages, unable to hide his concern. "Reverend Fredericks, you shouldn't be here."

"I knew that was how you'd feel, my son. You've always been so protective of me. That's why I didn't tell you yesterday I'd decided to join you."

"But, Reverend, this situation is highly dangerous. If anything went wrong . . . you're risking your position, all your good work. I'd never forgive myself."

"You're charged with no such burden, my son. The decision is mine alone. I'm quite sure I was meant to be here for this moment. We're in this together for the good of generations to come. In this task we're each but humble servants of the Lord."

"I understand, sir. And your presence gives me strength, as always. My only concern is for you."

"Duly noted, my son. But remember, I'm here merely as a witness to history. *You're* the sacred arm of our savior. Our people's destiny flows through *your* hands. It is *I* who should be concerned for *you*."

✦

This was getting ridiculous. Josh checked his phone—it was after eleven thirty already. How much longer until the newlyweds paraded out of the church into the open?

Earlier, the three of them had walked out to Fifth Avenue and watched wedding guests being dropped off at St. Patrick's. When the bride and groom arrived, Sammi had tugged Josh's sleeve and pointed to the stretch limousine that delivered them.

"It's jet black," she'd whispered.

"Aren't most limos?" he'd replied.

"I guess. But there's also *that*." She'd pointed skyward. The morning sky had been uncommonly blue and clear. But, as the wedding party arrived, two charcoal clouds appeared, lurking ominously overhead.

Now, high above Rockefeller Plaza, the skies were growing darker by the minute.

Josh shot up off the bench and threw his hands up. "We told them he's in the building. You'd think they would've sent in the cavalry and be guarding the doors. I haven't seen one person go in since I called. And do you see anyone even looking at the entrance? Where's the damn FBI?!"

"What if there's *no* FBI?" Mark interjected. "I mean, what if Kwan is bogus?"

"Why would you say that?" Sammi asked.

He tugged at his glasses. "I'm somewhat familiar with FBI procedures. I've studied them."

Josh shook his head. "Because they arrested you once?"

"They didn't arrest me." His fingers were wagging. "Just brought me in for questioning."

"Yeah, for a *week*."

Mark turned to Sammi. "One of the members of my orbital team hacked into a spy satellite looking for data on UFOs."

"But why," she asked, "do you think Kwan might not be an FBI agent?"

"I was a little suspicious when he never called for a forensics team to check out Judge Maloch's house. I don't think the FBI would be satisfied with some local police evidence search."

"You're first telling us this now?!" Josh barked.

"I was processing." He adjusted his glasses again. "When that woman who answered the phone told you to get out of here before you 'screw it all up,' that sort of clinched it. That's not FBI speak. She would've told you to 'stand down' or to 'get to a safe place.'"

Sure, if she were straight out of Central Casting. "Maybe on TV. She seemed pretty shocked that we were in New York. I think she just reacted."

"Let's find out." Mark pulled out his phone. "Read me the phone number Kwan gave us for his team at the office. I'll run it through my phone validator app."

"What's that?" Sammi asked.

"It checks the LRN database. Every phone number has a location routing number assigned to it. Phone systems need to know if a phone number is assigned to a cell phone or a landline. The protocols for system connection are different."

Josh read him the number as Mark keyed it in.

"Yup," Mark said. "That office number Kwan gave us is a cell phone." He nodded, smugly, at Josh. "Like I said, bogus."

"He's working for the Chinese!" Sammi blurted.

"Holy crap," Josh said, "you've got to be right."

"We thought they were involved," Sammi continued, "until we found out who Judge Maloch's killer was really working for. If the Chinese leadership believes that Falun Dafa's 'one with great inborn quality' is about to arrive, no one would have a greater incentive to stop that person."

"Well, we can't just let this happen." Josh swung his eyes toward Fifth Avenue. "I think I spotted a cop before, out there." He wheeled and raced toward the street.

A policeman was standing by the corner hot dog vendor, about to bite into a pretzel. "Excuse me, Officer," Josh said. "I need you to come with me immediately."

"Sorry," the policeman responded. "Off duty. Just finished an overnight in the worst part of the Bronx. I'm wiped and starving. Just call it in." He started to turn away.

Josh slapped the pretzel out of the man's hand.

Before the officer could react, Josh took off for the building the judge's killer was in. The policeman, bellowing choice words, sprinted after him.

He was in the revolving door when the policeman grabbed it from outside; he barely squeezed through to the dimly lit lobby. A security guard at the desk stood up as the police officer burst in.

Before the officer could say anything, Josh all but screamed, "I'm sorry about the pretzel, but someone's about to be murdered!" He took a breath. "You're the only one who can stop it."

Sammi's voice came from behind the man. "It's the truth."

Mark, puffing, added, "You don't . . . have much time."

The policeman eyed Sammi and Mark, then turned back to Josh. For the first time, it hit Josh how young the guy was; he looked barely in his twenties.

"Tell me the short version," the policeman said.

Outside the building's glass doors, Steven Lee came to a momentary halt as he spotted the familiar threesome standing in the lobby with a policeman. When a small group entered, he followed closely behind them, angling his face toward the wall as he circled the lobby. He entered an unoccupied elevator and hit the button for six. He'd wait to set the timer until he passed the third floor.

Back at that dingy Miami motel room, he'd told Ms. Bollinger that what he'd inserted into Jackson's sneaker was solely a tracking device. Planting Semtex plastic explosive there, after all, would not have seemed like standard FBI procedure. No need for tracking now anyway, since Mr. Sutton had called in and told him that Jackson was on the fourth floor. That call—directed to a burner phone—had been automatically forwarded, like the prior one, to Han Chee-hwa's informant and handled per their preestablished protocols. Guess it wasn't such a bad thing that Mr. Sutton and friends had ignored a direct order from the "FBI" and come to New York.

It was time. As always, he would follow the dictates of *The Art of War*. The most skillful attack was on an opponent who does not know what to defend. He pressed two buttons on the side of his watch and simultaneously used his thumb on a third button, setting the delay.

✦

Billy Ray ripped open two of the express mail packages he'd been carrying. His change of clothes was inside. Nothing like a multi-use decoy.

He sat down on a chair and pulled off his sneakers, leaving them on the floor a few feet from the Reverend. Picking up the fresh clothes, anxious to get out of the overly tight FedEx uniform he'd "borrowed," Billy Ray started toward the office.

The Reverend stood up in his path and waved him back. "That's all right, my son. Why don't you change out here? I'll step inside."

✦

Steven Lee opened the door to the roof. His rifle was waiting, hidden in the air-conditioning system a few steps away. Crouched and holding the weapon low at his side, he walked to the roof's ledge, which looked out on Fifth Avenue.

He knelt and placed the rifle on the ground next to him. Eyeing the great double doors of the cathedral across the intersection, he knew his sightline was perfect.

Above him, the midday sky was an ominous blanket of black.

✦

The short version.

"Officer," Josh explained, "we found out an assassin's planning to kill Judge Deborah Fenton when she comes out of St. Patrick's Cathedral after her wedding ceremony that's going on right now. We tracked the man to the fourth floor of this building."

Affirming nods from Sammi and Mark were all the corroboration the young officer seemed to need before following them onto an elevator.

And he *was* young. He was also big. Josh figured about six foot four and at least 220 pounds. The officer introduced himself as John Merogin—a name that sounded awfully familiar. An eerie image he'd seen before flashed through Josh's mind: a man holding molten steel bars in his bare hands.

The elevator slowed as it approached the fourth floor.

✦

"All decent in here," Billy Ray called out as he hitched the belt on his jeans. When the Reverend stepped back into the room, Billy Ray asked, "Our contact leave a little something for me?"

"In the closet in the office." The Reverend had that fatherly look in his eye. "You ready, my son?"

"Long as the equipment's up to snuff, most definitely." As he stepped past the Reverend he added, "Are you, sir?"

In the back of the office, on the top shelf of the closet, Billy Ray found an attaché case. He opened it on the desk and couldn't help but be impressed. The scope far exceeded his specifications. Even disassembled, this was some fine rifle.

✦

Kyle Fredericks figured the question had been rhetorical. Alone in the reception area, he answered it anyway, in a whisper. "It's in *his* hands, my son. I'll accept whatever *he* has planned for me."

He bowed his head. As he glanced down, he noticed Billy Ray's ratty sneakers on the floor next to him. He'd be glad to spring for a new pair when they got back to Gatlinburg.

✦

Steven Lee checked his watch. The yellow indicator was down to its last bar. The thread was about to reach the desired temperature.

It would be just hot enough to ignite the Semtex he had planted in Billy Ray Jackson's sneaker.

✦

Billy Ray was assembling the rifle when a blast in the next room shook the floor. "Reverend?!" Please God, no! He dropped the gun and leaped into the smoky reception area. With his first glimpse of the room, he started wailing. Bloodstains ran up the walls all the way to the ceiling.

It felt as if someone had plunged a spear through his heart.

✦

The elevator doors had just opened when Josh heard the sound.

Felt it as much as heard it. Like the pulse from a car with a trunk-sized subwoofer.

"What was that?"

"Some kind of controlled explosion," Officer Merogin said. "Came from that room." He pointed at suite 414.

"How do you know that?" Sammi asked.

"We're taught to open our peripheral vision at crime scenes. When the vibration started, I scanned the hallway. That door swelled."

Officer Merogin drew his revolver, approached the door, and knocked. No answer. He announced himself and knocked again. Still no response.

He tried the door handle. It was unlocked.

The officer pulled the door open. Josh peered around Merogin's shoulder. Through the hazy smoke and cloudburst of fire sprinklers, he saw the judge's killer, catatonic, tears streaming down his cheeks, hunched over apparent human remains that were drenched in blood.

Merogin raised his gun and entered the room. He stepped in close, examining the scene.

Without warning, the killer's rage erupted. He roared at the top of his lungs, startling the young policeman, then burst for the door. His bull rush knocked Merogin flat on his back; the officer's head smacked hard against the tile floor. Josh, Sammi, and Mark dove out of the way.

The man went screaming down the hall.

✦

The vows were exchanged, and the instruction to "kiss the bride" passionately adhered to, accompanied by *oohs* and *ahs*.

Newlywed Deborah Othniel turned to face the joy-filled room, gleefully clasped her husband's hand, and stepped down to the long central marble aisle. A broad beam of sunlight pierced the towering stained-glass windows, and the glistening stone beneath her feet was splashed in cobalt blue. As she paraded along the aisle with her new husband, her white bridal gown shimmering in the reflected hues, she glowed in the warmth of family and friends.

Ushers opened the double doors to the street.

At the doorway, Deborah clenched her husband's hand tightly. It seemed every neuron in her cortex was firing. She sensed a new horizon beckoning, a level of vision beyond anything she had experienced.

But then the beam of sunlight was swallowed by a coal-black sky, and her excitement was lost to a flash of terror. For what would such clarity lead to?

✦

"Officer?" Josh frantically nudged Merogin. The man was out cold and his gun lay on the floor next to him. Josh grabbed it.

"What are you doing?" Sammi pleaded.

"I've shot a gun before." He had, back in his programming days, with a buddy who took him to a range west of Miami a few times.

"At a person?"

He shrugged and turned for the door. It was almost noon. He had to get to the roof, though he didn't want to think about the last time he was on one. He looked back at Sammi. "Come on. We might already be too late."

✦

Anticipation of the kill was a primordial emotion, something Steven Lee shared with hunters and assassins across time.

The rush he'd felt before the sanction of Zhou Yuanxin was incredible. And now, within a matter of days, he had surpassed it. He was traveling in rarefied air. These were no mere assignments. They were preemptive strikes against the restructuring of civilization.

On one knee, left elbow steadied on the roof ledge, he raised the rifle to his shoulder, bringing the scope near his right eye. To remove any challenge from the ever-darkening skies, he turned on the night vision assist. His mind cropped the image. There were no hot dog stands, no taxis, no crowds, no buildings, no sounds.

His eyes tracked the bride in her wedding gown as she stopped and waited, alongside her new spouse, to greet their exiting guests. How ironic: a new life begun . . . and ended.

He never missed from this range.

He moved, methodically, through his well-practiced routine: setting the barrel down solidly in the palm of his left hand; curling his fingers around it; firming the butt end against his right shoulder; leaning his head slightly to the side; bringing the edge of the scope to his right eye; drawing his target into view—the woman . . . her face. He locked the dead center of her forehead in the crosshairs.

He began to squeeze the trigger with a smooth, steady sweep of his right index finger.

✦

The huge knife penetrated the side of the man's head with so much force that it knocked him out of his shooter's stance and dislodged the rifle from his grip. In a flash, Billy Ray was on him, viciously twisting the knife in the man's brain. This animal needed to be punished, needed to feel Billy Ray's pain, the Reverend's pain. He kept twisting the blade, though the first wound had surely been fatal.

Finally, he let the lifeless body drop. As shattered as he'd been, Billy Ray had sussed this out the moment he'd seen the Reverend's blood-soaked remains. The feds don't try to blow you up in your room. They come in numbers and take you away. It had to be Han's man. He wanted to eliminate the competition and take the glory for himself. He'd planned to work from this roof, just like Billy Ray.

Now, his fury calming, his hunter's senses took over. In the corner of his mind, he heard a small creak—the door to the roof was opening.

✦

Josh eased the door open and stepped out on the roof with Sammi behind him. The judge's killer was crouched over a body and a rifle.

"Don't move!" Josh shouted, and raised the gun.

Scowling, the huge man stood, pulled out his knife, and charged.

Josh aimed and fired, but the recoil was enormous, the policeman's gun almost jumping out of his hand. He fired again, but, unable to steady it, missed for a second time. The man raised his knife, readying to throw it.

Josh grabbed Sammi and dove with her behind the rooftop air-conditioning unit.

The door to the roof swung open again. Merogin.

The officer had barely stepped out when the large knife plunged into his chest, knocking him against the wall; he collapsed to the floor.

Staying low behind the large metal box, Josh swung the gun right, then left, then right. He'd get only one more chance. But which side would this animal come from?

He heard a thump and the floor vibrated. Of course! He fell to his back, clenched the gun firmly in his hands, locked his elbows, and began firing straight up at the sky. In a flash, the huge frame came overhead, directly into the path of Josh's bullets.

The man landed just past them, face down, his body twitching. Josh held Sammi close, with the gun at the ready. With blood pooling from the man's torso, he finally went still.

Sammi ran to Merogin.

The officer lay face up, the knife handle protruding from his chest. As Sammi reached him, he stirred, then slowly got to his knees. He looked over at the nearby body.

"What happened?"

"I shot him, had no choice. But, Officer . . ." Josh stared at the knife.

"Oh, this." Merogin placed both hands on the handle, yanked out the blade, and tossed the knife to the side. He unbuttoned his shirt to reveal a Kevlar vest with a slanted cut above the left breastbone. "Good thing it hit me at an angle. These vests don't do so well with knives."

Mark sheepishly poked his head out from the doorway. "How did you know to shoot upwards?"

"A man that large, who moved like that? It occurred to me back at Sammi's uncle's house that this guy had to be a hell of a middle linebacker back in the day. Middle linebackers who are that gifted don't go *around* the pile; they leap over it."

"I'll be needing that back now," Merogin said.

Josh handed over the gun, and the officer approached the body. Merogin kicked out with his leg and rolled the man over. The broad chest was a mass of red. He'd taken three bullets in the upper torso. "He's dead, all right."

Josh fought off a shiver. He'd just killed someone.

A big hand touched his shoulder. "You owe me a full explanation," Merogin said softly, "and a pretzel."

Josh slowly pulled his eyes from the corpse and nodded. "I promise to tell you the long version, but after I get you that pretzel, would you mind calling a certain Miami detective for me? I'd like to not be arrested when I step off my plane back home."

✦

At the first cracks of gunfire, Han Chee-hwa, who'd been standing near Fifth Avenue at the northeast corner of Rockefeller Plaza, had riveted his eyes across the intersection, directly on the new bride. She and those near her were looking around, unsure, in the echo chamber of surrounding office towers, exactly what they had heard and where the sound had come from.

When the ensuing burst had gone off, pedestrians cowered against buildings, and others bolted for doorways. Han had stood his ground as the wedding party scrambled back inside St. Patrick's.

Why had there been so many shots? He'd lost count after the first five. More crucially, why had none of those shots hit their target?

Then came the question that cut him to his core.

What if General Chang's operative had been caught in the act?

From his days in prep school, Han knew how the American media functioned. They were that dangerous combination of unfettered and relentless. The only question was *when* the dots would be connected from the death of Zhou Yuanxin to Steven Lee, and from Steven Lee to his true employers.

General Chang had warned him more than once that the new leadership was far more concerned with avoiding unseemly publicity than with chasing old demons across the globe—but he had pigheadedly pursued his plan. What would they do to *him* if this all went spectacularly wrong?

Bitter memories flooded in: abandonment in the slums by his mother; the death of his uncle and banishment by his cousin. He felt the long-suppressed suffocating pressure of a great stone on his stomach.

Orphaned twice before, Han could not keep the thought from his mind. He was about to be cut loose for a third and final time.

From the edge of the rooftop, Josh peered down at the mostly abandoned sidewalks. A number of policemen were emerging. *Now* they showed up. Cars, taxis, and buses whizzed by. The black limousine still lurked in front of the church.

People cautiously ventured out again. The streets filled. The city's sounds flowed back: Horns blared, brakes screeched, voices merged in a grand opera.

The double doors to the church opened and a couple came through. No white gown—not the wedding couple. They rushed to the black limo, got inside, and the driver pulled away.

"Look." Sammi was pointing up the street.

A glistening ivory carriage was heading down from the direction of Central Park led by a magnificent white horse. The driver steered the carriage to the curb, directly in line with the front doors of St. Patrick's.

The bride and groom came out of the church surrounded by well-wishers. As they worked their way toward the carriage, a sliver of brilliant blue sliced through the ashen clouds. It seemed to move as one with the bride's every step. She stopped and raised her eyes to the heavens. From across the street, six stories up, Josh swore he could see her broadening smile as the sliver of blue opened and slowly captured the sky.

He stared, transfixed, as she reached the curb and the carriage driver extended his hand to assist Deborah Othniel to her seat.

On her *white mount*.

Three days ago, Judge Maloch had proclaimed what this precise moment would change. Now, as Sammi's arms encircled Josh, he exhaled a breath he'd been holding in for far too long and recalled Judge Maloch's word:

"*Everything*."

INCIDENTALS

Falun Dafa is a spiritual belief with tens of millions of practitioners spread across the globe. The essence of its teachings regarding higher levels of consciousness, the allegations of its horrific treatment by the Chinese government, the controversies regarding its claimed alt-right and intolerant positions, and even the extraterrestrial musings of its founder are precisely as represented in this book. All biblical citations herein are from the King James Bible, verbatim.

The various legal issues and dictates scattered across these pages represent realities imposed upon diverse cultures over the centuries. From testimony prohibited based on religious affiliation under Justinian's Code, to the banning of cross-class marriage in Mongol-ruled China; from "bagging" as the punishment for parricide in third-century Rome, to "trial by ordeal" in eleventh-century England and the Venetian roots of patent law known as "privilege"—all these are real.

The achievements of Sir Thomas More, and his famous trial for refusing to take King Henry VIII's oath, including the actual words he spoke in his defense; the rise to power of the child duke of Normandy who would become William the Conqueror; the efforts to unify the laws of the Frankish kingdom by Charles the Great, whom we now know as Charlemagne—these stories are filled with historical accuracies (though I have used a literal translation of a Charlemagne Capitulary for my purposes). And the secret rooms in the Doge's Palace at Saint Mark's Square in Venice—where Gabrieli Triani learned of, and lost, his *privilege*—are there for you to see to this day, merely by booking a "Secret Itineraries" tour.

But the essence of this book lies not in what we know to be true. It asks "How?" *How* do our major "truths"—those moments of staggering significance—come into our lives?

Are they simply a matter of chance? We certainly don't always choose them. Is it possible, on some level, they choose us? Whether by God, Darwin, both, or neither, can our lives be fully explained without some factor of destiny?

Or is destiny merely our own little corner of *The Words*?

ACKNOWLEDGMENTS

The writing and many rewritings of this first novel occurred in two main stages: the early drafts written before I was ready to write it, and years later, the numerous revisions as I attempted to learn something about the craft. I am deeply indebted to two of my educators in that regard, Margaret "Peggy" Lucke, my editor during those early years—whose thoughtful counsel I wasn't fully ready to utilize—and Tanya Egan Gibson, my editor in recent years, who brilliantly pushed me through leaps I desperately needed.

For the final polish, and the professionalism they provided in taking these pages from digital hopefulness to printed (and e-book) reality, I am ever grateful to my wonderful team at SparkPress: my publisher, Brooke Warner; editor, Megan Milton; and art director, Julie Metz; along with my copy editor, Mikayla Butchart. Huge thanks to the sales and distribution people at Simon & Schuster and my publicists, Crystal Patriarche, Grace Fell, and Leilani Fitzpatrick at BookSparks.

Above all else, thanks to my incredible wife, my Deb, who encouraged me to write in the first place, has enthusiastically read every draft, and always has been my greatest supporter, my most honest critic, and the most wonderful soulmate and life partner ever conceived. Thanks to my amazing children, David, Dan, and Lauren—each of whom read drafts and provided meaningful input, with Lauren providing invaluable input on cover design as well—and to Fatim, Daron, and Stephen—who also read a draft—and to Dylan, Elton, Bode, Jovi, and our newest little love. Having you in my corner means almost as much as the pride I have in each of you.

Thanks to Sheldon and Linda Siegel for your input on the manuscript and invaluable guidance.

Thanks to all my other friends and family who read and commented on drafts, tolerated my rantings about story ideas, and have inspired and continue to inspire me daily. If I neglect to mention anyone, please know that I'm working from years of memory. Thanks to Jack Fields, Max and Dorothy Finkel, Merryle, Ryan, and Amanda Israel, Gregg Fields—who counseled me on the chemicals used in Gabrieli Triani's experiments—Kyra and Jordan Fields, Norman Finkel and Marilyn Zalcman, Paul and Regina Finkel, Barbara Millstein, Jen Finkel, Eric and Sophie Olsen, John and Michelle Berman, Bob and Helen Moore, Roslan and Patimah and family. Thanks to Sheldon Regenbaum and Caron Sanua Regenbaum and family. Thanks to Benjie and Lisa Schreier and family. Thanks to Tami Lesser and Craig Glover. Thanks to Danny and Shirley Lichtstein and family. Thanks to Dan and Deena Sokoloff and family. Thanks to Rich and Judy Kapner and family. Thanks to Ross Mankuta and the Mankuta clan. Thanks to Eric and Lauren Dwoskin, and Elizabeth Dwoskin and Leonard Medlock. Thanks to Kathryn Keslar Curley, Tim Curley, and family. Thanks to Terry Gross and family. Thanks to Evan and Susan Goldstein (my first non-family pre-reader volunteer) and family. Thanks to Gay and Harry Abrams and family. Thanks to Marc and Rhonda Reibman and family. Thanks to Steve and Joan Kirson and family. Thanks to Jeff Sherman. Thanks to Bob and Marge Gillece. Thanks to Stephanie Cassatly. Thanks to Margot Parker, Joel Spolin, and family. Thanks to Alex and Mary Kate Bedard. Thanks to Craig, Gail, Evan, and Inessa Bachove.

And finally, a special thank-you to our dear friend the late Jacki Browne, and my late, eternally sweet mother, Myrna, who each deeply believed in this book from its scattershot beginnings and, of far greater personal import, deeply believed in me, even when I had doubts as to both.

ABOUT THE AUTHOR

Author photo © Emma McGowan of Ether & Smith

Gary Fields earned his law degree from the University of Miami and his degree in mathematics/computer science from SUNY Albany. He has designed computer systems for Fortune 500 companies and built a law practice specializing in community associations. He's written hundreds of songs, performed professionally as a solo acoustic artist, been a leader in civic activism in his community, and coached youth sports for eighteen years. *The Book of Judges* is Gary's first novel. He is currently working on a sequel. Gary and his wife, Debbie, now live in Southern California, close to the rest of their family.

Looking for your next great read?

We can help!

Visit www.gosparkpress.com/next-read
or scan the QR code below for a list
of our recommended titles.